the Growing Pains of Jennifer Ebert,

Aged 19 Going on 91

D

David M Barnett is an author and journalist based in West Yorkshire. After a career working for regional newspapers he embarked upon a freelance career writing features for most of the UK national press. He is the author of the critically-acclaimed Gideon Smith series of Victorian fantasies, published by Tor Books, and teaches journalism part-time at Leeds Trinity University. David was born in Wigan, Lancashire, in 1970 and is married to Claire, also a journalist. They have two children, Charlie and Alice.

By David M Barnett

Calling Major Tom
Hinterland
Angelglass
The Janus House and Other Two-Faced Tales
popCULT!
Gideon Smith and the Mechanical Girl
Gideon Smith and the Brass Dragon
Gideon Smith and the Mask of the Ripper

the Growing Pains of Jennifer Ebert,

Aged 19 Going on 91

DAVID M. BARNETT

First published in Great Britain in 2018 by Trapeze.
This paperback edition published in 2018 by Trapeze,
an imprint of The Orion Publishing Group Ltd
Carmelite House, 50 Victoria Embankment
London EC4Y 0DZ

An Hachette UK company

3 5 7 9 10 8 6 4 2

A CIP catalogue record for this book is
available from the British Library.

ISBN (Mass Market Paperback) 978 1 4091 7510 0

Typeset by Born Group

Printed and bound by CPI Group (UK), Croydon, CR0 4YY

www.orionbooks.co.uk

This one's for Mum.
Thanks for everything, and helping me be who I am today.

The Woman in the Window

(1944, dir. Fritz Lang)

The look she is going for is Lauren Bacall.

That was the plan, anyway. Blood-red lipstick, come-hither eyes and hair with waves to knock the sea legs out from under any man. What Jenny Ebert has achieved, after four hours on a packed train and thirty minutes standing in the hammering downpour, is more *drowned rat*. The midnight-blue silk dress she'd bought for a song at a charity shop near home and poured herself into seems to have hitched up and twisted in all the wrong places, and she's sure it's shrunk in the rain, meaning she's in danger of pouring herself *out* of it. The shoes-to-die-for are slowly and sadistically killing her. And the fog of hairspray she'd employed to keep her hair ice-cool and Hitchcock-blonde is now running in chemical rivulets down her forehead and into her eyes, stinging them and blurring her vision.

Jenny looks down at her bags and considers digging in them for either her umbrella or her anorak. Would Bacall do that? No, she would not. She'd probably have a dozen men fighting to hold umbrellas for her. She looks around but there's not a Humphrey Bogart in sight on the concrete apron in front of Morecambe train station. Instead there are small knots of students waiting with their few new starters cases and cardboard boxes of kettles and toasters and books. Those who didn't have the luxury of parents to drive them straight to their halls, or second and third years who are returning on this cold and wet October morning to already established digs.

Which of these will be her new friends, she wonders? She looks around the gathered tribes, the goths and the emos, the loners and the geeks. Mentally she puts a cross by each of them, looking around

1

for people like her. People like she is now. The cool people, the night people, the ones for whom style and class are effortless. Oh, that reminds her. She opens the small black leather handbag dangling from her shoulder and pulls out the packet of Gauloises and a Zippo lighter. Attention to detail, that's the thing. She doesn't even smoke, not properly, but she's been practising, just enough that she doesn't lapse into a choking fit on the first drag now. As nonchalantly as possible, Jenny pulls a cigarette from the pack and hangs it loosely from those blood-red lips, flicking the top on the Zippo.

The lighter is advertised as wind- and rain-proof, and it does indeed burst into flame, cool and blue just like her. But the cigarette is already sodden and won't take, and it gets even wetter when a cab pulls up sharply in front of her, its tyres sending a shower of rainwater over her from the puddles forming on the tarmac in front of the station building. Jenny coolly gives the cigarette one more try, sucking on it hard as it catches reluctantly, and immediately lapses into a choking coughing fit.

The driver leans over and winds down the passenger window, looking her up and down. 'You'll catch your death, standing there like that.'

'Yes,' gasps Jenny, the puddle-water dripping from her nose. She coughs one more time, so hard she thinks she might throw up. 'No thanks to you.'

'The university is it, love?' The driver, a big man in his forties, estimates Jenny, brushing the crumbs of a just-imbibed pasty from a belly straining the buttons of his shirt. 'Cutting me own throat here, but there'll be a minibus along in a minute going straight to the campus. Free for students.'

'I'm not staying on campus,' says Jenny, and through the open window hands him a scrap of paper bearing the address of her new home. 'Not yet. They're still building the accommodation blocks. I'm staying here until it's finished.'

She realises she's talking too much. Sultry and mysterious, Jenny Ebert. Sultry and mysterious.

He looks at the piece of paper for a second and then shrugs. 'OK.' He reaches under the dashboard and pulls a lever; the boot clicks open. 'Let's get your stuff in the back.'

Jenny watches as he loads up the boot with her cases, but she keeps a tight hold on one green sports bag, clanking metallically. 'I'll carry this with me,' she says.

'Family silver, is it?' laughs the driver. 'Let's get you moving, then.'

Jenny climbs into the back seat because that's what Bacall would do. She wouldn't sit up front, even in a knackered old Vauxhall Astra, because she had class. The driver gets into the driver's seat and punches the buttons on the dashboard meter. 'Bloody awful weather.' On the dashboard, beside his meter, is his hackney carriage licence, sporting a washed-out photograph that makes him look as if he's being hunted by the police for escaping from prison, and the name: Kevin O'Donnell.

Jenny looks out of the window at a gaggle of girls with stripy tights, face piercings and blue and pink hair falling over the shoulders of their uniform black T-shirts. As Kevin pulls away from the station forecourt he says, 'You'll be going out to the pub tonight, drinking snakebite and black? That's what students drink, isn't it? Snakey and black? You a first year? Never went to university myself.'

Jenny sighs with the realisation that she isn't going to get through this drive without conversation. She glances at his meaty left arm as he changes gear, at the faded tattoo that says *MOIRA* on a banner wrapped around a heart that is dripping with blood. She wonders if this is because he loves Moira, or because he hates her, because she squeezed his heart dry. She looks back through the window at a squabble of seagulls rising up noisily over the black slate roof of a down-at-heel hotel. 'Second year. But I'm new to the University of North Lancashire. I did a year at Loughborough but I've transferred.'

'Never been to Loughborough,' sniffs Kevin as they turn on to the seafront. 'East Midlands, innit? Never been there. Always strikes me as a boring sort of place, the Midlands. Neither one thing nor the other. Is that why you left? Too boring?'

'Too close to home.' The sea is so far out Jenny can't see it beyond the expanse of dark, wet sand that stretches out beyond the blue metal railings interspersed with bright red lifebelts.

The driver nods. 'Away from the old mum and dad. What've they gone and done to piss you off?'

3

'They talked too much,' says Jenny, which is the sort of thing a femme fatale would say.

It seems to work because Kevin says nothing for a long time, but then he points across towards the passenger window. 'See that statue? Eric Morecambe.' He starts to sing tunelessly. 'Bring me sunshine, da-de-dah. Bring me sunshine, do-de while. What you studying, anyway?'

Jenny cranes her neck to see the black statue, right hand up behind the entertainer's ear, left leg cocked up behind him, framed against the grey sky, until it disappears out of sight. 'Film studies. I'm hoping to specialise in film noir.'

'Film noir,' says the driver admiringly, and Jenny isn't sure if he's mocking her or not. 'That sounds grand. Like I said, I never went to university. Didn't have the brains. What's film noir, then, arty French stuff?'

'Crime movies from the forties and fifties. Some from the thirties. Mainly American, a few British.' With a slight feeling of alarm, Jenny realises they are heading along a lonely, deserted road which she doesn't remember from last time she was here. 'Where are we going?'

'Got to take the old coast road. Nobody uses it much since they built the bypass. But there was a landslip last month – half the bloody access road to your new place fell into the sea. You'll have to go up to the house from the front. Be there in ten minutes. Crime movies, eh? Funny old thing for a girl like you to be into.'

Out to the left the beach goes on and on until it meets a thin thread of sea. Well, not so much a beach, more of an almost endless expanse of mud. When she came to check the place out in summer they said there was a bus that ran along the coast road and into town, right to the university. She wonders who else will be living at the accommodation, wonders if they'll be her sort of people.

'Not much for you young 'uns to do out here. Nearest pub's a good two miles away. That's if the Cross Keys is even still open.' He reaches on to the dashboard and hands her a card. *SANDPIPER TAXIS*. He passes it over to the back then rummages in the storage space in his door, overflowing with used tissues and chocolate-bar wrappers, and tosses her a biro with a chewed end. 'That's us. Write my name on the back. Kevin. You and your mates want

4

taking into town for a night out, give us a call. Ask for me. I'll make sure you get special rates and get you back safe and sound.'

The taxi slows and pulls in against the pavement on the long, deserted road. 'I'm sorry,' says Kevin. 'This is as far as I go.'

When Kevin and Jenny have pulled her bags from the boot she stands on the narrow pavement, cracked and uneven and pitted with sandy puddles, and feels the salty spray driving off the Irish Sea over the roof of the old Vauxhall Astra, stinging her cheeks and lips. She wonders if salt water is ageing or preserving; if she stood here long enough, facing the tumultuous waves, would she end up prematurely ancient or be forever nineteen? Behind her she feels the oppressive weight of the rising land and the old house that perches on top of it. It's almost as though the very shadow of the house cast by the faint October sun that is sluggishly emerging between the rain clouds has weight and substance. Her blonde hair whipping about her face in damp tails, she says conspiratorially, 'Is that because there are dark doings up at the old house? Stories that people tell in whispers? I bet if it was night-time you wouldn't even bring me this close.'

He slips her notes into the breast pocket of his short-sleeved shirt and gives her a handful of change, and frowns. 'No, love. I mean, I don't think so. Just a normal place. I mean, this is as close as I can get due to that access road being out. I'll give you a hand up these steps with your bags.'

Jenny clutches the sports bag to her chest. He grins. 'Apart from the family silver, of course. Probably wads of cash in there, I bet. Costs a lot to go to university these days. They did grants for people back in my time, but I never went to university, of course.' He taps his temple with a thick forefinger. 'Not got it up here, me.'

At the top of the steps Jenny pauses to catch her breath and look up at the house. It is in the Gothic Revival style, probably once the home of some rich Victorian mill owner or coal magnate, built to overlook the storm-tossed sea. It's constructed of sturdy stone, darkly weathered by the elements, that seems black in the lee of the building. Over a set of weathered double doors there's a portico and tall, thin windows above offering glimpses of the staircase that turns up over the four storeys. To the left is a high-peaked gable on which sits, lopsided, a tarnished finial four metres tall. To the right is a rounded turret above a wide, angled bay window fitted with small, square-latticed windows.

In one of these windows Jenny sees the woman.

She is half hidden behind the thick curtains, but Jenny sees a halo of pale hair surrounding a thin face, her figure dressed in a black high-necked dress, an archipelago of pearls at her throat. She is looking down at Jenny, who suddenly feels self-conscious and puts up a hand to smooth her wind-blown hair. When she looks back, the woman has gone.

Kevin dumps her bags in the porch of the grand doorway. 'This is just temporary, did you say?'

Jenny nods. 'Only until they get the new accommodation blocks opened.'

He waggles the card she's still got in her hand. 'Well, just remember, I'm at your service. You can always rely on Kevin.' He stands back and looks up at the house, and shakes his head. 'Great time you'll have. Making new friends, going out on the lash. Lovely. I never—'

'You never went to university,' says Jenny. 'Yes, you said.'

He nods. 'Right. Well, cheerio, then!'

Jenny watches Kevin head back down the stone steps and execute a U-turn in the deserted road, the taxi dwindling into a dot along the long, straight, empty road that separates the wide, endless beach glittering with oily pools of seawater from undulating dunes swaying with tall grasses. Morecambe is at one end and Silverdale at the other, and in between there's nothing.

Nothing apart from the house, perched on top of a craggy rise overlooking the road and the beach, roosting there like a muster of crows, trailing a zig-zag flight of precisely thirty-nine steps from the flagged terrace in front of the building down to the coast road; and a rusty gate hanging from a post beside a wooden sign that has been weathered and warped by years of spray and wind and rain, occasionally baked by the sun into crisp, fragile boards, the painted words illegible now.

Taking a deep breath, Jenny hefts her bag more securely on to her shoulder and drags her cases across the gravel. Far to the left there is a tangle of orange temporary fencing, bringing an abrupt end to the road that has barely begun arching away from the big house. Beyond there is a black chasm, three or four metres wide, and then the road sweeps down and behind the grounds. She wonders whether it will be fixed before she goes to the proper accommodation blocks in town.

Hauling the rest of her bags over to the ones Kevin deposited on the broad stone step in front of the doors, Jenny pulls her phone out of her pocket. No 4G; she's barely got any ordinary signal. Stuffing it back into her coat, she considers the ancient bell-pull by the doors and the faded card, encased in Sellotape and pinned to the flaking wood, which she can just about make out says *NO HAWKERS OR COLD-CALLING.* If any door-to-door salesmen made it this far, they should get a medal, never mind an order for toilet brushes. Jenny bites her thumbnail for a moment, then knocks once, hard, on the door.

Her knuckles make a dull, almost imperceptible sound, but the door swings open, revealing the cool, tile-floored reception area she remembered from summer. The wide mahogany desk in front of her is unmanned. Dark doors to the left and right are closed; there is one wedged open behind the reception desk, leading to a narrow corridor. Beside the desk the staircase sweeps up and turns to the left.

There is nobody here. Jenny frowns. She'd have thought at least someone would be there to meet her. She wonders if the others have arrived yet. She glances back at the main door and pulls it closed. Should it be unlocked like that? Wondering which way to go, Jenny is drawn by a thump and a volley of shouts to the door on the right. Putting her cases and bags against the desk, she listens at it for a moment, then twists the handle. She can hear voices from inside the room, and cautiously pushes at the door until she can peer quietly round it. Are these her new housemates?

Jenny takes a deep breath. This is what it has all been leading up to, all the pain, all the big decisions, all the careful reinvention of herself. A new start, with new people, and a new Jenny Ebert. She puts her head into the room, just so she can see them.

They are all ancient, occupying that sprawling age group that could be anything from sixty to a hundred. All of them.

She's in the right place.

2

Among the Living

(1941, dir. Stuart Heisler)

'There's a cream cracker under the settee!'

The young man with a shock of black, curly hair and a pained look on his face holds out his hands. 'No cracker! I hoovered this morning!'

Edna Grey sighs. He's a good boy, Florin, but he's very highly strung. And extremely easy to wind up. Edna has just let herself into the day room and settled down on the sofa in time for Mrs Slaithwaite to point at the other couch and claim sight of the non-existent cracker.

Edna says mildly, 'She is just having a joke with you, Florin.'

Florin implores Edna with his hands. 'But I hoovered, Mrs Grey! I always hoover!'

'There's a cream cracker under the settee!' repeats Mrs Slaithwaite, sitting in her usual chair by the fireplace with her huge hams of arms folded over a long, shapeless cotton dress, her white hair wispy on her ruddy head.

Florin pulls a face at Mrs Grey and drops to his knees in front of the wide sofa. Joe, Mr Robinson and Mrs Cantle are sitting on the sofa, and Florin peers between the stockinged legs of the latter. Mrs Cantle giggles. 'Ooh, you are awful, Florin.' The sofa faces the ornate fireplace, the carpet overlaid with a Chinese rug in muted colours. Florin waves his arm underneath the furniture. 'No cream cracker, Mrs Slaithwaite. It is as clean as a whistle.'

Mrs Slaithwaite harrumphs and turns her attention to the television on the wooden cabinet beneath the wide bay window. Edna looks back at Florin. 'She always says this. It's from an old television programme, before your time. She is just having fun with you.'

Edna considers the occupants of the settee. Mr Robinson has a short back and sides, his grey hair flattened over his head with pomade, a thin moustache beneath his hawkish nose, and is wearing a green knitted waistcoat over a buttoned-up shirt and a tie sporting a regimental crest; Mrs Cantle, thin and birdlike in a pale blue cardigan, is staring absently at three crushed paper handkerchiefs in her gnarled hands; and Joe – Ibiza Joe, he likes to be called – is a spectacled man with a shiny bald pate but long hanks of hair hanging from the back and sides of his head to a coarse-looking multi-coloured poncho.

'Hoovered, my left bollock,' says Mr Robinson, with what Edna has come to realise is his customary brusqueness. 'He's a lazy little swine, that one.'

'No!' says Florin in anguish. 'Mr Robinson, that is not nice.'

'Second Lieutenant Robinson to you, boy.' He directs a pointing finger and frowning stare at Florin. 'Lazy. Little. Swine.'

Joe turns his gaze on Mr Robinson 'Give it a rest, Robbo,' he says. 'The lad hoovered. I saw him myself.'

'Has anybody seen my jewels?' says Mrs Cantle. Edna smiles to herself. *Good work, Margaret*, she thinks. 'I've only got three here. I had four. Someone's taken one of my jewels.'

Mr Robinson snorts. 'Bloody jewels. They're dried-up snot-rags.' He juts out his jaw. 'And don't tell me he's hoovered, Joe, you bloody hippie. They're all the same, that lot.' He turns his gaze back to Florin. 'Lazy little swine.'

Florin ignores him and crouches down in front of the old lady, who is shaking her head at her balled-up tissues. 'Mrs Cantle. These are not jewels. These are handkerchiefs.'

'Bloody nut-jobs!' shouts Mr Robinson. 'Handkerchiefs, love, hand-ker-chiefs. Listen to the lad. Though if they were bloody jewels, he'd probably have them off you. Can't trust *his* lot as far as you can throw 'em!'

'Mr Robinson!' says Florin.

'Second Lieutenant!' he fires back.

'Mr Robinson, that is not nice. It is racist.' Florin folds his arms and stands in front of him. 'And do not get yourself worked up. Remember your angina. Have you had your medication this morning?'

'Robbo,' says the other man, Joe, cleaning the lenses of his glasses on the corner of his poncho. 'You are getting a bit over the top.'

'State of the bloody world today,' mutters Mr Robinson. He looks around. 'Bloody angina tablets. Where's the *Daily Mail*? And don't call me Robbo. That's what the lads in the regiment called me.' He points a finger at Joe. 'Proper men. Not bloody peaceniks like you.'

'Can someone help me push the chairs back?' says Florin. 'The yoga lady will be here soon.'

'Oh sweet Jesus,' says Mr Robinson. 'The bloody yoga lady.'

Mrs Cantle stops counting and puts a hand to her mouth. 'Oh. How long will the yoga lady be here? I'm expecting my son to come to visit today.'

Florin crouches down in front of her again and takes Mrs Cantle's tiny, bony hands in his. 'We have no visitors in the diary for today. I'm sorry. Maybe it is tomorrow?'

'I'm sure it was today,' says Mrs Cantle, shaking her head.

Mr Robinson puffs his cheeks out and blows air loudly through his lips. 'He's not coming. He's never bloody been, has he? We don't even know if he exists. He might be as made-up as your bloody jewels.'

Mrs Cantle glares at him. 'He is coming! He wouldn't just let me come here and not visit!'

Mr Robinson folds his arms. 'Give over, love. We've all just been left here. Nobody ever comes to visit any of us. We've been taken to the edge of the world and dumped. You, me, Ibiza bloody Joe over there, all of us. Nobody wants us and we're all alone. Sooner you can face up to that, the quicker we can all get on with the business at hand.'

'And what's that, Robbo?' says Joe. 'What's the business at hand?'

Mr Robinson shrugs. 'Waiting for a lonely, lingering death. What else is there?'

There's a long silence punctuated by a dull crack and everyone looks towards the TV just in time to see a black plastic remote control bouncing off the screen. 'Mrs Slaithwaite!' screeches Florin. 'You nearly broke the television!'

Mrs Slaithwaite sets her lips in a grimace and folds her arms over her ample bosom. 'It's not like there's anything on worth watching.' She holds Florin's gaze, then indicates the sofa with a nod of her big head. 'Anyway. There's a cream cracker under the settee.'

Florin makes a sound like an elephant and closes his eyes, breathing deeply. Then he retrieves the remote control. 'Does anybody want *Judge Rinder* on before the yoga lady comes?'

'*Judge Rinder* my left bollock,' says Mr Robinson, finally locating the *Mail* under Mrs Cantle's behind and tugging it out ferociously. 'I can't believe we fought a bloody war for this.'

Before the room descends into shouting chaos, Edna addresses them all. 'We've also got the students arriving today. I have just seen one from upstairs. Young woman. Very nicely dressed, I should say. Not like most of the young ones today.'

Mr Robinson rattles the pages of the *Mail*. 'Oh God, is that today? I don't know what the Granges are thinking of. What a stupid bloody idea. Fill the place with kids? It's supposed to be a rest home. *Rest* being the operative word. What sort of rest are we going to get with students tearing up and down the corridors?'

'I'm quite looking forward to it,' says Joe, which Edna expects him to. She might have only been at Sunset Promenade two weeks, but she's getting something of a handle on the residents. Mr Robinson is a reactionary old fool who thinks the world and everything in it has been designed purely to annoy him. Mrs Slaithwaite is a bad-tempered old woman who delights in causing others misery. Joe is a teenager trapped in the body of an old man, constantly trying to relive his glory days. Mrs Cantle . . . Edna glances at Mrs Cantle, studiously counting her balled-up tissues.

From the corner of her eye Edna notices that the door to the day room has been slightly ajar, and that there's been someone quietly watching them. The girl. The one she saw from the window. Curious clothes for a young girl. It was a lovely dress, but didn't look too good on her, like she'd been sleeping in it. Hair like a bird's nest. And whoever told her she could walk in those heels . . .

'I understand at least two of them are Chinese,' says Mr Robinson. He shakes his head as though this is a personal slight. 'I mean to say—'

'I think it will be good for you all,' says Florin. You can say one thing for the lad, thinks Edna. He works like a horse. He's the main carer at Sunset Promenade, does all the cooking and cleaning, while the owners, the Grange brothers, seem to spend most of their time locked in their little office, as far as Edna can tell, arguing. Probably about money.

She looks around the day room, at the large mirror over the fireplace, at the curtains hanging from the wide bay window, at the mismatched collection of rugs scattered across the floorboards. It's a big house and there aren't many residents. Edna wonders how it can possibly be financially viable. The short answer, of course, is that it isn't, which is why they're filling up the empty rooms with students. But it's an odd set-up. For starters, they don't charge a lot of money to the residents, not a quarter of what most places ask. And they don't demand you sell your home, if you have one, to pay for your care. Not that anyone else apart from her owns their own place, from what she's gathered in the past two weeks. They're all hard-luck cases, seemingly hand-picked by the Granges, as though the brothers are performing some kind of labour of love. The whole thing is very haphazard and lackadaisical. With the number of rooms in Sunset Promenade they could be making a lot more money if they took referrals from the local social services, but they don't seem to do that. And while this place is a bit remote – Edna glances out of the window to see black clouds rolling in from across the Irish Sea – the land it's on is probably worth a small fortune.

Still, she supposes the Granges know what they're doing. It's not for Edna to question their methods, just to be glad that they've allowed her to come and stay. She isn't at all sure what she would have done had they not welcomed her here, not sure at all. The others, Mr Robinson and Joe and Mrs Slaithwaite, said she was lucky to get in, that the Granges were very fussy about who they took on as residents.

Nonsense, she'd said. There's no such thing as luck.

There's only good planning.

Edna looks at the others in turn. She wonders if they know how *old* they all look, and then decides they don't. Without a mirror in

12

her sightline, she herself forgets that she's almost eighty-eight. No one feels old, not when they're all sitting together like this. Not in their heads. It's only when you see that reflection, or you try to move, that you realise you're not as young as you were. That's what people say, isn't it? *I'm not as young as I was.* Nobody says, *I'm older than I used to be.*

Mr Robinson pats the sofa and gently pushes on Mrs Cantle's bony back, looking behind her. 'Has anybody seen my magnifying glass?' he says. 'You know I can't read the paper without it.'

'You don't want to read that rag,' says Joe. He shuffles forward on the sofa and reaches for his cane, leaning on the chair arm. 'Ooh, give us a lift up, Florin, lad.'

Florin obliges, carefully helping Joe to his feet. The old man stands there, resting on his stick, catching his breath and shaking his head.

'It's there, Joe, you bloody hippie!' declares Mr Robinson, leaning rudely across Mrs Cantle to snatch up the big magnifying glass that the other man has been sitting on. As he does so, Mrs Slaithwaite makes a loud belch.

'Them sausages you serve up for breakfast don't do for me,' she scowls at Florin.

'My son does lovely sausages,' says Mrs Cantle wistfully, then begins to cry quietly. 'I'm sure he'll come to visit today. Where are we, anyway? Is it Corfu? Or Egypt?'

'Bloody hell,' mutters Mr Robinson, peering through his magnifying glass at the newspaper. 'Bloody Egypt.'

And here they all are, thinks Edna. Here *we* all are. Joe shuffling forward, his cane tapping the floorboards; Mr Robinson squinting at the type in his newspaper, struggling even through the lens of the magnifying glass; Mrs Slaithwaite banging her chest with her fat fist; Mrs Cantle counting her imaginary jewels and crying for a son who will never come.

'Well,' says Edna, standing up. 'I think if no one minds, I'll go and relax in my room for a while.'

But no one says anything. They're all far too busy getting on with – as Mr Robinson so succinctly put it – the business at hand.

3

Double Indemnity

(1944, dir. Billy Wilder)

As quietly as she can, Jenny pulls back out of the room and closes the door. Her housemates. She wonders exactly how she's going to cope with this. There's still no one at reception, and she wanders over to see if there's a bell she can ring. Tacked on to the wall by the desk is a print-out from the website of *North Lancashire News*. Her photograph is on it, blurry, standing outside the house, glancing at the camera as if caught by surprise. Which she was, she remembers. She wishes they'd said they wanted to give it to the local press. She'd have said no. She takes the Blu-Tacked sheet from the wall and studies it closely.

North Lancashire retirement home in pioneering scheme to house students with pensioners
By NLN Staff Reporter

The Sunset Promenade care home near Morecambe is pioneering a new scheme to provide accommodation for students from the University of North Lancashire at the start of the new academic year in October.

The scheme is based on a Dutch model that has proved incredibly successful and while it has been taken up by other care groups in Europe, this is the first project of its type in the UK.

Brothers Barry and Garry Grange, who run the independent Sunset Promenade, have received grants from various European social care funds to finance the scheme for the first year.

Barry Grange told *North Lancashire News* that Sunset Promenade would be providing accommodation for the students at a far lower cost than they could expect to pay on campus or in private rented accommodation.

He said: 'In return, they will spend some time with our residents, and the interaction between young and old will be beneficial to everyone. It will give the students more of an insight into the lives of older people, and their presence will help to revitalise those who live here.'

Students who have signed up for the scheme include Jenny Hibbert (pictured), who is transferring to the University of North Lancashire this year from Loughborough, John-Paul George, who has spent his first year living on campus, and two overseas students from China who are studying at the university's School of Business.

They'd got her name wrong, Hibbert instead of Ebert, a mistake Jenny's grown used to; that should make her a bit more difficult to track down, at least. She ponders John-Paul George. Jenny wonders if he's going to be her sort of person. Same goes for the Chinese students. And just how much interaction is going to be required with the old people in that room? She'd met with Barry Grange in the summer after hearing about the scheme and coming up to check it out. He'd been a bit vague about all that. Jenny tacks the sheet back on the wall where she found it and decides to go and find Mr Grange, starting, as she turns, to find a woman standing right beside her. No, not *a* woman. *The* woman. The woman from the window. She was sitting in the day room when Jenny sneaked a peak in, and must have come out while Jenny was looking at the cutting. She is almost as tall as Jenny, slim yet not scrawny like Mrs Cantle with her handkerchiefs. Her eyes blaze with an icy-blue intelligence and her long white hair is styled in an ornate braid pinned into a bun at the back of her head. Her black dress, Jenny sees now, is actually a smartly cut skirt and top. She fingers the pearls at her neck while she regards Jenny, then says, 'Can I help you?'

Jenny lets out a long breath. 'The door was open. The front door. I just let myself in. I thought there might be someone here to meet me. I was a bit surprised the door was unlocked.' She realises she's babbling, and stops. 'Erm. My name is Jenny. Jenny Ebert. I'm one of the students.'

The woman smiles. 'I'm Edna Grey.'

Edna continues to watch her. Jenny says, 'I think someone was expecting me today?'

'Possibly,' says Edna. She turns and walks towards the reception desk, her heels tick-ticking on the tiles. She stops and regards Jenny's cases with a critical eye. 'Probably someone is. I'd go in the day room and find Florin.' She looks back at Jenny. 'He's Polish, or some kind of Eastern European, anyway. Good English. He'll be able to help.'

Jenny waves a hand to the door she'd been peering round. 'Do you live here?'

Edna smiles. For the first time Jenny notices her lips are bright red. Her make-up is, in fact, rather immaculately done. She says, 'As do you, I understand.'

'Temporarily,' says Jenny, trying to smooth down her ruined dress. 'Just until they sort out the accommodation at the university. I'm not really sure . . . not sure I belong here, to be honest . . .'

Edna looks at her curiously and says, 'Have you read *Alice in Wonderland*? Do you remember what the Cheshire Cat says when Alice says she doesn't want to go among the mad people? He says that they're all mad, including Alice. And she says, well, how do you know I'm mad?'

Jenny stares at her. What is she talking about? Edna walks towards the carpeted stairs, stands on the first one and clears her throat. Holding her hands together lightly just below her sternum, she says clearly, '"You must be," said the Cat, "or you wouldn't have come here."'

Jenny watches Edna climb the stairs with an almost regal bearing, and as she disappears round the corner, the front door bursts open and what appears to be a large quantity of rolled-up mats spills on to the tiled flooring. A woman with a shock of red hair, her ample figure squeezed into a bright green leotard, tumbles in behind them, scattering CD cases across the floor. Jenny turns and picks up one that stops at her feet. *Pan Pipe Moods Vol. 3.*

'Hello!' booms the woman, her voice as loud as her hair and her clothing, as she stoops to gather the mats. 'I'm Molly. They call me Mad Molly, ha ha, no idea why. One more for yoga, is it? I've got a spare leotard you can borrow.'

Oh God, thinks Jenny. Is this what they mean by *interaction*? She wonders if she's been hasty accepting this offer, thinks that perhaps she should have tried harder to find some accommodation in town until the new blocks were ready. But this place is cheap, and she seems to find something about its location satisfying; the rain-lashed remoteness . . . for a while, at least.

Yoga, though. With old people . . .

But she is saved by the opening of the door behind the small reception desk and the emergence of a short man in a green woollen tank top and blue bow tie, who puts the spectacles hanging round his neck from a silver chain to his eyes and peers at Jenny.

'Ah! Miss Hibbert!'

'Ebert,' says Jenny. This is Barry Grange, whom she met when she came to look around Sunset Promenade.

He blinks and smiles broadly. 'Ebert. Of course. Welcome to Sunset Promenade! You're the first one to arrive.' Barry looks at the pile of bags and cases at Jenny's feet, then at Molly, who has finally gathered up her mats and CDs.

'I thought she could join in the yoga!' says Molly.

Barry smiles. 'Maybe next week, Molly. I think perhaps we'll let Miss Hobart—'

'Ebert. But "Jenny" will be fine.'

Barry looks through his spectacles at her again, and nods. 'We'll let Jenny and the rest settle in first, I think!'

'Fine!' says Molly, and breezes through the door into the day room, where Jenny hears a volley of groans and the man on the sofa – Mr Robinson? – saying loudly, 'Oh, good Christ, the bloody yoga lady . . .'

Barry Grange claps his hands together. 'Well! Come into the office and meet my brother Garry. He runs the place with me. He was away on business when you came over summer. And we can get you a nice cup of tea in there. I hope you don't mind me saying, dear, but you look like a drowned rat . . .'

Barry and Garry Grange are less like twins, thinks Jenny, and more like the mirror image of each other. There's a definite difference in Garry's demeanour; a slight crinkling of the brow, a narrowing of the eyes, an occasional flaring of the nostrils. Which is perhaps just as well, she thinks as she sits in a dining chair in the cramped office, nursing a mug of tea. Because how else would you tell them apart? Both with salt-and-pepper hair, unusually lush and thick for their ages – Jenny guesses at mid-fifties – and thick, black eyebrows which rear up alarmingly when they frown, which Garry does more than Barry. Slightly jowly, and cultivating small paunches, on the spectacles that hang round their necks from shiny chains and given to putting on with a flourish and a flick of the little finger. But what fascinates Jenny most – to the point that she can barely concentrate on the speech that Barry Grange is delivering like a particularly over-enthusiastic Scout leader welcoming a troop of small boys to their first camp – is that the twins are dressed identically too. From the ground up, they wear shiny black brogues, brown woollen trousers with a crease down the front so sharp you could shave your legs with it, a button-down Oxford shirt with a faint ochre check and a green tank top seemingly designed to enhance the contours of the twins' stomachs. However, as if in grudging concession to other people's sanity, the twins both wear a bow tie in a different colour: blue for Barry, green for Garry. She fixes on to that detail like a fog-bound sailor trying to keep the smothered beam of a distant lighthouse in sight.

'This is all so very exciting for us,' says Barry for the umpteenth time, clasping his hands together at his breast. He stands in front of the old mahogany desk while Garry sits behind, the latter's fingers steepled beneath his chin, leaning on a wide blotter pad with his elbows and scrutinising the newcomer.

'I suppose I should tell you a little bit about Sunset Promenade,' says Barry. 'We're what you might call a rest home, or a retirement home. We're not a nursing home. We have five residents. They are all senior but none of them have any acute medical needs – we're not set up for that. It's more like a . . . a long-term hotel.'

Garry snorts behind him. Barry falters slightly, then recovers and says, 'It is true that some of our clientele have certain . . . *characteristics*, let's say, that are concurrent with their general advanced age, and with that can come some specific . . . challenges, but by and large we are one big happy family here at Sunset Promenade.'

Another snort.

Jenny is about to say that she's hoping not to have to be there very long when there's a frantic knocking at the office door. Barry dashes to answer it and the yoga lady, Mad Molly, tumbles in. She brushes her red hair from her face and says, 'Oh, Mr Grange! And Mr Grange!'

'Who were you expecting to find in our office?' says Garry, frowning. 'Butch Cassidy and the Sundance Kid?'

'Ha ha!' barks Molly. 'Anyway, I've been looking for young Florin, but I think he must be off cooking up one of his lovely lunches.' A cloud passes over her face. 'Ever so slight problem in the day room. It's Ibiza Joe.' Her voice lowers and she says conspiratorially, 'I was running them through the Salutation to the Sun and I think it's set off one of his episodes . . .'

Then there's a low, sonorous *bong* that makes Jenny jump, spilling her tea on her dress. It's hardly going to be worth cleaning, the state it's in. Garry sighs.

'That'll be more students,' he says to Barry. 'You go and let them in, and I'll go and talk Joe out of whatever ravy-wavy flashback he's got himself stuck in.'

Barry nods then beams at Jenny. 'Come along, then. Time to meet your new housemates.'

✳ 4 ✳

Guest in the House

(1944, dir. John Brahm)

Jenny glances around at the other students in the dining room. Including her, there are four of them. Of the two Chinese students, one is a thin, pretty girl with smooth skin who is listening attentively to Barry, her shiny black ponytail bobbing as she nods at everything he says. She wears black leggings and a black shirt, styling them out like a supermodel, which makes Jenny momentarily envious. The other is a short, thick-waisted boy with round glasses and a bowl haircut, who steals shy glances at the girl. Sitting at the end of the row is a gangly white boy perched on the edge of his chair, his knees in his skinny black ripped jeans and his elbows poking from his Beatles T-shirt tangling together like the limbs of a spider. He keeps pushing his long hair off his face, revealing a large, angular nose and a forehead dotted with blackheads. He catches Jenny glancing at him and grins broadly, rolling his eyes in a theatrical manner.

'I should perhaps explain why you're all here,' says Barry, and Jenny has to bury her chin in her chest to hide her smile. It's like a scene from one of her old films: the shifty, disparate characters eyeing each other in the wood-panelled study of the remote mansion house, lightning crashing outside, as the soon-to-die Machiavellian host declares, *You might be wondering why I've gathered you all here this evening* . . . She blinks and concentrates on what Barry is saying. 'As we told you at the application stage, we got the idea from a similar scheme running in Holland. At Sunset Promenade, we currently have some vacant rooms' – a snort from Garry so huge Jenny fears he's going to choke – 'So, we thought, why not kill two birds with one stone?'

20

The Chinese boy uncertainly raises his hand. He's wearing a green football shirt with yellow insignia and it rides up to show his belly. Barry smiles brightly at him. 'Liu. Or Bo. I'm sorry, I'm still not used to which comes first.'

Bo Liu, or Liu Bo – Jenny is unsure of the name protocol as well – ignores the invitation to explain and instead scrunches up his face beneath his black bowl of hair. 'Mr Barry. Why must we stone birds to death?'

Jenny feels a giggle rise and looks away as the other girl leans forward and glares angrily at the boy. She snaps something like '*bái chī*', then says in flawless English, 'It is a metaphor. It means to solve two problems at the same time.'

She sits back and folds her arms, Bo looking crestfallen and blinking behind his thick spectacles. Barry, his grin plastered to his face, says, 'Thank you, Ling. Liu. Liu. Ling.'

The girl sighs and leans forward. 'In China we have a given name – mine is Ling – and a family name, which for both of us is Liu. The correct form is Liu Ling. But we understand this makes things difficult for English people, so it is fine if you refer to me by my given name, then my family name – Ling Liu.'

Barry looks up from making notes. 'So I call you Ling?'

She sits back. 'You call me Ms Liu.'

Garry smirks while Barry smiles wanly. 'Ms Liu. Of course. Well, while we're doing introductions . . .' He looks down at his papers and then up again. 'Jenny. Or . . . Ms Ebert?'

'Jenny's fine,' she says, giving a small wave, little more than an opening and closing of her hand. Bo smiles shyly at her and Ling gives her an impassive glance. The lanky boy pushes his hair off his face and waves back.

'And Mr George,' finishes Barry.

'John-Paul,' he says in a melodious Liverpool accent. He breaks out into a wide grin. 'But everybody calls me Ringo.'

Bo frowns. 'Why?'

'John-Paul George,' says Ringo. He shrugs, his bony shoulders rising and falling like tectonic plates. 'Liverpool, isn't it?'

'I don't get it,' says Bo.

Ling clenches her fists and mutters something sharp and spiky which Jenny is sure must be a swear word. 'His name is John-Paul George. Like the Beatles. So they call him Ringo.'

Bo's face lights up as though Ling has flicked a switch at the back of his head. He smiles broadly and breaks out in cracked-voice song: 'All your loving, do-de-do-de-do-doo!'

'It's all *my* loving, la,' says Ringo, not unkindly.

Ling is less benign. '*Bái chī*,' she spits.

'What's that mean?' says Ringo, rearranging his legs underneath him. It appears to Jenny that he has too many joints in his limbs.

Bo frowns, repeating the phrase softly to himself, searching for the English equivalent, then brightens again. 'Idiot,' he says. 'She is calling me an idiot.'

Barry claps his hands. 'Well. Now that we're all acquainted . . . why don't we show you to your rooms? And then once you're settled, you can meet the residents.'

As they are filing out of the office, the telephone on the desk rings. Barry squeezes back past them to answer, then puts his hand over the mouthpiece and motions to his brother, mouthing something at him that Jenny doesn't catch. Garry sighs and snatches the phone from Barry, who says, 'Guys . . . could you all make your way down the corridor and head up the main staircase to the landing on the first floor? We just need to deal with something but this won't take more than a moment. Wait for us there.'

'This is brilliant, isn't it?' says Ringo.

Jenny glances at him. 'Really?'

He punches his hand into his palm, eyes shining. 'Yeah! Out here, away from everything, mixing with all these different people, nothing like the usual uni experience . . .'

She pauses and turns to face him. 'Those are all the reasons I'm wishing I'd never come here.'

Ringo blinks. 'So why did you come here?'

'I've transferred from Loughborough. The new accommodation blocks aren't ready.'

'Why Morecambe?'

'Do you always ask so many questions?'

Ringo considers this. 'Yeah. Do you always avoid answering them?' Before Jenny can retort he looks her up and down and says, 'I like your style, by the way. Forties femme fatale.'

She smiles despite herself. Thank God. Someone's actually recognised what she's going for. 'Well, thank you,' she says.

'A good look,' he nods. 'But that dress is knackered, well and truly. So, why'd you transfer? Did something happen?'

Sultry and mysterious, Jenny tells herself. Sultry and mysterious. 'A girl's got to have some secrets,' she says, and carries on through the reception area to where the others are waiting.

Jenny Ebert wasn't always Lauren Bacall. Far from it. In fact, it was *not* being Lauren Bacall that directly contributed to her decision to leave Loughborough. Because when Jenny Ebert was at Loughborough, she was boring.

After sixth form, which was as awful as Jenny thought things could get, she had an idea of reinventing herself, of emerging like a butterfly from a cocoon into the brave new world of higher education. No longer would she be the boring old girl who sat at the back of the class, hiding behind her hair, diligently getting on with her work amid the whirlwind of raging hormones and sexual tension and planning of wild parties that she never got an invitation to, that she was forever on the outside of, looking in. She would become a new Jenny, a liberated, independent woman who nobody knew and who would throw off the shackles of the old, dull, unliked Jenny who had struggled through school. She would make new friends and sleep with boys and be invited to the wild parties.

But the cool kids at university seemed to avoid her, just as they had at school, as though her dullness was an infectious disease they were afraid of contracting. Instead she attracted the attention of girls who were just like her, or rather the persona of her she was desperate to cast off – monochrome girls with a deficiency of social skills who thought a wild night in was discussing *Jane Eyre*. Her new, artfully ripped black jeans and T-shirts proclaiming obscure bands and purple eye make-up were no armour against them. They saw through her disguise and recognised her for what she was: one of them.

She was studying economics, which she hated with a passion, and which she suspected contributed to the boringness she wore like a cheap scent. So in a last-ditch attempt to save her own sanity and soul, she decided to drag the dull friends out who clung to her and never did a thing that wasn't commonplace, and get rip-roaring drunk.

That very night, in fact. It was May, and there was a party at the students' union for something or other. Her friends were like a disapproving Greek chorus when she floated the idea, but she cajoled, persuaded and bullied them into going. She skipped lectures that afternoon and put all her clothes in to wash in the student laundry.

Had Jenny been one for signs and omens, she may have taken the fact that the washing machine broke down, with all her clothes in it, as some kind of portent of doom. With scant hours to go, a repairman desperately tried to gain access to the machine, full of water and everything she owned, which was in no way going to be dry for the evening. She nearly gave up there and then, standing in the laundry room in her dressing gown and pyjamas, crying furiously. But no. She wouldn't let herself fail. With not even a pair of knickers to wear, she set about begging and borrowing a full outfit from her friends.

From Charlotte she procured a summer dress, quite attractive, in pale blue with white polka dots, but three sizes too big, a situation deftly solved with the application of a line of safety pins down the back to pinch it in and give it (thought Jenny in the spirit of looking on the bright side) a rather punky feel. Bereft of any underwear at all, she obtained a too-small bra from another of her hall-mates, Imogen, and from the third, Mia, a pair of knickers that covered her belly button and were adorned with a picture of a bashful teddy bear and a thought bubble that proclaimed them to be Saturday's underwear. The pants were only relinquished with the strict guarantee that they would be hand-washed, thoroughly dried and returned the next morning in time for them to be worn by the rightful owner on the appropriate day. Jenny wondered if she couldn't perhaps have Sunday's or Monday's knickers instead, a suggestion that was greeted with the same horrified reaction she might have expected had she said she was planning to wear them to an all-in mud-wrestling tournament.

So, adequately if not very satisfactorily attired and with only minutes to spare before the big night out, Jenny Ebert was ready to paint the town red.

It was, of course, an unmitigated disaster.

✳ 5 ✳

Party Girl

(1958, dir. Nicholas Ray)

In the foyer, at the foot of the staircase where Jenny first saw that curious woman, her green sports bag is sitting, unzipped, on top of her other cases. She rushes over to it, heart pounding.

'What's that?' asks Ringo, by her side, looking at the wide metal discs spilling out of the bag. 'Old film canisters?'

Jenny counts them – four – and zips up the bag, angrily turning towards Ling, who is waiting there impatiently. 'Did you see who did this?'

Ling raises an eyebrow. 'It wasn't me, if that's what you're thinking.'

'I never said it was!' retorts Jenny. Her hands are shaking. 'I just asked if you'd seen who'd done it.'

Ling shrugs and looks back to the office. 'It was like that when we got here. I didn't take much notice of it, to be honest. Where are the Granges? Are we being taken to our rooms, or not?'

'Hey, are you all right?' says Ringo. '*Are* they movie canisters?'

'Yes, thirty-five millimetre,' says Jenny distractedly. She takes a deep breath. 'Maybe the bag just came open,' she says. She can't start going around accusing people of tampering with her stuff. That's not the way to get off on the right foot. But if anything had happened to them . . .

'What's on them?' presses Ringo.

Jenny rubs her face. She feels damp and rumpled and she just wants to get out of this dress and have a shower or, even better, a bath. She's getting a headache and she pretty much wishes she was anywhere except Sunset Promenade. 'It's just stuff for my course,' she says, hoping that'll shut down his questions. 'Does he ever stop?'

From the closed door leading to the large room where the residents were sitting she can hear the muted sounds of tinkling bells and flutes. She wonders what tortuous shapes Mad Molly is trying to coax the pensioners into.

'Bugger, forgot my rucksack,' says Ringo. 'Wait for me on the first floor, I'll just go back to the office for it.'

Ling is already taking the turn on the staircase, sturdy Bo huffing up close behind her. As Ringo disappears back down the corridor, Jenny is momentarily alone. She briefly wonders what the others think of her. Was this really going to be the place that would crack the cocoon of dull Jenny Ebert and allow the real her to emerge? She feels suddenly that she's made an awful mistake agreeing to come here. She shouldn't have let herself be talked into it; she should have waited to see if a room came up on campus, or if she could have got into a shared house in town. Would a femme fatale live in a lonely house overlooking the Irish Sea, with a bunch of pensioners for company? Would Lauren Bacall put up with someone like Ringo wittering on at her?

Jenny has to register for her course tomorrow; she resolves to ask if she can transfer out of Sunset Promenade. She's sure the Granges will be able to find someone else to take her room here.

Jenny climbs the thickly carpeted stairs and at the top they open into a wide, wood-panelled landing, with several doors leading – she presumes – into bedrooms. The polished wooden floor has a wide rug on it, and there's a battered chaise longue underneath the window that could do with a bit of a clean. Beyond she can see the storm-tossed grey waves of the sea.

Ling and Bo are nowhere to be seen. Jenny moves towards the chaise longue to wait for Barry and Garry when a movement catches her eye through an open door. She pauses and looks in to find the old lady she saw downstairs, the one with the pale blue cardigan and the nest of wiry white hair. She is perching on the edge of her bed like a little sparrow, peering into an open drawer in the bedside cabinet. She looks up sharply and smiles.

'Hello, dearie,' she says in a warm, high voice. 'Are you one of the scholars?'

'One of the students, yes. I'm Jenny. Are you not doing the yoga?'

'Not with my hips,' sniffs the lady.

'You're Mrs Cantle, right?'

The old lady frowns. 'Yes. I'm supposed to be, aren't I? At least I think so.'

Jenny's heart sinks, just a little. She thought this was meant to be a rest home, that the residents were supposed to have most of their wits about them. Mrs Cantle brightens and says, 'Do you want to see my jewels?'

Ah, yes. The jewels. Jenny remembers the old man telling her off as Mrs Cantle counted the balled-up paper handkerchiefs in her hand. She's not sure what you're supposed to do in these situations: put them right or humour them? She'll have to ask Barry what the correct protocols are. Mrs Cantle is beckoning to her.

'Come on. Look at my jewels.'

Jenny smiles tightly and steps into the room. It's quite big, with a double bed covered by a thick bedspread, a dark mahogany wardrobe and tall windows hung with heavy curtains. The room is at the rear of the house, looking out towards hills crowned with thick grey rain clouds. Somewhere out there is Morecambe, and the university, and the life Jenny should be carefully constructing for herself. She decides she'll tell Mrs Cantle her jewels are very nice and quickly get out.

'Come on, dearie,' says Mrs Cantle. She pulls out the bedside drawer further. 'Have a look at my jewels. I'll turn the lamp on so you can see them better.'

Jenny pads over the thick rug and glances down at the drawer. 'Yes,' she starts to say. 'They're love—'

Her words catch in her throat. Mrs Cantle smiles proudly.

The drawer really is full of jewellery. Rings, brooches, pendants. The glare from the bedside lamp above them fills them with light, infusing the gems with red and green and blue life. Jenny is no expert, but she's pretty sure they're genuine. Diamonds. Rubies. Emeralds. Sapphires. They must be worth an absolute fortune.

'All right, Jenny?' She jumps, then quietly pushes the drawer closed and turns to Ringo, who is leaning in through the door. 'Getting to know everybody?'

'Is this your boyfriend?' asks Mrs Cantle.

'No!' says Jenny, more forcefully than she means to. She smiles at Mrs Cantle. 'It was lovely to meet you. I'm sure we'll get properly introduced later.'

'Bye, dearie.'

Mrs Cantle gives her a wave as she walks out on to the landing with Ringo, just as Barry and Garry are mounting the stairs. Jenny shakes her head. 'I can't believe it. Jewels.'

Barry smiles. 'Ah, you've met our Mrs Cantle, then?' He gives a wide, exaggerated grin at the old lady, still sitting on her bed, and ushers them all past her open door. He drops his voice to a whisper. 'Gets a little . . . confused, sometimes.'

'Can't remember her own name half the time,' scoffs Garry.

'But those jewels—' begins Jenny. She's about to say they should be in a safe rather than a drawer, but Garry cuts her off.

'I know. Always going on about them. Bits of tissue paper and handkerchiefs.' He shakes his head.

'Still, she's not doing anyone any harm,' says Barry. 'Now where have those other two got to?'

Jenny opens her mouth, then shuts it again. It's not for her to say anything. If she's expecting everyone else to keep their noses out of her business, she's going to have to learn to do the same.

It all went swimmingly at first. She sat with Charlotte, Imogen and Mia on a table in the corner of the students' union and bought a round of ciders with tequila shots. The other three sipped their ciders but only Imogen tasted the tequila, pulling a face. Jenny downed her shot, then the other three as well, and went back for another round.

'I want to go home,' said Charlotte. She didn't like crowds. Imogen put her hands over her ears and rocked backwards and forwards; she didn't like loud music. Mia said, 'Don't forget, I need my Saturday knickers back first thing tomorrow.'

'Sod this,' said Jenny. 'I'm going for a dance.'

This was far more like it, she thought as she pushed herself into the sweating crowd, throwing her hands in the air and dancing to the music. Imogen's bra was pinching her but she tried to ignore it, and Mia's knickers felt like rice paper against her skin. This was probably the most fun Mia's Saturday knickers had ever had on a Friday night. What tales they'd have to tell the Sunday knickers when they got put back in the drawer.

And perhaps, thought Jenny hazily, there'd be even more tales to tell. She felt the heat of a body up against hers, moving behind her. She pushed back against it, enjoying the sensation of an actual male moving in rhythm with her.

'What's your name?' a voice shouted in her ear.

'Jenny!' she shouted back, moving closer, moulding herself against him. 'What's yours?'

'Brendan! What are you studying!'

'Economics!' she yelled. This was going extremely well. 'What about you?'

'Sports journalism!' cried Brendan.

She didn't know what to say after that so she was rather relieved, and somewhat thrilled, when Brendan began to plant kisses on her bare back above where Charlotte's dress was pinched together with the safety pins. Jenny shivered as he went lower, between her shoulder blades. She put a hand behind her, feeling his thigh. So this was how easy it was!

Then he stopped. She patted his thigh encouragingly. He said something she couldn't quite make out.

'What?' she shouted, turning her head slightly.

'Ifff khott baa vrasss snokkk on visss phoggn savdddi pemcch.'

'What?' she yelled again, trying to turn to face him.

'Owww! Don't! Don't move! I've got my brace stuck on these fucking safety pins . . .'

But Jenny was already committed to the manoeuvre, and as she turned she felt a safety pin twang and part company with the dress.

'Jesus!' said Brendan, and she saw him properly for the first time, his eyes watering, the glinting safety pin stuck in the metal of his braces. He wasn't very attractive, and he looked rather annoyed.

Jenny felt a draught as Charlotte's dress billowed around her chest. Unfettered by the safety pins – she felt another one ping out of place – the dress was assuming its three-sizes-too-big original form, and Jenny's slim frame just couldn't hang on to it. She watched, helpless and with horror, as it slipped off her shoulders, straight down to her waist, then pooled around her feet. At that moment the music stopped while the DJ changed the track and, as if unhappy that there was a break in proceedings, Imogen's bra strap decided to fill the vacuum by loudly snapping and flinging itself bodily as far from Jenny as it could. She clapped her hands to her breasts, eyes wide, as a growing circle formed around her and she was suddenly blinded by the flashes from a dozen camera phones and deafened by the bitter sting of laughter.

'I'm bleeding!' wailed Brendan, and he was, blood pumping from his mouth. It was like something from a horror film.

'I'm naked!' Jenny screamed back at him.

He wiped his mouth with the back of his hand and looked her up and down. He smiled, his teeth covered in blood, the safety pin still sticking out from his brace. 'Don't suppose you fancy coming back to mine?' he lisped. 'I've got a frozen pizza.'

Jenny closed her eyes, but that didn't drive away the sound of laughter and the flashing of camera phones and the image of an evil, leering teddy bear with a thought bubble that proclaimed, 'Oh, shit.'

The Young and the Damned

(1950, dir. Luis Buñuel)

'You know what the problem is with young people today,' begins Mr Robinson.

Mad Molly, the yoga lady, has put them through their paces and gone, like a Lycra-clad whirlwind. The students are being shown to their rooms and doubtless, thinks Edna, being bored rigid by Barry Grange. Mr Robinson is peering at them all, one by one, through his magnifying glass.

'Don't you have spectacles, Mr Robinson?' asks Edna.

He turns the magnifying glass on her. 'I do, but they hurt my ears. Lenses are like bloody jam jar bottoms. Heavy.'

'I like your magnifying glass,' chuckles Mrs Cantle. 'It makes you look like Sherlock Holmes.'

Mr Robinson tuts and says again, 'The problem with young people today—'

'Oof,' says Joe. He is walking, with difficulty, up and down the hearth rug, leaning heavily on his stick and rubbing the small of his back. 'I might have to start giving that yoga a miss. I don't think it does it for me.'

Mr Robinson frowns at him. 'I do stretches every morning before breakfast, Joe. A man should keep himself in shape. That's one thing the army taught me. There's no reason you can't be fit and healthy in old age. Anyway, young people today—'

'I met one of them,' says Mrs Cantle. 'I showed her my jewels.'

'Did you, Margaret?' says Edna. 'And did she like them?'

Mrs Slaithwaite, who has been staring at the muted television, blinks and stares at Edna. 'I don't know why you encourage her.'

She's an odd one, that Mrs Slaithwaite, thinks Edna. In fact, they all are. Odd in their own ways. But that's what comes of living a long life, she supposes. Everyone's earned the right to have their own little quirks. People are like trees. The older they get, the more rings in their trunks; the broader their wealth of experience. When you've had a lot of life, you're allowed your foibles.

'That's what's wrong with young people today,' she says out loud. 'They haven't had enough life.'

Joe stops his shuffling up the rug and looks at her. 'Well, they wouldn't have, would they? On account of them being young.'

But Mr Robinson is waving his magnifying glass at her. 'No! She's right! Correct, Mrs Grey! They haven't lived enough. I mean to say, Joe, these kids that are coming in . . . they're what, nineteen? Twenty? What had you done by that age?'

Joe sticks his lip out and ponders. 'I left school at fifteen. Started work with the corporation. Highways. Up at six every morning, digging ditches, come rain, hail or shine.'

'Exactly!' Mr Robinson slaps the magnifying glass down on his lap in triumph. 'We just got on with things. Didn't fanny about. I bet these kids can't even tie their own bloody shoelaces.'

'Too busy on their phones,' says Mrs Slaithwaite, folding her arms. 'I could strip off and do a belly dance in front of them and they wouldn't look up from their phones.'

Edna grimaces and Mr Robinson mutters, 'Steady on, Mrs Slaithwaite. I felt my breakfast come back up then.'

'Cheeky bugger,' she says, and jabs viciously at the remote control, turning up the sound on the TV. There is a line of people sitting on chairs on a stage. One woman is crying, another one is gesticulating, and a young man in a baseball cap and tracksuit bottoms between them looks bored.

'Oh, I don't like this show,' says Mrs Cantle. 'Everybody is always shouting.'

'Irresponsible, that's what it is,' says Robinson. He points at the TV. 'I don't even need to watch this to know that he's a ne'er-do-well; just look at the way he's dressed. He's probably got that one pregnant while he's supposed to be with the other one.' He shakes his head. 'Seen it all before on this programme. Young people. No sense of responsibility, that's what it is.'

'There were people of our generation who didn't live up to their responsibilities, Mr Robinson,' says Edna mildly. Old people weren't all paragons of virtue throughout their lives, she knows that for sure.

'What do you call fighting in a world bloody war?' shouts Mr Robinson. 'What's that if not responsibility? If it wasn't for people like my father, this lot wouldn't have the freedom to walk around with their eyes glued to their bloody Tweeters and BookFaces. And what's that all about, anyway? Taking photos of your bloody dinner and putting it on the internet for everybody to look at? Wetting yourself every time some pop star says something they think is half clever? Telling everybody you've just "checked in" to the public bloody lavatories? That's what's wrong with young people. Think the world revolves around them and their skinny lattice.'

'What?' says Joe, looking at him. 'Lattice?'

'I think you mean *lattes*,' says Edna. 'Skinny lattes. Coffees made with milk.'

Mr Robinson blinks. 'I thought it was lattice. Like some sort of . . . pie, I suppose.'

Mrs Cantle giggles. 'Oh, you are funny, Mr Robinson. I could just eat a nice pie, though. I wonder what young Florin has on the go for lunch?'

'Nothing you'd want to take a photo of and stick on BookFace,' mutters Mr Robinson. He shakes his head. 'Lattes. Bloody coffee. What's wrong with a scoop of Mellow Bird's? Everything's got to be posh and foreign or they won't touch it.' He slaps his knee. 'Entitlement, that's what it is. Bloody entitlement.'

Mr Robinson does, despite his blustering, have a point, thinks Edna. She has often despaired at the self-absorption of the younger generation. Always looking inwards, never at the wider world, unless it is, of course, on the screen of their phone. And she is quite impressed with his deployment of the word 'entitlement'.

'There is a sense, I agree,' she says, 'that many of them think the world owes them a living.'

'The world owes you nothing,' replies Mr Robinson firmly. 'We all know that; that's why we've ended up in here. You make your own luck in life. You can't rely on anybody else.'

That, too, is true, thinks Edna. That is very true. Relying on others, trusting people . . . well. Had she not been so trusting, perhaps she would have had a better life. A happier one, at least.

'We rely on the lovely Grange brothers, though,' points out Mrs Cantle. 'They keep a roof over our heads, and young Florin serves us up three meals a day.'

'Not through the goodness of their hearts,' says Mr Robinson. 'We bloody pay for it.'

And – with perfect dramatic timing, thinks Edna – Garry Grange chooses that moment to let himself into the day room. He looks around and scowls at Mr Robinson.

'I was just coming in to tell you that Barry's showing the students to their rooms, then we're going to bring them through to meet you,' he says. He looks at Mr Robinson. 'And I don't wish to appear harsh, Mr Robinson, but if you're finding that life at Sunset Promenade isn't to your liking, then you are of course free to find alternative accommodation. None of you is a prisoner here.'

'I didn't say I didn't like it,' says Mr Robinson lamely.

Garry looks at all of them in turn. 'You do realise that you're all lucky to be here? For the fees you're paying? If I were you lot I'd count my blessings instead of complaining. And I should mention that we've got an inspection at the end of October, to see if we can keep our licence. They might want to speak to some of you about life at Sunset Promenade. If you know which side your bread's buttered on, you might want to think about just how well this place is run for the prices we charge.'

It is extremely well priced, considers Edna. She and Mrs Cantle only arrived two weeks ago and Garry Grange is right, she's never heard of a rest home run like this one. They don't take referrals from social services, instead going on what Barry Grange told her was 'instinct'. If they think someone's a good fit with Sunset Promenade, they offer them a place. The fees can barely cover the cost of the residents' meals, let alone the full expense of them living here. Fortunately, she won't be here long. Not now that the plan is underway.

'How do you keep this place going?' she wonders aloud. 'There are only five of us, and Margaret and I arrived only recently.'

'My brother thinks the four students will help,' sighs Garry, sitting down on the sofa next to her. 'But he's got his head in the clouds.'

'It's the grants and whatnot,' says Joe. 'That's what keeps it going, isn't it?'

Garry nods. 'That's Barry's purview, to be honest. I couldn't be bothered with it all, I don't mind admitting.' Is there a begrudging note in his voice? 'He's got all these grants and funds he taps into, always making applications and writing emails. If it was up to me . . .'

If it was up to you, we'd all be out on the street, thinks Edna. Garry has never made any attempt to hide the fact that he has little patience with the whole idea of Sunset Promenade. Even in the past two weeks she has heard the muted arguments emanating from the office. For Garry Grange, the home is a business; for Barry it's a vocation. She wonders how they got into the game in the first place.

'And where do all these wonderful grants come from, dear?' asks Mrs Cantle.

Garry sighs again. He sighs a lot. 'Europe, mostly. Which, as you can imagine, is a bit of a worry at the moment.'

Mr Robinson shakes his head violently. 'Bloody typical. I bet they're all going to dry up, aren't they? Be just like the bloody Europeans, that. Withdraw the funding out of sheer spite.'

'I presume that's why we're getting the young people,' says Edna. 'Am I right, Mr Grange?'

He nods. 'Yes. Extra funding source. Bringing together the generations, that sort of thing.' He shakes his head to make the point that he thinks it's all a waste of time. 'But we've only got it for six months, to prove we can make it work. Which I can't say I'll be hugely surprised if it doesn't. All I'll say is, things might not be so rosy come Easter . . .'

Joe sits down on the sofa heavily and with a huge grunt, and leans forward on his stick. 'Mr Grange, are you saying there's a real danger the money could dry up?'

Garry pulls a face. 'I'd rather none of you had this discussion with the young people. We don't want to scare them off before they've even unpacked. Or paid their rent.' He pauses and looks thoughtfully around the day room, peering at the walls, at the ceiling. 'This is a good location and a solid old building. I can't imagine there'd come a time when there isn't a care home at Sunset Promenade.' He stands up. 'I'll go and see how my brother's getting on with the students. We'll bring them down shortly. I believe Florin's putting on a bit of a buffet.'

Edna watches him go. He chooses his words carefully, that one, she thinks. *I can't imagine there'd come a time when there isn't a care home at Sunset Promenade.* But not necessarily *this* one, run *this* way, perhaps . . .

Mr Robinson picks up his magnifying glass and glares through it at a fight that's breaking out on the TV. Men in black jackets are separating the combatants and someone's thrown a chair at the presenter.

'Don't tell the students this place is in trouble,' he says, mimicking Garry's voice. 'Got to bloody mollycoddle them all the time. That's the trouble with young people today . . .'

✴ 7 ✴

Whispering City

(1947, dir. Fedor Ozep)

The trouble with old people, thinks Jenny, as she stands with her face upturned to the spray of hot water from the shower, is that they think they know it all.

Granted, she is only going off the experience of her own parents, but she can't see that these people, with another two or three decades on her own mum and dad, are going to be any more humble or exciting.

This is not quite the start of the new, improved Jenny Ebert that she was imagining. Still, it's only until the new accommodation blocks are finished. And tomorrow she's going in to uni for registration, so she'll be able to set her plans in motion properly then. In the meantime, at least she's got a big room and an en-suite bathroom with a good shower.

Jenny's room is at the front of the house on the third storey, overlooking the road and the dunes and the endless sand. There's a double bed and a dark mahogany wardrobe set against busy floral wallpaper, and under the window is an old, solid desk with one of those blotting-paper mats on its scratched and scuffed surface. There are only two electric sockets, one of which is hidden just behind the wardrobe, as Jenny discovers when she looks around for somewhere to plug in her phone. The reception hovers between one dot and *NO SIGNAL*, which only compounds the growing feeling of isolation that rolls in like the misty sea spray pushing lightly against the sash window.

Jenny slips into her fluffy bathrobe. It's got unicorns on it; she's going to have to buy something more appropriate, maybe a silk one. As she towels her hair, Jenny looks at her folded clothes in her luggage and wonders if there are enough hangers in the wardrobe to accommodate them, when her door swings inwards and Ringo lopes in, throwing himself face down on the bed, then rolling over to look at her.

'What are you doing?' she says, pulling her robe tighter at the neck.

Ringo shrugs, his shoulders rising and falling like waves. 'Thought you might want some company.' He holds up a tiny, ornate key. 'You left this in the lock outside the door. Might want to put it somewhere safe.'

Jenny hooks her foot over the lid of the small case displaying her underwear and flicks it shut, turning to glare at him. 'Is the bed comfortable? Only I haven't even sat down on it myself yet.'

Pushing himself up by his elbows, Ringo presses down on the mattress with the palms of his hands. 'About the same as mine. OK, I suppose.'

'I was being sarcastic,' mutters Jenny, taking the door key from him and returning her attention to the interior of the wardrobe to count the hangers.

Ringo shuffles along the bed and inspects the pile of film canisters propped up against the little TV that Jenny is planning to place on the desk. He picks one up with his long fingers and looks at the hand-written label. 'What's this? I've never heard of it.'

'Nothing,' says Jenny, taking it off him and putting it back on the stack.

'What are you studying? I'm doing creative writing.'

'Film. Look, I—'

'What shall we do later?' interrupts Ringo. 'Is there a pub nearby? Do you think Bo and Ling drink? Should we eat first? Will we get our tea here? What time do you think this thing with the oldies will finish? Will we—'

'For God's sake!' says Jenny, putting her hand over her eyes. She turns round and takes a deep breath. 'Ringo. What are you doing in here?'

He shrugs, surprised. 'I just thought . . . you know. Housemates and all that?'

She covers her mouth with her cupped hands and listens to the sound of her breathing for a moment, eyes closed. 'Look,' she says eventually. 'I know you mean well. But it's bad enough being stuck out here without feeling . . . feeling so *harassed* in the first five minutes.'

'Sorry,' he says, rolling over on to his back but making no move to leave. 'Did you not want to come here, then? To Sunset Promenade?'

'I transferred, and there were no places on campus. They told me I could come here for a cheaper rate until something turned up.' Jenny pauses. 'We've been through this. Did you come here on purpose?'

''Course,' says Ringo. 'I thought it was a dead interesting idea. I want to be a writer, see. Good experience, this. Where are you from, then? I can't place that accent.'

Jenny mumbles something non-committal. Ringo barely draws breath. 'Why'd you transfer?'

'I just did. Now if you don't mind—'

Ringo stares at the ceiling. 'Something happened, didn't it? I bet something happened.'

The washing machine still hadn't been fixed, so Jenny went to the launderette half a mile away as soon as it opened at eight, which was fine because she'd been up all night, huddled in her bedclothes, sobbing. She washed Charlotte's dress, Imogen's bra and Mia's knickers, and tried not to think about last night. She had wanted it to be so perfect, like a movie. And it had been like a movie. Some sort of awful mash-up of *Dirty Dancing* and *Carry On Camping*.

On the way back to the halls, she passed three people who gave her a second glance. There was a knot of students lounging in the morning sun outside the building, all looking at her and whispering. One boy started to whistle the tune they played when there was a stripper on stage. Face burning, she ran up the stairs to Mia's room.

'Saturday's knickers,' she said. 'Washed and tumble-dried.'

'Finally! I can get dressed,' said Mia. 'Did you iron them?'

Jenny was just about to leave when Mia's phone pinged and the other girl looked at it, then at Jenny, and giggled.

'What?' said Jenny crossly, taking the phone from her. On the screen was a picture of her standing on the dance floor, hands over her chest, dress around her ankles. 'Oh my God. Who sent you this?'

'It's the third time I've had it,' said Mia slyly. 'I think quite a few people took photos.'

Charlotte and Imogen had both seen the photo as well. Jenny checked her phone, switched it off and on again and rechecked it. Nobody had sent it to her. She didn't know what she was most appalled by, the fact that people had taken photos of her in her darkest hour and sent them all round the university, or that boring old Mia, Charlotte and Imogen had actually been deemed worthy enough to send them to while she hadn't.

I've wasted a whole year, thought Jenny, sitting on her bed, knees drawn up to her chin. I've wasted a whole year on those girls and now I'm the laughing stock of Loughborough. They're whispering and pointing and they always will. I'll only ever be the girl whose dress fell off. For the next two years, that's all I'll be.

She turned on the TV. There was an old movie playing. *Dark Passage*. Humphrey Bogart and Lauren Bacall. One of her favourites.

'Don't you get lonely up here by yourself?' asked Bogie.

'I was born lonely, I guess,' said Bacall and Jenny together.

Jenny buried her face in her hands. She could probably complain. It was practically revenge porn, wasn't it, sharing photos like that? Wasn't that against the law now? If only she could be more like Lauren Bacall. Things like this would never happen to *her*.

She slowly lifted her face and studied Bacall on the small TV screen. Who was to say she *couldn't* be Lauren Bacall? She could be anything she wanted. That was the whole point of going away to university, wasn't it? To reinvent yourself.

She could be Lauren Bacall. She *would* be Lauren Bacall.

Just not here.

'Nothing happened,' says Jenny. 'Sometimes people just do things because they want to.'

'Every good character needs motivation,' says Ringo. 'At least, in all the best stories.'

Jenny stares at herself in the mirror. She needs to blow-dry her hair. She needs to find something to wear. She needs to put on her make-up.

'Well, this is a pretty boring story so far.'

'I don't believe you,' says Ringo. 'Something exciting must have happened to you at some time.'

Jenny digs in her case for her hairdryer and rollers. She wonders if she'll have time to get her hair wavy before they all have to meet the old people. Then she thinks, is it worth it? Just to sit with a bunch of pensioners? And then she shakes her head. Would Bacall say that? Would she ever look anything less than fabulous? No, she would not. And Jenny Ebert is going to do no less.

She looks at Ringo. 'I need to get ready. I'll see you downstairs, all right?'

He nods and unfolds himself from the bed. 'Tell me one thing about yourself. One thing you haven't told anyone since you got here.'

Jenny sighs. 'All right.' She looks at him. Sultry and mysterious, right? Just give him enough. Enough for a taste of the enigma of Jenny Ebert. She looks down at her hands, then back at Ringo.

'My parents are both dead.'

* 8 *

Out of the Past

(1947, dir. Jacques Tourneur)

Ringo sits up, eyes wide. 'No way.'

'It's not that uncommon,' says Jenny, feeling uncomfortable in his stare.

'Totally right,' says Ringo. 'My parents are dead too! How did it happen? My mum had this rare disease and it was dead quick at the end, like, six months. My dad had a heart attack a year later. Everybody said he died of a broken heart. Which I suppose he did, really.'

Jenny groans inwardly. This is not what she wanted. 'Car crash. But I don't want to talk about it.'

'Did they die together? Can you remember the last conversation you had with them? I can. Clear as day. Last thing I said to both of them.'

Jenny shakes her head. She is not doing this. She closes her eyes and touches her temples lightly, then forces a smile. 'Ringo. Look. I don't mean to sound . . . well, it's just . . .' She takes a deep breath. 'I don't want to be in some sort of orphans club, all right? I came here to put it all behind me. I really don't want to talk about it.'

'Talking helps,' he says, and Jenny briefly wonders if he ever actually stops. 'It's bad to bottle it all up.'

'Do you think you can go now?' Jenny says quietly. Her legs are shaking and she needs to sit down.

Ringo finally makes for the door. 'Yeah. 'Course. See you later, at the meeting, all right?'

She nods and waits until he shuts the door behind him before letting her legs give way and dump her unceremoniously on the edge of the bed, the duvet crumpled with the angular indentation of Ringo. And she cannot help but think of the last proper conversation she had with her parents.

'Why are you so bloody boring?' screams Jenny. She feels like her head might explode. She wants to punch something, smash anything, destroy everything. She looks around wildly, sizing up targets. The vase on the polished dining table. The ghastly ornate mirror on the wall. The porcelain figure of the man sitting on a wicker basket, fishing rod by his feet.

'Language, young lady,' says her father with a tutting sound and a sad, solemn shake of his head.

'Jenny,' says her mother, wringing her hands, dressed in her quilted housecoat.

'There's no talking to her when she's like this,' says her father. He is wearing a cardigan over a white shirt checked with pale beige, his hair neatly parted and smoothed down with cream. Her mother touches a hand to her forehead. She'll have one of her headaches coming on. Jenny laughs out loud, an ugly, humourless sound. They're like something out of an old sitcom.

'Boring!' yells Jenny. 'Fucking boring!'

'We just think you've acted in haste,' says her father reasonably. 'We just wish you'd have spoken to us first before you told Loughborough that you were leaving. Perhaps we could have got around this.'

'There's nothing to get around,' says Jenny, the anger dissipating. 'I hate it. I've left. I'm going to North Lancashire at the start of the new term.'

'To study film,' says her father, rolling the words around his tongue as though they are in some foreign language. He shakes his head again in his sad, solemn way and the wind rises within Jenny. She wants to smash and destroy everything in this boring little room all over again. 'What good is that? At least the economics degree might have got you somewhere, set you up for a good job. But film studies?'

The raging gale blows all reason out of Jenny. 'I don't want a good job! I don't want a boring job, like you! What did you think, I'd follow you into the exciting world of accountancy, where you've wasted your life for the past forty years? Why can't you just support me for once in your lives!'

'I'd hardly say wasted,' says her mother quietly. 'We've had a good living out of your father's career. You've wanted for nothing. How can you say we haven't supported you?'

Jenny clenches her fist and growls. 'I don't mean "support me" like that. I mean encourage me. Let me follow my dreams.'

Her father snorts. 'Dreams? Whoever made a good living out of dreams?'

'I don't want a good living,' seethes Jenny. 'I want a good *life*. And how can you say I've wanted for nothing? How can you say that when you've kept *this* a secret for all these years?'

Jenny unwinds the extension lead and plugs it into the socket by the bed, running it along the wall and behind the desk so she can connect the TV. She angles it towards the bed, then sits back against the headboard, looking at the blank screen and then beyond, at the rain-spattered window. Is the weather here always bad? She squints through the rivulets racing down the pane. Barry has told them all about the dangers of this stretch of coastline and how the sea can come snaking in, circling around the unwary, cutting them off and forcing them into patches of quicksand. 'The tide can come in faster than a horse can gallop, that's what they say around here,' he warned.

Jenny thinks it all sounds rather thrilling.

She points the remote at the TV and it bursts into a crackle of static. She'll need an aerial lead. As she feels around the skirting board behind the desk for evidence of one, she wonders if it was the age of her parents that made them so boring, or if they were just made that way. Back then, when she had that last conversation with them at the tail end of summer, her father was about to turn sixty-one, her mother fifty-nine. They'd had Jenny very late; her mother had been forty when she got pregnant. She often wondered why they'd waited so long for children, but they never spoke about it. Jenny had ached for some conversation on the matter, some confession, some explanation. Perhaps they'd tried

45

for years and it had never worked. Maybe they'd had failed pregnancies before. Might it have been a complete surprise, a shock to a couple who had never intended to have children? There were a dozen possibilities, a hundred chances to perhaps make themselves more interesting, add more depth and texture to their lives. But they never volunteered any information, and by the time Jenny was old enough to wonder about it, she'd grown so far apart from them that even the revelation that they'd found her under a mulberry bush would have been too little, too late for her to care any more.

Someone raps on the door and Jenny's heart sinks at the prospect of Ringo back for another round of rapid-fire talking, but it's Barry – which she ascertains after a quick look at the bow tie that accompanies the face peering round the door ('Blue for Barry, green for Garry, easy-peasy!') – come to ask if everything's all right with the room.

'Hello!' he beams. 'Hope you're settling in OK. I must say, this is all very exciting for us, you know. It's a bold new venture for Sunset Promenade.'

'I was wondering if there was a way to connect the TV?'

Barry, as if desperate to be useful, hops at an alarming speed over to the wardrobe, pulling from behind it a coiled brown flex held together with a little wire tie. 'Here you are!' He glances around at the DVD player and pile of cases, some blank, some with the lurid titles and cover images that Jenny finds so strangely comforting. 'You're doing film studies, correct?'

Jenny nods, taking the aerial lead from Barry and unspooling it as he picks up a handful of the DVDs, fanning them out in his hands. '*The Asphalt Jungle*! And *The Big Sleep*. You like old movies, then?'

Barry closes one eye and points his fingers at her like a gun. '*Pew! Pew!* When men were men and women were dames, eh? Exciting stuff.'

Jenny finishes connecting the aerial lead and looks out of the rain-drenched window. 'I watch them for the moral ambiguity, the self-destructive alienation and the existential crises,' she says absently. She realises after a moment that Barry's gone silent, and she turns away from the relentless rain to find him watching her somewhat pensively. She forces a smile and points a finger-gun back at Barry. 'And for the femmes fatales and handsome men, obviously. *Pew! Pew!*'

Barry finds his broad smile again and lays the DVDs back on the pile. 'Well,' he says, clapping his hands together. 'Another half an hour to get settled, then perhaps you'd all like to meet the residents? We'll convene again at the bottom of the main staircase at . . .' Barry glances at his wristwatch. 'Quarter past? Lovely. Oh, did I mention the power cuts? I don't know if it's because we're so far from the main power lines, or so far from town, or the wind and the sea, but we do sometimes get power cuts. Mainly when it's bad weather.'

Jenny looks pointedly out of the window. 'Is it ever anything but bad weather?'

Barry laughs. 'Oh, it's lovely in summer.' He pauses, considering. 'When it's not raining. Anyway, I just wanted to say . . . don't worry if the power goes out. We have a back-up generator that kicks in. Eventually. And that sees us through until the power comes back. Happens every couple of weeks or so.' He smiles broadly again and taps his watch. 'Anyway! Quarter past! Don't be late!'

When he's gone, Jenny busies herself with setting up the TV and DVD to her satisfaction and putting her laptop on charge, then is just putting her clothes in the wardrobe on a selection of plastic hangers – stamped with the logos of dry-cleaning businesses and high-street shops she's barely aware of, other than that they purvey old-lady clothes – when there's a brisk knock at the door and Ringo pops his head round. 'Decent?' he says.

Jenny imagines pointing a finger-gun and *pew-pew*ing him full of hot lead. 'It's a good job I was.'

'I did knock this time,' he protests.

'It's still nice to wait until actually I've invited you in, though.'

He loiters on the threshold and digs the angular bulk of his phone from the pocket of his skinny jeans. 'It's nearly quarter past. Shall we go and meet the oldsters?'

Jenny closes her wardrobe doors. 'I suppose. Then I might get some peace around here.'

As Ringo waits for her at the door, he says, 'I think this place is in trouble, you know. Sunset Promenade. Remember when I left my bag in the office and had to go back for it? They were having a right barney.'

'Who? Barry and Garry?'

Ringo nods, wriggling his hips as he tries to get his phone back in his pocket. 'Something to do with that phone call they got before they made us all leave. From what I could gather this place isn't bringing in much money, which is why they're doing this thing with us, the students. There's some bigger company wants to buy it. I think Garry's keen but Barry doesn't want to sell.'

'Wow,' says Jenny, casting around for her phone, purse and room key. 'You picked up a lot of information just from calling in to get your bag.'

He gives a crooked smile. 'I might have listened at the door for a bit.'

'Sneaky,' says Jenny, and as she ushers him out and closes the door behind her, she's put in mind of double-dealing Joel Cairo in *The Maltese Falcon*, and she wonders if, in this movie, Ringo is going to be played by Peter Lorre; if he's the sort of character who listens at doors and barges in uninvited, who hears and sees more than he lets on, who you never know whether you can trust or not until the final reel.

* 9 *

Stranger on the Third Floor

(1940, dir. Boris Ingster)

'. . . and this is Jenny Hibbert,' says Barry Grange. 'She's reading film studies.'

'It's Ebert,' says the girl. She's quite attractive, supposes Edna Grey. Something of the past about her. Long blonde hair, blow-dried into a wave. A symmetrical face. Could even be a beauty, and rare style for a young person: a pencil skirt, some nylons with a straight seam, a pair of six-inch heels in black patent and a nice, tight, roll-neck sweater. Even be fit for Hollywood, maybe, if you scrubbed all that panstick off and did it properly.

'Of course,' says Barry, wringing his hands. 'Ebert. Sorry. Sorry, sorry.'

Edna wonders where the other brother is. He hates them all, she knows; hates all the old people. She wonders if he sees shadows of his own mortality in them, if he worries which one he's going to end up like. She looks down the line at her fellow residents. Perhaps Garry will become reactionary and bigoted like Mr Robinson. Dull-witted but quick to anger like Mrs Slaithwaite. Maybe he'll be another Ibiza Joe, high as a kite one minute and down in the doldrums the next. More likely he'll follow Mrs Cantle's path, a brittle existence where the shell of reality can be brought crashing down by the mere tap of a toffee hammer.

At least I know he won't end up like me, thinks Edna Grey. Because I shouldn't even be here. Right on cue, Garry bursts into the common room, holding a sheaf of papers and shaking his head from side to side. His twin gives him a little wave.

'Ah, my brother's here,' says Barry. 'Garry, we've done all the introductions . . .'

Garry looks up from the papers and blinks, as though he's just awoken from a dream and can't quite get his bearings. 'Ah,' he says. 'Right.' He folds the papers up and waves them at Barry. 'This has just come. Bloody postman's getting later and later. You'll need to read it sometime. About the grants.'

'Is there anything from my son?' asks Mrs Cantle. 'He might send me a postcard to say what time he's arriving.'

'No visiting today, Mrs Cantle,' says Florin. He's very good, thinks Edna. Got quite a soothing voice. She wonders what will become of people in places like this if all the foreigners go home, and they stop letting new ones in. Half the home-grown youngsters she sees on the streets seem too feckless to cook their own lunches, let alone anyone else's. Let alone wipe backsides, if it ever comes to that, God forbid.

Barry claps his hands. 'So that's everyone introduced!' Edna watches him with cool curiosity, switching her attention back and forth between the brothers. Barry is obviously a screaming homosexual, while Garry has apparently been married but is now divorced. Edna can't think why, what with his sunny disposition and cheery demeanour. She smiles at her own little joke. Yet the twins dress identically, still, save for those differently coloured bow ties. An odd thing. It's as if they want to tell the world how alike they are, yet they seem to positively hate each other.

Garry casts a baleful gaze at the residents lined up on the carpet in front of the fireplace like he's the commandant in a prisoner-of-war camp, inspecting the inmates. Edna has an overbearing urge to whistle the theme tune to *The Great Escape*, but instead she says, carefully and quietly, 'You'll probably die first, anyway.'

Garry glares at her. 'What? What? Are you speaking to me?'

Edna continues, 'I was just thinking that you are probably wondering which one of us you'll end up being like when you get old, but then I thought that you'll probably die before you get to that stage. Men usually die first, don't they? And you smoke. And you're overweight.'

Garry's eyes widen and Edna sees the girl, Jenny, cover her mouth with her hand to hide a smile. Florin puts himself between Edna and Garry and murmurs, 'Mrs Grey, that is not nice . . .'

Edna smiles sweetly. 'Sorry, dear. I do forget myself sometimes.' She winks at Jenny Ebert. Yes, that's the ticket. Get the girl onside.

Barry claps his hands again. He does that a lot, as though he's a stage magician, drawing attention away from the trickery. Misdirection, they call it. The trickery in this case being the under-current of tension that Edna has noticed in Sunset Promenade ever since she arrived here. It's like when Dorothy drops into Munchkinland. It's all happy and singing and Technicolor, but underneath the house there's a dead body.

Mr Robinson is straightening his tie and coughing quietly, which, Edna recognises with mild dread, means he's about to start speaking. Holding forth. He's a silly old fool. Insists on everyone calling him Second Lieutenant and banging on about the war, but Edna's done the maths. He can't possibly have served in the Second World War, and would have certainly been too old for the Falklands. She briefly considers Vietnam or Korea, but she is sure he'd have mentioned it more if that was the case.

'On behalf of the residents of Sunset Promenade, I'd just like to give a warm welcome to all the new recruits,' says Mr Robinson. Not on my behalf, thinks Edna. Mr Robinson isn't done yet. 'While I'm sure Messrs Grange have been – or will be – updating you vis-à-vis the rules and regulations of the home, I just wanted to say that we'd all appreciate it if you could observe a strict lights-out at ten o'clock and ensure that there is no music or loud television noise to disturb the residents, and no drunkenness, drug-taking or fornication—'

Barry laughs nervously and claps his hands. *Look at me! Don't look at him!* 'Ha ha, thank you Mr Robinson. Obviously, we do all have to get along together, and of course we'd appreciate a measure of temperance in terms of . . . of alcohol, and absolutely, of course, no drug-taking—'

'Boo!' shouts Ibiza Joe, giving a thumbs-down with both hands and winking theatrically at the four students.

'No drug-taking,' says Barry more firmly. 'And no . . . no . . .'

'For-ni-ca-tion!' announces Mr Robinson with clipped military precision.

Barry takes off his glasses and squeezes the bridge of his nose between thumb and forefinger. He heaves a sigh and says, 'I think it's all just about common sense.' Mr Robinson blows a breath of disappointed air through his pursed, thin lips and shakes his head sadly.

Ling clears her throat. 'I can only speak for myself, obviously, but I am not planning to indulge in anything other than hard work.'

'Me too!' says Ringo, winking theatrically at Jenny. Interesting, thinks Edna. Is there a burgeoning romance between the two? She'll have to watch that. It could be a problem, or it could be an opportunity . . . she files the thought away for future reference.

A silence descends on the common room, the four students on one side, the five residents on the other, the Grange twins at one end, Florin at the other. It is eventually Florin who says, 'Mr Barry? The sandwiches and cakes . . . ?'

Another clap of the hands. 'Of course! Young master Florin, who is an absolute marvel in the kitchens, has been working feverishly all morning on a welcome feast.' He waves his hand expansively to the corner of the room where several plates of sandwiches wilt under smothering cling film, and a chocolate cake crowned with strawberries – imported, thinks Edna, at this time of year – dominates. There's a sense of sudden relief that you could almost poke your finger into as everyone moves towards the table, apart from the Chinese boy, who hesitantly raises a hand.

'Yes, Bo?' says Barry.

'Please . . . what is fornication?'

The Chinese girl stops dead and turns to look at Bo. Edna has, of course, heard the phrase 'looking daggers' many times, but it's the first occasion she's actually seen anyone do it to such an astonishing degree. The girl would make a wonderful actress, she thinks, if she could replicate that on screen.

'*Bái chī*,' says the girl – Ling? – and although Edna, of course, doesn't know what it means, she can tell by the way Bo hangs his head like a puppy who's been kicked that it isn't anything good.

'Perhaps we can all mingle, get to know each other over sandwiches and cakes!' shouts Barry. 'There is tea and coffee and some fruit juice, I believe, Florin?'

'No gin?' suggests Mrs Slaithwaite.

'No gin,' says Florin firmly.

'No gin, no drugs, no fornication,' says Ibiza Joe morosely. 'Welcome to Sunset Promenade.'

Sandwiches in hand, the residents and the students do indeed begin to mingle. Edna can see Mrs Cantle shuffling towards the Jenny girl, but she swiftly puts herself between them. Ibiza Joe has zeroed in on the lanky boy, no doubt wondering if, with his long hair and sallow complexion, he might be able to help him with his constant mission to relive his youth . . . or at least the youth he wished he'd had. Mr Robinson is talking to the other two, which fills even Edna with a low-level feeling of alarm.

'So are you related, then?' demands Mr Robinson.

The boy opens his mouth to speak but Ling says, with icicles dripping off every word, 'Liu is the fourth most common surname in China, Mr Robinson.'

'It's Second Lieutenant Robinson,' says Mr Robinson proudly, smoothing the corners of his thin moustache. He digs in his pocket and pulls out a leather case, opening it to reveal a shiny medal on a multi-coloured ribbon. He'd shown it to Edna on her first day. 'What do you make of that, then? Don't suppose you see anything like this in China, eh? What are you doing over here, then?'

'We are both at the International Business School,' says Ling. She casts a disgusted look at Bo. 'Though I don't know what good it will do *him*.' She says that phrase again, and Bo brightens up and says to Edna, who he can see is listening, 'It means idiot.'

Edna turns back to Jenny, who is sniffing suspiciously at one of the egg and cress sandwiches. She looks at Edna and says, 'You're the one I met on the stairs. The *Alice in Wonderland* lady.'

'Edna Grey,' says Edna, holding out her hand. 'And you're Jenny . . . Ebert?'

'Yes, pleased to meet you properly,' says Jenny, juggling her cup of juice and paper plate of sandwiches in the crook of one arm so she can take Edna's hand. 'Ebert's right. People usually get it wrong but I've stopped bothering.'

'They've put you on the third floor, haven't they? How are you finding it up there?'

'Fine,' shrugs Jenny. 'I've got a room at the front of the house. Nice sea view, if it ever stops raining.'

Edna watches her drink her juice and risk a nibble of the sandwich, then says, 'You're studying film, is that right? I suppose it's all about those computer effects and flying saucers and whatnot these days.'

Jenny shakes her head, swallowing the mouthful of sandwich. She really could be quite lovely in the hands of a good make-up girl, thinks Edna. 'No, it's not film-making I'm doing. Film studies. We do learn about the techniques and stuff, but it's also about the importance of films, their place in our culture, what they mean, that sort of thing. I'm specialising in film noir. That's—'

'Oh, the old crime movies!' says Edna. Jenny looks impressed and Edna feels annoyed. Why do young people think that old people know absolutely nothing?

'Yes,' says Jenny. 'Sorry, I didn't mean to sound patronising. It's just that I usually have to explain to people what it means.'

'I used to go to the pictures to watch them all the time. Of course, we didn't call them anything as fancy as "film noir". They were all just movies to us. I remember *Gilda*, and that one with Victor Mature – *Kiss of Death*. Oh, and *Criss Cross*. I did use to like Burt Lancaster.'

Jenny stares at her. 'Wow, you know your stuff.'

Edna shrugs. 'I just have a good memory for things I enjoyed.'

But now Jenny is screwing up her face. '*Gilda* was nineteen forty-six, *Kiss of Death* nineteen forty-seven, and *Criss Cross* was . . . forty-nine, I think? You don't look old enough to have watched them at the cinema.'

Edna lays a thin, liver-spotted hand on her arm. 'Bless you, dear. It's a fact I could pass for older when I was a girl, and they weren't as strict at the pictures as they are these days. But I'll be eighty-eight on my next birthday, so I was quite old enough to watch all of those at the cinema.'

Jenny is studying her face and figure with admiration. 'I hope I look as good as you at eighty-eight.'

'You're a kind girl,' says Edna, smiling. 'It's true, I have taken care of myself, I suppose. Good food, regular exercise . . . it all helps.'

She follows Jenny's gaze to Mrs Slaithwaite – big, blousy and ruddy, and glowering with unmistakably rising fury at the chocolate cake, for some imperceptible reason – and Mrs Cantle, hunched over on the sofa, sorting her balled-up handkerchiefs into piles.

'You look brilliant,' says Jenny quietly. 'What's your secret, really? Were you an athlete or something?'

'No,' says Edna, smiling. 'Nothing like that. Just a . . . secretary.'

Suddenly, Mrs Cantle throws up her arms and begins to shout in her high, feeble voice, 'Police! Police! Someone's stolen my jewels!'

As Florin rushes over to calm her, Edna sees Ibiza Joe excuse himself from Ringo and head over to the window, where his shoulders begin to shake. He is crying again. Up one minute, down the next.

'For God's sake!' booms Mr Robinson, furiously straightening his tie. 'What sort of impression do you lot think you're making on these young ones?'

Jenny and Edna lock eyes as Barry, who has been sitting in the corner reading the papers Garry brought in, suddenly realises what is happening and dithers on the carpet, unsure whether to see if Ibiza Joe is all right or to try to calm Mr Robinson, whose face is turning puce.

'This is going to drive me mad,' murmurs Jenny. They both turn to look at Mrs Slaithwaite, still standing by the table bristling with unbridled anger. At that moment the floodgates open and Mrs Slaithwaite, raising a white, doughy hand, screams, 'I FUCKING HATE CHOCOLATE!' then brings her fist down violently, right in the middle of the cake.

Florin, who has been busy picking up all the paper cups discarded on the floor, falls to his knees, his hands flying to his head, and shrieks, 'No!' even as a large dollop of chocolate ganache slaps into his forehead, sticking there with a strawberry protruding like a third eye.

'Bloody hell,' laughs Ibiza Joe, suddenly gleeful. 'She's gone bananas!'

Jenny looks properly shocked at the outburst from Mrs Slaithwaite. Edna sees her exchange a glance with Ringo, and edges closer to them.

'She's mad,' says Ringo, shaking his head.

Jenny catches Edna's eye and smiles thinly. 'We're all mad – isn't that right, Mrs Grey?'

'"You must be," said the Cat, "or you wouldn't have come here",' smiles Edna. 'It was lovely meeting you, Jenny Ebert, but I think this means the party's over.'

10

Suspicion

(1941, dir. Alfred Hitchcock)

Breakfast is taken in the dining room, with a large silver pot full of steaming porridge at the centre of the long table, and on a trolley neat piles of toast and bowls of prunes and fruit.

'Porridge!' says Joe happily, digging in with the long-handled spoon. 'Sticks to your ribs, this!'

Jenny takes a place at the far end of the table from Joe, Mrs Grey and Mrs Cantle. Mrs Slaithwaite hasn't shown up for breakfast, which Joe announces is a normal state of affairs. 'She'll be down just after everything's cleared up, demanding poor old Florin puts her some kippers on.'

Ringo is lounging on a chair at Jenny's end of the table, arms draped over the back, picking at a piece of toast, while Ling and Bo sit together pushing their spoons around a bowl of fruit each. There's a distinct chasm between the two groups at either end of the table.

Jenny has accepted a bowl of porridge and is instantly regretting it. She stands her spoon up in it and watches it slowly list to one side like the mast of a stricken ship, and decides she'll probably just stick to the coffee. Mrs Cantle sees her abandon the breakfast and calls, 'Would you like some prunes, dear? Best thing for keeping you regular. Why, I've been eating prunes for years and every morning at nine o'clock sharp I—'

'Hush, Margaret,' says Edna mildly. 'I believe that's what the young people today would refer to as "too much information".'

'I'm surprised Robbo's not here, though,' says Joe. 'He's usually first at the table.'

As if on cue, Mr Robinson marches into the dining room. 'All right,' he says. 'Who's got it?'

'Got what, Mr Robinson?' says Mrs Cantle. 'The porridge? It's right here.'

'My medal,' seethes Mr Robinson. He puts his fists on his hips and regards the room. 'I had it yesterday. I was showing it to this lot.' He waves his hand in the direction of Bo and Ling. 'Now it's gone.'

Bo shrugs and Ling says nothing. Ringo offers, 'Maybe you just put it down somewhere?'

Robinson zeroes in on him. 'You don't just *put down somewhere* a thing like that, laddie. I've treasured that for more than seventy years. I had it when I was talking to you lot and now it's gone.'

Jenny sips her coffee uncomfortably. What exactly is he implying? That one of them has taken it? Then she remembers her bag, unzipped, the film canisters spilling out. Maybe someone has taken it. She glances at Ringo, Ling and Bo.

'Robbo, it'll turn up,' says Joe. 'Have you asked Florin?'

'It's probably him who's nicked it,' sniffs Mr Robinson. 'You can't trust 'em, you know.'

'That's so offensive,' mutters Ringo, mostly to himself.

But it doesn't escape Mr Robinson, who glares at him. 'Sit up straight. Lounging about like that. Who do you think you're talking to?'

Ringo shrugs and takes another bite of his toast. 'All I'm saying is, you can't go round saying things like that about people, and you especially can't make generalisations like that.'

Robinson folds his arms. 'Well, all I know is that my medal's gone missing. And it's either that Florin or one of you lot.'

Jenny frowns. Normally she'd be quite happy to let someone like Ringo handle an argument like this. But Lauren Bacall wouldn't stand by quietly while someone cast aspersions upon her. She clears her throat and says, 'Why one of us? I'm not being funny, but why can't it be one of *you* lot?'

Mrs Cantle nudges Mrs Grey. 'Is she saying we stole the medal, Edna?'

'I'm not quite sure what she's saying,' says Edna, looking pointedly at Jenny.

'For heaven's sake!' says Ling, finally breaking her silence. 'I can only speak for myself, but I have no interest in your medal and am certainly not a thief. It is just a piece of metal; why would I want it?'

Mr Robinson stares at her in uncomprehending fury. 'Just a piece of metal? Do you know what that represents, missy? Do you know the sacrifices that were made for that medal?' He shakes his head. 'Typical. Just bloody typical. No sense of history, of achievement, of pride.'

Mr Robinson stalks back to the door and points at the students. 'I'm not going to let this lie. There'll be a reckoning, mark my words.'

When he's gone, Joe says gently, 'You'll have to forgive him for getting upset. You young ones . . . you don't understand.'

'I understand he was calling us thieves,' says Ringo. 'Us, or Florin. Like old people are incapable of doing something like that.'

Edna frowns. 'Well, it's possibly true that we do have more . . . respect for things like that.'

Joe nods. 'You're not really sentimental at your age, are you? Which is as it should be. Old things aren't important to you.'

Jenny stirs her porridge and looks at Joe. If only he knew.

Across the Ebert kitchen table are scattered the contents of two cardboard boxes that are so old they can only be called boxes by dint of the fragile cardboard being held in a rough cube shape by perished packing tape.

'I want a good *life*,' says Jenny. 'And how can you say I've wanted for nothing? How can you say that when you've kept *this* a secret for all these years?'

This is strewn across the table, between Jenny and her parents. Curling, typewritten scripts bound with thick, rusting staples. A slim, black leather viewfinder, like one half of a pair of small binoculars. A stack of celluloid loosely spooled on tarnished metal reels, spilling out in 35mm tails. A worn, faded clapperboard, dusty with chalk marks. A brown notebook with the name *W. J. DRAKE* stamped on it in flaking gold leaf.

'Who is W. J. Drake?' says Jenny, her voice cracking.

'Was,' says her mother. 'He was my father. Your grandfather. William Drake.'

'And this . . . ?'

'He made films.'

'Not very successful ones,' says her father. 'None you've ever heard of. Practically bankrupted himself and his family.'

Jenny rubs her temples viciously. She cannot believe this is happening. 'All these years . . . my own granddad was a film-maker. All these years you've kept this locked away in the attic.' She rounds on her father. 'When I wanted to apply for film studies at Loughborough, and you talked me out of it.'

'I still think economics is of immeasurably more—'

'You talked me out of it! And all the time all this was upstairs. Gathering dust. My own granddad made films. And nobody thought to even mention it to me!'

And suddenly her mother is angry, too. Jenny has rarely seen Barbara Ebert lose her temper. But now her thin cheeks redden and her nostrils flare, and she turns her flashing green eyes on her daughter.

'And a lot of good it did him!' shouts Barbara. 'Your father's right. It brought him nothing but trouble. He chased a dream all his life that he never caught, and he dragged the family down with him in the process. You have no idea, Jenny. Tell her, Simon.'

Simon Ebert heaves a sigh. 'William Drake flew by the seat of his pants and seemed to think that he was destined for greater things than those around him. He played fast and loose with his own money and everyone else's. And ultimately, he was a failure.'

The anger is blown out of Barbara Ebert's sails, leaving her becalmed in her own pine-clad kitchen. Jenny looks from her to her father, in his maroon pullover and blue slacks, and she suddenly loathes them both for their ordinariness, which seems to have been put into even sharper relief under the shining glare of the revelation of William Drake.

'Maybe he was a failure,' whispers Jenny. 'But at least he tried.'

'He didn't care about anyone!' her father suddenly shouts. 'Just like you! It looks like the worst of him skipped a generation!'

'Simon . . .' says Barbara, laying a hand on his arm.

'Good!' Jenny shouts back. 'I'm glad! It would have been wasted on you with your boring little lives!' She begins to scoop the reels and scripts back into the boxes. 'I'm taking these to my room. I imagine they'll be useful when I start my film studies course at the University of North Lancashire. Between now and then, it really wouldn't bother me if we didn't speak at all.'

Leaving her mother sobbing quietly in the kitchen, Jenny thunders up the stairs to acquaint herself with the lost world of William J. Drake, and to photograph her treasures to share on Twitter. Not that anyone in the world will care.

'Still think this is an interesting, exciting thing to do?' asks Jenny, as the small bus rattles into the turning circle at the front of the main University of North Lancashire campus. One bus runs every two hours along the old coast road, and not after six in the evening. She's kept Kevin the taxi driver's card in her purse; she has a feeling she's going to need him quite a lot if she doesn't want to get stuck in the rest home after the sun's set.

'You mean living at Sunset Promenade?' says Ringo, hopping out into the rain. Jenny has remembered her umbrella this time and puts it up to protect her hair; Ringo slides underneath it without being asked. 'Yeah, why not?'

Ling and Bo get off the bus behind her; Ling hasn't spoken a word all through the journey other than to hiss sharply at Bo when he tried to sit with her; instead he hung his head low and walked to the back of the bus. As Ling strides off towards the university gates, Bo walks cautiously behind her. Jenny wonders if she'll ever understand those two.

'Well, for starters, the fact they think we're a bunch of crooks.' Jenny pauses at the wide entrance road on to the campus and looks at the mix of squat buildings and tall blocks. Towards the rear of the site she can see the scaffolding-clad new blocks, which should have been ready by now but are behind schedule. Had they been ready, she'd never have set foot in Sunset Promenade, and wouldn't be feeling mildly furious like she does now.

'Yeah, that was a bit full-on,' says Ringo, following her gaze. 'Hey, just think, if they hadn't fallen behind on the construction we'd never have met.'

She gives him a sidelong glance. 'No, I don't suppose we would. Have you got lectures today?'

'Nah, not until next week. To be honest, creative writing's a bit light on lectures. Didn't even need to be in today. Thought I'd come and show you round.'

Jenny smooths down the front of her dress with her free hand. 'That's kind of you. But I think I'll be fine.' She looks around at the students rushing through the rain, wondering which ones are *her people*. Where do the cool kids hang out? Where are the classy ones, the stylish ones, the ones who have fun? She's not making the same mistake she made at Loughborough; she's not getting saddled with the wrong people. She gives Ringo another quick glance. 'Honestly. I think it's better if I explore by myself, get used to the place.'

Ringo shrugs and extracts himself from the shelter of the umbrella. 'Cool. I'll catch you later, then. I saw Florin cooking up some kind of stew for tea.'

Jenny pulls a face. 'Is there a Nando's around here?'

Ringo laughs. 'See you back at the ranch.'

Jenny watches him go and lights herself a Gauloise. He lopes across the university grounds, high-fiving a guy in a long coat, turning to walk backwards as he chats to a group of girls hidden under anorak hoods, hopping leggily over a puddle on the tarmac. She takes a drag of her cigarette and lets the smoke leak from her lips, imagining herself in black and white.

Registration is in the atrium of the main building, and just involves signing a few forms and arranging course payment from her student loan. There's a freshers' fair in the bright, airy space, and though she's officially transferring as a second year she browses the stalls and noticeboards, lingering by the film club stand. A big guy with a beard and a *Terminator* T-shirt hands her a flyer.

'Don't you watch proper films?' she asks, perusing the list of upcoming dates.

He sniffs. 'Bet you're doing film studies, aren't you? There's nothing wrong with those.' He jabs a finger at the list of science-fiction blockbusters and superhero movies. 'That's what people like.'

Jenny decides she won't be attending the film club after all, and joins the queue shuffling towards the desk to register for her course.

When she's signed everything and given them her full address –
'though it's only until the new accommodation block opens' – she
notices two girls also registering for her course. Jenny appraises
them critically; both are casually but expensively dressed, exuding
style. Taking a deep breath, she goes over to introduce herself.

The girls are called Amber and Saima, and they look Jenny up
and down for a moment. 'Nice dress,' says Amber.

'We're going to the refectory for a coffee, if you want to come,'
adds Saima.

Jenny orders an espresso and a glass of water, not because she
likes it but because she thinks it's the sort of thing a femme fatale
should drink. They find a table near the wide glass windows. Saima
takes a lock of Jenny's hair in her fingers and says, 'That must take
you ages. I like it. Well retro.'

'What's the tutor like?' asks Jenny, sipping her espresso and
practising that Bacall look, chin on chest and eyes cast upwards.
It's more awkward than it looks on screen.

'Fran?' says Amber. 'He's all right, I suppose. Quite young.
Looks a bit like that guy.' She clicks her fingers and turns to
Saima. 'What's his name?'

'Idris Elba,' nods Saima. 'He's fairly easy-going.'

'I hope I haven't missed too much from the first year,' says
Jenny. 'I wanted to come straight in as a second-year transfer, not
start the course from scratch.'

Saima pulls a face. 'It was a lot of French stuff. And narrative
structure. I can't even remember most of it.'

'Fran likes old stuff,' says Amber. 'Really old stuff. Like, black-
and-white stuff.'

Idris Elba and old films, thinks Jenny. Maybe things are looking
up after all.

'Hey, do you know that guy?' asks Saima.

Jenny looks up and out of the window. Ringo is outside standing
on the wet grass, waving maniacally with both hands, drenched
by the rain.

'I know him, I think. He's a right weirdo,' laughs Amber.

Jenny puts her head down and peers into the dregs of her tiny
coffee cup. 'No,' she says quietly. 'I don't know him.'

Why does saying that make her feel so bad? She barely knows Ringo. Out of the corner of her eye she can see him throwing shapes, doing some crazy semaphore thing, his arms outstretched.

'Oh my God,' says Saima. 'What's he doing? He's such a doofus.'

Jenny turns slightly so her back is against the window and she can't see Ringo any more, and laughs hollowly. 'What a doofus.'

11

The Sound of Fury

(1950, dir. Cy Endfield)

'Twenty-two,' calls Florin. There's a collective sigh from those gathered in the day room.

'Not like that, dearie,' says Mrs Cantle, her felt-tip dabber poised over her bingo card. 'You have to say "two little ducks".'

'Quack, quack!' say Ibiza Joe, Mrs Slaithwaite and even Mr Robinson, in unison.

Jenny, who is sandwiched between Edna and Mrs Cantle on one sofa, exchanges a glance with Ringo, who is squashed between Ibiza Joe and Mr Robinson on the opposing one. They both look towards Bo and Ling to await the inevitable.

Bo raises an uncertain hand but Ling, nostrils flaring and eyes closed, holds out her own palm to fend him off. 'It is because the two number twos look like ducks,' she says with barely controlled anger.

Bo ponders, then smiles broadly and shouts out, 'Quack, quack! Bingo!'

Ling waves her arms. 'You do not have bingo! You only say that when you have filled the whole card! You do not even have twenty-two!'

Florin, who is sitting on a stool in front of the television, turns the handle on the plastic bingo cage. The balls roll around and he stops turning, flips open the lid of the cage and pulls out another ball. 'Two little ducks . . . eighty-eight!'

'Oh, for God's sake!' says Mr Robinson, hurling his dabber down on the carpet. 'That's two fat ladies, isn't it? How can eighty-eight be two little ducks? We've just bloody had two little ducks.'

Florin's face contorts with anguish and he says, 'I am still learning! Give me a chance!'

'Shake 'em up!' shouts Mrs Slaithwaite. 'I'm sweating here.'

Jenny feels Mrs Cantle's bony elbow nudging her arm. 'You've got eighty-eight, lovey,' she says, pointing at Jenny's card. Jenny quickly blots it with her red dabber.

'OK,' says Florin, reaching in again. 'Number ten . . . Maggie's den.'

'Boo!' shouts Ibiza Joe.

'Shut up,' snaps Mr Robinson. 'Best bloody leader this country had since Churchill.'

Jenny glances at Ringo and he shrugs and pulls a face. Their gazes both shift towards Bo.

'Who is Maggie?'

'Thatcher!' rumbles Mr Robinson. 'Damn fine woman.'

'Ruined this country,' says Ibiza Joe.

'We wouldn't be in the mess we're in now if she was still with us,' counters Mr Robinson reverently.

'Yes,' says Ling. 'She will forever be remembered in China as the leader who negotiated the rightful return of Hong Kong.'

Mr Robinson tugs at his moustache and stares at her. 'Well, I never said she was perfect, did I?' He stabs his retrieved dabber viciously at his card. 'So what do you pair want with us, anyway?'

'Bit aggressive, Robbo,' murmurs Ibiza Joe.

Ling folds her arms and stares back at Mr Robinson. She is very stylish, almost effortlessly so, thinks Jenny. She is wearing a black dress with a wide white belt and a kind of flower-petal-shaped white collar. Jenny suspects that if she wore that she would look like someone dressed as a nun at a Halloween party. Ling looks like Audrey Hepburn. With an audible and rather challenging click, Ling puts the top on her dabber. 'You want to know why Liu Bo and myself are here? *Only* Liu Bo and myself?'

Mr Robinson shrugs and holds his dabber out, clicking his own top on with a flourish. That's the gauntlet down, then, thinks Jenny. 'Yes, just you two,' nods Mr Robinson.

'And by "here" do you mean in this house, or at the university, or in your country?'

'All of it.'

Florin tries an experimental turn of the bingo cage, but everyone glares at him and he stops. Ling says, 'Very well. We are in this house because the University of North Lancashire has failed to complete construction of its new accommodation blocks in time. This is a slipshod approach that would not have happened in China. We are at the University of North Lancashire because it offers an internationally renowned package of courses in business management and targets overseas students, which impressed my father. We are in your country because there is money to be made from your own incredible stupidity.'

There is a collective intake of breath, withdrawing so much air from the room that Jenny imagines she feels momentarily faint. She looks at Ling with a mixture of shock and admiration.

'Who's she calling stupid?' says Mrs Slaithwaite loudly.

'Bloody cheek of it,' Mr Robinson mutters.

Ibiza Joe frowns. 'What do you mean, exactly, miss?'

'She means you're bloody stupid – she just said so, didn't she?' scoffs Mr Robinson. 'That's what they think of us, isn't it? It's all coming out now.'

Ling says something to Bo and he lets loose a torrent of Chinese at her. She nods thoughtfully and says in English, 'It is your Brexit. In China, we were shocked that you would embark on such a thing with what seemed to us no proper planning or contingencies. China has invested a lot of money into the United Kingdom; this came as a surprise to us and the Chinese do not really like surprises.'

Mr Robinson waves his hand dismissively. 'Ah, what do you know about it? I've been saying it for years, we're better off bloody out of Europe. We don't need their meddling human rights nonsense and their interfering with everything. Deciding whether bloody bananas are too straight or too bendy.'

'We don't need no bloody Germans or French or anything!' shouts Mrs Slaithwaite, a red flush climbing up her doughy neck. 'They don't call us Great Britain for nothing!'

'Yes!' shouts Mr Robinson, pointing at Mrs Slaithwaite. His blood is up. He points his dabber at Florin, waving it like a magic wand that could make him disappear in a puff of red, white and blue smoke. 'It's you lot who should be worrying. No more gravy train for the likes of you.'

'Calm down, Robbo,' says Ibiza Joe. He looks at Florin. 'He doesn't mean it, lad.'

Suddenly, Ringo springs up from the sofa like Tigger, surprising Jenny. He rounds on Mr Robinson. 'You don't even know what you voted for! It won't even affect you for long! It's us that have to live with it, and we weren't even allowed a vote because we weren't eighteen!'

Ibiza Joe stands too, holding out his hands for peace. 'Ringo, lad, you have to realise . . . we were sold a pup with Europe. Back in seventy-five, I voted to go in.'

'So did I,' says Mrs Cantle. 'It all sounded rather wonderful.'

'But it wasn't what they said it would be,' continues Joe. 'We thought we were joining a big club, that it would be all pals together, but then it was all this money going to Europe, and them telling us what to do . . .'

'But you didn't think about us when it came to voting to come out again,' says Ringo, exasperated. 'You forgot you'd had it all very nice . . . you could afford to buy a house, you got to go to university for free if you wanted, you've all got pensions. We don't have anything like that, because you've wrung it all out of the country and now you've taken away any chance we had to be a part of something.'

'We don't need that lot!' sneers Mr Robinson. 'They're queuing up to deal with us. America, India, Russia, China . . .'

As he tails off everyone looks towards Ling. She nods. 'Exactly. We're queuing up to deal with Britain. And we've got the upper hand. You need us more than we need you.' She sits back, a satisfied smile on her face. 'Like I said, there is money to be made from your stupidity.'

There's a long silence, then Mrs Slaithwaite sighs and says, 'Bollocks to it all, anyway. We'll either be dead or doolally by the time it's all sorted.'

'That's kind of the point,' says Ringo, banging his knuckles on his forehead and sitting down again. '*We* won't.'

Edna leans forward and says, 'But this is your chance to make it work for you, surely? I must say, I do find that there's a certain paucity of . . . spirit among the younger generation. This is a situation you cannot change; surely you should make the best of it?'

'You sound just like my parents,' says Jenny, finally breaking her silence. Ringo gives her a puppy-dog look from across the room and she glares at him. She doesn't want his sympathy. 'They wanted me to stay doing a degree I hated in a university I hated. They wanted me to just keep at it.'

'Like Winston Churchill said,' nods Mr Robinson with a satisfied smile, 'Keep Buggering On.'

'But what if we don't want to?' says Jenny, exasperated. 'What if we don't want to make the best of a situation we never asked to be in?'

'We never asked to be bombed in the war but we had no choice,' says Mrs Cantle. 'We didn't just roll over and die.'

'Where would you lot be if we had?' says Mr Robinson triumphantly. 'Bit of Blitz spirit, that's what your generation needs. Suck it up and crack on. That's the ticket.'

Jenny folds her arms and sits back. Why are old people so bloody infuriating? Why do they think their way is the only way? Why can't they see that the world's changed so much since they were young, that it's a different place with different rules?

'This is never going to work,' she mutters.

Edna looks at her. 'But it's too late now, isn't it? It's all underway. That's our point, Jenny. You're on the path now. It might seem unfair, but if it doesn't work it's down to you.'

Jenny looks around at them all, at the day room, at Sunset Promenade. 'I wasn't talking about Brexit,' she says quietly. She waves her arm over her head. 'I was talking about all this. Us. You. Under the same roof. It's never going to work.'

The room goes quiet, a silence broken only by the rattle of the balls in the bingo cage that Florin has started turning again. Everyone shifts to look at him as he puts his hand in the plastic barrel and pulls out a ball. He ponders it and says hesitantly, 'Um . . . one and one . . . legs eleven?'

'House!' bellows Mr Robinson, stabbing at his card with a flourish. He brandishes it around the room, flapping it in Jenny's direction. 'Ha! Put that in your pipe and smoke it!'

Jenny stands up and Ringo follows suit. She looks at Florin. 'I think I'll skip dinner tonight, if you don't mind.'

'Me too,' says Ringo.

'But I have made a stew!' says a stricken Florin.

Ling stands also, Bo right behind her. She says, 'I, too, am not coming for stew.'

Bo hurries after her as she leaves the room with the others, then turns to the bereft Florin and says, 'Can you save me stew? One bowl? No, two?'

As Jenny stalks through the doorway, she hears Mr Robinson cackling. 'That bloody showed them! They don't like it up 'em, do they, these kids? Now come on, Florin lad, get those balls back in that cage and let's have another game. I'm on a winning streak here.'

✳ 12 ✳

The Dark Mirror

(1946, dir. Robert Siodmak)

Fran does indeed look quite like Idris Elba, though younger –
only in his twenties, thinks Jenny – and rather more clean-cut.
He wears chinos turned up to show his ankles and sockless feet
shoved into battered Adidas trainers, and his slim, muscular
frame inhabits a collarless shirt, the sleeves rolled up to his
elbows. A plain gold wedding band glints in the light from his
desk lamp as he taps heavily on the keyboard in front of him.
A thought comes from nowhere; she wonders if she's his type.
The rain is lashing against the single window of his office, which
is cramped with a filing cabinet and bookshelves sagging under
all kinds of volumes of film theory and scripts of classic and
obscure movies.

'Well,' says Fran. He picks up a pencil and taps the rubber on
the end against the wood of his desk.

Jenny doesn't know what she's supposed to say to that, so
just smiles. Eventually he says, 'It's quite unusual to switch from
economics to film studies.' Then he frowns. 'Isn't it?'

'I suppose,' says Jenny. 'I really took economics because my
parents pushed me towards it. But I hated it. And Loughborough.
And I'd heard good things about your course.'

Fran takes the compliment, beaming. 'Yes, well, we are considered one of the best. It's also a bit unusual to start a course in the
second year. I must say, I was doubtful at first. You have missed a
lot. However . . .' He draws the word out, absently drumming a
light cadence on the desk with the pencil. 'The assessment project
for the end of the third term was actually fairly light. And you

managed to complete the assignment over the summer, as was one of the conditions of your acceptance.'

'What did you think of it?' says Jenny. She had indeed completed the assignment over the summer, a five-thousand-word mini dissertation. To be honest, she found it a bit of a breeze. She wonders if she should have spent more time on it. She's been given a place, obviously, but Fran would be well within his rights to have her start the course from the first year, should he want to.

He sits back in his chair and swivels away from the monitor. 'Your area of expertise appears to be film noir. Why's that?'

Jenny takes a deep breath. 'Because . . . everything's uncertain. And chaotic. It feels like we're alienating each other with everything we do, even with all our technology and social media. Because we're damned if we do and damned if we don't, there's no escaping that. Because the good guys don't always win, crime sometimes pays, and the road to hell is paved with good intentions. The themes of noir are as relevant today for my generation as they were in the forties.'

Fran pulls an impressed face. 'Cinema of any era is a dark mirror that reflects our modern lives, for sure. But Jenny . . . so young, yet so cynical?'

Jenny returns the challenge with what she fears might be a sneer. 'What's a nice girl like me doing in a genre like this, you mean?'

'Woah. I didn't mean it like that.' He muses. 'Well, yes, I suppose I did. Which takes me back to my original question: why film noir? Why all that . . . that existential angst?'

'I'm a teenager. I'm supposed to have existential angst.'

Fran blows through pursed lips. 'Well, you'd think so. Back in my day, for sure. Today . . . well, let's just say it's nice to meet a student railing against the moral ambiguity of an uncaring universe instead of complaining about the campus wi-fi coverage.'

'That's life. Whichever way you turn, fate sticks out a foot to trip you up,' says Jenny, suddenly a tough-talking Yank. Fran raises an eyebrow. Jenny blushes slightly and mutters, 'Tom Neal in *Detour*, nineteen forty-five.'

'I'll take your word for it. You know your stuff. Who's your favourite director?'

Jenny leans forward. 'Have you ever heard of William J. Drake . . . ?'

Fran sits back, looking at her curiously. 'Now that's some top-level name you're throwing out. One for the cognoscenti. I might be tempted to think you've picked the most obscure director you could to impress me. But I think you've more about you than that. So, impress me.'

Jenny takes a deep breath. 'He only made four movies, in the late nineteen forties. They did all right but they never really became classics. Mainly because the studio went bust and the liquidators seized everything, all the reels, all the equipment.' She pauses. 'He was supposed to be working on a fifth when he just let it all go.'

Fran shrugs. 'It says as much on Wikipedia. Impress me some more. Which is your favourite of his films?'

Jenny smiles. 'Now you're trying to catch me out. If you read the same Wikipedia entry I did, you'll know that he released *Ice in my Heart*, *Alone with Everybody*, *The Firebugs* and *Off Devil's Head*. They did well enough at the box office and he got a good reputation in the British film industry. Even Hollywood was beginning to take notice. But unless you were around in the forties you won't have seen them . . . they've never been on TV or released on video. All the copies of them were destroyed when he closed his studios.'

Fran nods. 'Very good. I'd love to have seen them. I've read the reviews, of course, from the time, and they've been described in books on the genre. They sound very good.'

'They are.'

Fran raises an eyebrow. Jenny goes on, 'I have what are probably the only surviving thirty-five-millimetre copies of all four of them. I had them transferred to DVD over the summer.'

She's gratified to see his eyes widen. 'But . . . how? Where did you find them? They'd be worth a fortune to the right collectors. Hell, I'd pay a fortune for them, if I had a fortune.'

'William J. Drake was my grandfather.'

Fran sits back and whistles. 'Well. That sounds like your final project all sorted, then.'

Jenny blinks. 'So I'm in, then? I can start the second year?'

He grins. 'I should say so.' He peers at his monitor. 'Ah, you're staying at the old folks' place. Sunset Promenade, right? I read about that in the university newsletter. Here, let me print you out the course notes and module handbook.'

Jenny's heart bangs. Why is he asking that? Why is he taking an interest in where she lives? She gives him another appraisal. He is very good-looking, she thinks. Maybe that is something the new, improved Jenny Ebert would, and indeed, *should* do. An affair with her lecturer. That's a very femme fatale thing. A flight of butterflies goes crazy in her stomach at the audacious idea of it.

'Yes,' she says. 'Sunset Promenade. It's . . . different. I was hoping to get into halls of residence on campus but the new blocks aren't finished yet . . .' She glances at his wedding ring. Is he divorced, perhaps, just wears it out of habit? She blinks as he starts talking again.

'Well, it's been lovely meeting you, Jenny. Such a breath of fresh air to get someone who already has such a knowledge of film.' He gathers the print-outs and taps their edges on the desk to collate them all neatly. He jots a number down on the top sheet. 'Here you go. I've put my mobile on there in case you have any questions before the lecture sessions begin. My office number's in the handbook, but to be honest I'm not here a lot.'

Jenny takes the sheets and stares at the phone number, almost unwittingly committing it to memory instantly. She wonders if everyone has his mobile. As she stands up and shoves the papers in her bag, Fran reaches into the pocket of the jacket hanging over the back of his chair and pulls out a battered blue pack of Gauloises. He shrugs and gives her a smile. 'We all have our weaknesses.'

Jenny decides to walk into town before getting the bus back to Sunset Promenade, explore Morecambe a little. She also has to go to the local branch of her bank, get all her accounts transferred over here. She wanders up Marine Road, past the Eric Morecambe statue that Kevin showed her on her first day, the rain driving almost horizontally from the sea. She ducks into a side street populated with the usual shops you get anywhere, past a generic fried chicken outlet, and, as she's hurrying towards where Google Maps tells her the bank is, she sees Barry Grange, huddled inside a raincoat and walking just ahead of her.

Jenny feels like a detective from one of her movies as she shadows him along the pavement, then realises he's going to the same place as her. She puts her head down – purely for the fun of it – as he looks around before stepping into the bank, then follows him in, shaking out her umbrella in the foyer.

It's a small branch with two open desks near a paying-in machine, and just one teller position open. There's a small queue and Jenny loiters near a rack of leaflets about loans and mortgages, watching Barry as he stands by one of the vacant desks, taking off his raincoat. Through a glass door a man in a suit emerges, greeting Barry by name.

'Mr Grange, sit down. Awful weather.'

Barry looks perturbed. 'Isn't Mr Costigan in?'

'Didn't you know?' says the man. 'He's retired early. On health grounds. I'm Mark Lewis. I'm handling the business accounts now.' The man sits and logs on to the computer at the desk. He reads for a moment, frowning, then says, 'You're looking to borrow?'

Barry sighs and sits down, glancing around. Jenny holds a leaflet on ISAs up in front of her face, then peers cautiously over the top of it. Barry has turned back to the banker. 'Yes. Just short-term. We've got a new revenue stream just underway but we need a little . . . bridging funding.'

'Ah, yes,' says Mr Lewis. 'The students. You mentioned that to Mr Costigan last time. There's a note on your file.' He taps at his keyboard. 'Hmm. Remind me, Mr Grange . . . your current funding . . .'

'We've had some very good years – Mr Costigan would tell you that,' says Barry quickly. 'It's mainly been through various grants and hand-outs from quite a few social funds. That's how we keep costs down so much for the residents. But most of this money comes from Europe, and for some time we've been quite worried about what was going to happen to that, with all the European Union stuff that's going on . . .' Barry pauses. 'We've been approached by a big company, the Care Network. They want to buy us out, take over Sunset Promenade. We've got an inspection coming up at the end of October and we're set to pass with flying colours, I think, which would make us an especially attractive proposition.'

'Well, that's a positive sign in this climate, isn't it?' says Mr Lewis encouragingly.

Barry shakes his head. 'For Garry and I, perhaps. Not for Sunset Promenade. Not for the residents. No one would run it like we do. It would lose its . . . soul. But if we don't sell, then we're relying on the grants continuing. And we've been having quite a lot of communications with the various funds these past few months. None of them will commit to renewing our funding past the end of the year.'

'Oh.'

Jenny edges closer, pretending to use the paying-in machine. That did sound quite bad.

'That's why we brought the students in. That enabled us to access some different funding. Everything has to be about interaction, innovation, social responsibility, you see. It's helped for a while, but we're already in the middle of October, and come Christmas . . .' Barry shrugs sadly. 'Unless we can prove our viability as a going concern we won't be able to renew our licence to operate as a rest home. We might have to make a choice between selling up or closing down.'

Barry falls silent as Mr Lewis taps at his keyboard for a while. Eventually the banker says, 'Well, I'm pleased to say that it's extremely positive—'

'It is?' says Barry, brightening.

'—that you've got this potential offer for the business on the table,' finishes Mr Lewis. 'Because, although Mr Costigan might have been a little . . . generous with your borrowing needs in the past, I'm very much afraid that in the current climate and with the uncertainty over your continued funding streams . . .' Mr Lewis holds out his hands, palms upwards, apologetically.

'Computer says no,' says Barry hollowly.

Mr Lewis smiles. 'Quite.'

As Barry stands up and begins to climb into his raincoat, Jenny puts her head down and hurries towards the door, all thoughts of putting her own accounts in order forgotten. Outside in the rain she crosses the road and pretends to stare into a shop window, instead watching in the glass the reflection of Barry Grange as he walks slowly out of the bank and up the street, his shoulders slumped.

What, she wonders for the umpteenth time, has she wandered into at Sunset Promenade?

In a Lonely Place

(1950, dir. Nicholas Ray)

A foreboding soundtrack issues from the TV as white text begins to scroll up the screen.

In 1539, the Knights Templar of Malta paid tribute to Charles V of Spain, by sending him a Golden Falcon encrusted from beak to claw with rarest jewels – but pirates seized the galley carrying this priceless token and the fate of the Maltese Falcon remains a mystery to this day—

As the screen turns to black and a view of the Golden Gate Bridge fades in, with the words *SAN FRANCISCO* writ large across it, the wind is abruptly knocked from the sails of the argument. Jenny looks at each of the residents in turn as their eyes graze towards the TV and the music takes on a jauntier tone.

'Now,' says Mr Robinson, sitting back and folding his arms, as if the movie has somehow proved all his points. 'This is what you call a picture.'

'They don't make them like this any more,' agrees Mrs Slaithwaite.

'Ooh, he was handsome,' says Mrs Cantle, nudging Jenny. 'He's Humphrey Bogart. He was a famous—'

'I know who he was,' says Jenny, more sharply than she intended to.

'Of course she does.' Jenny feels the weight of Edna's stare from the side of her. 'I mean, everyone knows Humphrey Bogart.'

'What is this, anyway?' says Ringo, leaning forward to peer at the TV.

'*The Maltese Falcon*!' they shout in unison, and Ringo puts his hands up in mock surrender.

Mr Robinson shakes his head, frowning but happy. 'See? Not a bloody clue, these kids. It's all that bloody YouTube and supermen and—'

'*The Maltese Falcon* was John Huston's debut as a director,' Jenny says, quietly but forcefully enough to cut Mr Robinson off. 'It premiered in New York on the third of October nineteen forty-one, and got three Oscar nominations. It's based on the nineteen twenty-nine novel by Dashiell Hammett, who had worked as a private investigator himself for the Pinkerton Agency.' She looks at Mrs Cantle. 'Apparently Bogart wasn't the first choice to play Sam Spade. The producers wanted George Raft.'

Mrs Cantle screws up her face. 'I think I met him once.' She leans forward and looks across Jenny at Edna. 'Did I meet George Raft, or—?'

'I'm sure I wouldn't know, dear,' says Edna frostily, and keeps her eyes on the screen, where Sam Spade is looking at the gun that killed his partner Miles Archer, his hands shoved in the pockets of his trench coat, muttering, 'They don't make 'em any more.'

'He's not wrong – they don't, like Mrs Slaithwaite says,' says Ibiza Joe. 'Not like this. Bloody good film.' He looks across the day room at Jenny. 'You know your stuff, though. You like the old pictures?'

Jenny nods, being drawn into the movie, although she's seen it more times than she can count. 'They're sort of my speciality.' Especially this one, she thinks.

When she is eight years old, Jenny says to her mother, 'Why are you not as young as all the other mummies?'

'You just came to us later, when we were a little bit older than the mummies and daddies of the other children in your class,' says Barbara, wrestling Jenny into the purple quilted coat that comes down to below her knees and which she hates. It is a cold day, Jenny remembers still, close to Christmas, the gloom of dusk settling at school home-time as the winter marches on to its midpoint.

'You look nearly as old as Lisa's granny,' Jenny says, matter-of-factly. If she sees the look of sudden shock on her mother's face, she does not register it.

'Lisa Holmfirth's grandmother has at least ten years on me,' says Barbara stiffly. 'Besides, she had Lisa's mummy when she was very young, and Lisa's mummy had *her* very young . . .'

'Is it better to have babies when you are young or old?' says Jenny as they walk, hand in hand, along the pavement, Jenny skipping between the flags that are not cracked. It is bad luck to stand on a cracked paving flag, Jasmine told her a week ago, and Jenny has been diligent in avoiding them ever since.

By the time they get home Jenny has forgotten she asked the question, and that she did not receive an answer, and her mother sits her down in front of the TV in the living room and puts it on to CBBC. She brings Jenny a drink of juice and a nutritious but not very tasty cereal bar to snack on, and says she is going to have her dinner ready in an hour. When she has gone, Jenny sips her juice and pushes the cereal bar between the cushions of the leather sofa – along with yesterday's, and the day before's – and stares at the TV for a bit. There is something on about children living together in a big house, and Jenny wonders what that might be like. None of the children seems very happy. Jenny finds the show quite tedious and reaches for the remote control, cycling through the channels until a grey screen bursts out from the parade of colour. Jenny stops flicking and listens to the music for a moment. She is a very good reader for her age and she watches the list of unfamiliar names that appears, followed by the title of the film.

The Maltese Falcon.

Jenny sits back on the sofa and slowly sips her juice, eyes fixed to the TV.

An hour later when Barbara comes back into the room she looks at the TV, then at Jenny, then back at the film. 'What on earth are you watching?'

Jenny looks at her. 'The stuff that dreams are made of.' She has remembered the line said by the craggy-faced man in the hat.

Barbara picks up the remote and points it at the TV. 'You're supposed to be watching CBBC.'

'That's boring!' says Jenny. 'I'm watching this! It's got people being killed and hitting each other and a statue that everybody wants.'

79

Her mother frowns at her. 'You'll watch what I say you watch, young lady.'

Jenny sticks out her lip and folds her arms. 'Keep on riding me and they're gonna be picking iron out of your liver.'

'Jenny Ebert! Go to your room at once!'

Jenny slides off the sofa and stalks past her mother, holding her gaze. Barbara folds her arms and raises one eyebrow. 'Don't you have anything to say to me?'

Jenny looks away and carries on walking towards the door. 'The best goodbyes are short. Adieu,' she says, then runs upstairs to her bedroom.

'Do you miss your mum and dad?' asks Ringo, watching her from the floor by the window, where he's contorted himself into a sitting position. She doesn't even know why he's in her room. He just sort of followed her upstairs after they'd watched *The Maltese Falcon*.

'What sort of question's that?' she says. 'Do you?'

'Of course I do. Damn. Look at that.' Ringo has a long dark stain down his T-shirt, which he's rubbing at ineffectually. 'Florin's dinner. What exactly was in that casserole, anyway? It tasted weird.'

Jenny wriggles off the bed and goes to her wardrobe, fishing out a fresh T-shirt. It says *THE RAMONES* on the front – a band she's never even heard the music of, but suitably retro enough to be cool, she thinks. It still has the tags hanging from the back, which she surreptitiously rips off before tossing it across the room to Ringo. 'Put that on,' she says. 'You're starting to smell.'

'Cheers,' he says, and peels off his own T-shirt. Jenny looks away then back at Ringo; there's not an ounce of fat on him, she thinks with a tinge of envy. There are supermodels who would kill for a figure like his. He drags the Ramones T-shirt on and it hangs off him, hatefully, better than it ever would on her. He looks down and clicks his tongue appreciatively. 'Nice one.' Then he balls up his dirty T-shirt and says, so conversationally it throws Jenny, 'Are you lonely?'

Is this a come-on? Should she feel worried? No one saw them come upstairs; no one knows they're up here together. She's just told him to take his T-shirt off, she realises. Would people see that as some kind of invitation? What if he tried something on? Jenny's pretty sure a solid kick in the balls would snap Ringo in two, but are people going to think she's led him on? Then she becomes angry, with him and herself. She didn't ask him to come in here. Whatever he does, it's not her fault, it's his.

'You can go now,' she says.

'What?'

'You can go now.'

He looks so crestfallen she almost feels sorry for him, but he unwinds his legs and pushes himself up to a standing position, scooping up his T-shirt. Ringo lopes to the door and before he leaves he turns and says, 'I know what it's like, you know. To lose parents. There are lots of people you can talk to. It doesn't have to be me. That's why I asked you if you remembered the last conversation you had with them. It's one of the things they asked me when I went for therapy. It helps you realise that nothing was your fault.'

Jenny says nothing and Ringo nods, smiles and lets himself out.

Everything was her fault.

'Jenny!' calls Barbara Ebert. 'We're going out and we'd like you to come with us.'

Jenny sits in her bedroom, head cocked to one side, considering her mother's words issuing up the stairs. She's at the desk poring over the script of one of her grandfather's films. It's dog-eared and frayed and held together with a massive split pin driven through the top left-hand corner. On the top sheet is a brown ring, a stain from a coffee cup. It smells faintly of tobacco. Jenny has been holding the document, eyes closed, drinking in its smells, imagining herself back when this script was in the hands of an investor or actor or producer, newly typed. She wishes she could put herself there – forever – in 1946. If the past is another country, then get her a one-way ticket and stamp her visa right now. She ignores her mother and runs her fingertips over the page, feeling the almost imperceptible indentations the hammers have made on the paper, and pictures him, her grandfather, William J. Drake himself, bent over his typewriter bashing at the keys.

'Jenny.' Her mother has let herself into her room, standing at the door. Jenny ignores her; she's been doing that since she found all of her grandfather's stuff in the attic a week ago.

'We've got a surprise for you,' says Barbara, perching herself on the edge of Jenny's bed. 'Me and your father. But you'll have to come with us to get it.'

Half an hour later, still not having spoken, Jenny is in the back seat of the car, looking out of the window at unfamiliar country roads. Her father is driving and her mother burbling on about inconsequential things. Then her father pulls into a small industrial estate and parks in front of a single-storey unit.

'Won't be a tick,' he says, and disappears inside.

Jenny peers at the sign fixed to the breeze-block wall. *ALLEN & SMITHEE AUDIO-VISUAL SERVICES*. She raises an eyebrow, but feigns indifference to the expectant looks her mother is casting over the back of her seat. Some crap to buy her off, she shouldn't wonder. Some utterly pointless, empty gesture that will hit so wide of the mark it'll prove once again just how little her parents know her.

When her father emerges with a cardboard box, Jenny takes out her phone and begins scrolling through her social media accounts, though she barely has any followers or friends on them. Simon Ebert slides into his seat and hands the box to her mother, who passes it to the back. Jenny sighs and takes it, and opens the cardboard flaps.

'We thought you might like—'

'Oh my God!' exclaims Jenny, holding up the first plastic case. 'You've had Grandad's films transferred to DVD!'

'Well, yes,' says Barbara. 'We were going to find a film projector and we can still buy one but we thought it might be better to protect the originals and just watch these . . .'

'Thank you!' beams Jenny. This is the first thing they've done for her that actually makes her happy, she thinks. Dad starts the car and pulls back on to the country road.

They've been driving for a quarter of an hour, Jenny inspecting the DVDs and holding the original 35mm reels up to the light from the window, when she realises they aren't going back the way they came.

'Where are we going now?' she says.

Her mother turns in her seat and smiles. Jenny freezes. She knows that smile. 'Well, as you're so pleased with those DVDs we thought you wouldn't mind doing something for us.'

'Doing *what* for you?'

'Well, it's not really for us, it's for you,' says her father with forced warmth.

'Where are we going?' demands Jenny, replacing the film and DVDs in the box.

'No one's saying you can't do the film stuff as – as a hobby,' says Barbara, her face stuck in a wide grin as though she's some kind of robot. 'But as a, well, potential career . . .'

'Look,' says Simon Ebert, glancing at Jenny in the rear-view mirror. All pretence at friendliness has melted away. 'We've been in touch with your tutors at Loughborough. They've agreed to reverse your decision to leave the economics course. I mean, we had to jump through a lot of hoops, let me tell you, but they're letting you keep your place.' He gives a self-satisfied smile. 'I like to think my standing in the local business community certainly opened a few doors. Greased a few wheels. You just have to go in and sign the papers saying you've changed your mind.'

'That's where we're going,' says Barbara, her smile still set as if in stone. 'Then we can go straight home and you can watch your grandad's films.'

Jenny realises she's been clenching her fists so tightly that her knuckles have gone white and her nails are digging into her palms. 'How. Fucking. Dare. You,' she breathes.

'Jenny!' snaps her father. 'I won't have language like that in front of your mother!'

'Turn this car around,' says Jenny levelly. 'I'm not going to Loughborough.'

'You'll do what you're told, young lady. You'll do what's best for you.'

'Jenny,' says Barbara. 'We only have your own interests at—'

'Turn around!' screams Jenny, lunging forward into the space between the front seats before her seatbelt snaps her tight. Her father tries to push her away with his left arm and she grabs on to it, screaming, 'Turn around turn around turn around!'

'Simon!' shrieks Barbara, and Jenny's father forces her off him, pushing her away into the back seat, but he's pulling down at the steering wheel with his right hand and the car is spinning off the road and on to a grass verge lined with trees and there's a squealing of brakes and a smell of burning rubber and a sudden crumple of metal and that's all that Jenny Ebert remembers.

✳ 14 ✳

Crime Wave

(1954, dir. André De Toth)

Edna stands by the bay window in the day room, looking down at the deserted beach. She wonders how people cope with this sort of life, long-term. She's almost climbing the walls with boredom. Perhaps she's been on her own for too long, got used to nobody's company but hers. Moments like this one, with no one else about, are precious things to be cherished.

But then . . . she turns around as the door opens and Ibiza Joe shuffles in, leaning heavily on his cane. Perhaps one does get used to company. And maybe . . . once you've spent some time with other people around you, does that make it more difficult to return to a solitary existence? She thinks to ask Joe how long he's been on his own, but something about his demeanour stops her. He looks pale, ashen even. His hair is lank and lifeless. And when he looks up at her, his eyes are red-rimmed. He's been *crying*.

'Joe?' she says. 'Is everything—?'

'It's gone,' he whispers hoarsely. 'It's been taken.'

She guides him with a hand on his elbow to the sofa and sits him down, perching beside him. 'Taken? What has?'

'When Robbo was banging on about his medal, I just thought he'd put it down somewhere and forgotten about it,' he says. 'But now it's happened to me, too.' He looks up at Edna. 'The photograph of my lad that I had on my bedside table. It's the best one I've got. My favourite one. Somebody's been into my room and taken it.'

Edna pats Joe on the shoulders. She knows he's had sadness in his past – who hasn't? – and that he had a wife and a child,

85

though she doesn't know why he's on his own now, or why he spent his later life partying like he was a teenager. Then again, she hasn't been at Sunset Promenade long. She turns as the door opens and Mr Robinson marches in, putting his magnifying glass up to his face and searching for the newspaper. He notices the pair of them and scowls.

'What's up with him? Having another one of his episodes?'

She knows that Joe's over-indulgence in his partying days means that he has abrupt mood swings, part of the reason he's on his own now and needs care, she understands. But this doesn't seem to be one of those. She shakes her head at Mr Robinson and says quietly, 'Joe's lost something.'

'Not lost,' he says, looking up at Mr Robinson. 'Stolen. Picture of my little lad. It's gone. Just like your medal.'

Mr Robinson slaps his magnifying glass into his palm in fury. 'We've got a bloody thief among us! We need to get the police involved. I'll go and get the Granges immediately.'

Edna holds up a hand. 'I'm not sure we should be so hasty, Mr Robinson.'

He frowns at her. 'Why not? I'm sure you don't have something to hide, Mrs Grey . . .'

Edna smiles sweetly. 'Well, of course not, and I'm sure you're not implying I had anything to do with either your medal or Joe's photograph.'

'Well, naturally,' says Mr Robinson, disgruntled. He sits down on the sofa opposite. 'But why not alert the appropriate authorities?'

'Just a feeling I have,' says Edna. 'Obviously, you have all been here much longer than Mrs Cantle and I, but I get the feeling that things are not all right at Sunset Promenade. I hear the brothers Grange arguing quite a lot, and I suspect it is about money.'

'You're not wrong there,' says Joe morosely. 'Especially lately. I know they're trying to keep it quiet from us but there's something going on here.'

Mr Robinson smooths his moustache and nods vigorously. 'I see where you're coming from, Mrs Grey. Any problems that involve the police . . . you think that might reflect badly on their management of this place? Might have financial repercussions?'

Edna shrugs. 'It's possible, don't you think?'

'Then what?' says Joe. 'What about my photo of my lad, and Robbo's medal?'

Mr Robinson clicks his fingers. 'We'll sort it out ourselves. Let's get everybody in here. Give the villain a chance to confess first.'

Edna claps her hands. 'An excellent idea, Mr Robinson. I knew you would be the one to reach some solution.'

He smiles modestly. 'Well, Mrs Grey, quite . . . I am known as something of a problem-solver.'

They all turn towards the door as it opens inwards and Jenny and Ringo step inside. Mr Robinson rubs his hands together. 'And here are our first suspects right now.'

It goes precisely as Edna expects it to, which is not what Mr Robinson was anticipating at all, she feels. Neither of the young people reacts very well at all to the suggestion that one of them – or, as Mr Robinson strongly hints, the pair of them, working together – is responsible for the missing items.

'Who do you think we are, Bonnie and Clyde?' says Ringo angrily. 'Why would we even want your medal and Joe's picture?'

'You tell me,' smirks Mr Robinson. He thinks he's got them on the ropes, Edna can tell. He's taking Jenny's silence for guilt. Edna can see the girl's just building up to a furious explosion. Mr Robinson adds, 'It's funny that it's only us residents who've been targeted, and it's only since you lot arrived.'

'On my first day someone rifled through my bag, which contains very valuable items,' says Jenny through gritted teeth. 'So does that still put me in the frame, or make me a victim?'

'*Everyone's* under suspicion, love,' says Mr Robinson. 'Except me and Joe, obviously. But everybody else . . . Mrs Grey and Mrs Cantle only turned up two weeks before you. Mrs Slaithwaite. It could be any of them.'

He catches Edna glaring at him and stutters, 'B-but of course, the chances are it's one of you lot.'

'Why?' demands Jenny.

'Why what?' says Mrs Cantle, letting herself into the room, with Mrs Slaithwaite behind her. 'Ooh, are we playing a game?'

'It better not be too long, *Countdown*'s on soon,' says Mrs Slaithwaite.

'Oh, this is no game,' says Mr Robinson. He really is enjoying this, thinks Edna. 'This is deadly serious.' He points his finger at Jenny and Ringo. 'One of these . . . or the Chinese . . .' Mr Robinson's eyes widen and he clicks his fingers. 'Or that Florin! He must be on only tuppence ha'penny a week! I bet he'd clean you out as soon as look at you!'

'I've had enough of this,' says Ringo, standing up. 'I'm going to see Barry.'

'No, don't, lad,' says Joe. 'We've agreed we'll sort this out ourselves. For fear of causing trouble with the home, like.'

'*We* haven't agreed anything,' says Ringo. 'Come on, Jenny.'

'Hang on,' says Jenny. She puts a hand on Ringo's arm and he sits down again. 'He might have a point about involving the Granges.'

Interesting, thinks Edna. The girl obviously knows something about this place. She wonders if one of the brothers has confided in her about something. Or if she's overheard them talking. It's no real secret that Sunset Promenade is run in a fairly precarious financial manner. Edna wonders just how unsteady the situation is. She says to Jenny, 'What's this about your bag, though, dear? What was in it?'

'Film canisters,' says Jenny. 'Quite rare thirty-five-millimetre prints.'

'Film canisters,' scoffs Mr Robinson. 'Who the hell would want film canisters?'

'Who'd want your medal?' counters Ringo. 'Who'd want Joe's photograph?'

'Well, before any of you say it, it's not me,' says Mrs Slaithwaite, settling down in her chair and looking around for the remote control. 'I don't think it's any of us oldies.'

'That's quite right,' nods Mrs Cantle. 'We used to be able to leave our doors unlocked, you know. You couldn't do that these days.'

'Yeah, yeah, and the Kray twins loved their mum as well,' says Ringo. 'You think you have a monopoly on honesty? You think we don't understand loss?'

'I'm just worried for my jewels,' says Mrs Cantle, wringing her hands.

'Oh, for God's sake,' says Mr Robinson. 'Look, love, we're dealing with actual thefts here, not a bunch of tissues you think are diamonds.'

Jenny looks as if she's about to say something, thinks Edna. She watches the girl carefully, but in the end Jenny shakes her head slightly and obviously thinks better of it. That's interesting. The girl's got a secret . . . and did a look pass between her and Mrs Cantle? Very interesting indeed.

'This is getting us nowhere,' says Mr Robinson.

'I agree,' says Ringo, standing up again. This time Jenny doesn't stop him. 'The fact is, if things have gone missing, it could be any of us. Or it could be nobody. Maybe you've just lost them. That happens when you're old.'

Edna watches him walk to the door, and Jenny joins him there and says, half to herself, 'Yes, we all lose things from time to time. And that happens when you're not so old, as well.'

15

The Letter

(1940, dir. William Wyler)

Fran is wearing dark chinos today, with a pink polo shirt. He sits on the desk at the front of the lecture room, swinging his feet, which are shoved, sockless, into blue deck shoes. It's a good look, Jenny decides from her place in the front row.

There are only eight of them in the lecture, and only Jenny is studiously taking notes in longhand from the PowerPoint presentation on the big screen. Fran has already said the notes will be available on the course intranet page, but Jenny likes the sense that she's absorbing the information through osmosis by writing it down, rather than just scanning through some document sheet online later.

'Archetypes,' Fran is saying. 'Those basic characters that recur again and again.' He makes a show of squinting into the unlit room until his gaze settles on Jenny. She feels a slight thrill. He smiles broadly. 'Jenny. Let's look at your speciality. Film noir. What are the archetypes we might find in the classic film noir?'

Jenny swallows and glances around at the other members of the group. Amber and Saima are constantly on their phones messaging friends or, Jenny imagines, juggling their hectic social lives and fielding relentless exciting invitations. There's a pale boy with a haunted expression who dresses in black; an ebullient, overweight Irish boy with roughly bleached hair who always wears board shorts and has *PRIDE* tattooed up one calf. Even the two lads who seem to spend every lecture doing online sports quizzes on a laptop are looking at her expectantly. She takes a deep breath. This is your chance, she thinks. This is your opportunity. Impress them. Make them like you.

'Well, there's the, uh, hardboiled detective, of course,' she says. 'He's tough, solves problems with his fists, dogged and determined. He's a loner, he's in it for the money . . .' She tails off, wondering how much she's meant to say. She glances around again. The two guys have gone back to their sports quiz.

'Then we have the femme fatale.' Saima gives a little laugh. Jenny ploughs on. 'She's sexy but incapable of love, she's mysterious but untrustworthy. She's sort of everything that was considered bad about women back in the nineteen forties.'

'That's so you,' says Saima to Amber.

Jenny frowns. No. That's so *me*.

'The other side of that is the good woman,' says Jenny. Fran gives her an encouraging smile. 'She's not as exciting as the femme fatale and represents all those things like stability and family life, the American Dream. She'll be in love with the hero but he'll realise that he can never have those things—'

Fran puts up a hand. 'Good. Excellent. I wanted to stop you there, though, because we're finding out how the archetypes in a genre help to drive the theme. So we've got this triangle here . . . the tough detective and the two women, who are really two sides of the same coin. On the one hand, he craves the stability of the good woman, but he's drawn to the femme fatale, even though ultimately he knows she'll betray him in some way. Why is that? What do we call that?'

The question is open to the group. Amber puts her phone down long enough to say, with a shrug, 'Because the femme fatale is more exciting? I mean, who wants a good woman?'

As everyone starts talking Fran holds up his hand again. 'There's one aspect of film noir especially, one theme, that's very common and addresses this very point. Jenny? You know what it's called?'

'Fatalism,' she says. 'Nothing we do makes any difference. We are who we are, and we're at the mercy of life. And life is always against us.'

There's a momentary silence, then Amber mutters, 'Jesus. Sounds a barrel of laughs.'

But Fran is nodding. 'Good, Jenny. Good. Fatalism. Noir is essentially about existentialism. The futility of the individual in a huge world that operates like a machine. There's the duality of the hardboiled hero; he at the same time tries to break the cycle by operating outside, or at the fringes of society, but also accepts his fate . . . that he can never be what he perhaps secretly wants to be: at the heart of society.'

Fran claps his hands together. 'OK. Assignment for next time.' A volley of groans swells up. 'Look at your favourite genre. Identify the archetypes and how they inform the main theme or themes. And for extra credit, maybe write a few lines about friends or family, which one of the archetypes you think they fit into.'

As everyone starts to pack up, Amber raises a hand. 'Shall we go for a drink? Like, all of us?' she looks around the room. 'This week? In town?'

The geek nods enthusiastically. The outsider shrugs. The two sports guys make affirmative noises. Fran considers, then grins. 'Cool. Bit of a social. What about the Smugglers?'

And that's how easy it is, thinks Jenny. That's how normal people make friends, and organise things, and have a proper social life. They just speak up and get things done. The room empties around her and she sits there for a moment and thinks that things are definitely looking up.

Jenny is the first of the students back at Sunset Promenade. On the reception desk are four letters, neatly spread out, addressed to each of them along with the university franking mark. As she picks hers up, the door behind her opens and Ringo seems to unfold himself into the lobby.

'Now then,' he says.

'Have you actually been into uni?' says Jenny. 'I was beginning to think you weren't bothering attending any classes.'

He dumps his bag by reception and leans over her shoulder, inspecting the letters. 'Creative writing, innit? You can't stick writers in a room and expect them to listen to somebody droning on. We've got to experience life if we're going to be any good.'

'And experiencing life means sleeping in till noon every day?'

Ringo shrugs and reaches round her to take his letter. 'Thinking time. Hey, that reminds me. I owe you. For one of my modules we have to do a series of interviews with people on one subject.

I'm going to do the residents here. Ask them about their favourite movie or something. You gave me that idea.'

'Good luck,' says Jenny. 'I wouldn't mind if I never spoke to them again after yesterday.'

Ringo peers at his envelope. 'What's all this, then?'

Jenny waves her unopened letter. 'I don't know yet. I'm not a mind-reader.'

Ringo starts tearing into his and Jenny does the same, suddenly anxious. He pulls his letter out first, scans it and says, 'Woah.'

'Don't tell me!' says Jenny, extracting the sheet of University of North Lancashire headed paper and reading it through. She turns round and looks at him. 'Oh. They've found us rooms.'

'Due to an exemplary effort on the part of the sub-contractors, we now have one of the projected four new halls of residence close to being ready for occupation,' reads Ringo. 'As a student who originally opted for campus accommodation and was temporarily housed in Sunset Promenade as an interim measure, we are pleased to offer you first refusal on one of the new rooms.'

'I can read, you know,' says Jenny, staring at the letter. Rooms. On campus. She has a sudden vision of herself in the lecture hall, not sitting alone but with Amber and Saima scrolling through their phones and laughing at private jokes and arranging their social lives. Together.

Ringo stuffs the letter in his pocket. 'I'll give them a ring later, say thanks but no thanks. You want me to say you're staying as well?'

Jenny stares at him. 'You're staying? Here? In Sunset Promenade?'

Ringo shrugs. 'Well, yeah. Of course. Aren't you?'

She looks at the letter again. 'I . . . why would I stay? After everything that's happened . . . and it was always only going to be temporary.' Then she says, though she doesn't know why, 'I'm going for a drink this week. With people from my course.'

Ringo looks at her oddly, in a way Jenny can't quite fathom. 'Great,' he says briskly, then hefts his rucksack on to his shoulder. 'Right, I'm going for a lie-down.' He winks. 'Thinking time.'

As Ringo climbs the stairs, Bo and Ling come in through the front door, arguing as ever. Jenny wonders, not for the first time, what is going on with them. Bo follows Ling around like a puppy dog; he's obviously infatuated, and she's just as obviously told him she's not interested. Jenny wonders what it takes to remain so doggedly determined in the face of such insurmountable odds; either incredible stupidity or a massive amount of faith that you will eventually succeed.

Ling says something sharp to Bo and strides across the lobby, ignoring Jenny. Bo pauses, considering for a moment, then hurries after her. A lesson in never giving up, thinks Jenny, or behaviour bordering on obsessive and stalkery? She says to them, 'Hey, did you know Mrs Grey and Mrs Cantle only came here two weeks before we did?'

Ling stares at her. 'We've had letters.'

Ling and Bo head to the reception desk and pick up their envelopes. Jenny hovers on the bottom stair as Ling slices hers open with a long thumbnail and Bo tugs ineffectually at his, accidentally tearing it, and the letter, straight down the middle. He gives Ling a hangdog look. 'Sorry.'

Ling sighs and begins to read her letter to herself, then pauses and reads it out to Bo. He stares at her for a moment, then says, 'We can leave here?'

Jenny clears her throat and says, 'What are you going to do, Ling? What about you, Bo?'

A rare smile breaks out on Ling's face. She's even more beautiful when she smiles, thinks Jenny. Then Ling throws her arms around Bo, embracing him tightly, the letter clutched in her hand, her eyes tight shut.

'Oh, Bo! It's wonderful! We can leave this mad place! We can go!'

'Can we be together?' says Bo.

'Of course we can!' says Ling happily. She kisses his cheek. 'We'll always be together!'

Jenny realises she's staring at them, then hurries on up the stairs. Maybe she just doesn't, and never will, understand people at all. When she gets to the top she looks at the letter again. She can leave this mad place, too. Finally, Jenny Ebert can be who she came all this way to be. No more prunes for breakfast, no more bingo, no more arguing with old people. She can finally lay the ghosts of Loughborough to rest and get on with the life she wants. The life she deserves. With a spring in her step, Jenny heads to her room to think about how brilliant it's going to be from here on in.

16

The Turning Point

(1952, dir. William Dieterle)

After dinner, Barry asks Jenny if she'll gather the rest of the students in his office, and when they all troop in he's sitting behind his desk, Florin standing beside him. He looks up at them and shakes his head.

'This isn't going very well, is it?'

Jenny and Ringo glance at each other. Florin hops uncomfortably from foot to foot. Ling, as ever, remains impassive, while Bo appears not to really understand what's going on. Barry continues, 'So far I've heard three separate arguments raging. Three! God knows how many more you've had. Just be glad I'm dealing with this and not my brother. If he wasn't out tonight . . .' He shakes his head. 'He'd be pushing to have you all out, you know. Seriously.'

Barry looks pleadingly at Jenny. 'We talked about this. It's supposed to be *engagement*. Not . . . not all-out war.'

Florin says, 'It was not so much war, Mr Grange. More a . . . discussion. And we did start with the bingo the first time and things just got . . . out of hand . . .'

'Your residents are all small-minded bigots,' snaps Ling, folding her arms.

'Oh dear,' says Barry. 'Oh dear, oh dear.'

'The soldier man is very racist,' offers Bo.

Barry begins to rub his temples. 'Oh dear. Oh dear.'

'Mr Robinson *is* quite a racist,' agrees Florin.

Barry rubs his face from forehead to chin with the palm of one hand, as though he might wipe away everything he's seen and heard. 'Mr Robinson . . . well, all of them, really . . . you must realise . . . they're from a different generation . . . you wouldn't really understand what it's like for them . . .'

No, of course we wouldn't understand, thinks Jenny. Nobody but old people can possibly know what it means to be sad and lonely. The thought makes her angrier than she felt during the big row in the day room. Why should old people have cornered the market in tragedy?

Barry takes off his glasses and kneads his eyes. 'This place, Sunset Promenade . . . it was always more than just a desire to be *nice*,' he says. 'It's a vocation. It's a legacy.' He replaces his spectacles and looks at them. 'Do you know why we do this, Garry and I?'

Jenny shakes her head. Barry says, 'It's to do with our mother, really. This used to be her home. We grew up here, as boys.' He smiles wistfully. 'It was a wonderful place to live. You might think it was remote for a couple of children, but oh, the adventures we had here, in the dunes, down on the beach. Every day was different, every playtime we were transported to the prairies of the Wild West, or some distant planet, or the foothills of the Himalayas. We counted ourselves very lucky.'

Barry pushes his chair back and stands up, looking through the office window to the grounds behind Sunset Promenade. 'But towards the end of her life, she was lonely, was Mother. Our father had died when we were quite young and she spent most of her later years alone. Garry and I had our own lives to lead – we took jobs, we had relationships. Garry married, but it didn't last. We always found ourselves drifting back to Sunset Promenade.'

He turns to look at the students. 'Mother didn't have many friends, shut away up here. When she was dying, she said to us that this place shouldn't be empty, shouldn't be the sort of home where nobody came, which town children told ghost stories about, where the rooms echoed with emptiness. She said it should be full of life. And she knew there were people out there who didn't have the opportunity she'd had, to live in such a wonderful place. So she asked us if we'd find them, and take them in, and give people who'd lived long and perhaps not so happy lives the chance to see out their days in our home.'

Barry leans over the desk, picks up a sheaf of papers and waves them. 'Grant applications. Funding requests. Begging letters.' He drops them back on the desk, their figures and charts seemingly challenging him to go on, to put sentiment and the wishes of a long-dead old woman over the pragmatism and practicalities of real life. 'So we did. We advertised locally and we had people approach us – sometimes directly, sometimes through their children. We took in the lost and the lonely, and those who had nothing in the bank but so much to give. We've seen people arrive as strangers and leave as friends. When they take their last breath, they know that they aren't on their own, that there are others like them, that nobody, no matter how lonely they are, truly has to be alone.'

There's a long silence, broken by Ling. 'We're leaving,' she says abruptly. 'We have had letters from the university. One of the accommodation blocks is almost ready. We will be able to move there in a week, possibly two.'

Barry smiles sadly and nods. 'Right. Well, I knew this day would come. Perhaps not so quickly, but I knew it would come, one way or the other. Either the funding would run out or you would get fed up.' He sighs heavily. 'The great experiment has failed. I suppose Garry was right all along.'

'We're not all leaving,' says Ringo. He looks at Jenny. 'At least, I'm not.'

Barry raises an eyebrow. 'What? But why?'

Ringo shrugs. 'I don't know. I wanted to come here. Yeah, it's not been perfect, and we have had big rows, like you say, but . . .' He looks around at the others. 'It's not been all bad, has it? Remember when we watched the old movie that was on telly? What was it, Jenny?'

'*The Maltese Falcon.*'

'That's right, *The Maltese Falcon*. We all got along then, didn't we? Mostly?'

Barry looks thoughtfully at Jenny. 'That's your bag, isn't it? Old films? I saw all those DVDs in your room.' He closes one eye and points a finger at her. '*Pew! Pew!*'

'It's almost like it's a connection,' says Ringo. 'Between them and us. Or Jenny, at least.'

She scowls at him. What's he up to?

Barry sits back. 'Hmm. The current strand of funding we have is specifically for initiatives that aim to combat loneliness among older people and encourage interaction between the generations. To continue receiving the money, we have to prove that we're trying to bring young and old together. I wonder . . .' He shakes his head. 'But what's the point? You're all leaving.'

'Only Ling and Bo have said they're definitely going,' says Ringo. 'What were you going to say, Mr Grange?'

Barry's eyes light up. 'Well, I was just thinking . . . Jenny has all these wonderful old movies . . . wouldn't it be a marvellous thing if we could perhaps show them to the residents? We could make it a feature, an event, every week. A film night!'

'But, like you said, we're all leaving . . .' says Jenny.

'Maybe with a discussion after each film,' suggests Florin. 'Like a film club!'

'Discussion, yes, but not all-out war,' frowns Barry.

'But,' repeats Jenny, 'we're leaving.'

'I could bake a cake!' says Florin happily.

'Not chocolate,' warns Bo. 'Not after that Mrs Old Lady went the bananas on it.'

Ling glares at him, then at Barry. 'Bo and myself are not leaving for another couple of weeks. I suppose we could show our support for the first one at least.'

'But,' says Jenny again.

'The Lonely Hearts Cinema Club,' says Ringo with a grin. 'Sounds ace.'

Barry's eyes widen. 'That's perfect! The Lonely Hearts Cinema Club. I love it!'

Jenny stands up. 'But. We're. Leaving.' She glares at Ringo, then says to Barry, 'I'm sorry. It's a lovely idea and everything but . . . I've already decided. I'm going. I'm sorry.'

'What the hell was all that about?' fumes Jenny as she and Ringo ride the bus to campus.

He shrugs. 'I think it's a great idea.'

She waves the letter at him. 'But we're leaving!'

'I'm not. Ling and Bo have told the accommodation office they're taking rooms. I suppose you have as well, then?'

Jenny stares at the letter then out of the window as the bus negotiates the coast road. It's raining again. Obviously. 'No,' she says. 'Not yet. I'm going to sort it today. You should too, if you know what's good for you. You don't want to be shut up in that place on your own.'

'You make it sound like a horror film.'

'Isn't it? Dawn of the nearly dead, with attitudes to match. Besides, there's practically a crime-wave going on there. Someone messed with my bag, Joe and Mr Robinson's stuff has been taken. It would frazzle my wits living there for much longer.'

Ringo wipes condensation from the glass with his sleeve. 'Solve the mystery, then.'

She looks at him. 'What?'

'Solve the mystery. Catch the thief. It'll be like one of your old movies. All of us locked up in a big, lonely house, raining all the time, the electricity can go off at any moment. And there's a villain on the loose!'

Jenny shakes her head at him and grabs her bag as the bus pulls into the turning circle outside the university. Ringo stays there, scrolling through messages on his phone. Jenny looks at him. 'Come on, we're here.'

'I'll see you later,' he says. 'I'm going to ride the bus back.'

She laughs. 'Why, have you forgotten something?'

Ringo shrugs. 'I just like to ride buses. Gives me inspiration. Especially this one, along the coast road. Don't you think it's brilliant? Dramatic? I love the rain all the time. I thought you would, too. Like I said, doesn't it rain all the time in your old films?'

He does have a point there, concedes Jenny. It did rain all the time in film noir. She wonders just how femmes fatales managed to keep so perfect-looking in all that rain. The bus driver beeps his horn and looks round from his cab. 'You two getting off, or what?'

'I am,' says Jenny, hurrying forward down the aisle. She turns to Ringo. 'You're really staying on?'

He nods. 'I like to get my money's worth. Besides, I'm interviewing Ibiza Joe this morning, for my project. I was thinking of calling it 'Ringo's Stars'. What do you think? Because I'm doing the interviews and the old people are the stars, but they're also talking about films. Which have stars. Do you get it?'

'I get it.' Jenny wrinkles her nose. 'I think it's awful.'

'I think I'll do it anyway.' He waves at her. 'Cheerio. Don't forget to go to the accommodation office. Those rooms in the new block will get snapped up quickly.'

Jenny waves the letter at him and gets off the bus.

'It sounds a fabulous idea,' says Fran after the lecture.

Jenny scowls at him. 'Are you all ganging up on me?'

'I don't see the problem,' says Fran, gathering up his papers from the lectern and sliding them into his brown leather briefcase. 'You've got the films, you've got the expertise. It could be your project for this term. Write it up.' He looks at her. 'You could even show them your grandfather's films. You've had them transferred to DVD, right? That could go towards your final dissertation.'

'Hmm,' says Jenny. She hadn't thought of that. 'But there's only one problem. I'm leaving Sunset Promenade. The new block is ready. I've been offered a room.'

Fran shrugs. 'I suppose you'll be more in the thick of things on campus. Still, it sounds interesting, rooming in a rest home. Good experience. I'm all for new experiences.'

Jenny thrills slightly. What is he trying to say? She does the Bacall thing again, chin on her chest, looking up at him. 'It's too late. I've made up my mind.'

After leaving the lecture theatre, she goes straight to the accommodation office, letter in hand, and stands outside the door, pondering. She doesn't see Saima and Amber until they grab her arm, making her jump.

'Hi,' says Amber. 'We're going to the refectory for a coffee, if you fancy it?'

Jenny looks at the letter. 'I was just—'

'Did I see you on the bus with that lanky guy?' butts in Saima. 'The one with the curly hair? Ringo, is it? Creative writing or something? He's a weird one.'

'So weird,' nods Amber. 'He asked me out last year.' She giggles.

100

Jenny scowls. Ringo asked Amber out? 'Did you go?' she says. Amber laughs. 'No way. He's so weird. Always reading books.'

'Weird,' agrees Saima.

He's all right, Jenny wants to say defensively, but instead she mutters, 'Yeah, he's weird.'

'Coffee, then?' says Amber. 'Or should we meet you in the refec?'

Jenny ponders, then shoves the letter into her bag. 'Yeah. Coffee. I'll do this later.'

Ringo's Stars

Ibiza Joe

Are you recording this? On your phone? Ha ha. Marvellous. So
. . . what do you want me to do? Just say my name and talk about
a film? Any film? Right. A film that has some sort of meaning for
me. OK. So. My name is Joe Holmes. Everybody calls me Ibiza
Joe. Liked a bit of a party, I did, in me day. Back in the eighties.
I mean, I was old for it even then, I admit that. Oldest swinger
in town, me. But you're only as old as you feel, right? What?
Embarrassing dad? Ha ha. Um. No. No, not really. I mean . . .

No, it's OK. I'm all right. It was just when you said that.
Embarrassing dad. Made me think. Don't like to think about it
much, to be honest. I suppose that's why I did all the parties, Ibiza
and all that. So I didn't have to dwell on things. I'm only sixty-
nine, you know. I know I look older. That's the partying. And the
drugs. Cognitive impairment, they call it. I get a lot of short-term
memory loss with it. Some depression as well. I know! You'd never
guess to look at me, would you? Life and soul of the party, me.

Yeah, I suppose that *was* the problem. What you said, though
. . . embarrassing dad . . . there was a film on that day. On the
telly. They used to put these old films on in the afternoons. Monday
Matinee slot, they used to call it. You won't remember it. Too
young. I remember that day clear as crystal, though. I'd taken the
day off work and my wife, Shirley, she didn't work at all. Not since
our lad was born. Brian. What? Oh, nineteen seventy-seven this
would be. He'd turned seven a month before. I remember Shirley
was in the kitchen washing up after our dinner. We'd been to the
chippy for a treat, but Brian hadn't been hungry once we got it

home. And there was this film on the Monday Matinee. *Jason and the Argonauts*, it was. Cracking film. Our Brian was made up. He loved all that stuff, Greek myths, gods and monsters and such. Couldn't take his eyes off the screen. Shirley came into the front room just at that bit where the baddie is sowing those dragon teeth and the skeletons are springing up out of the dirt. You seen that? Cracking. Our Brian's face was like . . . his jaw was on the floor. You lot today would probably think it was a bit tame, not up to all the computer stuff they do with the films now. But Brian's face was a picture. Shirley was like, come off it, Joe, he'll have nightmares! He shouldn't be watching this! And I was like, give over, Shirley, look at him! He thinks it's the best thing since sliced Hovis!

What? No, it wasn't the summer holidays. It was March. Brian hadn't been too well. Aching in his bones and his joints. I said it was just growing pains, but Shirley had insisted on taking him to the doctor's. You know what mums are like. I remember that day, watching those skeletons, and Brian had lain across me on the sofa. I had a brew, nice big cup of tea with four sugars. Builder's tea. Earned my money on the motorways. Took me away from home a lot. I watched them building the Preston by-pass when I was a lad. Did you know that was the first motorway in Britain? Part of the M6 now. Soon as I left school I went and signed up to work on the motorways. First one I did was the M1. Every bloody inch of that I worked on, from London up to Leeds, over the best part of ten years.

I don't know if it was watching all them skeletons in the film, but Brian said to me, Dad, my bones are hurting me. Do you think the doctors can stop my pains? Clear as day, I remember that. And I said to him, look, lad, you don't want to stop growing yet, do you? You're only seven. You've got a lot of growing up to do.

No, no, it's all right. I'm fine. See, I was between jobs, and the reason we were all at home was that we had to go to the hospital to see the doctor about Brian's pains. After Shirley had taken him to the doctors they'd done all these blood tests and everything. I thought it was just to keep her quiet, really. Look like something was being done. But what can you do about growing pains? Not a lot until you've grown up.

I remember Shirley being quiet when we walked into the hospital at Preston. Brian had forgot his bones were hurting him and was skidding along the corridor floor. They were always well polished in them days. All the hospitals were really clean, cleaner than they are now. We had to wait in this bit of the hospital for kids and there were paintings all over the wall. Brian was good at drawing and painting, and I remember him looking at these pictures. Snow White and the Seven Dwarfs, I think it was. He had his head on one side, like he was in an art gallery or something. He came running over to me and said, Dad, when I grow up I want to be an artist.

I always remember that.

When we finally got in to see the doctor he asked us to sit down at this desk. He asked Brian how he was feeling and Brian said, all right, my bones were hurting earlier but we watched this brilliant picture called *Jason and the Argonauts*.

Good lad, said the doctor, and he gave him this little toy truck to play with and told him he could zoom it up and down his office floor if he wanted.

I started apologising to the doctor, I don't know why. Said something about we were sorry we'd caused all this fuss for growing pains and we knew he was busy with proper poorly folk. Shirley told me to shut up. I was a bit surprised because she didn't usually talk to me like that, not unless we'd had a couple of drinks and she was getting a bit ratty. I looked at the doctor and then I saw the look he had on his face.

We've had a look at the blood tests, he said. We've gone over the results of all the tests. I'm sorry about this, Mr and Mrs Holmes, but Brian is suffering from a rather advanced case of childhood leukaemia.

I swore. I think I said the F-word. I asked him if I could smoke and the doctor nodded, but Shirley gave me one of her looks and I put my Woodbines back in my pocket. Sorry, I said to her, to the doctor, you're right, we don't want to make the lad any worse.

I'll give that doctor credit, he looked us both in the eye when he said it.

Mr and Mrs Holmes. I'm afraid it couldn't be any worse.

What do you mean, I said to him.

This time it was Shirley's turn to swear. When I looked at her she was crying. I didn't really understand what was going on, to be honest. She said to me, it's cancer, Joe. It's cancer. Brian's got cancer.

And all I could think about was that bad guy sowing those dragon teeth in the ground and skeletons springing up. And I looked at Brian, whizzing this toy truck around on the floor underneath the coat stand in the corner, and it was like . . . I don't know. Somebody had sown dragon's teeth in my lad. My little seven-year-old lad. And now monsters were breaking out inside him. I tried the word out a couple of times. Cancer. Cancer. It sounded uglier the more I said it, felt more like something you might call a monster.

Then Shirley said to the doctor, how long have we got with him?

Give over, I said, though my own words sounded like they were a bit . . . hollow, you know? Does that make sense? Like they were the right words but at the wrong time. I said, it's not like that, love. They can do all sorts these days.

The doctor looked at this pile of notes in a file and for the first time I noticed how thick it was, how much stuff they'd been writing down about our Brian. About what was going on inside him. About the monsters in his blood.

Mr and Mrs Holmes, said the doctor. Then he sighed and pulled a packet of Park Drive out of his shirt pocket. He offered one to Shirley and she shook her head and he offered one to me and I took it. I had a box of Swan Vestas in my pocket and I struck one and lit the doctor's fag with it, then my own.

Then he said again, Mr and Mrs Holmes. We think about six months.

I'm sorry. No, it's not your fault. You weren't to know. I didn't think I was going to talk about this when you asked to film me. I try not to think about it. But it was that picture that was on. *Jason and the Argonauts.*

I think I'd like to stop now, if that's all right.

* 17 *

Ice in My Heart

(1947, dir. William J. Drake)

'You heard, didn't you?' says Barry Grange.

Jenny is in the dining room, picking over a plate of cold chicken and salad from the kitchens, and Barry has come in to fuss around the trolley of plates and serving dishes, though she can see he's itching to speak to her.

'I'm sorry?'

'You were at the bank,' says Barry. 'I saw you leaving and then you were standing across the road, watching me in the window. Like a spy.' He closes one eye and points his fingers at her and says, *'Pew! Pew!'*

Jenny thinks about lying, then sighs. 'Yes. Sorry. I should have said hello but you looked a bit . . . busy.'

'So you heard,' nods Barry. 'You know how much trouble we're in.'

Jenny takes a deep breath. She's been expecting this ever since the letters came. She's been rehearsing what she's going to say. *I'm sorry. It was good of you to open your house to us. It was always going to be temporary. I'm sure you'll have no trouble filling the rooms.*

'I'm not going to try to persuade you to stay,' says Barry. 'But I wondered . . . you know this latest round of grants is dependent on intergenerational interaction, as they say?'

Jenny nods. 'And I know you thought the film club idea would be perfect, and if I was staying it would be, but—'

Barry holds up his hand. 'Just hear me out. Didn't you say it would be a couple of weeks before the rooms are ready? How about if you just did a couple of film nights? One, even? It would just give us something to show the funding people . . . it might really help. Even one. And we've got a really important inspection coming up, and this might help to show we're serious about engagement between the young and old . . .'

Jenny bites her lip. Then smiles. One film night. What harm could there be in that?

The first – and only, thinks Jenny – meeting of the Lonely Hearts Cinema Club is scheduled to take place the very next evening. When the residents are all having their dinner in the dining room, Jenny takes the opportunity to check the DVD player in the day room and sorts through her stack of movies on the carpet, trying to decide what to show them. She's sitting there, lost in the covers, and doesn't hear Ibiza Joe come in and sit down on the sofa.

'Big film night tonight, then?' he says, making Jenny jump.

'Yes, just trying to decide what to put on.'

'Let's see what you've got then,' he says, and she hands over a clutch of DVDs. As he looks through them, Jenny watches him for a while. His face is lined and weathered, the top of his head smooth and liver-spotted. She wonders why he wears his hair so funny, hanging down from the back and sides on to his collar. Today he's wearing a Led Zeppelin T-shirt, faded and pitted with holes, and skinny black jeans crinkled up around his ankles, and his moccasin slippers.

'Why do they call you Ibiza Joe?' she asks, impressed at her own boldness.

He looks up and smiles at her, showing teeth cracked and stained with nicotine. Jenny remembers what Edna said, about him being up one minute and down the next. Bipolar, presumably.

'Just a nickname I picked up in the eighties. Spent a few summers out there, especially when all the acid house business was kicking off.'

Jenny stifles a laugh, then realises he's serious. 'You used to go out there? Raving?'

Then Joe spreads his hands and closes his eyes, throwing shapes at her and nodding to a beat only he can hear. Jenny stares at him and he opens his eyes and says, 'I was mad for it. Watching the sun set over the sea, the White Isle coming alive after dark, all the beautiful young people, the music, staying out until the sun came up again.' He watches her face for a moment, then says, 'I know what you're thinking: old fart like me, no business having it large.'

'I wasn't!' protests Jenny, though that is exactly what is running through her mind.

He shrugs. 'I wasn't that old then. Only in my late thirties. I suppose that's old to you, though. Don't trust anyone over thirty, right?'

'My parents were quite old when they had me,' says Jenny, as though that could bridge some common ground between them. 'Were you not married then? I presume no kids?'

Joe looks down at the DVD covers again. 'I was, once. I did have.'

Jenny wants to ask what happened, but his mood has palpably altered, as though a cloud has passed in front of the sun. He's no longer animated; the internal beat that was keeping his foot tapping on the carpet has been silenced.

'You've got some oldies but goodies here.' He holds up one of the cases, blank but for a hand-written sticker on the front. 'What's this? *Ice in My Heart*? I don't think I've ever seen this one.'

'Not many people have,' says Jenny. 'That was one of the films my grandad made. William J. Drake. He was a director back in the forties. He wanted to make American-style crime dramas set in London.'

'What's it about?'

'Jewellery heist,' says Jenny, replaying the opening reel in her head. 'Then the gang members fall out and start picking each other off. There's a cracking femme fatale in it, an actress called Joyce Palermo. She was in another of my granddad's films but didn't seem to do much else. I'm surprised, because she's got amazing screen presence.'

Jenny realises she's babbling, which she always does when she gets on to the subject of her films, and shuts up. Ibiza Joe looks impressed, though.

'I think we should watch that one tonight.'

'Oh, I don't know,' she says, taking the DVD back from him. She feels oddly protective of William J. Drake's movies; she's worried that people wouldn't like it and that she would end up having to defend him. 'Maybe they'd like to see a more famous one.'

'I think they'd appreciate seeing one you have a connection to,' says Joe. 'But you decide.' He pushes himself up from the sofa and stretches his arms. 'I'm going to have a little nap before dinner.'

At the door, he turns back to Jenny. 'It's great having you kids here, you know. Makes me feel alive again. Thought I was going to live out my days without seeing another young face.'

She feels she ought to say something about the stolen photo that made him so sad. 'It wasn't me,' she says. 'Mr Robinson's medal and your photo. It wasn't me. I promise.'

He smiles at her. 'Don't worry. I'm sure it'll turn up. Just one of those things.'

'A mystery,' says Jenny.

He laughs. 'It's a mystery how some of us get up in the morning.'

'What are you doing here, Joe?' blurts out Jenny. 'Why did you come to live at Sunset Promenade?'

He shrugs. 'I was lonely, I suppose. I think I still am. I think we all are. But at least we're lonely together.'

After loading up the DVD Jenny feels like she should say something by way of introducing the film. The residents are assembled on the various sofas and chairs, Ringo is sprawling on the hearth rug and Bo is staring attentively at her while Ling taps at her phone. Florin sits in a dining chair at the back of the room. Barry Grange is there, standing by Florin, but of course not Garry, whom Jenny hasn't seen much of since she arrived. She stands by the TV and clears her throat.

'Well,' she says. 'Thank you for coming—'

'Not much bloody choice, have we?'

'Shut up, Robbo.'

'—to the first, erm . . .'

'Meeting of the Lonely Hearts Cinema Club!' says Ringo with a big grin.

Barry Grange applauds loudly from the back of the room.

Mrs Slaithwaite glares at him. 'I'm not lonely. I'm on my own. There's a difference.'

'Lonely Hearts makes us sound like we're looking for love,' says Joe.

'Oh, for God's sake, get the bloody film on. What are we watching?' demands Mr Robinson.

Jenny clears her throat, her head light, and feels she's made a terrible mistake. 'This is called *Ice in My Heart*,' she says quickly. 'It's a British film, released in nineteen forty-seven. It stars George Storm and Joyce Palermo, with Eddie Monk in his first supporting role. Monk went on to take leading roles in *Off Devil's Head* and *The Firebugs*, before he died in a plane crash in nineteen fifty. It was directed by William J. Drake.'

Jenny turns to aim the remote control at the DVD player and Mrs Grey says, 'And who was he, dear? The director? Drake, did you say?'

Jenny looks back at her. 'He was my grandfather,' she says, and for some reason she can't put her finger on, her stomach flips and churns, as though she's given away a terrible secret.

As the music strikes up and the title appears over a stylised artistic depiction of London, Barry Grange dims the lights and Jenny takes a seat on the carpet next to Ringo. The painted image morphs into an aerial shot of the city at night, taken, Jenny knows from reading her grandfather's papers, from the lantern at the top of the dome of St Paul's Cathedral, the capital's tallest building in the 1940s.

'London!' says the voiceover briskly. 'A city shattered by war, yet triumphant. But in the labyrinthine streets there were men not only concerned with rebuilding the city, but also amassing their own fortunes . . . by any means necessary!'

Jenny has watched this opening more times than she can possibly recall, studied every camera angle, every inflection of every voice, pored over the typefaces used in the titles and credits. So engrossed is she that she doesn't even notice that Mrs Slaithwaite has already begun to loudly and defiantly snore.

'Bloody good picture, that,' says Mr Robinson when the final credits have rolled. Jenny can't help but feel a flush of pride in her cheeks.

'It was very exciting,' agrees Mrs Cantle. 'Just goes to show, no honour among thieves.'

Jenny sees Mr Robinson and Joe glance at each other. 'Less said about that the better,' mutters Joe.

'Has your stuff not turned up yet?' says Mrs Slaithwaite.

'Oh, you are awake,' says Florin. 'I was just about to make cocoa.'

'I wasn't asleep,' says Mrs Slaithwaite crossly. 'I was just resting my eyes.'

'You bloody snore loudly enough for a woman who was awake,' says Robinson. 'And no, my medal hasn't turned up, nor has Joe's photograph.' He narrows his eyes and looks around the room. 'The thief is still among us.'

'Let us not have that argument again,' says Ling with a sigh.

'No,' agrees Joe. 'Let's not.'

'Just know we haven't forgotten,' says Mr Robinson.

'Oh!' says Bo. 'I nearly forgot!'

Ling stares at him as he fumbles in his trouser pockets and pulls out two paper bags. 'I went to the shops in Morecambe. I got you these.' He hands a bag each to Mr Robinson and Joe.

Mr Robinson takes his suspiciously and peers inside. 'What the bloody hell's this?'

Joe pulls out a cheap vinyl photo frame, with a generic stock picture of a smiling family inserted behind the plastic glass. He looks at Bo, frowning. Mr Robinson delves into the bag and takes out a golden disc, attached with Sellotape to a length of pink ribbon.

'I saw you were sad about losing your things,' says Bo, suddenly embarrassed. 'I made you a new medal, Mr Robinson. It is chocolate.'

Mr Robinson stares at the chocolate coin in his hand. Bo continues, 'And I thought you could put another photograph in that, Mr Joe.'

Jenny winces, waiting for Ling to call him an idiot in her own language, but she stays silent and quietly pats Bo on the arm. Mr Robinson opens his mouth to speak, then evidently thinks better of it and closes it again. He glances at Joe with what Jenny is sure is a helpless look.

'That's very kind of you, son,' says Joe softly. 'Very . . . thoughtful.' He stares meaningfully at Mr Robinson.

'Erm, yes,' says Mr Robinson. 'Very thoughtful.'

Ling gives Bo a rare and quite beautiful smile.

There's a long silence, then Mrs Slaithwaite says, 'Did somebody mention cocoa?'

'Not for me,' says Mrs Cantle, stifling a yawn. Does a look pass between her and Edna? thinks Jenny. 'I think I'll get off to bed.'

As Mrs Cantle lets herself out of the day room, Jenny removes the DVD from the player. Edna says to her, 'That was quite a marvellous film, Jenny. Your grandfather was a very talented director.'

'Thank you,' she says.

'I'd imagine we'd all like to see the other ones he made.'

Jenny nods. 'Well, yes, we'll have to see. I mean, Ling and Bo are leaving next week, and I've been offered a room in the same block . . .'

'Oh,' says Edna. 'Well. I'm sure we'll be sorry to see you go.'

'How many for cocoa?' says Florin, counting the hands that go up.

'I'll take one,' says Barry. 'Well, I think that went rather well—'

He is cut short by a blood-curdling scream from the floor above.

Ringo's eyes widen. 'Mrs Cantle!'

Jenny, Barry and Ringo rush from the day room to the stairs, Edna and Mrs Slaithwaite behind them. Joe struggles to his feet, helped by Florin, who hands him his stick, while Mr Robinson cries, 'Let me at 'em! They'll rue the day they messed with us!'

Ringo is first at the open door to Mrs Cantle's room, where she is sitting on her bed, the drawer to her bedside cabinet wide open. She looks up with a stricken face as Jenny and Barry join Ringo at the door.

'My jewels! Someone's stolen my jewels!'

Barry sighs. 'Mrs Cantle. You're just over-tired, I think.'

'Oh good Christ,' says Mr Robinson from halfway up the stairs. 'Not the bloody jewels again.'

'They were here, they were in my bedside table,' insists Mrs Cantle. She points to the empty drawer.

'Florin,' calls Barry gently. 'Help Mrs Cantle calm down and get ready for bed. Don't worry, Mrs Cantle, it'll all seem better in the morning.'

Everyone turns to leave, Ringo rolling his eyes at Jenny as he heads back down the stairs. Only Jenny remains at the door as Florin appears and consoles Mrs Cantle. Her imaginary jewels again, she knows everyone is thinking.

But Jenny has seen them. She knows they're real. And like Mr Robinson's medal and Joe's photograph, they've been stolen. Jenny suddenly feels cold on the staircase landing, and looking up and around at the closed, blank doors of the residents' rooms, she has the inescapable sense that someone is watching her.

18

They Won't Believe Me

(1947, dir. Irving Pichel)

Edna sips her tea in the communal living room, watching the afternoon sky darkening over the storm-tossed sea through the big bay window. What a godawful place this is, she decides. Does it rain here perpetually? It seems to have done ever since she arrived. It feels like the end of the earth, and she wonders if she'll ever see the sun again. Perhaps when this is over she might think about a holiday somewhere. Edna turns away from the window to consider the other residents. Mr Robinson is huffing and puffing his way through the *Mail*. Joe is shuffling up and down the hearth rug in his slippers. Mrs Slaithwaite is glaring at a puzzle magazine. So angry all the time, that Mrs Slaithwaite. Edna has wondered on more than one occasion what she's doing here. She evidently dislikes the company of others; indeed, often goes out of her way to cause friction. Why put yourself through living in a place like this, cheek by jowl with strangers, if you hate other people so much?

Young Florin comes into the room holding Mrs Cantle's arm and sits her on the chair nearest to Edna. Mrs Cantle looks very upset – has been since the episode last night with her so-called jewels. Mr Robinson glances up and frowns at Florin. The headline on his newspaper screams *DOOR TO CLOSE ON EU MIGRANT LEECHES*.

'Hello, Margaret,' murmurs Edna. Mrs Cantle looks at her with shining eyes.

'Did you hear about my jewels, Edna?' she says in a tremulous voice. A little too tremulous. Don't overdo it, girl.

'Yes. Terrible business.'

Mr Robinson is staring at them from the sofa. Ears like a bat, that one. He makes a snorting noise. 'Bloody jewels. I don't know why everyone's pussyfooting around the daft old mare.' He leans forward and enunciates loudly and carefully, 'There are no jewels, love.' He taps his temple with his forefinger. 'All in here, innit? If you had a drawer full of bloody jewels you wouldn't be marking time in God's second-class waiting room, would you?'

Mrs Cantle gazes out of the window at the thrashing waves. The tide is in as far as it comes, now, almost up to the rocky breakwaters near the main road. 'Main road' being something of a misnomer, of course. Hardly anyone ever uses it.

'This is the worst cruise I've ever been on,' says Mrs Cantle, looking at the sea.

Mr Robinson barks a laugh. 'Sweet Jesus, she thinks she's on the *Queen Mary*.'

'Mr Robinson—' begins Florin.

'I know, I know,' he sighs, then says in an exaggerated impression of Florin's accent, 'That eez not nize.'

Florin stares at him impassively. Mr Robinson taps the front of his newspaper. 'See this? Writing's on the wall for you lot. They'll be shipping you back off to Poland soon.'

'I told you, I am from Latvia,' says Florin, with what strikes Edna as incredible control. If Mr Robinson were talking to her like that, she'd be force-feeding him that right-wing rag by now.

Mr Robinson shrugs. 'Poland, Latvia, what's the difference?'

His rant is cut short by the entrance of the students, Jenny and Ringo. They're both scowling at Mr Robinson, and the lad, Ringo, says to him, 'The war was a long time ago, Mr Robinson. You should try to move on.'

Edna pinches her nose between her fingers. Red rag to a bull, that. Mr Robinson puffs out his chest and turns on the sofa to face the boy.

'Don't you even bloody dare, lad. The war made this country. Made our name. Showed everybody that we weren't for backing down.' He glares at Florin. 'That we weren't for being taken for mugs.' Mr Robinson appraises Ringo. 'I mean to say, look at the state of you. Hair down to your shoulders, not an ounce of meat on you, muscles like knots in cotton. You know what this country needs? Another bloody war. Sort you kids out, that's for sure. You'd have to step up to the mark bloody quick-smart, wouldn't you?'

'Leave it out, Robbo,' says Joe, but without much conviction. He's been subdued since he did that interview with Ringo, which they're all supposed to do. She wonders what they talked about. Edna can practically see Mr Robinson's moustache bristling. His blood's up. He stands, slapping the paper on the sofa.

'No, come on, let's have this out.'

Ringo laughs. 'What, do you want to go outside and sort this out like real men, or something?'

'Ringo,' says Jenny. 'Just leave it.'

Mr Robinson sneers at him. 'Oh, you'd like that, wouldn't you, lad? Pushing an old man around? An old man with a heart condition?' He shakes his head. 'God knows what this country's come to.'

Mr Robinson is about to say more when something outside catches his attention. Edna looks out of the window to see a big man with dark hair, wearing knee-length shorts and a short-sleeved shirt despite the inclement weather, struggling up the stone staircase to the terrace in front of Sunset Promenade, carrying two wide plastic boxes stacked together.

'It's the grocery man,' she says.

'Bernie!' says Mr Robinson.

'Ah, all those boxes to bring up the steps!' says Florin.

Mr Robinson rubs his hands. 'That's all right, lad, we'll help. Joe, come on. You too, Ringo, build up those muscles. Just in case there ever is a bloody war.'

Edna sees Ringo glance at Jenny and shrug, then follow the men out of the day room. Florin raises an eyebrow and says, 'Well, that is very helpful, thank you.'

As Florin follows the men to sign for the grocery delivery, Jenny crouches down in front of Mrs Cantle. Edna moves away, feigning interest in Mr Robinson's abandoned newspaper, but not far enough that she can't hear.

'Mrs Cantle,' begins Jenny quietly. 'What did they say about the jewels?'

'Oh, they don't believe me,' says Mrs Cantle sadly. 'They think I've just invented them.'

'But I saw them,' whispers the girl urgently. 'I know they were there. Have they really gone? You haven't just . . . moved them, and forgotten where you put them?'

'I never take them out of that drawer,' says Mrs Cantle. She screws up her face. 'It was very important, I was to leave them in the drawer.'

Jenny nods and stands up. 'I'm going to have a word with Barry,' she says.

Edna watches her leave the room, then throws the newspaper back on the sofa. She turns to Mrs Cantle. 'Just going to powder my nose, Margaret. Won't be long.'

Mrs Cantle nods and looks out of the rain-spattered window again. 'Worst cruise ever.'

In the hallway, Edna sees Jenny pausing outside the office. There are raised voices coming from behind the closed door; the Grange twins are having another of their arguments. At the open door Florin is signing the chitty for the grocery delivery and taking the first of the boxes. 'I'll get this into the kitchen,' he says. 'If the rest of you would like to help Bernie with the other boxes . . . but do not strain yourselves.'

'It's a right carry-on, the access road still being out,' says the grocery man. 'Got to park down on the coast road and hump these boxes all the way up those stairs.'

'Are you from Merseyside?' says Ringo, clocking his accent.

'Near St Helens,' says Bernie, looming in the doorway. 'You Liverpool? One of the students who's moved in?'

'Never mind the bloody small talk,' says Mr Robinson impatiently. 'You got any *extras*, Bernie?'

Bernie grins broadly and takes the lid off the bottom box. 'Thought you lads might have a bit of a thirst on. Well, you will when you've helped me carry another eight boxes up those steps. I brought you two of each for starters.'

In the box are eight two-litre Pepsi bottles, filled with liquids of varying shades of brown. Mr Robinson holds one up to the dull daylight.

'Home brew?' says Ringo, plucking out another.

'Bernie's a genius,' says Joe, seemingly rallying after his depression. 'He does a lovely India pale ale.'

Mr Robinson is gazing into the depths of the dark liquid in the bottle he's holding. 'Bernie's stout is not for the faint-hearted. It's a proper, proper man stout. Here, Joe, give him the money while I get this lot inside.'

'Is anybody going to help me with the rest of the food?' says Bernie.

Mr Robinson slaps Ringo on the back. 'Off you go, lad. You're not going to let a bunch of old men do the heavy lifting, are you? Glass of ale in it for you later.'

As Mr Robinson hefts his contraband up and starts to ascend the stairs, Edna turns her attention back to Jenny, still poised outside the office, listening intently at the door. The girl jumps back as the door is suddenly wrenched open and Garry Grange emerges, a phone clamped to his ear. Barry is hovering behind him, and looks at Jenny.

'Yes, we have received the offer,' Garry says into his phone.

'Can I help you, Jenny?' asks Barry.

The girl backs off towards the stairs. 'No, no, just . . .'

Garry covers the phone with his hand and hisses at Barry, 'They might be willing to up the offer.'

Edna busies herself inspecting the sheets pinned on the noticeboard. Yoga. Bingo. A day out to the Isle of Man. She shudders. Catching Barry's eye she says loudly, 'Are you talking to me, dear? You'll have to speak up, I haven't got my hearing aid in. Deaf as a post without it.'

Barry smiles, evidently satisfied, and says quietly to Garry, 'Tell them we're thinking about it.'

Garry pulls a face at him. 'We can't think about it forever. They're going to go cold on us.'

Barry shakes his head vehemently. 'It would be the end for Sunset Promenade, Garry. You know that. These people couldn't afford the Care Network's fees. They wouldn't have the sort of life they have now. God knows what would happen to them.'

'Just hold on a second longer,' says Garry through gritted teeth

118

into the phone. Then he covers it again and whispers fiercely, 'Don't you think I know this? But we have to do something, and we have to do it quickly. We have that inspection at the end of the month . . . if we signed before that, we wouldn't have to run ourselves ragged worrying about it. It would be the Care Network's problem.'

'No,' says Barry firmly. 'No. We pass this inspection, and we'll think about their offer. You can't bully me on this one, Garry. It's too important.'

Garry shoots daggers at him and heads back into the office, slamming the door behind him. Edna continues to stare at the noticeboard, humming tunelessly for good measure, as she hears Jenny approaching down the stairs again.

'Mr Grange? I wondered if I might have a word. I know you're really busy with everything but there's just something quite important . . .'

'A problem shared, and all that,' says Barry raggedly. 'What's up, Jenny?'

'It's about Mrs Cantle's jewels,' she says. Edna perks up. Here we go. The game's afoot, as Sherlock Holmes used to say. 'When we came in and she was crying about them being stolen . . .'

Barry rubs his face. 'Oh God, the jewels. I know we said we're not a care home, as such, more a residential place, but when people get to this age, they're bound to have certain . . . episodes. I hope it hasn't frightened you in any way.'

'No, it's not that,' says Jenny hurriedly. 'It's just, these jewels—'

'I know, I know. Completely non-existent.'

'But—'

'Yes, but it's a good job she doesn't really have any jewels,' nods Barry. 'I mean, can you imagine if this was true? If she really had a load of valuables stolen? With an inspection due? There would be an inquiry, there would be . . . oh God, it doesn't bear thinking about. We'd be closed down within the month, I'm sure of it.'

Jenny says nothing, just stares at him. He looks at her. 'Was that it, Jenny? Was there anything else?'

She smiles. 'No, Mr Grange, that's everything. I just wanted . . . I just wanted to say we're all enjoying staying here.'

Barry grins warmly. 'That's lovely, Jenny. Thank you. Now, if you'll excuse me . . . paperwork, paperwork, paperwork! It never ends!'

Edna turns and hurries back into the day room as Barry closes the office door on Jenny. She finds Mrs Cantle still staring out of the window. 'Margaret,' she says quietly. 'I think it's probably best if you don't make too much of a fuss about those jewels any more.'

Mrs Cantle blinks at her. 'Are you sure? Have I—'

'You've done well, Margaret,' says Edna brightly. 'Excellent work. I'll take it all from here, though, I think . . .'

* 19 *

Her Kind of Man

(1946, dir. Frederick de Cordova)

Jenny Ebert is a femme fatale. And tonight she is going to prove it. She opens the wardrobe door and looks in the full-length mirror mounted on the inside. So far, so good. Then Jenny closes her eyes and shucks off her dressing gown, opening one eye in a squint to consider her reflection. Black knickers edged with lace, matching bra. Her boobs look good, she concedes. She grabs the handfuls of flesh insulating her hip bones. Not so good. With the palm of one hand she pushes in her stomach and takes a deep breath. Maybe she should have bought some higher-waisted pants. Maybe she should have bought a corset. She wonders if Edna or one of the other old ladies could lend her one of those, what did they call them, girdles?

Jenny twists a half-turn and considers her bum. Twice as big as Ling's, she decides. She still hasn't spoken to anyone about what she saw – Ling embracing Bo like that in the hall – and she's decided it was none of her business anyway. Still, she wishes she had Ling's skinny ass.

Or maybe Fran prefers something to take a good hold of.

Jenny feels a slight thrill. Is she really going to do this? Can she see it through? She can't deny the looks he's given her, how he smiles at her in a different way than he does the other students. She briefly considers the ring on his left hand. Maybe he is trapped in a loveless marriage. Maybe that, too, is none of her business. A femme fatale doesn't worry about hurting the feelings of the good woman. If Fran's wife can't stop him straying, that's hardly Jenny's fault. She turns back to look at herself face on. She isn't too bad, is she? Maybe Fran does this all the time. Maybe he has a girl in every class. She tells herself she doesn't care. Femmes fatales are above that sort of thing. She gives herself one last look in the mirror.

What does Tom Neal in *Detour* say about the scheming Vera when he picks her up in a diner in Reno? *Not the beauty of a movie actress, mind you, or the beauty you dream about when you're with your wife, but a natural beauty. A beauty that's almost homely because it's so real.*

Which would have to do. Jenny takes her black dress from its hanger and steps into it, arranging the hem around her knees and smoothing down the front, then casts around for her heels.

Fran isn't going to know what's hit him.

In the hall Jenny hears raised voices coming from the dining room. Mr Robinson – as usual – and Florin. She pops her head round the door to see everyone seated, including Ringo, Bo and Ling. Florin is in the process of ladling a thick, green soup into everyone's bowls and looks up as the door opens.

'Jenny. I did ring the bell for dinner.'

'Oh, I'm going out,' says Jenny. Ringo looks up at her and back to his soup. 'I might just have a buttered roll, though, if that's OK?'

'You need more of a lining in your stomach than that, girl, if you're having it large,' says Ibiza Joe.

'*Someone's* looking very lovely,' says Mrs Cantle.

'Never bloody mind her,' says Mr Robinson angrily. 'I want to know what me laddo here has to say for himself.'

'A brief recap,' says Edna quietly, dabbing the corners of her mouth with her napkin. 'Ling and Bo have announced they're leaving Sunset Promenade to take up rooms at the university. Mr Robinson has voiced the opinion that it's the wrong people leaving. He seems to be becoming increasingly wound up by that newspaper he's reading and has something of a bee in his bonnet about our European friends, such as dear Florin. Which is rather reckless of him, as it is Florin who ensures he has his angina pills every day and he is not someone I would want to unduly upset, were I in his shoes.'

'He wouldn't dare!' says Mr Robinson, arms folded. 'And I wasn't having a go at him personally, just saying that what we should be doing is encouraging relationships with the likes of the Chinese and facing up to the fact that it's these Poles and whatnot who don't have anything to offer the country now.' He points his spoon at Florin, who is carrying the soup tureen, then lets it clatter into his yet-to-be-filled bowl. 'Then himself got all upset and started giving me the verbals. He should remember who pays his wages.'

'Hear, hear,' says Mrs Slaithwaite, folding her arms.

'Mr Robinson,' says Florin, taking a deep breath. 'I am just a little . . . upset today. It is my daughter's birthday.'

'I didn't know you had a little girl, lad,' says Ibiza Joe. 'Having a party for her?'

'She is in Riga, with her mother,' says Florin quietly.

'Is that in Wales?' says Mrs Cantle. 'What sort of soup is this?'

Jenny looks at her phone. She needs to be going, but wonders where this is heading. Florin puts down the tureen heavily on the table. 'It is in Latvia. My wife Irma lives there with Juta, who is three today.' He looks mournfully around the table. 'I should be with them.'

Mr Robinson nods and smooths his moustache. 'Oh yes, I can see where this is going. You're trying to get them over here, aren't you? Bring 'em in the back door. Get a nice council house, is that it? Some benefits?'

'Now hang on a minute, Mr Robinson,' says Ringo warningly. 'You're going too far again.'

'It is all right,' says Florin. 'I tell you about my family. Irma worked until she had Juta. We met together in the same job.' He picks up the tureen again. 'It is cabbage soup, Mrs Cantle.'

'That'll play havoc with me guts,' says Mrs Slaithwaite, letting a spoonful of the green soup fall into her bowl. 'I wouldn't sit downwind from me tonight.'

Moving down the table, Florin says, 'It is difficult to find work in Latvia now because so many people have left to work in other places. A – what you say – vicious circle? The place we worked had to close down so I had to come to England to find a job.'

'No call for wiping old folks' arses in Latvia, then?' says Mr Robinson.

'Mr Robinson!' admonishes Edna. 'Not at the dinner table.'

Florin smiles sadly. 'We did not work at a place like this, Irma and I. We worked at a university. But so few students were coming there that her department was reduced in size and she could not go back after Juta was born, and my department was closed down altogether. Wages are very low in Latvia compared to England.'

'Cleaners, were you, love?' asks Mrs Cantle kindly.

Florin moves the tureen over to Mr Robinson's end of the table. 'No. Irma was a professor in European literature and I was a lecturer in particle physics.'

There's a long silence in which Mr Robinson gapes at him until Florin says, 'Anyone for bingo after dinner? Two little ducks, quack, quack. See, I have been practising.'

Then he ladles a bowl's worth of soup into Mr Robinson's lap, who leaps up and starts yelping at Florin. At Florin's profuse but evidently insincere apologies, Jenny takes the opportunity to withdraw.

The Smugglers is heaving and dark; people are packed on to a tiny dance floor while a DJ plays nineties indie music. Jenny smooths down her dress again and glances at herself in a tarnished mirror near the entrance, then makes a beeline for Amber and Saima, who are sipping from bottles with straws in them. They're both wearing short dresses; they both look better than her, and as though it's taken them far less effort to look so good.

'Hi!' says Jenny, loud and bright to be heard over the music. She self-consciously touches her face; her make-up feels garish and overdone compared to theirs.

'Hi,' says Amber.

'How's life in the nursing home?' says Saima.

'Ha ha!' barks Jenny. Too much, calm it down. 'Ha. Yes. Well, not for long. Got a letter today. I can move into the new hall on campus.'

'Cool,' nods Amber.

'We live in Cocker Hall,' says Saima. 'I mean, what a name, right?'

'They're all named after rivers in Lancashire,' explains Amber. 'Apparently. Cocker, though.' She shakes her head.

'Cool,' says Jenny, suddenly bereft of anything to say. 'Cocker, though, right. Ha ha.' She pauses, watching Amber and Saima sipping their drinks. 'Well! I'll get us some booze, right? What are you on?'

They waggle the bottles at her and Jenny fights her way to the bar and returns with three of them. She doesn't even know what it is, except it's sickly-sweet and packs a bit of a punch. Jenny hands them out and says, 'So, how're you liking the course? How're you liking Fran?' She gives a theatrical wink.

Amber shrugs. 'S'OK, I guess.'

'Actually a bit boring,' says Saima.

'Yeah, bit boring,' agrees Amber. She squints at Jenny. 'You seem to like it, though. You like those old black-and-white films, right?'

Saima makes a face. 'Ugh, black-and-white films, though.'

'I know!' yells Jenny, glancing around, trying to see Fran. 'I mean . . .' She pulls a face. 'Ugh, what was I thinking, right? What sort of stuff are you into?'

Another round of shrugs. Amber says, 'Y'know . . . whatever's out.'

'I only picked the course because it looked easy. I thought we might just, like, watch Netflix or something,' says Saima.

'Yeah,' says Amber. She brightens. 'Like *Pretty Little Liars* or something. That was cool.' She shakes her bottle. 'Drinks?'

By the time they're finishing their third, Jenny feels bold enough to say, 'Hey, when I move into halls maybe we could hang out?'

'Cool,' says Amber.

'Got to be better than being with all those stinky old people,' says Saima.

'Oh, they're not that bad . . .'

'Old-lady smell,' says Amber, wrinkling up her nose. 'Eww.'

'Dirty old men,' agrees Saima. 'I bet they look through your keyhole.'

'Eww,' says Amber again.

'I know!' says Jenny. 'Can you imagine? Living with a bunch of dirty old men?' She feels a pang even as she says it. Why are you being so horrible? she thinks.

'I bet the old ladies are as bad,' says Amber. 'Do they all wear surgical stockings and smell of wee?'

125

Saima bends forward and pretends to be walking with a stick, her hand on the small of her back. 'Are they always banging on about the war? Ooh, when I were a lad we didn't see a banana until nineteen fifty-plonk.'

'They're actually quite nice,' protests Jenny quietly. Then remembers Mr Robinson. 'Mainly.'

Amber and Saima exchange a glance, and Jenny thinks it's time to get on with the business at hand. She excuses herself and says she's going to the toilet, then muscles her way to the bar and orders another bottle of whatever she's been drinking, with a shot of tequila for good measure. She does it at the bar, wincing as it burns her throat, then turns and immediately spies Fran, in a loose pink shirt and black jeans, listening intently as the beardy guy with the geek T-shirts – Alan? – talks animatedly at him. Grabbing her bottle, Jenny lurches through the crowd towards them, suddenly feeling a little light-headed. She glances down at her cleavage and pulls the front of her dress down a bit, not looking where she's going, and suddenly stumbles into Alan.

'Jenny!' says Fran with palpable relief. He's actually pleased to see her. He turns back to Alan. 'Well, Alan, that's been really interesting, and I'll certainly think about putting some of your ideas into practice.'

'Good,' says Alan. 'Because I've—'

'Well, thanks again,' says Fran firmly. 'I just need to speak to Jenny about her coursework now.'

Finally taking the hint, Alan lumbers off towards the bar, spotting Amber and Saima and waving madly at them as they try to hide behind a tall guy queuing for a drink.

'Phew,' says Fran, with a grin that lights up his face and makes Jenny's stomach flip. 'Lovely guy, but he doesn't half go on.'

Jenny realises she's staring at him with puppy-dog adoration and tries to rearrange her face into something cool and subtly seductive. Femme fatale, she reminds herself. Femme fatale. Fran is leaning with his arm outstretched on the wall and Jenny decides it's time to go big or go home. She taps the gold band on the ring finger of his left hand. 'You been given a pass out, then?'

Fran raises one eyebrow and shrugs. 'Sam's very understanding.'

Jenny squeezes in closer to Fran to let a guy with his hands around three pint glasses get past. When he's gone she stays there, up tight against him. 'How long have you been married?' she says.

'Two years,' nods Fran, taking a sip from his bottle of lager. He glances down at how close Jenny is to him – and, she's sure, taking in an eyeful of her boobs – then pats his pockets. 'Think I'll go outside for a fag,' he says. 'Horrible habit but . . . we all have our vices.'

Did he hold her gaze for a little longer than he needed to when he said that? 'Yes,' she says breathily. 'We all have our vices. I'll come with you.'

It's pouring down again, of course, and there's a huddle of smokers in the doorway. Fran takes Jenny's bare arm and she thrills at his touch as he leads her round the corner of the pub, where a canopy keeps off the worst of the rain. He holds out his packet of cigarettes at her with a querying look. Trying to ignore the photograph on the box of someone sticking out a tongue swollen with tumours, she nods and takes one. She leans in to Fran as he lights her cigarette from a Zippo before lighting his own.

'I do like to see the students out of the lecture halls,' he says, inhaling deeply. 'I've got a busy day tomorrow and I should get an early night, but . . .' He shrugs. 'Sam's working away this week, so you know what that means.'

Jenny feels the alcohol swirling around her stomach and the cigarette making her head light and fuzzy. 'Yes,' she says huskily. 'I know what that means.'

'I knew you would,' he laughs. 'You're on my wavelength. I'll probably sit up until the small hours watching old movies. We're two of a kind, aren't we?'

Jenny keeps her eyes locked on his as she takes another deep drag, then flicks the cigarette away nonchalantly. She's quite impressed with how cool that must look. 'Yes,' she says again. 'Two of a kind. A pair of loners. Ships passing in the night.'

Then she leans in, pushing her hands against his chest, forcing him against the wall and putting her mouth on his. Putting her mouth on his hard, unyielding lips. She tries to force her tongue into his mouth but those lips are solid and impassable. Gently he takes her by the wrists and pushes her away from him.

'Erm,' he says. 'Jenny.'

'I've seen the way you look at me,' she says. 'I know what you want. Let's go back to yours.'

He blinks rapidly and bites his lip. 'I was just being friendly . . . I think you might have the wrong idea . . .'

'I won't tell anyone,' she whispers urgently. 'I won't get you in trouble. I—'

'Jenny!' he says more forcefully. He closes his eyes and takes a deep breath. 'Jenny. Look. Even if you weren't my student . . . I love Sam.'

'Of course you do,' she says, touching his face. 'I'm not trying to get between you.' She considers what a proper femme fatale might say. 'I don't want you forever. I just want you for tonight.'

Fran rubs his face with one hand and shakes his head. 'Jenny. Even if I didn't love Sam, even if I was that sort of person, I wouldn't be doing this with you.'

She feels her face burning. She looks down at herself. 'Am I that bad?'

He laughs. 'You look gorgeous. I imagine half the guys in that pub have given you the once-over.'

'But not you,' says Jenny quietly. 'You'd never betray her, would you?'

Fran nods kindly. 'I would never betray Sam. But Sam's not a her. Sam's a him.'

The booze and the cigarette and the sudden, crushing embarrassment all convene in Jenny's gut. Oh my God, she thinks. How could I have got this so very wrong? I have made a play for a married man. A married man who is married to a man. For a moment she cannot decide which is worse. That she has thrown herself at someone who firmly told her he was in a long-term relationship, that she has so brazenly assumed he was straight, or that she has been so roundly and publicly rejected. Then the weight in her stomach suddenly shoots upwards, and emerges as a multi-coloured stream of vomit that splashes over the front of Fran's pink shirt, dragging with it hot tears of shame.

20

Two Smart People

(1946, dir. Jules Dassin)

The next morning, Jenny stays curled in her bed until long after ten, her faced streaked with mascara tears, her eyes red and swollen from crying. Stupid, stupid, stupid girl. She has no lectures with Fran until next week, but she's not sure she will ever go back. She's blown it. She can imagine him going back into the pub after she'd fled, covered in her vomit, laughing with Amber and Saima and Alan and all the rest about how idiotic she'd been. She stifles a sob and puts her face into her pillow, hugging herself tightly.

Standing under the hot spray of the shower, Jenny watches the remnants of her make-up swirling in the water around the plug hole. There goes the femme fatale, quite literally down the drain. This is Loughborough, all over again.

Jenny had come to Lancashire to reinvent herself, but maybe some people just can't change. She will always be boring. She will always get it wrong. She pulls open the curtains and sees the distant figure of Ringo on the beach, skimming stones into the grey sea. Pulling on her raincoat, she heads out.

'Hi,' says Ringo. He has a small pile of stones and pebbles, and is crouching down, building a tower from them in the wet sand; the widest, flattest stones first. He looks critically at the gathered pebbles and selects the next one for the stack. 'How was your night out?'

'Utterly awful.' Jenny stands there, hands jammed into her coat, watching him work. He doesn't invite her to continue but she suddenly can't help herself. 'I made an idiot of myself in front of my lecturer, the people on my course are shallow and awful and I drank so much I threw up.'

'Standard,' nods Ringo. He finally glances up at her. 'God, you look terrible.'

'Thanks for that.' She turns to go.

'Wait,' he says. He places another pebble on the stack and it topples over. He sorts through the stones for the biggest one and starts again.

'What are you doing?' she asks with exasperation.

'Exactly what you're doing. Trying to build something that just isn't going to work.'

Jenny gives a long sigh. 'Go on, then. Tell me what you're talking about.'

Ringo balances a second stone, and then a third, his hands flanking the growing tower until he's sure it's stable. He says, 'You're trying to create a new life for yourself. Trying to make a new Jenny Ebert.'

'You don't know anything about me!' she snaps angrily.

He shrugs. 'Maybe you don't know anything about yourself. And I do know what you're going through, Jenny.' He adds another stone. 'It happened to me, remember?' Ringo stands up and gazes out to sea. 'Today's the third anniversary of my mum's death.'

'Oh,' she says. She really wishes he hadn't gone there. 'I'm sorry.'

'Not for you to be sorry about.' A pause. 'I do understand what's happening to you, you know.'

She bites back her angry response. Today's not the day for an argument with him. Instead she just says levelly, 'Oh?'

Ringo's gaze remains on the sea. 'You feel responsible. For their deaths. I can tell. You think it was your fault.' Finally he turns to her. 'Was there an inquest? I presume so. I couldn't find anything online.'

'You've been googling me.' Calm, Jenny. Calm.

'I wasn't prying.' He obviously was. 'I was just interested . . . after what you told me, about them dying in a car crash . . .'

'It sounds quite a lot like prying, Ringo.'

He holds up his hands in surrender. 'I just wanted to be sure before I spoke to you . . . in case there'd been any trouble with the law over the crash.' Suddenly he takes her hands in his, surprising her. 'I can help. I've been there. Been where you are now. I know what it's like.'

Jenny pulls her hands free, a little more roughly than she planned to. 'I'm fine.'

'You don't know who you are,' insists Ringo. 'You want to change yourself. I *know*. Believe me. You think that person you were . . . it's all their fault, so you want to leave them behind and become someone different. That's why you're so self-obsessed.'

Jenny's mouth drops open. 'What did you just say?'

He crouches down again, resumes carefully constructing his pebble tower. 'Self-obsessed. I don't mean that as an insult.'

'Oh, sure, you meant it in the *nice* way.' She can feel her hands curling into fists; she can barely subdue her growing rage now.

A sudden cold wind whips up, blowing her hood against the back of her head, lifting Ringo's hair aloft like fronds of seaweed on the tide. 'I did too, believe it or not,' he says. 'I mean, you're so convinced that you need to reinvent yourself that you're ignoring the people around you – you're missing stuff.'

'Such as?'

Ringo shrugs. 'Ling and Bo. They're brother and sister.'

Jenny opens her mouth to speak and then closes it again. 'What? How do you know?'

He laughs. 'Because I asked them. You were all like, "ooh, what's with them, what's the mystery, what's going on here, so weird", and I just asked them. Bo is a bit of a business genius, and he dotes on Ling. She's got all the social skills, all the patter, the looks, but she has to work twice, three times as hard as Bo to get the academic results. She resents him a bit for that, which is why they talk to each other like they do, why she pretends she isn't really anything to do with him. But they're devoted to each other, really.' He looks up at her. 'All these people around us, Jenny, they all have stories. They're not just . . . extras in the background of yours.'

Jenny glowers at him. Because she knows he's right. 'But Ling said they weren't related when Mr Robinson asked.'

'No. She just pointed out that their surname is the fourth most common one in China. She didn't actually answer his question.

131

She was just challenging his assumptions.' Ringo looks up at her, his hair whipping across his face. 'Sometimes people are just what they appear to be. Like you, Jenny. You might think that after your parents' deaths you have to change, to not be that person any more, but you don't. Sometimes you just are what you are.'

Maybe she wasn't the femme fatale after all – that idea had crashed and burned anyway, after last night. Maybe she was more like the hardboiled detective, the guy who is swept along in the story, ultimately powerless in the face of everything. It doesn't matter what you do; you are who you are. Jenny Ebert will always just be Jenny Ebert. She looks down at the tower of pebbles Ringo is building. Soon the tide will come in and wash them back to their natural state, scattered and chaotic. She kicks the tower and it collapses, the stones slapping on to the wet sand. Does it matter that she chose to do that? The end result is the same, whether she kicks over the tower or the tide washes it away.

Ringo stands up. 'Have you phoned the uni yet? Told them you're taking up one of the rooms in the halls? You should do it soon, before they all go.'

'I'm going to call them now,' says Jenny. She looks at the scattered stones, sees the constant and inescapable collapse of every new identity she tries to create for herself. Then she turns round and begins to walk back up the beach towards Sunset Promenade.

As Jenny rounds the stairs she sees Mrs Cantle sitting on her bed through her open door. The old lady waves at her. 'Hello, dearie.'

She beckons Jenny through the doorway. Strewn around her on the bed are postcards from various exotic locales, dozens of them: Tenerife, Cape Town, Naples, Hong Kong, Singapore.

'Someone's sent you a lot of lovely postcards,' says Jenny.

'Oh, they haven't been sent to me. I'm sending them to my son,' smiles Mrs Cantle.

'Collects them, does he?'

Mrs Cantle frowns. 'No, I don't think so, dearie. I've got them out of order, though. Not sure where I'm supposed to be going next.'

Jenny perches in a space on the bed between the postcards. 'Mrs Cantle . . . about your jewels.'

Her face suddenly darkens. 'Yes. They've gone. Been stolen.'

'Are you quite sure?' says Jenny. 'Perhaps you put them some-where else? And forgot?'

Mrs Cantle shakes her head vehemently. She opens the drawer of the bedside table. 'They were here. They're always here. And then they were gone. And Edna told me what you said, that I can't tell Mr Grange because they'll come and close Sunset Promenade down.'

'So someone's definitely taken them? Someone here?'

Mrs Cantle shrugs. 'I suppose they must have.'

Jenny thinks about all the people in Sunset Promenade. The residents, the students, the staff, the Grange twins. Any one of them could have done it. Then she remembers something.

'Mrs Cantle, is it right that you and Edna only came here two weeks before me? Did you come together? Are you friends?'

'Friends, yes,' says Mrs Cantle brightly. 'Neighbours, really. It was all Edna's idea. Said it would be good for us.' She frowns and picks up a postcard. Limassol. On the back it is blank, but there's what appears to be a Cypriot stamp affixed to it. 'I think, all things considered, I would have rather gone on the cruise.' She looks up at Jenny. 'Do you think I should call the police? About the jewels?'

'Maybe not yet,' says Jenny slowly. 'Let me speak to a few people.'

The old lady's face brightens. 'Oh, that would be lovely. Maybe you can find them for me. You look like a clever girl.' Then she frowns. 'Oh, but you're leaving us already, aren't you? So soon.'

Jenny pauses. 'Mrs Cantle, have you ever tried to be something you're not?'

'Oh, all the time, dear. But I think I prefer being the old me.'

'But what if you don't like the old you?' presses Jenny. 'What if you want to be a new you, but you don't know who that should be?'

Mrs Cantle thinks about it. 'Then you just have to wait until you do know. You have to give things time, don't you, dear?'

*

133

Jenny's mind is racing as she mounts the stairs. Maybe she can change, after all. But maybe Ringo's right. She's been trying too hard. Trying too hard to be someone completely new and nothing like who she really is, with all her baggage from her parents weighing her down. But perhaps she's been going about things the wrong way. Perhaps she doesn't need to be a different Jenny Ebert.

Perhaps she just needs to be a *better* Jenny Ebert.

She's so wrapped up in her new idea that she almost runs into Edna as she rounds the stairs to the next landing. Edna is wearing a long skirt and a pair of red high heels, a tailored blouse and a string of pearls around her neck. Her platinum hair is piled artfully on her head. Jenny can't help hoping once again that she looks half as good as Edna if she ever makes it to anywhere near her age.

'Less haste, more speed,' says Edna mildly, as Jenny sidesteps her to avoid a collision. Edna puts her head to one side and considers her. 'Are you rushing to pack so you can leave this place?'

'Do you think I should leave?' says Jenny. 'Would you, if you were me?'

Edna makes a show of thinking about it. 'Well, I'm not at all sure. Living at the university is more *normal* for students, perhaps. Maybe you'll be happier, doing all the things you're supposed to be doing. I think the real question is, what would there be to keep you here?' She looks around, then whispers conspiratorially, 'The young man, perhaps?'

'Ringo?' says Jenny, barking a laugh. 'God, no. I mean, he's nice and everything, but . . .'

'I think he's quite taken with you, you know.'

Jenny shakes her head. 'No.' She thinks about it. 'It's possible he's taken with the idea of who he thinks I should be, but that's not the same.'

'Not the same at all,' agrees Edna. 'So, what else might there be to keep you here?'

'It's a mystery,' says Jenny slowly.

'You mean, you don't quite know yourself?'

'No. I mean . . . there's a mystery.' Even as she speaks, she finds things are becoming clearer to her. 'There's a problem.' She looks at Edna for a long time. 'Can we talk? In your room, perhaps?'

Edna nods and leads her into her room. It's immaculate, with silk sheets, a vase of fresh wildflowers and a framed black-and-white photograph on the wall: a portrait of an absolutely stunning woman in her twenties wearing a pale evening dress, a halo of light around her head coming from a window or some other light source behind her, and a dark, unreadable, enigmatic look on her face. It takes Jenny a few moments, then she says, 'Oh my God, was that you?'

Edna smiles tightly. Jenny's eyes widen. 'Wow. You were absolutely beautiful. I mean, it's amazing.'

'I had my admirers,' agrees Edna with an indulgently self-satisfied smile. 'However, you mentioned a mystery.'

Jenny wrenches her eyes away from the portrait. 'Mrs Cantle. She's your friend, right? You came here together, not long before the students arrived?' Edna nods. Jenny continues, 'These jewels she keeps going on about . . . they're real.'

Edna raises one eyebrow. 'She's a lovely woman, Jenny, but is given to fanciful notions.'

Jenny shakes her head. 'I've seen them. The jewels. They're real. And they're definitely gone. Someone's stolen them. Someone at Sunset Promenade! And probably the same person who stole Mr Robinson's medal and Joe's photo.'

'Then we should go to the police immediately.'

'No, no, no, we can't. Because if there's an investigation . . . this place is hanging by a thread, all the funding's up in the air, the grants and everything. Garry wants to sell it on to a big care home chain. If there's any whiff of scandal, if the police are involved . . . the money could dry up, the place will have to be sold and we'll all be out on our ears because no big company is going to run it like Barry Grange runs it.'

Edna looks at her curiously, then her eyes widen as the implications sink in. 'Ah. I see. But why are you coming to me with this?'

'Because you're Mrs Cantle's friend,' says Jenny. 'And because . . . well, I don't know why but you're the only person I actually trust completely in this place. So I thought you might help me.'

'But help you do what, Jenny?'

'Solve the mystery!' says Jenny, eyes shining. 'Find the jewels, and everything else that's missing!'

Edna considers this for a moment, then looks back to Jenny. 'But why would you want to do this?'

Perhaps I don't need to be a different Jenny Ebert.

Perhaps I just need to be a *better* Jenny Ebert.

'I think it's something I have to do,' says Jenny. 'I don't really know why, only that I can't *not* do this.'

'But . . . you're leaving Sunset Promenade, aren't you?'

Jenny thinks about the room waiting for her on campus, thinks about the nights out with the likes of Saima and Amber. Thinks about that exciting student life she's been aiming for. Thinks about being . . . just like everybody else. Is that what Bacall would do? Would she be commonplace? Or would she do the unexpected thing . . . ?

Ringo's Stars

Mr Robinson

Seems like a bloody waste of time to me, all this, but I suppose if everybody else is doing it, then all right. Have to show willing, haven't you? Have to do your duty. Just don't expect me to bang on and on for ages. I know your game, see, lad. Want us to pour our hearts out, don't you? Find out what makes us tick? We're not exhibits in a museum, you know. We're just ordinary people.

Right, so. I liked the scary stuff when I was a boy, the ones about aliens and monsters and ghosts. Pictures about things that had no right to be here being sorted out, kicked up the arse and sent on their bloody way. Yes, you can read into that what you want.

It was July, nineteen forty-two. Long, hot summer. Not like the bloody damp squibs we have these days. Everything was better back then. Everything. Yes, even though there was a bloody war on.

I don't think I was supposed to be in that film, probably far too young. It was the Palladium on Church Street. What? Preston. Just down the bloody motorway. That's where I grew up. The Palladium, though, wonderful place that was. In summer they kept a door at the back of the screen ajar because it got so hot. You could sneak in when the lights had gone down. That's what I did. You didn't even know what picture you'd end up watching half the time.

Cat People, it was. Ever seen it? No? Cracking film. About this poor bloke who marries this conniving woman. Serbian, I think she was. Eastern European, definitely. She's from this yokel village up in the mountains where they're all witches or some such; they can turn into big cats. She turns into this big bloody panther and kills this doctor chap. What? *Spoilers*? Look, pal, the film's nearly

137

eighty bloody years old. If people haven't seen it by now it's not my bloody fault.

Anyway, the reason I'd gone to the pictures in the first place was that my mum and my sister were getting the house ready for Dad coming home. He'd been away, fighting the good fight. Keeping the world safe. They said I'd just get underfoot while they were making bunting out of old newspapers. They'd all saved their rations to get eggs and suchlike to make a big cake. I couldn't wait to see my dad, hear about all his adventures sticking it to the foreigners. He'd been on a mission, see, somewhere near Russia. Couldn't talk about it, obviously. It was all very hush-hush. Had to be, you see? Not like today. You'd all probably be giving the secrets away on bloody Tweeter or something if we had another war. Don't know when to keep stuff to yourselves, your generation. In fact, I bet half of you wouldn't even turn up for a war. You'd be all, oh, is there a war on? I didn't notice. I'm so wrapped up in my video game or my computer or something. Can they come back tomorrow?

Sorry, yes, I'll stick to the bloody point, then. So I sat through *Cat People* twice, watched this conniving Serbian woman turn into a panther and kill this fella – well, I've already bloody spoiled it once, haven't I? Doesn't matter now. I was itching to get home, though, and after the second showing I ran all the way there. I thought my dad would be home by then, but he wasn't. Everybody was just sitting around the front room, saying nothing.

They'd made a lovely cake, though. Victoria sponge. And there was a pie, and sandwiches, and some lemonade. Even a couple of bottles of stout for my dad.

Then I noticed everybody was crying. My mum couldn't even speak and my sister, Vera, called me over and gave me a big hug. Dad's not coming home, she said, just like that.

Has he gone on another mission? I asked her.

No, she said. His ship was sunk. We just got the telegram.

And that was bloody that. I just sat there, wondering if it would be bad to ask if we could still eat the cake, looking at my mum crying her eyes out, that newspaper bunting hanging over the fireplace. And all I could think of was this bloody Serbian woman turning into a panther and going round killing everybody.

✳ 21 ✳

So Dark the Night

(1946, dir. Joseph H. Lewis)

Stomach churning, Jenny walks into the lecture hall and takes her usual seat. There are no whispers, no subdued giggling. Amber and Saima are on their phones, and Saima glances up as she walks in. 'What happened to you at the Smugglers? We lost you.'

'Oh, I got a phone call. Emergency. Had to go.'

Saima turns back to her phone. Amber shrugs. 'Rubbish night, anyway. We might go to the Sugar Shack next week, if you want to come.'

The lecture passes uneventfully. Fran is neither friendlier nor colder than he has been with her in the past. As everyone files out at the end, she lingers until it is just him and her. She approaches him at the lectern as he puts his papers in order and stuffs them into a battered leather bag.

'I am so sorry—' she begins, but he holds up a hand.

'Nothing to be sorry for. It's forgotten.' He cracks a crooked grin. 'I had to wash that shirt twice, though.'

'But what I said . . . what I did . . .'

Fran looks at her. 'Jenny. I was flattered. You were drunk. We should all be thankful I'm gay, because otherwise I might have taken you up on your offer and we'd all be in a load of trouble right about now. Please don't let this affect anything.' He glances around to make sure they're alone. 'You're my best student, by a country mile.' He ponders. 'Best student for years, actually. You make this job worthwhile for me. You've got a great future ahead of you. Let's draw a line under this, yeah?'

As she's leaving, Fran says, 'I'm glad you seem to be settling in

139

all right. I suppose once you leave the old folks' home and move into student halls you'll feel more a part of campus life. Be able to do the things everyone else is doing. Be like the rest of the students.'

Jenny looks at him for a long time. 'Do you think that would be a good thing? To be like everyone else?'

'Do you?'

Jenny sighs. 'It's the right thing to do, isn't it? The sensible thing to do. Live the proper student life.'

Fran leans in to her and says, '"When your head says one thing and your whole life says another, your head always loses". Humphrey Bogart in *Key Largo*. But I guess you already knew that.'

'So, you're staying then?'

Jenny lights the last of the Gauloises with the Zippo and crushes the packet, stuffing it into the pocket of her coat. She inhales deeply and then breathes out a plume of smoke into the cold, night air. She's sitting with Ringo on the wall at the front of Sunset Promenade, the lights of the house behind them. It's cold, but at least it's not raining. High above, the stars are actually twinkling and the moon is full.

'It looks like it,' she says. She wriggles her toes in her boots. She's abandoned the slinky dresses and high heels, and it's such a relief not to have to put the rollers in and blow-dry her hair every morning. Goodbye, Lauren Bacall. It was nice knowing you. Nicer than trying to be you, at any rate. She says, 'For as long as this place is open, I suppose.'

Ringo weighs a stone in his hand and tosses it high and hard, across the road, on to the sand. Jenny tuts. 'You shouldn't do that. There might be someone walking on the beach.'

'Nobody ever comes here,' says Ringo. 'You think it's that bad, then? The situation here? You really think it's going to close down?'

'Be sold off, I should imagine. Which amounts to the same thing.'

'So why stay, then? You might miss out on the room in the accommodation block.'

She shrugs. 'There are more blocks to finish. I'm sure we'll both be offered rooms eventually.' She looks at him, taking another drag on the cigarette. 'It's the mystery. The thefts. I feel like . . . I can't save the home but I want to do something to help. This is the only thing I can think of.'

'Robbo's medal and Joe's photo?' He laughs, then stops when he sees she's serious. 'Um, OK then. It's a mystery, I suppose. From femme fatale to hardboiled hero in one fell swoop,' says Ringo with a cracked grin. She smiles, too. At least he's been taking notice. She looks across at the black sea and the black sky. It's like a void out there, save for the occasional winking light on a ship or gas platform. She picks up a stone and hefts it as hard as she can. It clatters to the road far below.

'Hey,' says Ringo. 'You told me off for that. There might have been a car.'

'There's never a car,' she says, and grinds her cigarette out under her heel.

'And you don't need me to tell you that's bad for you,' says Ringo.

'It was my last one, anyway. I didn't even like them, to be honest. It was all part of the image. Along with the silk dresses and the hair.' She looks down at her ripped jeans. 'These are much more comfortable.'

'I liked you in your dresses,' says Ringo. She feels his shoulder touching hers, lightly, through their coats. 'You looked classy.'

'I suppose,' says Jenny. For some reason she has an almost unbearable urge to lay her head against his shoulder. She resists. 'Looking classy all the time is a bit of an effort, though, to be honest.'

She has to keep reminding herself that she can't trust anyone at Sunset Promenade. That someone's responsible for the thefts. She can only be sure that it isn't her, and for reasons she can't put her finger on she trusts Edna Grey as well. Does she distrust Ringo? Not exactly, she supposes. But maybe she doesn't know enough about him. Maybe it's time for the detective to do some detecting.

Jenny says slowly, 'You must have only been young when your parents died. That must have been difficult for you.'

She can feel Ringo looking at her, no doubt in surprise, then he says, 'Yeah, it was. I was fifteen when Mum died, sixteen when

Dad had his heart attack. He looked after me when Mum had gone, and when he died I went to live with my Auntie Lisa. She only lived in the next street. I've got three cousins, though, and their house was only the same size as ours, so it was a bit cramped. Soon as I'd done my A-levels and got a place here I moved out.' He looks across the waves. 'Feels weird, boiling it all down to a couple of sentences like that. I thought my world had collapsed at the time. It was Armageddon.' Jenny feels his breath on her hair. 'But I don't need to tell you about that.'

'It gets easier, though' she says carefully.

Ringo ponders. 'It gets . . . different. You come to a day where you've gone to bed at night and you realise you haven't thought about them, not at the front of your mind, and you feel guilty. You feel guilty because you've had a day where you haven't been upset and you don't think you deserve that, and it feels disrespectful. Then you have another day like that, and you don't feel as bad as the first time, because you realise that just because they're not right there . . .' Ringo bangs his fist on his forehead. 'Just because they're not right *there* all the time, it doesn't mean they're not *here*.' She doesn't have to look at him to know he's put his fist to his heart.

'How did you get through it?' she whispers.

'The Beatles, of course,' says Ringo. She feels him shiver with cold at her side. 'And books. I read stories to escape, and then I started writing stories and that helped me find my way back.' He looks at Jenny. 'You can't write stories unless you understand people. So I decided I'd always be around people from then on.'

'I'm sorry for what happened to you,' says Jenny.

'Don't be,' says Ringo. 'It's happening to you. It happens to everyone, eventually. Since I started doing this project . . . ah, man. You should hear the stories they've told me. Ibiza Joe lost his kid and it sent him off the rails. Mr Robinson's dad died during the Second World War. That's why he's the way he is. That's why he hates foreigners.'

'A lot of people lost family in the war,' says Jenny gently. 'They don't all become reactionary old racists.'

'Sssh,' says Ringo, and points across Jenny. She follows his finger to see a figure quietly letting itself out of the front door and padding along the terrace at the front of the building, away from them. Ringo mouths, *It's Mr Robinson.*

'What's he doing?' whispers Jenny.

Wrapped in a duffel coat, Mr Robinson is standing on the corner of the terrace, holding his magnifying glass up in front of him, pointed at the night sky.

'He's looking at the moon,' says Ringo wonderingly.

'Let's go inside,' says Jenny. 'It's cold.'

'No,' says Ringo, standing up. 'Let's go and talk to him.'

'I don't think he'd—' But Ringo is already loping across to Mr Robinson, and Jenny gets up and quickly follows.

'All right, Mr Robinson?'

He looks away from the magnifying glass and squints at them. 'Halt! Who goes there? Oh. You two. What do you want?'

Ringo nods upwards. 'Are you looking at the moon?'

'Yes. I suppose you're going to take the bloody mickey out of me now, aren't you?'

Ringo grins. 'I've got a telescope in my room, you know.'

Mr Robinson makes a *pshaw* noise. 'Bloody Peeping Tom, are you? You won't find any scantily clad beauties on this beach, let me tell you. Not even in the height of bloody summer.'

'I like astronomy,' persists Ringo. 'Do you?'

Mr Robinson holds up his glass again. 'I like the moon,' he says softly. 'Only I can't see it very well any more. Look after your eyes, you kids, if you don't do anything else.'

Jenny watches Ringo circle behind Mr Robinson so he can see through the magnifying glass as well. 'Look. Mare Imbrium. Big dark patch to the left.'

'Yes, I know. The Sea of Rains,' says Mr Robinson, glancing at Ringo with what Jenny thinks can only be a grudgingly impressed look. 'And that little white dot just underneath it . . . ?'

'That's the crater, Copernicus.'

'I wish I could see it better.' He waves the magnifying glass. 'This helps. But not much. Over to the right there, you know what that is?'

'The Sea of Tranquility,' replies Ringo.

Mr Robinson nods. 'June the twenty-first, nineteen sixty-nine.' He looks at Ringo and Jenny. 'I cried that day. Bet you have no idea why. Bet it's one of those "ooh, it happened before I was born so why would I know that?" things.'

Jenny doesn't, in fact, know, but Ringo says quietly, 'The day we landed on the moon.'

'Aye, lad,' says Mr Robinson. There's a long silence. 'Cried like a baby. It was all so . . . so hopeful. One small step for man. Felt like the start of something. One giant leap for mankind.' He looks at Ringo. 'I thought everything was going to change then. I thought . . .'

Mr Robinson puts the magnifying glass down, still looking up at the moon, which Jenny knows must be only a white blur to him now. He says, more to himself than anyone else, 'During the war, when my dad was home, he took me to the pictures. There was a film on about men going to the moon. Rubbish it was, really, but I liked that sort of thing. Took you away from all the horror. I said, "Dad, will men ever go to the moon?" And he said to me, "Aye, lad, I hope they do. And I hope they build a big rocket and take all the bloody blacks and Jews and whatnot and send them up there and keep them out of the way of good, honest, hard-working folk".'

Mr Robinson blinks and stares at Ringo and Jenny, as though surprised they're still there. 'And I said to him, "Dad, if they do, can I go with them?" And you know what he did?'

Jenny shakes her head. Mr Robinson looks at his feet. 'He hit me. Back of my head. Hit me so hard I fell over and burst my nose on the pavement. And he said that was only half of what I'd get if he ever heard me talking like that again, going to the bloody moon with the blacks and the Jews.' Mr Robinson looks up at the moon one last time. 'I think I'd better go in now.'

They watch him go and then Ringo says, 'Mr Robinson? It's not too late yet, and I . . . I wondered if you wanted to look at the moon through my telescope? We haven't really had many clear nights and it's full and . . .'

Mr Robinson is looking at Ringo with a curious gaze. He says, 'This isn't some sort of trick, is it?'

Ringo shakes his head. 'It's a fairly powerful telescope. I bet you'd be able to see the moon great through it.'

Mr Robinson rubs his face and Jenny realises with sudden shock that he's surreptitiously wiping away a tear. He says, 'You know what, Ringo lad, that'd be grand. Thank you.'

Ringo turns and smiles at Jenny, and she is surprised to find that she's lightly clasping his hand in hers. She gives it a squeeze, then lets go. As Ringo follows Mr Robinson back into the house, she ponders that missing jewels and stolen medals aren't the only mysteries hiding behind the windows of Sunset Promenade.

✳ 22 ✳

Alone with Everybody

(1948, dir. William J. Drake)

For the second gathering of the Lonely Hearts Cinema Club, Jenny decides to follow *Ice in My Heart* with the next William J. Drake movie, *Alone with Everybody*, about a detective who is framed for a murder and imprisoned, along with a good number of crooks and gangsters his testimony has helped to put away.

Making good on his earlier promise, Florin has baked a cake for the occasion, a huge Victoria sponge oozing with cream and jam and dusted with icing sugar like a winter tableau. Not a speck of chocolate anywhere to raise Mrs Slaithwaite's unpredictable ire. Florin has wheeled a large urn of tea into the day room as well, and not only has Barry Grange taken a chair by the door, but Garry has pitched up, too. Even Bo and Ling are there, by way of a goodbye, as they are leaving Sunset Promenade the next day for their rooms in the newly opened hall.

Ringo, of course, is delighted that Jenny is staying. She finds him difficult to read, if she's honest. On the one hand, he's exuberant and excitable with everyone and over everything, like a bouncing puppy. But on the other, she feels that he's taking a special interest in her, directing some of his energy into . . . what? She doesn't know. She really wishes she had never spoken to him about her parents dying, because he seems fixated on it, as though it's somehow his responsibility to guide her through it. Last night she paused at his door on her way down to dinner. He was playing that Beatles song over and over and over: 'Eleanor Rigby'. The one about lonely people – wondering where they all come from, wondering where they all belong.

He seems all right tonight, though, huddled in a corner with Ibiza Joe and Mr Robinson, each of them sipping tea and laughing as they enjoy some refreshments before the DVD goes on. A right little gang of boys, thinks Jenny, with a flush of something she can't quite identify . . . humour? Pride? A little jealousy? She sidles up to them under the pretence of refilling her teacup, listening in to their conversation with her back to them.

'Yes, she's a damned handsome woman, that Edna Grey,' says Mr Robinson quietly. 'Damned handsome.'

'She's a looker and no mistake,' agrees Ibiza Joe.

'Bit old for you, Joe,' laughs Mr Robinson. 'Don't you prefer hanging around people young enough to be your grandkids?'

There's a pause, then Joe says softly, 'It was never for *that*, Robbo. I never went to the clubs and festivals for that sort of thing . . . It was more just to be around young people.' He pauses quietly for a moment, then says to Mr Robinson, 'She's too good for you, is Edna. Well out of your league, man.'

'Get out of it, you bloody hippie,' retorts Mr Robinson. He takes in a deep breath. 'Wait, what are you saying? That you'd have a better chance with her than me?'

Jenny glances over her shoulder to see Joe shrug with a mischievous grin. 'You said it, Robbo.'

'*Pshaw*,' sniffs Mr Robinson. 'I'll tell you what, let's have a little competition. You, me, her. May the best man win.'

Joe smiles, spits on his hand and holds it out to Mr Robinson, who pulls a face and cautiously places his palm against Joe's, who says, 'You're on. And don't worry – I will.'

Jenny hurries back to the sofa with her tea. God, what should she do? Tell Edna? Just leave them to it? She glances back at the huddle of boys; Ringo has noticed her listening in and looks over, shrugging as if to say, *nothing to do with me, but what can you do?* In the interest of being a better Jenny Ebert, she gifts him a lopsided grin and his face lights up. A little secret, then. Just between the two of them.

Jenny is sitting, once again, between Edna and Mrs Cantle. Mrs Slaithwaite is in her chair, staring impassively at her puzzle book. Jenny has to say, Mrs Cantle doesn't seem unduly concerned about the loss of her jewels. Perhaps they haven't been stolen at all; maybe she really has just mislaid them, put them in a bag or another drawer and forgotten about them. Maybe there's no great mystery to be solved. But if that's the case, what will Jenny do then? How can she become a better person if she doesn't have this? Failed femme fatale . . . what if hardboiled investigator fails as well? Where does she go from there?

She looks at Ringo again, sizing him up critically. Is she the good woman? Stability, family life, all those boring things? That's the life her parents would have chosen for her: a nice little economics degree under her belt, a few years in accountancy like her father, then married off to someone with a good job, a nice house in the suburbs, popping out children, employing that economics degree to balance the household budget. And why is she looking at Ringo when she thinks this? Because he's the only boy to have shown any interest in her since she got here?

As if reading her mind, Edna nudges her gently and murmurs, 'I bet the young man was pleased that you decided to stay.'

Jenny looks at her. 'Why do you say that?'

'Just that with the Chinese students going, if you'd left as well he'd have been on his own here. With all us oldies.'

'I'm sure Barry and Garry will be getting some other students in to take up the empty rooms,' says Jenny, though with the new hall opening she isn't quite convinced that will be the case. She glances at Edna. 'You don't think . . . the twins . . . ?' She nods her head at Mrs Cantle.

Edna purses her lips thoughtfully. 'A motive, you mean? For the jewel theft? Because of their money troubles?'

Jenny glances back at Barry and Garry, talking quietly near the door, and then nods enthusiastically. 'It's possible,' she whispers.

'Have you thought about everyone else? Other possible motives?' says Edna. 'Perhaps we need a list . . . everyone's names and any potential reason they might have for stealing the jewels.'

'I'll do that,' says Jenny excitedly.

'Are we watching this film or not?' shouts Mrs Slaithwaite, which is a little rich, thinks Jenny, as she slept through the last one entirely.

Jenny nods and inserts the DVD into the player. Edna touches her arm. 'I am interested, though, dear . . . how did you get these old films on to those discs?'

'Oh, there's a lot of places do it,' says Jenny. 'Why, do you have something you want to get converted to DVD? I could sort it out for you.'

'Just an idea I have, some old memento,' smiles Edna. 'I'm sure I can find the right place.' She nods to the TV. 'Hadn't we better get on?'

The conversation in the room dies down and all eyes are on Jenny. She clears her throat. 'Well. Hello again. For the next film I've chosen another one directed by my grandfather, William J. Drake. This is the second film he made, and it's called *Alone with Everybody*. In the leading role of the private investigator who is wrongly convicted of murder, Drake cast a newcomer, Edwin Morrell, with George Storm – who starred in the first film we saw – taking a much smaller part. From my grandfather's notes I think that there'd been some kind of falling-out between Drake and Storm, and they didn't work together again after that.'

'I wonder what that could have been about?' says Edna.

'A woman,' nods Mrs Cantle. 'The leading lady, I shouldn't wonder.'

'The notes didn't go into detail . . . the main female role opposite Morrell in this picture is taken by Joyce Palermo again . . .'

Edna raises an eyebrow. 'The woman who was in the first film? I didn't think she was up to much, to be honest.'

'Doesn't hold a candle for you, Mrs Grey,' shouts Mr Robinson across the room. He gives Joe an exaggerated wink and mouths, *One – nil.*

Edna stares at him. 'What on earth are you talking about?'

'Anyway . . .' says Jenny. 'If we could dim the lights again . . . I'll get it started.'

Jenny counts it as a victory that Mrs Slaithwaite appears to have stayed awake for the whole of the film, but that's offset by the gentle snoring of Mr Robinson from the far sofa. She stops the DVD after the final credits have rolled and says, 'Right . . . does anyone have any questions to start the discussion?'

'Can we have a comfort break first?' asks Edna. 'Just five minutes.'

'Aye, I'm dying for a slash,' agrees Mrs Slaithwaite.

'Cracking picture,' says Ibiza Joe.

'That poor fella, though,' says Mrs Cantle. 'Locked up with all those bad sorts in prison. And when they put him into that cell on his own, and turned out all the lights . . .'

'Hold that thought,' says Jenny. 'That's a good point to start the discussion. In fact, I'll just get my grandfather's notes from my room while everyone's having a quick break.'

Jenny walks out with Edna, who heads for the communal toilets on the ground floor. 'That was thrilling, dear,' she says. She cocks her head to one side. 'You seem to be enjoying hosting these film nights. I must say, on behalf of all of us, we're very grateful.'

'I *am* enjoying them,' says Jenny. 'I feel like, half the time in this place, everyone's just one wrong word away from a meltdown. But when we're all watching the films it's as though . . . I don't know.'

'We're together. At least for an hour or so,' smiles Edna encouragingly. 'It's a good thing you've done. Now, I really must powder my nose.'

Jenny races up the stairs to her room, pulling her case from under her bed. It's here she keeps all the original scripts and notes written by her grandfather, along with the other memorabilia and mementos. The 35mm canisters are still in their bag, under her bed. She has wondered if she should put them somewhere safer; they are potentially very valuable. Besides, the old nitrate-based film is extremely flammable; William J. Drake's oeuvre could burn down Sunset Promenade with one spark. She'll just have to be careful.

She is sorting through the scripts, looking for the hand-written pages that refer to the making of *Alone with Everybody*, when a sudden click makes her jump. The door to her room has swung shut. She frowns. Has it ever done that before? No matter, she has the notes. Jenny is just pushing the suitcase back under the bed when everything abruptly goes black.

*

150

It's only a power cut, Jenny realises with relief, when she remembers to breathe again. Barry had told her, back on her first day, that Sunset Promenade was prone to outages. Something about a back-up generator, too, wasn't there? Jenny waits for a moment, crouching on the carpet by the bed, the sheets of paper in her hand. How long does it take an emergency generator to kick in? Jenny stands up and feels her way round the bed. There's no light coming in from outside, and she's left her phone downstairs, so can't even use the torch on that. Taking short steps, she heads with her hands outstretched towards the door, coming up hard against the woodwork and sliding her fingers down to the handle. She's sure that once on the landing her eyes will become more accustomed to the dark, and besides, the generator should surely—

The door is locked.

That's impossible. She never locks the door. Not even after Mrs Cantle's jewels were stolen did she lock the door. She twists the handle again and pulls at the door, but it's stuck fast. Not just jammed, but solidly shut. Locked.

Jenny's fingers probe at the keyhole, but of course the key isn't in it. She can't even remember where it is. Ringo gave it to her on her first day, and she dropped it somewhere . . . in the bowl on the chest of drawers, maybe? But if it's there, how come the door is locked? Then she feels a sudden shiver of fear down the nape of her neck. It's dark and it's silent and here she is, trapped in her room right up on the third floor.

Someone's locked me in, she thinks, knowing how crazy it sounds, but the thought is somehow amplified by the darkness. She gropes her way to the chest of drawers and feels around in the bowl on top. Her fingers brush a handful of small change, a phone charger, but no key.

What if someone's locked the door from the inside? What if they crept in while she was rifling through the suitcase? What if they're in here with her now? She spins round, peering into the blackness, listening intently for the slightest of sounds, perhaps from the en-suite bathroom.

When the door handle rattles, Jenny can't help but scream. Then the lights come on and relief floods through her. She tugs at the door and it swings open, and on the other side is the slight frame of Mrs Cantle.

'Are you all right, dearie? I thought I heard you shout out.'

Jenny puts a hand on her chest and breathes rapidly. 'It was the power cut. I thought . . .' What did she think? She bends down to retrieve her grandfather's notes from the floor as Mrs Cantle steps into the room.

'How do you think I felt? I was sitting on the loo.'

'The door,' says Jenny weakly. Already the terror she felt is receding in the bright light, seeming insubstantial and silly. The door was obviously not locked, it was merely jammed or stuck, and in her rising panic . . . She looks at the chest of drawers and there, sure enough, not in the bowl but sitting by the edge nearest the door, is the small, ornate key, right by where Mrs Cantle is standing. Jenny snatches it up and stuffs it into her pocket.

'I think there'll be a nice cup of tea on in the day room,' says Mrs Cantle. 'Can I hold your arm down the stairs, just in case the lights go off again?'

'Of course,' says Jenny, looking back at the drawers as she pulls the door closed behind her. The key was there all the time, she thinks. Except she's pretty sure it wasn't.

Ladies in Retirement

(1941, dir. Charles Vidor)

'Hello!' bellows the green-and-red rocket that bursts into the day room, mats unfurling in front of her to herald her arrival.

Mr Robinson, on the sofa, slumps behind his *Daily Mail*. 'Oh, God. The yoga lady.'

'I'm not turning the telly off,' announces Mrs Slaithwaite. 'I want to see how much they sell this shit-hole of a house for after they paid all that money for it at auction.'

'Ha ha!' yells Mad Molly. 'Now, let's get these sofas and chairs pushed back. Where's that nice young man? Florette?'

Florin pops his head round the door and his face falls. For once, thinks Edna, he and Mr Robinson seem to be of the same mind.

'Florette!' shouts Molly. Does that woman ever do anything quietly? She is balancing a stack of CDs under her arm, and they suddenly burst out and clatter all over the floor. 'Be a love and push the sofas back. I'm running late and I've got Pilates with the Women's Institute at eleven.'

'Oh, come on,' says Edna. 'We can't just sit on our behinds all day. We need to exercise.'

Mr Robinson folds his newspaper and looks at her appraisingly, smoothing his moustache. 'I must say, Edna, you certainly look after yourself.'

Edna raises an eyebrow. Before she came to Sunset Promenade, she attended her local gym three times a week. They'll doubtless be wondering where she has got to. Nothing too strenuous, of course, but some brisk walking on the treadmill, a little exercise-bike action, even some light weights. It's nice to be appreciated, she thinks, even by someone like Mr Robinson.

'Dancing is a good way to keep fit,' says Joe, who's been leaning on the mantelpiece. 'You should let me take you dancing, Edna.'

She blushes, despite herself. 'Oh, Joe. I doubt we'd manage more than a couple of turns at our age.' She's being kind, of course; Edna could still cut a rug with the best of them. Joe can barely walk without his stick.

'Rubbish,' says Ibiza Joe. 'We should go out with the young 'uns, show them how to really enjoy themselves.'

Mr Robinson shakes his head wonderingly. 'You really are a case, Joe. A right bloody case.'

'Chop, chop!' calls Mad Molly, clapping her hands together. 'Are we all here?'

'Mrs Cantle doesn't partake,' says Edna. 'On account of her hips.'

'I'd have those hips sorted out in no time,' harrumphs Molly. 'Still, we must crack on. Come on, let's loosen up a bit, then while we're on the subject of hips, everybody take a mat and let's get down and start with the Cobbler's Pose.'

'Bloody cobblers is right,' says Mr Robinson, surprising no one as he says it every single week.

'Good for the groin as well,' says Molly, plonking her Lycra-clad bum down on her mat and putting the soles of her feet together in front of her.

Is Edna imagining it, or do Mr Robinson and Joe both glance at her when Molly says that?

'Aaaaand stretch!' shouts Molly, hitting the play button on her portable CD player and filling the room with the sounds of the Guatemalan rainforest.

'You're all being marvellous today,' booms Molly after half an hour. 'I'd like to move us on a step. Everybody on all fours; we're going to try the Downward Dog.'

Edna finds it all quite untaxing, if she's honest. She follows Molly's lead and begins to slowly push herself up, straightening her knees. She glances around and can see the others are struggling;

Joe hasn't got off his knees and Mr Robinson is turning a shade of puce. He needs to be careful, with his heart, she thinks.

'Downward Dog? More like son of a bitch,' gasps Mr Robinson, collapsing back on to his knees. 'That's enough for me. I'm buggered.'

Mrs Slaithwaite has given up after ten minutes, and only Edna is holding the pose along with Molly. Edna blinks as Joe, rubbing his back in surrender, appears to wink at her.

'And relax,' instructs Molly. She jumps up to her feet and runs her hands through her wild, red hair. 'Excellent session. Especially Mrs Grey.'

'Maybe we should do some extra practice on our own, Edna?' says Joe. Mr Robinson glowers at him with undisguised loathing.

'I'm sure Molly's sessions are enough,' says Edna primly. As everyone starts to roll up the mats, she adds, 'I think I'll go and check on Mrs Cantle.'

It's curious, she thinks as she climbs the stairs. She's almost started to forget the reason why she came to Sunset Promenade in the first place. She has to bring herself up short sometimes, remind herself what she's doing. You aren't here to enjoy yourself, she says to herself. The funny thing is, though . . . she pauses at Mrs Cantle's open door and knocks briskly, disturbing her friend from her reverie.

'Hello, Margaret. The yoga lady's gone.'

Mrs Cantle smiles sadly. 'I wish I could take part, Margaret. But, you know, my hips . . .'

'Edna,' says Edna kindly. 'I'm Edna and you're Margaret.'

Mrs Cantle rolls her eyes. 'Oh, yes. Sorry. I am such a silly.' She looks down at the pile of postcards in her hands. 'I've forgotten where I'm supposed to be.'

Edna sits down beside her. 'Let's see . . . how long has it been? Four weeks? That would mean . . .' She gently takes the cards and sorts through them. 'What about Egypt? That sounds plausible.'

'Egypt,' says Mrs Cantle. 'I would quite like to see Egypt, Margaret.'

'Edna.'

'Edna. I would quite like to see Egypt, Edna.'

Edna pats her hand. 'One day, Margaret.'

'Only . . . will we be here long, do you think? I am missing my little house.'

Edna smiles. 'You just get on with enjoying yourself here. Don't worry about your house. Everything's fine.'

Edna stands and pauses at the door. 'We should go out, you know. If it ever stops raining, we should go out. Get some fresh air.'

Mrs Cantle nods absently, then looks up. 'Are you enjoying it here, Mar— Edna?'

Edna ponders. For so long she's been on her own, and that's the way she's liked it. Her own house, her own things, her own little routines. Seeing people when she wanted to, locking herself away when she didn't. Locking herself away with all those thoughts, all those memories, all that . . . she brushes it away. Never mind. Not something to dwell on now. She smiles again. 'Funnily enough, Margaret, I do believe I am.'

After lunch the Chinese students are preparing to leave for their new home. A large minibus has arrived, driven by a rough-looking chap who seems to know the girl, Jenny. He's had to park on the road at the bottom, and he and Florin are transferring Bo and Ling's bags as the Grange brothers and the residents shelter from the rain in the porch of Sunset Promenade.

'How you settling in, love?' he shouts to Jenny as he hefts up two more bags. He disappears down the steps and emerges again, five minutes later, to grab the last of the luggage. 'You still got my card? I can get the minibus any time, if you and your mates wanted a night out.' He squints at the gathering under the porch. 'You could all go. Young and young at heart, eh?' Kevin looks at Ling and Bo. 'This is the last of them. Come down when you're ready.'

Ibiza Joe and Ringo exchange a glance. They're up to something, those two. There's an awkward silence, Ling standing under a yellow umbrella, Bo beside her, getting drenched. Then Barry Grange steps forward. 'Well, ah, obviously we're sad to see you go . . .'

'Not as sad as the bank manager will be,' mutters Garry Grange.

'But . . .' says Barry, glaring at his twin. 'But we have enjoyed your time here, and hope you will be very happy in the new halls of residence.'

Another long silence. Then the boy, Bo, says haltingly, 'I think you are all very nice people. I will miss you all. Even you, Mr Racist Soldier Man.'

'Is he talking about me?' says Mr Robinson loudly.

Ling clears her throat. 'I am afraid I cannot echo my brother's sentiments,' she says curtly. 'Living here has been appalling.'

The silence this time is shocked. Ling looks at them all in turn, defiance in her eyes. 'In China we have a big problem with old people. They are living too long and the state does not provide for them. Families are splitting up, children moving away.'

'Like us!' says Bo.

'Hush,' says Ling. 'Here, in this place, in Sunset Promenade, you are very lucky. The Grange brothers are doing a very special thing. They are financing this place at a loss. It is obvious to see. They are subsisting on grants and hand-outs to make sure you people have a comfortable life.' Ling shakes her head. 'And all you do is bicker and argue and fight. You have the idea of bringing young people in to make a different atmosphere, but the young people just fight with the old people. Nobody ever counts their blessings. I have never known so many people living together but so . . . apart.' She shrugs. 'You might as well be on your own.'

Nobody speaks. Edna strokes her chin lightly. The girl is not wrong. She glances around at them, at Ibiza Joe and Mr Robinson, at Ringo, at Mrs Cantle, Mrs Slaithwaite, Jenny. At herself.

Ling touches Bo on the arm. 'Come on, it is time.' She looks back at them all, standing on the porch. 'You act like you have all the time in the world. You don't. You should be nicer to each other.'

It is Ibiza Joe who speaks first. 'To be fair, love, you haven't been very nice to Bo while you've been here. We didn't even know he was your brother.'

'He is an idiot in many ways,' says Ling. 'But in others, he is a genius. We cannot choose our family but we have to live with them.'

'We didn't choose each other in this place,' says Mrs Slaithwaite.

Ling looks at her. 'No, you didn't. But you can choose to be friends, or at least, not enemies. You don't have to be alone. Not when you are surrounded by people.'

Then she turns and heads towards the steps. She doesn't look back. Bo smiles and waves at them, and hurries after her. Edna and the others wait and watch until they've descended out of sight.

'Well,' says Barry Grange. 'That was . . .'

'Food for thought,' says Ringo softly.

Mr Robinson raises an eyebrow. 'My arse,' he says. 'It's bad enough having to live with you lot, let alone have to be friends with you.'

Mrs Slaithwaite laughs. 'You're not wrong.'

Ibiza Joe pulls out from beneath his poncho a pack of cards. 'Anyone fancy a game of rummy before lunch?'

'Bloody rummy,' scoffs Mr Robinson as they all turn to head back inside. 'Three-card brag, that's a man's game.'

'Ooh, I do like a hand of find the lady,' says Mrs Cantle. 'Or pontoon.'

'OK,' says Mr Robinson, disappearing through the door, the rest of them around him. 'But we're not playing for matchsticks or bloody buttons; cash pot only. Pennies and tuppences. Who's in?'

'I will start lunch,' says Florin, 'while you play cards.'

'And we've got some paperwork to sort out,' says Garry pointedly, steering his brother to the office. 'Now that we've got two empty rooms.'

Edna follows everyone else into the day room. Ibiza Joe starts to shuffle the cards but Mr Robinson snatches them off him. 'Give them here. You shuffle like a girl.'

'I'll tell you what,' says Joe, surrendering the cards. 'That taxi man . . . we could all get in his minibus, you know.'

'I'd love a night out,' agrees Mrs Cantle, clapping her hands.

'Are you allowed?' asks Jenny.

Ibiza Joe laughs. 'We're not prisoners here, love. We can come and go as we please.'

'We just don't please to very often,' says Mr Robinson, dealing out the cards on the coffee table. 'Where would we go?'

'Well,' says Ringo, looking shifty. 'Joe and I, we've been having a chat, and we were thinking about doing something, you know, to bring us together. But the question is, what would we all enjoy?'

'I'm not going to a nightclub with bongo-bongo music,' says Mr Robinson firmly. Edna wouldn't have put it quite like that, but she has to agree. She's not packing herself into a student nightclub.

Jenny says, 'Well, to be fair, Mr Robinson, I don't think Ringo and I would be up for an afternoon tea dance either.'

They stare at each other across the table, then Ringo pulls out a cutting from the local paper. 'That's why we thought this was a good idea. It's at some place called the West End Working Men's Club, so it's not going to be all students. And it's a disco, so it's going to be lively.' He hands the advert around.

Mr Robinson stares at it and says, with a touch of loathing, 'A Halloween disco? Fancy dress encouraged? You're not serious, are you?'

Ibiza Joe laughs delightedly. 'I think it's brilliant! A night out! What do we say?'

Ringo shrugs. 'Sounds like a right laugh. You in, Jenny?'

Jenny frowns. Edna watches her to see what she'll do. She needs to lighten up, that girl. Then she says, 'Why not?'

'Oh, say we can go, Edna,' says Mrs Cantle. 'I haven't been out in such a long time. What about you, Mrs Slaithwaite?'

Mrs Slaithwaite picks up her cards. 'Don't see why not.'

'Fine,' sighs Mr Robinson, as though his permission is required. 'Fine. Let's do it. When is it?'

'Saturday!' says Ringo.

'Bloody hell. What are we going to wear? We're not really going in fancy dress, are we?' says Mr Robinson, slapping down his cards. 'You, missy, Jenny – are you going to book that cabbie?'

'Book him for what?' asks Florin, popping his head round the door. 'Where are you going? I came to say lunch is ready in the dining room.'

'Just going out on Saturday night,' replies Ibiza Joe, maniacally nudging Ringo. 'New art exhibition at the museum.'

Florin nods and disappears. Edna says, 'Why did you tell him that?'

Joe cackles. 'Because it's always more fun if you feel like you're doing something wrong.'

Mr Robinson shakes his head and says, witheringly, as he stands up, 'You're off your nut, Joe, you know that? We're going to an art exhibition dressed as the bloody Addams Family, are we? I wonder what's for lunch?'

Florin opens the day room door again to let them all file out. 'Cabbage soup!' he says.

Mr Robinson sighs. 'Cabbage soup. Oh, sweet Jesus.'

'Try to keep it in your bowl and not in your lap this time, Robbo,' says Joe.

They all laugh, and even Mr Robinson's bluster as he blames Florin for the incident seems to be tinged with the slightest hint of self-deprecation. Edna watches them go for a moment, then falls into line behind them. Will wonders never cease?

Then, as she takes her seat at the dining room beside young Jenny, she realises that once again she's almost allowed herself to forget just why she is here.

Almost.

Ringo's Stars

Edna Grey

I was sixteen when I went to the cinema to watch David Lean's marvellous adaptation of *Great Expectations*. Have you seen it? No, I don't suppose you would have. I should speak to Jenny about old films. But you're familiar with it, of course? You've read the novel? Good.

Martita Hunt played Miss Havisham. Absolutely wonderful performance. Argentinian-born, she was. Learned her trade on the stage. One of the greats. Her Miss Havisham, though . . . she terrified me. Sitting there in her cobwebby mansion, crumbling along with her home. I think it was the age of her that frightened me. I was a teenager, and if you don't mind me saying so, Ringo, I was quite striking at that age. Being an old lady . . . that seemed a terrible thing, one I could barely imagine. I know that seems strange, looking at me now. But we were not always old, just as you and Jenny will not always be young. And when I was your age, the thought of withering away, all alone . . . it looked like the worst thing in the world.

I felt I had more in common with young Pip, of course. His life was all ahead of him; the world was his oyster. I was not born into riches, and for those of us who had lived through the war years . . . well, we were glad to be alive, but wondered what the brave new world held. Pip showed me that even someone with nothing could have greatness thrust upon them. He gave me hope.

I had so much hope in those days. And in the very year I watched that film, things did indeed begin to happen. I started to live out my dreams. Have you heard the saying that you should be careful what you wish for, though, Ringo? It is sound advice.

161

No, no, I'd rather not go into it, I think. Suffice to say that after a few years of living my dream, it all turned rather sour.

I watched another version of *Great Expectations* much later on in life. It was made for television. Had James Mason in it, and Michael York. No, I don't suppose those names do mean much to you. Miss Havisham was played by Margaret Leighton. Do you remember her from *Night of the Iguana*? No, of course not.

This was . . . nineteen seventy-something. Four, maybe? I'd have been in my mid-forties. Not quite as old as Miss Havisham, but older than Pip. Stuck somewhere between them. And life no longer seemed laid out in front of me. It felt as though it was behind me. Yes, I know, that doesn't seem old these days. But it was back then. Miss Havisham no longer frightened me. She fascinated me.

Did you know that Dickens himself said that Miss Havisham was only in her fifties? She was always portrayed as very old in the films, but she wasn't really. She'd been aged by tragedy. She wasn't just the scary old witch. She'd had a terrible life. She sat in her old house, wearing her wedding dress that hung off her in tatters. Why? Because she'd been jilted at the altar, dear, and she never recovered from that.

Don't you think that would be an awful thing? To let one event in your life mark out the rest of your days? And yet it happens, doesn't it? We let things happen to us, rather than allowing ourselves to influence and change the world. I think that's a decision we have to make ourselves: whether we're going to be the sort of person who life happens to, or the sort of person who happens to life, if that makes sense.

I suppose what I'm saying, dear, is that everybody who's had a life has a story of some sort. And I'm sorry if this one hasn't been very interesting. I suppose some of us have just had less eventful lives than others.

✳ 24 ✳

The Big Night

(1951, dir. Joseph Losey)

Kevin is waiting for them on the coast road at eight o'clock the following Saturday, and by some miracle the rain has let up. As Jenny descends the steps it's clear enough so that she can see lights winking across the bay. At the bottom she stops and looks up at the rest of them. And what a sight it is to behold.

The costumes were all Ringo's idea, really. He was very particular that they had to have outfits that reflected their personalities. Florin – as much of a wizard on the sewing machine as he is in the kitchen; not really much at all – had helped run up Ringo's designs using scraps of material foraged from around Sunset Promenade: old sheets, decommissioned curtains.

First down the steps is Ibiza Joe, his face slathered with white greasepaint, his mouth streaked with red, a black cape with a red lining draped over his shoulders as he carefully and breathlessly negotiates each step. He's the vampire, of course, forever young. Huffing and puffing behind him is Mr Robinson, two bolts at his neck, skin coloured a sickly grey-green. 'Bloody Frankenstein!' he'd said. 'Frankenstein's monster,' chided Ringo. 'The creature made in the image of his father.' Jenny wonders if Mr Robinson understands Ringo's subtleties, and decides not. He'd never have agreed if he did.

Mrs Cantle is a dark and forbidding fairy ('She's away with them most of the time,' Ringo had explained) with black wings and thick purple eyeshadow applied by Jenny, and behind her Mrs Slaithwaite wears a witch's hat and an old sack for a dress, tied at the waist with string, her face glowing green. 'Ee!' she'd said delightedly, 'I'm like that Grotbags off the kids' show donkey's years back. The one with that bloke and the bird puppet. The one that fell off the roof when he was fixing his telly aerial.'

'And what disguise will you choose for me?' Edna had said.

'Something glamorous,' Ringo replied thoughtfully. 'Something powerful.'

She'd allowed Jenny to blow-dry her hair high up on her head and apply temporary black-and-white colouring. 'The Bride of Frankenstein!' Ringo had said with satisfaction when she was finished.

'Elsa Lanchester,' Edna had murmured. 'I met her once.'

'Really?' said Jenny. 'How come?'

But Edna had shaken her head. 'I forget now.'

Bringing up the rear was Ringo. He was far too skinny for Batman, but he'd insisted. And he'd also chosen Jenny's costume for her. She was a werewolf, with bits of fur from a former resident's old coat (Jenny decided not to ask if it was real, and if so what animal it was from) poking out of the sleeves of a ripped shirt, her hair tousled, a delicate rivulet of blood running from her mouth. She'd asked him why, of course, as they all assembled at the top of the steps.

'Always changing,' Ringo had smiled. 'But your true nature will come out eventually.'

'Holy amateur psychoanalysis,' she'd said, smacking her fist into her open palm. 'And you've rather modestly chosen Batman for yourself . . .'

He'd looked up, jaw set determinedly, at the clouds scudding across the pale, indistinct moon. 'He lost his parents, too. He decided to devote his life to helping others.'

'Very noble,' said Jenny. 'Come on, let's get this horror show on the road.'

Jenny helps Mrs Cantle and Mrs Slaithwaite into the minibus and climbs in up front, next to Kevin. Ringo slides in alongside her.

'West End, is it?' says Kevin, checking in his rear-view mirror to make sure everyone's got their seatbelts on. 'Big night out?'

'Halloween party,' calls Joe. 'In case you thought we dressed like this all the time.'

'Bloody bongo-bongo music, I'll bet,' sniffs Mr Robinson. 'Don't see why we can't find a proper dinner dance.'

'Mr Robinson—' begins Jenny, but he cuts her off with a raised hand.

'I know, I know,' he sighs.

Then everyone chimes in. 'That is not nice!'

He holds out his hands. 'I'm trying, aren't I?'

As Kevin rams the minibus into gear and negotiates the dark, empty coast road to town, Jenny can feel Ringo's eyes on her through the holes in his mask. She picks self-consciously at a bit of fur poking from a gash in her ripped jeans and glances at him. 'What?'

'I was just thinking how great you look,' he mumbles, turning to stare out of the side window.

'Ha ha,' she says. 'You should see me on a full moon.'

'It's not just the costume,' says Ringo. 'It's everything. You seem . . . more relaxed in your own skin. Like you're not trying to be something you're not any more.'

Jenny sighs. 'It's like you said, I just need to give in. If the full moon says I've got to be a wolf, then I suppose I've got to howl.'

He shakes his head. 'I didn't say you have to give in. People are allowed to change. Take Bruce Wayne. He decided to become Batman. He could just as easily have sat in his mansion without working nights. He knew he wanted to fight the bad guys but he had to wait for inspiration . . . he had to see a bat flying through his window before he knew what he had to become. Sometimes we have to know what we want to change before we understand how we can change it.'

Jenny looks ahead as they turn into the more brightly lit roads that lead into the town, and signs of civilisation emerge at last. Sunset Promenade is so isolated, so on its own, that it's easy sometimes to forget that there's all this life just a couple of miles away. She still isn't convinced by Ringo's argument; she still believes that she is what she is, a product of Simon and Barbara Ebert, nature and nurture. She has their blood flowing in her veins, and she can never escape that. She can never be something different. But perhaps she can bend what she is, shape it a little. Be a bit closer to what she would like to be.

'All excited for the jolly next weekend?' calls Ibiza Joe. 'Isle of Man?'

Ringo leans over the seat. 'Are we invited?'

''Course,' says Joe. 'We go every year. Trip to Douglas. Lovely day out. All on the Grange brothers, as well.' He pauses. 'I suppose this'll be our last trip.'

'Three and a half hours on the ferry from Heysham,' mutters Mr Robinson, jerking a thumb at Mrs Slaithwaite. 'She was as sick as a dog.'

'All over the side,' agrees Mrs Slaithwaite. 'Puked my guts up. There *and* back.' She pauses, folding her big arms over her bosom. 'Anyway, did you bring anything to drink?'

'Oh, aye,' says Mr Robinson, delving into a sports bag sitting on the floor of the minibus. 'Bugger. Forgot to get some plastic cups from Florin.'

There's a hiss of escaping gas as he twists the top off the Pepsi bottle. 'Bernie's home brew,' he says with a wink.

'Ladies first,' says Mrs Slaithwaite, grabbing it from him and taking a deep swig. She hands it to Edna, who raises her eyebrows and then wipes the top with a handkerchief and takes a delicate sip, grimacing.

'Cracking stuff, isn't it, Edna?' laughs Joe. 'Come on, pass it round. We want to finish this before we get there.'

When the bottle comes to Ringo he gives Jenny an amused look, then puts it to his lips. She takes it next, keeping her eyes on Ringo as she takes a mouthful.

'Urgh,' she says, wiping her mouth. 'That's rank.'

'Give over,' says Mrs Slaithwaite, putting a big arm over the back of the seat. 'Pass it here, it's my go again.'

Mrs Slaithwaite takes a long draught, then passes the bottle on. She lets loose a wet belch and smiles happily. 'Bernie's a genius.'

Kevin pulls up outside a long, flat building on the edge of an industrial estate. There's a sign on the pebble-dashed wall proclaiming it to be the West End Working Men's Club, and strung across the entrance is a hand-painted banner announcing *HALLOWEEN PARTY – ALL WELCOME*. Even from within the minibus Jenny can hear the thump-thump of the bass.

'Can you come back for us in a couple of hours?' she asks.

Kevin shrugs. 'Tell you what, I'll just wait with the van. I haven't got any more jobs in the diary and there's no point going home and coming back.'

'Good,' says Mr Robinson. 'I can leave my bag in here. There's two more bottles of Bernie's home brew in it and I don't think they'll let me take it into this place. Keep an eye on it, will you, lad?'

'Hey,' whispers Ibiza Joe. 'Anybody got any pills before we go in?' He's directing the question at Ringo, really, who shakes his head, but it's Mrs Cantle who pipes up.

'I've got some Dulcolax in my handbag,' she says. 'Are you bunged up, Joe?'

'Ooh, I had some of that once,' says Mrs Slaithwaite. 'Took a double dose by mistake. You wouldn't have wanted to follow me into the toilet, I can tell you that.'

Joe curls up his lip. 'Ah, no, it's fine. Thanks anyway, Mrs Cantle.'

The doormen look them up and down as they assemble outside the minibus. The taller of the two says, 'What we got here, then? The Munsters?'

'Button your lip, lad,' says Mr Robinson, marching up to them. 'Seven for the party, please.' He turns to Ringo. 'The lad's paying us in. Get that student loan out, Ringo.'

As they file in through the small lobby, the heat and music hit them square on. Everyone's in fancy dress and the lights flashing around the room are purple and orange and green. Mr Robinson waves at Jenny and Ringo. 'Oi, you two. Get some drinks in. I'll have a pint of mild.'

'Gin and orange for me,' says Mrs Slaithwaite, looking critically around the room. 'Make it a double. No, a treble.'

Mr Robinson turns to Edna. 'Mrs Grey,' he says formally. 'Would you do me the honour of a dance? I am but a lowly monster, but you are the Bride of Frankenstein, are you not . . . ?'

'To this?' frowns Edna as the DJ drops something fast and furious.

Mr Robinson bows slightly. 'We can dance to our own beat, Mrs Grey. We have the class and the upbringing.'

Jenny glances at Mrs Cantle, who's following the conversation with a slight frown. What is Edna going to do? Surely she's not going to—

'It would be my pleasure,' says Edna. Mrs Cantle's eyes widen. 'Margaret, would you hold my purse?'

Jenny hears her name called above the music and sees Ringo at the bar, waving at her. She joins him and takes up one of the trays of glasses, following him as he threads through the crowd back towards the rest of them.

'Sunset Posse in the house!' declares Ringo, handing the tray round for people to get their drinks. 'Where's Robbo?'

'Over there,' says Jenny, pointing at the dance floor. 'With Edna.'

Ringo grins and nudges Joe. 'First blood to Robbo,' he says.

Joe just smiles. 'I'm biding my time, son. You can't rush into these things.'

'What is going on with you lot?' says Jenny with a grin. 'I overheard you talking . . . is there some sort of competition?'

Joe nods his head. 'For the affections of the wonderful Mrs Grey.'

Jenny laughs. 'You know that's really not cool, right? She's not a prize to be won.'

'Oh, girl, we did things differently in our day. I'm all for you young kids and your equality and your modern ways, but sometimes . . .' Joe shrugs. 'Sometimes a lady likes to feel special. Am I wrong?'

Jenny is aware of Ringo looking at her, and for some reason she can't meet his eye. Instead she scans the dance floor for Mr Robinson and Edna, and when she spots them her eyes widen.

Edna is like a beacon of serenity and grace, moving among the bouncing dancers as though she occupies a different space to them, drifting in and among them with Mr Robinson guiding her skilfully. Or so he thinks. While Mr Robinson is ostensibly leading her, it's obvious that Edna is the driving force, performing some subtle trick of allowing Mr Robinson to believe he's in charge while she, in actual fact, is directing them around the oblivious dancers. The glitter ball spins lazily overhead in counterpoint to their dance, making it appear for all the world that they are figures on an ancient movie screen. Slowly, as people notice them, space opens up around Edna and Mr Robinson – people take a step back, slow their dancing, stop to watch. By accident or design, a spotlight seems to fall on them. Edna is quite, quite beautiful, thinks Jenny, even in Halloween fancy dress. When the track finishes, a spontaneous round of applause breaks out from the hushed dance floor. Edna looks around and gives the tiniest of bows; Mr Robinson appears startled and smiles wanly smile before leading Edna from the dance floor as the DJ puts on the next track.

Edna drops Mr Robinson's hand as they approach, and he takes his pint of mild from Ringo and winks at Joe. 'You can throw in the towel now, if you like.'

As Edna excuses herself to find the toilet, Mrs Cantle says, 'Oh, I am glad Margaret's enjoying herself at last.'

'You mean Edna,' corrects Jenny.

Mrs Cantle puts her hand to her forehead. 'Oh, I am silly. Edna. Of course. I'm Margaret.'

Ibiza Joe steps up. 'Mrs Cantle? I don't suppose you'd like a dance as well?'

She wrinkles her nose and shakes her head. 'Sorry, love. Not with my hips. Maybe Mrs Slaithwaite . . . ?'

They all turn to where Mrs Slaithwaite is at the bar, fluttering a five-pound note at the barman and bellowing for another gin and orange. Joe frowns. 'Maybe not.'

'I'll dance with you,' says Jenny, surprising herself.

Joe blinks. 'Really? You'll have to be patient with me, love . . . you've seen what I'm like. And if I get short of breath, you'll have to sit me down.'

Jenny grins. 'Deal. Let's go.'

She glances back at Ringo, who gives her a huge wink and a thumbs-up. She's actually enjoying herself. This is almost easy. Why has she never been able to manage it before?

Joe starts to move along with the music, and Jenny falls in with him, facing him and aping his movements. She glances over at Ringo, who's pushed his Batman cowl off and is waving at her, giving her another thumbs-up. *Know what you want to change before you try to change it*, Ringo had said. But maybe you also had to recognise what you didn't want to change; had to see the things that were good, that you enjoyed, that you didn't hate about yourself. You didn't want to throw the baby out with the bathwater. And here, in this working men's club, dressed as a werewolf, dancing with a pensioner who can barely walk, being elbowed by a man in an octopus costume, the glitter ball overhead sending shafts of coloured light shimmering around the room, she suddenly feels happy.

Then she turns back to Ibiza Joe and he's got his eyes closed, and tears are running down his face.

* 25 *

Lonelyhearts

(1958, dir. Vincent J. Donehue)

'After our Brian died,' says Ibiza Joe, 'well, things went downhill quickly, as you can imagine. We nursed him through the last weeks of his life, watched him deteriorate and . . . I don't know, *shrink*, I suppose. Like the life was just leaking out of him.' Joe wipes his eyes and takes a mouthful of the bottle of lager that Jenny has bought for him. They are sitting at a table far from the others, sandwiched between a pair of zombies incongruously arguing about who should have done the washing-up before they left the house, and a large man who Jenny thinks is meant to be someone from *Game of Thrones*.

'When he'd gone . . . me and Shirley sort of drifted apart. He was the glue that held us together, was our Brian. Without him . . . Shirley wanted to try again, have another kid, but I couldn't. It felt like it was a betrayal, in a way. I couldn't imagine watching another little kiddie grow up, past the age of seven, doing all the things that Brian should have done.' He shakes his head. 'I started marking the time he'd lost, saying what he would have been doing if he'd been alive, what he'd be learning at school. Me and him going to the football. To the pictures. Birthday parties. "He's ten today," I'd say. "I bet he'd have wanted a nice model plane, or a toy boat." I think that was the last straw for Shirley. She said I was living in the past, and she wanted to move forward to the future. We split up.'

Joe watches the dancers for a moment, then continues, 'But she was wrong. I wasn't living in the past. I was living in the *present*. With Brian. Only he wasn't there any more. And when we got to the years when he'd have been a teenager . . . oh, I so missed the house being full of young people.' He looks at Jenny. 'I never had much of what you'd think of as teenage years myself. Worked from the age of fifteen, me and Shirley got married young. Felt like I'd gone straight from school to playing at grown-ups.'

'Is that why . . .' begins Jenny. 'The clubbing, and Ibiza and everything?'

He nods and smiles ruefully. 'I suppose I was having the youth I'd never had. Partying, raves, pills, up all night, watching the sun rise. I know young people laughed at me, thought I was the oldest swinger in town. But nobody cared, really. Nobody cared how old you were. Everybody was loved up and happy.' He stares at his feet. 'Even if it was just the drugs. At least they did the job. It was like, in some way, I was living Brian's life for him as well as the life I'd missed. When I was dancing on my own on some beach, round a bonfire, the sky paling in the east . . . it felt like he was with me.' Joe looks up at her. 'Does that sound daft?'

Jenny shakes her head and Joe says, 'And I might have still been at it today, even at my age, but for . . .' He shrugs. 'Too many drugs, too many late nights. Affected my brain. Spent some time in a mental institution, and when I got out I was suddenly old, and alone. Then I saw an ad for Sunset Promenade. Brian had gone, by then. But sometimes, like tonight, he comes back.'

Jenny reaches across the table and takes hold of Joe's hand, because she doesn't know what to say. It feels good, making that connection, and he seems to draw strength from her. Suddenly he smiles. 'We'd better get back to the others. We don't want them gossiping.' As Jenny pushes her way through the crowd, Joe takes hold of her arm. 'Jenny. Thank you. For listening.'

'It's bloody hot in here,' says Mr Robinson when they return. 'Is my make-up melting?'

'Do you want me to come outside with you, get a bit of fresh air?' offers Jenny.

'No, no, I'll be fine. I'll just go and keep that cab driver company for a bit, I think. Make sure he's not fiddling the meter.'

'Do you think we should all go?' asks Jenny, watching Mr Robinson push his way to the door.

'Oh, it's early yet,' says Edna. She looks at Mrs Cantle. 'Are you all right to stay for a bit, Margaret?'

'Oh, yes,' says Mrs Cantle. 'I'm having a lovely time. A nice young chap offered to come and do some gardening for me while you were dancing.'

'Gardening?' says Jenny.

Mrs Cantle frowns. 'I think so. I wasn't quite sure what he meant, to be honest. Something about weeds. He wanted to sell me some. Though I've no idea why I'd want to buy some weeds.'

'More drinks,' says Ringo quickly, heading off to the bar. Jenny follows to help, standing with him as he places the order.

'God, Joe's story is so sad,' she says.

'I know,' says Ringo. 'His kid, Brian? And why he went off to Ibiza, all that?'

Jenny nods. Ringo looks at her for a long moment. She glares at him. 'What?'

'Nothing,' he says, which just infuriates her more.

'Say it,' she demands. 'Something about me finally thinking about other people and not being so self-obsessed? Is that it?'

'If the cap fits,' says Ringo, paying for the drinks. She's about to speak again but he cuts her off. 'Help me get these back and then you and I are having a dance.'

Jenny hands out the drinks while Ringo makes for the toilet, and five minutes later she spies him talking to the band. Then he's beckoning her over as the next record starts, an old one she can't immediately place until the vocals kick in.

It's 'Eleanor Rigby'.

Ringo takes her hand and pulls her on to the dance floor, dragging her into the middle of the crush, the moving bodies pushing them close together. He smiles at her.

'You're obsessed with this song,' she says. 'I heard you playing it over and over.'

'Beatles, innit? It's kind of the law if you're from Liverpool – you have to love the Beatles.'

He takes her by her forearms and they sway together.

'It's not just that, though, is it?' Jenny presses. 'This song . . . it's about loneliness. Despair. Eleanor Rigby . . . she dies unloved, unmourned.' The priest is wiping the dirt from his hands. 'No one was saved,' says Jenny.

She frowns at him.

'John-Paul George, are you trying to *save* me? Is that what this is all about . . . Batman? You're the big hero and you want to save me?'

He brushes her question off with a smile, but she stops dancing. 'Ringo. Really? You think I need saving? From what?'

'From yourself,' he says, and leans in to kiss her.

'No,' says Jenny, the palms of her hands flat on his chest, pushing him away. 'No.'

Then she flees from the dance floor.

It's gone ten-thirty, so Jenny decides it's time to leave.

'Boo,' says Joe. 'I'm just getting warmed up.'

'I think Jenny's right,' says Edna. She looks around. 'What happened to Mr Robinson?'

Joe shrugs. 'Never came back. Hope he's all right.'

They troop out of the club to where the minibus is parked up, dark and quiet. There's no sign of Kevin in the front.

'I hope nothing's happened to Robbo,' says Joe. He tugs at the door on the side of the vehicle, and as it slides open smoothly, a lumpen shape comes tumbling out on to the tarmac.

'Robbo!'

Mr Robinson looks up at them from the damp ground through one eye, his greenish greasepaint streaked with sweat marks. To his chest he's hugging an empty Pepsi bottle. Joe bends down. 'He's been through a whole bottle of Bernie's home brew. Robbo! Robbo! Are you all right?'

'I am very, very drunk,' Mr Robinson says, enunciating each word carefully.

'Where's Kevin?' asks Jenny, peering into the minibus. Then another empty Pepsi bottle rolls out and bounces off Mr Robinson's chest.

174

A head emerges from between the seats. It is Kevin. He says, 'I, also, am very, very drunk.' He points at the tattoo on his arm and adds, 'I loved her, you know. Moira. No man could love a cat more than I loved my Moira.' Then he plants his face into the metal floor of the bus and starts to snore loudly.

'Great,' says Jenny. 'How are we meant to get home now?'

Mrs Slaithwaite elbows her to one side. 'I'll drive. Help me find the keys.'

'You can't drive!' says Jenny. 'All that gin and orange . . .'

'Constitution of a bull, me,' says Mrs Slaithwaite. 'I'm fine. Get these two tossers in the back and let's go.'

'I'm not sitting in the front with her,' whispers Jenny to Ringo as she climbs in the back and buckles up. Ringo ignores her and sits up front with Mrs Slaithwaite as she rams the keys into the ignition and turns the engine on with a crunch of gears. Great, thinks Jenny. Now he's pissed off at me. Why can't everyone just have fun without complicating things?

'All set?' says Mrs Slaithwaite, gunning the engine. She takes off her witch's hat and tosses it into the back. Then she lets the clutch up and the minibus squeals forward, laughing loudly as she wrenches the wheel. The minibus skids out of the car park and towards the coast road.

'Oh God oh God oh God,' says Jenny, fumbling for her phone. 'We should pull over. I'll phone another cab.'

'We'll probably get the nice Kevin chap sacked if we do that,' says Edna. 'After all, it's only ten minutes, isn't it? And Mrs Slaithwaite seems to be in control.'

They all grab on to each other as the minibus bumps up on to the pavement and a litter bin flies into the air, bouncing off the nearside wing.

'Maybe some music to distract us . . .' says Ringo, twiddling the knobs on the radio.

'None of that bloody bongo-bongo music,' slurs Mr Robinson from the back.

The sound of a Celtic fiddle issues from the speakers, undercut by a steady drum beat, and immediately everyone sits up.

'I love this song!' says Mrs Cantle.

'Proper bloody song,' says Mr Robinson, struggling to straighten up.

Then the piano kicks in and Jenny recognises it from a hundred ironic playings at sixth-form parties and student bars. Joe is bouncing in his seat, and even Mrs Slaithwaite is rocking her head from side to side.

'Come on, Eileen,' everyone sings in unison, and Mrs Cantle starts clapping along to the beat.

'Poor old Johnny Ray,' sings Joe in a surprisingly melodic voice. 'Sounded sad upon the radio, he moved a million hearts in mono.'

Kevin rouses himself, unexpectedly, to pick up the tune. 'You're grown!'

'So grown,' laughs Mrs Cantle.

'So grown!'

'So grown up!'

'Now I must say more than ever,' sings Joe, tapping Ringo on the shoulder, who responds perfectly: 'Come on, Eileen!'

Then even Jenny and Edna are joining in as the entire minibus lets loose with, 'Too ra loo ra too ra loo rye aye!', Joe adding a hasty counterpoint of: 'And we can sing just like our fathers . . .'

'Come on, Eileen,' bellows Mr Robinson from the back, waving the empty Pepsi bottle in time to the beat.

'Oh I swear, well he means!'

Ringo turns in his seat to look at Jenny.

'At this moment, you mean everything!'

I'm sorry, he mouths.

'You in that dress, my thoughts I confess!'

It's OK, she mouths back.

'Verge on dirty!'

But what's he apologising for? Trying to kiss her? Trying to save her?

'Ah, come on, Eileen!'

Then Ringo is saying, 'Oh, shit,' and looking in the wing mirror on his side of the vehicle. 'Mrs Slaithwaite, I think you'd better pull over.'

It's only then that Jenny notices the interior of the minibus is painted in blue lights, and the sudden squawk of a police siren is sounding behind them.

The minibus lurches to a halt and Mrs Slaithwaite winds down the window. The face of a young police officer peers in, raising first one eyebrow and then both as he takes in the scene. Ringo quietly turns off the radio, Mrs Cantle obliviously singing on.

'We are far too young and clever!' she trills, tailing off as she realises she's the only one singing.

There's a moment's silence, then Mr Robinson shouts from the back of the minibus, 'Turn the bloody music back on! I'm very, very drunk!'

* 26 *

Dead Reckoning

(1947, dir. John Cromwell)

Barry Grange is walking up and down the day room like some kind of regimental sergeant major, something sadly lost on Mr Robinson because he's as pale as a ghost and looks like he might be about to throw up everywhere, and it's not just the remnants of his Frankenstein's monster make-up. They are all standing in a line, staring at their feet, as what passes for a bollocking is being issued, Jenny realises.

'To say I'm disappointed in you is an understatement,' says Barry, shaking his head as he strolls up and down the line. 'Coming back here at all hours, making such a racket. The police!'

'There are no charges,' says Joe. 'Though I don't know how.'

'Told you,' says Mrs Slaithwaite with satisfaction. 'Strong as an ox, me. I can drink a shedload and it has no effect.'

Even the two police officers had been perplexed, getting Mrs Slaithwaite to blow into no fewer than three breath-test bags before they had to admit that, despite her proud assertion that she had been drinking gin and orange like it was going out of fashion, the tests barely registered any alcohol. They had been pondering taking her to the station for a blood test, but in the end had evidently decided that a minibus full of drunk pensioners and students in Halloween fancy dress wasn't really worth the paperwork, given the breath-test results, and had instead opted to escort the minibus home, which happened largely without incident. There was a crack in the windscreen caused by the head of an unfortunate seagull, which Mrs Slaithwaite could have conceivably swerved to avoid, but all agreed that was a small price to pay for getting home uninjured and without any kind of police record.

Barry stops and sizes up Ringo, then moves on to Joe. 'It was you two, wasn't it? You're the ringleaders.'

'We all wanted to go,' says Mrs Cantle. 'It was a lovely evening.'

Even Mr Robinson, sweating profusely, puts up a hand. 'Now then, Grange, there's no use trying to pin the blame on one or two individuals here. We were all in it together.'

Jenny stares at them, one by one, down the line. *We were all in it together.* She never thought she'd see the day that was said at Sunset Promenade, let alone by Mr Robinson.

Barry rubs his face. 'I wouldn't so much . . . but we've got the inspection at noon.' He looks at them appealingly. 'Florin said you were going to a . . . an art exhibition.' He glares at Florin. 'Why the hell would they be going to an art exhibition dressed like that?'

Florin shrugs and Joe grins. 'We only said that so you wouldn't get worried.'

'We're not children, dear,' says Edna quietly. She glances at Jenny and Ringo. 'Even the young people. And we can come and go as we please.'

'Yes, yes,' says Barry. He closes his eyes and takes a breath. 'This inspection . . . it's very important. It's about the renewal of our licence to operate as a residential home. The inspector . . . she might want to speak to some of you.' He opens his eyes imploringly. 'Please don't tell them you all went out and got roaring drunk at a fancy dress party.'

Mr Robinson salutes. 'Understood, Grange. Now, if no one minds, I might just go back to bed for an hour or two? Feeling a little under the weather.'

'Fine,' sighs Barry. 'But one last thing . . . if you have any more of that home brew hidden around the place, can you get rid of it? And can someone go and wake up that taxi driver and get him to move his minibus from the bottom of the steps?'

'You lot know how to party,' says Kevin, slumped in the back seat of the minibus, gratefully holding the bag of frozen peas Jenny has begged from Florin to his forehead. 'Christ. That home brew is lethal.'

'You won't want this, then,' says Jenny, holding out a carrier bag with the two remaining bottles she's had to forcibly separate from Joe and Mr Robinson's hands. 'We can't keep it here in case the inspector finds it.'

Kevin looks into the bag and groans, then says, 'Well, I won't see it go to waste. Thanks.'

'Are you sure you're OK to drive?' asks Jenny as he clambers into the driving seat.

He peers at the windscreen. 'Christ. What happened here?'

'Seagull.' She thinks it best not to mention the big dent on the nearside flank from where Mrs Slaithwaite hit the bin. He'll find it soon enough.

Kevin looks at her. 'I don't really want to know how we got back here from town, do I?'

Jenny wrinkles her nose and shakes her head. 'Not really.'

He glances at his watch. 'Eight o'clock. Blimey. Back on shift in three hours.' Jenny closes the door on him and he winds down the window. 'Great night. Give me a call next time you and your gang are going out.'

Back in the day room, Mr Robinson has departed for a nap and Joe is playing a game of solitaire on the coffee table. Mrs Slaithwaite is flicking quietly through the TV channels. Joe looks up when Jenny walks in and says, 'Cracking night, all told.'

'My head's banging,' confides Jenny. 'Bernie's home brew, I think.'

'Rocket fuel,' nods Joe. 'Are you feeling all right, Mrs Slaithwaite?'

She shrugs. 'Like I said. Nothing bothers me.'

'Did you enjoy yourself?' asks Jenny.

Mrs Slaithwaite turns her gaze on her. 'We went out for a night that wasn't completely awful. That doesn't mean we have to be friends or anything.'

'No, I don't suppose it does,' says Jenny, nonplussed.

Mrs Slaithwaite turns back to the TV and Joe pulls a face at Jenny. She says, 'Did you see where Ringo went?'

'I think he was going in to university today,' says Joe.

Jenny wonders if anyone had seen Ringo's clumsy attempt to kiss her on the dance floor. What was he thinking? More to the point, what had she been thinking? Did she like him? She couldn't decide. She certainly didn't *dis*like him, and he was all-right looking

. . . intelligent, funny . . . maybe a little intense sometimes, but that could be quite an attractive characteristic . . . Jenny shakes her head. Is she trying to talk herself into something?

Jenny decides to have a shower and ponders what Joe said to her last night. They've all got their own tragedies, their own triumphs. All stories, packed together to make a life.

But what stories make up the life of Jenny Ebert?

The discovery of her grandfather's film work. The car crash. Watching *The Maltese Falcon*. But they don't seem to have *made* Jenny; they seem just to have been sparks, things that pushed her in one direction, or another. They're not the base for anything, not the stones that build a tower, like the ones Ringo made down on the shore.

Has there even been a Jenny Ebert before now? Or just a chaotic mass of static, a confusion, a random scattering of stories? It feels like Jenny Ebert has only existed properly since she came to Sunset Promenade; seems as though it's only now her experiences and stories are stacking up properly, making a real pattern.

She's only started to feel like Jenny Ebert since she stopped trying to decide what Jenny Ebert should be.

Not having had the stomach for breakfast, Jenny feels pangs of hunger and goes down to the day room to see if she can find Florin to beg a snack. Mrs Cantle is reading a large-print romance novel. Mrs Slaithwaite is still watching the TV, and Mr Robinson – looking much refreshed – is harrumphing behind the *Daily Mail*. He keeps casting pointed glances at Joe, who's leaning on the mantelpiece, whistling softly to himself, and Edna, who's sitting in the window seat, watching the fresh downpour of rain sluicing the panes.

Jenny goes to sit with Edna, who looks at her and murmurs, 'Did you have any further thoughts towards our *investigation*?'

Jenny says quietly, 'I'm wondering if Mrs Cantle hasn't just mislaid the jewels, you know. Maybe we could ask if we can search her room properly.'

Edna nods and turns back to the window. Then she says, 'There's something else that has occurred to me. About the power cut we had, when you got locked in your room.'

Jenny laughs. 'I didn't get locked in. The door must have just stuck.' She pauses. 'Though it's never happened before, or since. Or just swung shut on its own.'

'Hmm,' says Edna. 'You see, the thing that occurred to me . . . Margaret's jewels went missing just after we watched the first of your grandfather's films, didn't they?'

'I suppose . . . But I don't see . . .'

'*Ice in My Heart*, wasn't it? About—'

'A diamond heist!' says Jenny, eyes wide.

'And the episode in your room occurred directly after the second film, *Alone with Everybody* . . .'

Jenny's hand flies to her mouth. 'About someone being imprisoned!' she whispers fiercely.

Edna nods. 'As I say, just something that occurred to me . . .'

Jenny looks around the room. Joe. Mr Robinson. Mrs Cantle. Her eyes settle on Mrs Slaithwaite, who's regarding her and Edna with something approaching contempt. Ringo showed her the transcript of his interview with Mrs Slaithwaite for the university project, and what she said.

You don't get it at all, do you? You're making me sad. You make me sad because you piss me off. It's as simple as that. Can you go away now?

It's her, she thinks. It's Mrs Slaithwaite. She's stolen the jewels and she locked me in my room. She's big enough, strong enough. She could have been holding the handle on the other side of the door. Trying to frighten me. But why would she steal Mrs Cantle's jewels? Just for the sheer hell of it? Or . . . what if Mrs Slaithwaite saw Mrs Cantle showing them to me? What if she knows that I'm the only other person in Sunset Promenade to know they exist?

What if she's trying to frame me in some way? To get rid of me? Because she doesn't like me?

Looking just as though she's been listening to Jenny's thoughts, Mrs Slaithwaite sits back and rests her head on the antimacassar over the back of her chair, folding her heavy arms across her chest with a self-satisfied smile on her face.

'I'm going to sleep,' she announces. 'Try not to wake me up with your inane babbling.'

'Sweetness and bloody light,' mutters Mr Robinson.

Jenny glances at her phone. It's half past eleven. She says, 'Do you think we should all be doing something . . . constructive when this inspector arrives?'

Mr Robinson looks at her. 'Like what? Don't suggest getting Mad Molly back in. Downward Dog my arse.'

Joe looks up. 'That's not a bad idea, though. Not Mad Molly, but something. I still feel a bit bad for old Barry after we got brought home by the police.'

'Oh, you did look funny, Mr Robinson,' says Mrs Cantle with a titter. 'All that green make-up on your face, and you couldn't walk straight.'

'Somebody should have stopped me,' says Mr Robinson. 'I've got angina, you know. You shouldn't have let me go and drink all that home brew.' He looks around. 'No sense of responsibility. Especially you young ones.'

'You just can't handle your ale, Robbo,' says Joe.

Jenny can feel everyone slipping back into their normal argumentative state and stands up to intervene. 'This inspector is coming soon and I think we owe it to the Granges to make a bit of an effort.'

'I hope that bloody Latvian's making an effort and not warming up that cabbage soup again for lunch,' mutters Mr Robinson.

'Cards!' says Jenny desperately, grabbing the deck from the coffee table. 'We enjoyed that before. Let's have a game of cards! What was that one called, where you get three of one thing and four of another . . . ?'

'Rummy,' says Joe. 'Great idea, Jenny.'

'Bloody rummy,' scoffs Mr Robinson. He folds his newspaper and tucks it down the side of the sofa. 'I suppose so, if it'll keep you quiet.'

Then there's the clanging of the doorbell and Jenny rushes to the day room door to see Florin answering and a woman with a severe face, carrying a briefcase, stepping over the threshold and looking around the entrance hall.

'She's here,' whispers Jenny urgently. 'The inspector! Everyone get round the table.'

Joe starts dealing the cards and nods to Mrs Slaithwaite. 'Wake her up.'

'Aren't we better leaving her asleep?' suggests Edna.

'Not if she starts bloody farting and snoring,' says Mr Robinson. 'Joe's right – wake her up and get her to either play or go and hide in her room.'

Jenny creeps over and whispers, 'Mrs Slaithwaite? Mrs Slaithwaite, the inspector's here. Would you like to play cards with us?'

Mrs Slaithwaite sits with her head back, eyes closed, mouth wide open. Jenny nudges her arm. 'Mrs Slaithwaite!' she says more loudly. She shakes her vigorously this time and hisses, 'For God's sake, I know you don't like me, but will you please just wake up?'

Mrs Slaithwaite's head lolls forward, her chins coming to rest on her chest. Jenny snatches her hand back as though she's been burned, then chances another brisk shake of her shoulder.

'Mrs Slaithwaite . . . ?'

Jenny turns back to the rest of them, sorting their cards, Mr Robinson huffing and puffing about the hand he's been dealt. Joe beckons her over. 'Just leave her, love. Come and have a look at your hand.'

'It's Mrs Slaithwaite,' says Jenny numbly. 'I think she's dead.'

Ringo's Stars

Mrs Slaithwaite

I've heard some of your interviews. Prodding and poking, like we're animals in a zoo. I don't see why I should do it. Do your bloody homework for you, I ask you. Still, anything for a quiet life.

I know your game. Fancy yourself a writer, eh? You think we've all got some kind of story, don't you? Some sort of tragedy. I heard Ibiza Joe, whining on about his dead kid. Mr Robinson, going to the pictures and coming home to find his dad had died in the war. Boo-fucking-hoo.

Guess what, lad? We're not different to you. We're just old. We were like you once, and one day you'll be like us. I don't like you; I don't like any of you kids. I'm not Ibiza Joe, trying to relive a youth he never actually had. I just want to be left alone. We all do. That's why we're here.

What? Why come here with other people if we want to be on our own? Just goes to show you know nothing. Because the best place to be left alone is with other people who want to be left alone. It's like that bloke who was on the news this year. The one who went to Mars. Major Tom. Right grumpy bugger, he was. But he did the right thing. Went where there was nobody else at all. I'd do that if I could.

See, we were all happy being miserable until you lot turned up. It was bad enough when that Grey woman and Mrs Cantle arrived a couple of weeks before you did, but at least they were like us. You lot, though . . .

And don't think it's just jealousy, don't think I wish I was young again, and seeing you makes me sad because I'm old and fat and my hair's falling out. I hated being young as much as I hate being old. You want to know why? You want a story? All right, here's one for you. Here's a film I remember going to.

It was *E.T.* Do you remember that? Dumpy little brown alien. Gets lost on earth and this whiny kid finds him. The government turn up and they're chasing them all over the place. Took my kids because they'd been mithering me to go for weeks. Never really was one for films like that myself. Stupid. Aliens and such. Can't happen, can it? So what's the point of making a picture about it? Anyway. I was thinking, if that was me I'd be handing the monster over to the government, not helping it escape. It was an alien, wasn't it? Shouldn't have been here. Horrible little wrinkly thing.

Right at the end the other aliens come back for it, its mum and dad maybe – to be honest, I wasn't taking much notice. Then everybody was crying and the little alien was telling the whiny little kid to be good, and that was it. I couldn't understand why they were all bloody sobbing around me, even my own kids. 'Good bloody riddance!' I shouted. 'Send the brown little turd back where he came from!'

And then I couldn't stop laughing. Nobody else was. My kids ran out and said I'd ruined the film for them, for everybody. I didn't care. It was just a fucking puppet. A brown, wrinkled turd of a puppet.

So don't judge me. We live in a world where people cry their eyes out over a puppet alien, so why should I give a toss about real people?

No. No, that doesn't make me sad. You don't get it at all, do you? *You're* making me sad. You make me sad because you piss me off. It's as simple as that. Can you go away now?

✳ 27 ✳

Cover Up

(1949, dir. Alfred E. Green)

They all sit there in silence for a moment, then everyone starts talking at once.

'Sssh!' says Jenny, though she's not sure why. She rubs her hand where she touched Mrs Slaithwaite's bare arm. Her dead, bare arm.

'Let me through,' says Mr Robinson. 'Let me take a look. She's probably not dead at all.'

He bends over and listens intently for breathing, then picks up her flabby arm and places three fingers on the inside of her wrist.

'Dead as a dodo,' he pronounces, letting the arm drop on to the chair.

'We'd better go and find one of the Granges,' says Mrs Cantle. 'Or Florin. He'll know what to do.'

'There's nothing to be done,' says Mr Robinson. 'She's carked it.'

'Oh my God,' says Jenny.

Joe stands up. 'Poor cow. Well, at least she died happy.'

Edna raises an eyebrow. 'Really?'

Joe shrugs. 'Well, by happy I mean miserable. But she was only really happy when she was being grumpy, wasn't she?'

There are voices from the reception hall and Joe makes to go and open the door.

'Wait!' hisses Jenny. They all stare at her. She looks back at Mrs Slaithwaite. She seems peaceful, as though she's still just sleeping. 'Wait. Is this going to look good? For the inspector?'

Mr Robinson raises an eyebrow. 'It's a rest home, love. People come here to die.'

'I know, but . . .'

Edna nods. 'Jenny has something of a point, I think. The Granges don't tend to cope too well under extreme pressure. Young Florin runs around like a headless chicken if the milk delivery's wrong. Can you imagine what's going to happen if we announce that Mrs Slaithwaite has just died?'

'Christ, you don't think it was Bernie's home brew, do you?' says Joe.

Mr Robinson looks at him. 'For God's sake, Joe, we all had it and we're still standing. And you saw for yourself; she hoovered up enough gin to stop an elephant in its tracks and still didn't show up on the breathalyser.' He shrugs. 'When it's your time, it's your time.'

They all look at Mrs Slaithwaite for a long moment. Joe says slowly, 'I don't suppose it would hurt if we just hung on a little bit before telling anyone . . . until the inspector's gone . . .'

Mr Robinson rubs his moustache vigorously. 'That's probably illegal, you know.'

'What if the inspector comes in?' says Joe.

'We just say she's asleep,' says Jenny. 'We'll say she sleeps a lot.'

They all jump as the door opens, but it's only Florin. 'Lunch is in five minutes,' he says.

Jenny looks at Joe. If they all go into the dining room, Florin's going to try to wake Mrs Slaithwaite. He'll have a meltdown. Joe says, 'Florin, I think we'd like to eat in here today.'

He looks around at everyone else and slowly they nod. 'Yes,' says Mrs Cantle. 'That would be lovely.'

Florin frowns. 'Why?'

Jenny smiles widely. 'It's my birthday!'

Mr Robinson nods. 'Yes. It's the girl's birthday. We'll have our lunch in here to celebrate.'

A grin spreads over Florin's face. 'A birthday! And just this morning I make a cake! I am right back!'

When he's gone Jenny sinks into the sofa. Joe pats her shoulder. 'It's all right, love, that was a masterstroke. We only need to wait an hour or so, then we can just pretend we've not been able to wake her up.'

Five minutes later the door opens again and Florin comes in

carrying a large chocolate cake blazing with candles. 'I did not know how old so I just put them all on,' says Florin proudly.

'Oh dear,' says Mrs Cantle. 'Chocolate cake, though. Mrs Slaithwaite's not going to like that.'

'I think she'll probably not mind, just this once,' spits Mr Robinson through gritted teeth.

Florin puts the cake on the coffee table and conjures from his pocket a roll of paper crowns. 'From Christmas!' he says. 'One for everybody! Mr Joe, Jenny, Mrs Cantle . . .'

'I'll hand them out,' says Jenny, snatching the rest. She gives a little laugh. 'My birthday, after all.'

'And blowers!' says Florin, fanning the plastic party trumpets on the table. 'Now everybody put the hats on and we can sing!'

Mr Robinson rolls his eyes as he unfolds his green paper hat and Jenny turns around, wincing, and puts one on Mrs Slaithwaite's head. She keeps herself between the corpse and Florin, pulling Edna and Mrs Cantle closer to either side of her.

'Now, we sing!' says Florin delightedly. 'Happy birthday, to you! Happy birthday, to you!'

Joe begins an accompaniment on one of the plastic blowers, and Florin tries to peer round Jenny. 'Come on, Mrs Slaithwaite, sing! Happy birthday, dear Jenny!'

At that moment the door opens and the Grange brothers, flanking the frowning inspector, step into the room.

'Happy birthday, to you!' finishes Florin. Joe's blower trails off.

Barry smiles nervously. 'Ah, hello everyone. This is Ms Calvin, she's inspecting us today. Erm, Florin, I didn't realise we had a birthday . . . ?'

'It's mine,' says Jenny.

'One of the students,' says Ms Calvin.

'Yes, the other, Ringo, he's at university today,' says Jenny.

Barry steps forward and says, 'While we're doing introductions, this is Joe, Mrs Cantle, Mrs Grey, Mr Robinson, and in the chair there is Mrs Slaithwaite. Are you well, Mrs Slaithwaite?'

Joe puts a finger to his lips. 'Sssh. She's having a doze.'

Ms Calvin raises one eyebrow. 'Through all that singing?'

'Well, she's deaf, isn't she?' says Mr Robinson.

Barry frowns. 'Is she?'

'As a post,' says Edna. 'I don't think she wants you to know. She's a bit embarrassed about it.'

'But we've all been helping her with it!' says Jenny. 'One big happy family here at Sunset Promenade!'

She sees the Grange twins exchanging puzzled glances. Jenny feels something hit her in the back of the thigh, and looks down to see Mrs Slaithwaite's arm flopping over the side of her chair.

'Oh, she's awake,' says Mrs Cantle, looking down too. Jenny stares at her and, wincing inside, picks up the arm and places it across Mrs Slaithwaite's chest.

'No, no she isn't, Mrs Cantle,' says Jenny, smiling but glaring. 'Sleeping like a baby.'

They stand staring at each other wordlessly, the residents on one side of the room and the inspector, the Granges and Florin on the other. The silence is shattered by a long, loud and very distinctively Mrs Slaithwaite fart.

'Jesus Christ!' yells Jenny, learning for the first time what it means when people say they jump out of their skin.

'Look, she *is* sleeping!' says Mrs Cantle.

The inspector wrinkles her nose. 'Yes, well. It's lovely to see you all enjoying yourselves together. Excellent work, Mr Grange and Mr Grange. Would now perhaps be a good time to see the kitchens before I conclude the tour . . . ?'

As they all troop out Jenny spins round. Mrs Slaithwaite is still unmistakably dead.

'Corpses can do that,' says Mr Robinson. 'Break wind. I've heard that before.'

Jenny collapses on to the sofa, staring at the serene face of Mrs Slaithwaite, the blue paper crown lopsided on her head. Edna is at the window, peering out. 'Looks like the inspector is leaving.'

'Thank God,' says Mr Robinson. 'Go and get the Granges as soon as they come back in, tell them we've just found her like this.'

'Hang on five minutes, Robbo,' says Joe, digging a spoon into a big wedge of cake. 'All hell's going to break loose as soon as we do that. Let's at least enjoy this before it does.'

*

Half an hour later, they all loudly feign concern at the fact that they cannot awaken Mrs Slaithwaite, and then distress when the Grange brothers and Florin fuss around her and decide that she has died. All except Jenny, who realises abruptly that she is genuinely upset. They are all ushered out of the day room while Florin covers the body and the appropriate phone calls are made.

'Should I leave her paper crown on?' asks Florin as they are leaving.

Garry Grange stares at him. 'Why on earth would you do that?'

Florin shrugs. 'She looks so happy,' he says. 'For a change.'

As they gather in the reception hall, the main door opens and Ringo walks in, looking at them all. 'What did I miss?' he says.

'Lovely chocolate cake,' says Joe, then checks himself. 'Oh, uh, and some bad news.'

Jenny feels her face crinkling up. 'Mrs Slaithwaite's died,' she says, and suddenly can't stop herself from bursting into tears.

Ringo frowns and steps forward, and Jenny gladly allows him to embrace her.

'The young,' observes Mrs Cantle. 'They don't deal with death like we do.'

Ringo shakes his head. 'Some of us understand it more than others. Jenny lost both her parents in a car crash over the summer.'

Jenny pauses for a beat. She can't actually believe he's said that, out loud, to everyone.

'You idiot!' she screams, battering her fists on his chest until he lets go. She wipes her hand over her snotty nose and glares at his uncomprehending face. 'You idiot!'

Then she turns on her heel and runs up the stairs.

Jenny is lying on her bed, staring at her phone, when there's a sharp knock at her door. Not Ringo; he would have just walked in. 'It's open,' she mumbles into her pillow. 'Unless someone's locked me in again.'

It's Edna. Jenny pushes herself up to a sitting position and hugs her knees to her chest. Edna says, 'Can I come in?'

Jenny nods and rubs her sleeves over her eyes. Edna perches on the end of her bed and looks around the room. Piles of DVDs, the werewolf costume still on the floor where Jenny stepped out of it after last night. 'Sorry it's such a mess,' she says. 'I wasn't expecting visitors.'

Edna stares for a moment at the bag of film canisters spilling out from underneath the bed. Jenny crouches down and zips up the green bag; she really should be more careful with these things.

Edna says, 'Ringo told us what happened. With your parents.'

'He had no right to,' says Jenny. 'That wasn't for him to tell.'

'I don't think he was being malicious; in fact, I'm sure he wasn't. He . . .' Edna pauses, searching for the right words. 'He thinks a lot of you, that boy.'

Jenny nods glumly and stares at her toes. 'I . . . touched her. Mrs Slaithwaite. I touched her. She was dead.'

Edna places a hesitant hand on Jenny's arm. 'I know. It's never nice.' She looks at Jenny curiously. 'Did you not see your parents . . . after the crash . . . ?'

Jenny shakes her head. She could kill Ringo. She really doesn't want to have this conversation, not now, not at all.

Edna continues, 'It happened so recently . . . Ringo thinks, and I may agree with him, that you might still be in shock . . . that the full effects of what happened might not have hit you yet . . .'

Jenny looks at her. 'I've completely come to terms with what has happened. With what I've done. You don't have to worry about me. I just don't want to talk about it. Ever. I'd rather you all just pretended you didn't know about it. Please.'

Edna seems to gather her thoughts for a moment, then says, 'That is your choice, and I will respect it. And I will speak to the others. But just know, Jenny, that we have all experienced loss in some form or another. We all understand.'

Jenny looks at her for a long time and wants to scream at her, tell her exactly what has happened, tell her the whole truth of it. But then what would Edna think of her, what would she think of what Jenny has done? Instead she says, 'Understanding doesn't necessarily help.'

Edna smiles. 'Of course not. Not at first, anyway. But eventually, you will find that someone who does understand you . . . well, they can be like angels.'

'Edna . . . who have you lost?'

Edna says nothing, just smiles again and pats Jenny's arm, and stands up and leaves the room, closing the door quietly behind her.

28

A Woman's Secret

(1949, dir. Nicholas Ray)

By the next morning, all traces of Mrs Slaithwaite have been removed from Sunset Promenade. It is as though she's never been there, save for the chair she always sat in, the cushion indented and moulded to the ghost of her not insubstantial backside and the TV remote control, which the others subconsciously leave on the armrest of the chair, even after changing channels. Mrs Slaithwaite's body was removed by the undertaker the day of her death, and the next day her daughter arrived at Sunset Promenade to take her belongings and sign the relevant papers.

Jenny chances upon the daughter, a plump woman in her forties, in the reception hall as Florin is carrying Mrs Slaithwaite's effects down the stairs. Jenny feels the need to say something, and murmurs, 'I'm sorry for your loss.'

The daughter turns her tired gaze on Jenny. 'Don't be. It's very kind, but I know you don't really mean that.'

Jenny begins to protest half-heartedly but the woman shakes her head. 'It's all right. I know she was an objectionable old cow.'

The woman looks down at the last of Mrs Slaithwaite's belongings. 'She has three children and there's not a single photograph of any of us, nor her grandchildren, in amongst her things. She made no secret of the fact that she didn't like us, didn't like anyone, really. That's why she moved here. She didn't have to. Any one of us would have had her stay.'

Jenny tells the woman about the interviews Ringo's been doing, and about how Mrs Slaithwaite wouldn't take part properly. The woman smiles without humour, but kindly. Jenny says, 'I think he just wanted to find out her story . . . what made her the way she was.'

'Sometimes people don't have a story, love. Sometimes they're just not very nice people. Just because someone's old it doesn't mean we have to look for *reasons*. I hate to say this, as her daughter, but she'd always been a horrible person and there was no mystery behind that, no tragedy. She just enjoyed being nasty, and that's all there was to it.'

Barry comes out of the office with all the necessary paperwork and asks Mrs Slaithwaite's daughter if there's going to be a funeral. The woman sighs. 'We've discussed it, of course. On the few occasions she actually bothered to talk to her family. She always said the happiest she'd ever been was on your trips to the Isle of Man. Said she wanted her ashes scattering there.' She shakes her head. 'I don't think there's much appetite for that in the family. I realise how awful this sounds.'

Barry hesitates, then says, 'We were going to run a trip to the Isle of Man soon, but to be honest, our finances . . .'

'I'll pay,' says Mrs Slaithwaite's daughter quickly. 'You have your trip. Scatter her ashes. You'd be doing us a favour.'

Barry nods soberly. 'Well, if you come into the office we'll make all the arrangements. Jenny? Could you be a dear and keep an eye on Mrs Slaithwaite's effects until we're finished?'

When Barry shuts them into the office Jenny stares at the three cardboard boxes and the bags of Mrs Slaithwaite's clothes. If the jewels and the medal and the photo are in these boxes . . . then the mystery is solved. Mrs Slaithwaite certainly had a motive for the thefts; she'd have been delighted by all the trouble and friction they stirred up. Looking quickly around, Jenny squats down and begins to rifle through the boxes, and then the bags of clothes. Nothing, apart from Mrs Slaithwaite's own trinkets, a couple of dog-eared paperback doctor-and-nurse romances, some loose change, a miniature whisky bottle. She stands up as Florin comes down the stairs with a black bin bag bulging with sharp corners, and Barry emerges from the office with Mrs Slaithwaite's daughter.

'I found these under her bed,' says Florin, opening the bag. 'They are all boxes of toffee. There are lots of them.'

The daughter's face crinkles. 'They were presents from her grand-children. She always said she loved that toffee.' She peers into the bag. 'She's not even taken the wrapping paper off some of them.'

'You want me to put them in your car?' asks Florin.

'The daughter shakes her head. 'No. It'll just upset the kids. You can have them, if they're within their use-by date. Or throw them away, if that's all right.'

As Florin hefts up the boxes and staggers out of the door with them, Mrs Slaithwaite's daughter pauses at the porch and looks back to Jenny. 'It's not that hard to be nice, is it? It doesn't cost anything.'

'Where the hell were you last night?'

Jenny stands at the open door to Ringo's bedroom, where he is lying on his bed, reading a battered paperback. He looks up at her and blinks.

'What?'

Jenny folds her arms. 'I waited up for you and you didn't come home.'

Ringo lays his book face down and sits up. 'Sorry, did I miss the bit where we got married?'

Jenny marches into his room and looks around. It's the first time she's been inside. There's a poster of the Beatles' album *Help!* on the wall. He loves his Beatles, thinks Jenny, and wonders how much of a cliché that is. He sees her looking and apes the arm movements the band members are performing on the cover. 'Semaphore, isn't it?' he says.

At the window is his star-gazing telescope, pointed out at the rain. Presumably where he had his little bonding session with Mr Robinson over the full moon. She glares at him. 'I don't care about semaphore. All I'm bothered about is—'

'As it happens, I went out for a drink. With some friends. I have been here for a year already, you know.'

'I don't even care about that!' says Jenny.

'Some people from your course were there. Saima and . . . Amber?'

'Oh.' Jenny frowns. 'What are you doing going out with my friends?'

Ringo puts his hands up in surrender and reaches for his book. 'They were just there. I was chatting to them. As it goes, I thought they were a bit dull, actually. For you.'

'And I suppose you told them about . . . about what I told you? About the car crash? Just like you spilled your guts to Edna?'

Ringo nods slowly. 'Ah. OK. I get it. That's what you're annoyed about.'

'Yes!' says Jenny, slapping her palm to her forehead. 'Why did you tell her that?'

'I didn't know it was a secret!'

'It's just not your thing to tell!'

They glare at each other across the room. Ringo sighs and throws up his hands again. 'All right! I'm sorry!'

Jenny sits on the edge of his bed. 'Look. I know you mean well, but . . . I just don't want to talk about it. To anyone. Promise me you won't tell anyone else?'

Ringo shrugs. 'Deal.' He looks at her for a moment. 'Who was that woman downstairs?'

'Mrs Slaithwaite's daughter.' Jenny gets up and inspects the telescope pointing through Ringo's window. 'She said there's no back-story to Mrs Slaithwaite. No reasons that she was a grumpy old woman. Nothing made her like that. Do you think it's true?' Jenny peers through the telescope's eyepiece. All she can see is grey.

Ringo closes his book and rolls over on to his back, letting his head hang off the back of the bed, regarding Jenny upside down. 'I suppose, if she said it. You and I, we like stories. You like your old films, I like my books. Stories are always wrapped up properly, aren't they? No loose threads. You only get people like Mrs Slaithwaite in real life because she'd be a rubbish character in a film. She just smashes cakes up for no reason. You heard of Chekhov's gun?'

Jenny looks up from the telescope. 'No. Is it a film?'

Ringo laughs. 'No. Anton Chekhov. Russian. Wrote plays and short stories. He said that if you make a point of saying there's a gun hanging on the wall at the beginning of your story, then at some point that gun has to be fired. Otherwise there's no point mentioning the gun at all.'

Jenny turns back to the telescope. She can still see nothing. Ringo says, 'All of which makes for nice stories, but it doesn't always happen in real life. Mrs Slaithwaite's daughter was right; sometimes people are just nasty without any rhyme or reason.' He rolls off the bed. 'Here, you need to focus that if you're going to see something. It's just, there's nothing to see right now. Only clouds and sea and rain.'

Jenny peers through the viewfinder. Ringo says hesitantly, 'Am I forgiven, then?'

Without looking up, Jenny says, 'It doesn't cost anything to be nice, does it?'

He sighs audibly. 'That's very big of you.'

Jenny finally looks away from the telescope and frowns at him. 'I was talking about you. It doesn't cost anything to be nice. So don't go around talking about people unless they ask you to, all right?'

She stands up. Mrs Slaithwaite is out of the frame for the Sunset Promenade crime-wave, it appears. Which means the crook is still at large. It's time she got down to some proper investigating.

'Where are you going?' asks Ringo. 'Can I come?'

She taps her finger on her nose and winks at him. 'It's a secret,' she says, and closes the door behind her.

* 29 *

The Firebugs

(1949, dir. William J. Drake)

On the day of the third meeting of the Lonely Hearts Cinema Club, Jenny is visited in her room by Mrs Cantle, who seems more distracted than usual. 'Are you all right?' Jenny asks.

Mrs Cantle smiles, but it's a distant smile. She says, 'Hello, dear, I wonder . . . do you have a mobile phone?'

'Of course,' says Jenny, producing it. 'Do you need something?'

'Might I borrow it? To make one phone call?'

'Of course. Don't you have a phone, Mrs Cantle?'

She frowns. 'I did have. I think I must have left it at home.'

Jenny hands the phone over. 'Here, I'll have to unlock it. There's a phone in reception, you know. I'm happy for you to use this but I could show you how to use the main one.'

'I need privacy,' says Mrs Cantle. She looks at the phone. 'Can I take it to my room? Just for a few minutes?'

Jenny nods. 'Here, give it back for a moment. Let me take the lock off completely so it doesn't turn off again. The keypad's here; just put in the number you want and press the green button.'

Mrs Cantle smiles. 'Thank you, dearie. Back in a tick.'

Jenny returns to the list she's made. Of suspects. Four crimes, if she counts being locked in her room, which she thinks must be connected to the others: Mrs Cantle's missing jewels, Joe's photo, Mr Robinson's medal. On one side of the piece of paper she has written everyone's names. She hasn't put herself down – she knows she's innocent – and she hesitated just a moment before adding Edna's. Nobody is above suspicion. Then she divided the page into two columns and above the right-hand side wrote *MOTIVE*.

She had hoped that the missing items would be among Mrs Slaithwaite's effects, but they weren't, and they haven't turned up anywhere else in her room. She can't have got them off-site because she never left Sunset Promenade. If Mrs Slaithwaite was her number-one suspect, Jenny supposes she has to be in the clear now, by dint of being dead and there being no hard evidence. Jenny taps the pencil on the paper, illuminated on the desk under the bright light of her lamp. For Mrs Slaithwaite's motive she has written *hates everybody*. It would have been a nice, tidy resolution. She puts a line through Mrs Slaithwaite's name.

Jenny moves down the list. Mr Robinson. Possible motives? To discredit Florin, perhaps? He hates foreigners. Pinning thefts on Florin would certainly get him sacked.

Ibiza Joe. This one she struggled with. Why would Joe fake the theft of his own photograph of his beloved Brian? The only reason would be to divert blame from himself, in the same way that Mr Robinson would also have had to pretend to be a victim with the theft of his medal. But whereas Mr Robinson could conceivably want to pin blame on someone else, perhaps Joe just wants the money? For what, though? She looks out of the window, at the darkening sky, at the rain and cloud. To get away, perhaps? To Ibiza? To live out his days where he was happiest after the loss of his child?

Next she has Florin. He has access to all the rooms. He could steal the items easily enough. But having got surely the biggest prize – Mrs Cantle's jewels – why would he hang around waiting to be discovered, and why bother taking the other stuff? A motive is obvious enough – he's going to lose his job one way or the other, either when Sunset Promenade closes or Brexit means life becomes too difficult for him. Maybe he's just putting something in reserve to provide for his family in Latvia. But why lock her in her room? Jenny taps the pencil again. Maybe because he suspects she's on to him, and wanted her out of the way while he carried out another theft that hasn't come to light yet? She makes a note to ask everyone to check their rooms, in case they haven't noticed something's missing.

Barry and Garry are on the list, of course. Sunset Promenade is teetering on the brink; they need money. It's almost too easy.

But it doesn't have to be a convoluted explanation. Sometimes the simplest answer is the most likely. Ringo? But what would his motive be? To get closer to her, perhaps? She chides herself silently. *You're not all that, Jenny Ebert.*

Then she's got Mrs Cantle and Edna Grey. Mrs Cantle is a tough one; why steal your own jewels? Either to put the blame on someone else, and discredit them for some reason? Or maybe because they haven't been stolen at all. She's just moved them and forgotten. They've all just put their supposedly stolen things down in the wrong place, and there's no crime, no mystery to solve. Jenny sighs and tosses the pencil down. She takes the list, screws it up and drops it into the wastepaper bin with the rest of her attempts to figure out the mystery – a dozen balled-up pieces of paper.

Maybe she should just get on with organising tonight's movie.

The film night is notable for its reduced audience . . . Bo and Ling are gone, of course, and now Mrs Slaithwaite too. Jenny is momentarily put in mind of one of those films with an ever-reducing cast as each character is quietly bumped off . . . *Ten Little Indians*, that sort of thing. She voices this in a light-hearted fashion as she loads the DVD.

'Of course, you know what the original title of that book was,' says Mr Robinson. 'And I don't mean this offensively—'

'Yes, well, I don't think we need to go there,' says Jenny quickly.

'Political correctness gone bloody mad,' mutters Mr Robinson. 'What are we watching tonight, anyway? Another of your gran-dad's films?'

'The third of four,' says Jenny. She pauses. 'Are you all OK with watching these? I have plenty of others . . . I just thought, as they're films not a lot of people have seen . . .'

'We're thoroughly enjoying them,' smiles Edna. 'I personally find them very interesting indeed.'

'Right . . . well, this one's called *The Firebugs*. It was released in 1949. You remember Eddie Monk, who was in the first film, *Ice in My Heart*? He became something of a favourite of my grand-father's, and this was his first leading role. It's about a gang of crooks who set fire to failing businesses so the owners can claim on the insurance, and the mob take their cut.'

'Don't be giving the Grange boys any ideas,' laughs Mr Robinson. 'This place being on its uppers as it is, I wouldn't put it past them to do something like that.'

'Mr Robinson,' says Florin warningly from his chair by the door.

'I know,' he sighs. 'That is not nice. Where are Tweedledum and Tweedledee, anyway?'

'They are very busy dealing with grant applications and funding submissions,' says Florin. 'To keep you in the manner to which you are accustomed, Mr Robinson.'

'Speaking of which, I hope we have another visit from Bernie soon,' says Joe. 'We've not a drop of home brew left.'

'Yes,' says Mr Robinson, glaring at Jenny. 'Especially as that one offloaded the last of it on the bloody taxi driver.'

'I thought you and he were getting on famously,' says Edna mildly.

Joe laughs richly. 'That's right, Robbo! What was it again . . . ?'

'I am very, very drunk!' everyone choruses, even Ringo and Jenny, and they all collapse with laughter.

Even Florin can't keep an amused expression from his face. 'Next time you go to an art exhibition, please invite me,' he says. 'It sounds a lot of fun.'

They watch the film in companionable silence, and at the end everyone agrees that it's their favourite one yet. 'Ooh,' says Mrs Cantle. 'That was so exciting when they kidnapped the hero's girlfriend and had her chained to that radiator as the building was burning down.'

'Yes,' says Edna. 'Joyce Palermo again, wasn't it?' She folds her hands on her lap. 'I'm curious, Jenny, surrounded by all these beautiful actresses . . . did your grandfather marry one of them?'

'No,' says Jenny. 'No, he didn't. He didn't marry anyone in the film industry.' She ejects the DVD. 'And that was his downfall.'

'It was my mother that saved your grandfather from ruin,' says Barbara Ebert in the kitchen of their house, the films, mementos and memorabilia of William J. Drake scattered between her and

Jenny on the pine table. 'Just remember that, Jenny. Without her, you wouldn't even be here to have this pointless, stupid argument with us.'

'Thank God for Joan,' says Simon Ebert, filling the kettle.

Jenny looks at him with loathing. A cup of tea at this time of night. Can't you even bring yourself to have a bourbon or a scotch, at least show some tiny flicker of being interesting?

'He'd made four films and was on the verge of bankruptcy,' says Barbara. 'This was back in . . . what, nineteen fifty-one? Fifty-two? My mother worked for the accounts department of one of his distribution companies. She was actually something of a financial genius, but back then the best a woman could hope for was a secretarial job.'

'That's why it's important you continue with your economics studies,' says Simon Ebert, stirring his tea. 'Joan and William struck up a friendship. She could tell that he had no future as a film-maker, but she saw something in him.'

'Her father was the director of a big financial company in London,' continues Barbara. 'She got William and him talking. At first about possible financing for his films, but as it became clear he was struggling to find success, they started talking more about positions within the company, proper jobs.'

'Steady jobs,' says Simon.

'At the same time . . . well, my mother and William, their friendship began to blossom into something more.'

'Nick of time, as well,' says Simon, putting a cup of tea down in front of Barbara. Right on top of one of William J. Drake's scripts. Fiercely, Jenny moves it off. 'Wasn't he just about to get married to some no-mark actress nobody had heard of? Imagine that.' Simon Ebert looks proudly around his kitchen. 'None of us would be standing here today if that had happened.'

'After his fourth film he left the industry completely,' Jenny says to the room as she replaces the DVD in its case. 'He was convinced by others that his future wasn't in movies. He had his head turned by the promise of a steady job. He got married. Had children. And that was the end of it.'

'Why would he give all that up?' says Joe. 'Sounds like he was on the verge of something big.'

Jenny nods. 'He was. He was working on a fifth film that everybody says would have made his name. But he just walked away from it.'

'Aye, well, sometimes you have to do the sensible thing,' says Mr Robinson, looking around. 'It's all very well chasing dreams, but you have to be realistic. Has anybody seen my magnifying glass?'

'Well, I think it's a shame,' says Mrs Cantle. 'They have been such lovely films. Very exciting. Did you say we've only got one left to watch?'

'Where did you last have it, Robbo?' says Joe.

'I always put it with the *Mail*,' says Mr Robinson. 'I put it down over there, by the television.'

Jenny nods. 'One more William J. Drake. *Off Devil's Head*.' She grins. 'You'll love it, I promise. He really went out with a bang.'

* 30 *

On the Night of the Fire

(1939, dir. Brian Desmond Hurst)

The Grange brothers are arguing again. Edna stands outside their office, pretending to scan the noticeboard behind the reception desk, listening to their raised voices.

They aren't very discreet, she decides.

'You're just putting off the inevitable.' That from Garry.

'There's every chance the decision will go our way,' says Barry. 'We've got until the end of the week, at least. Why are you so pessimistic?'

'Because every day that we cling on to this place is another day losing money hand over fist.'

There's a pause, then Barry says, almost too quietly for Edna to hear, 'Do our mother's wishes mean nothing to you?'

Garry speaks in a less strident tone. 'Of course they do. How can you even think that? But we have to weigh up what's better. Putting Sunset Promenade in the hands of a professional, capable organisation that can keep it running for a long time, or admitting defeat and watch it go down the toilet. I know what she would have done, if she was faced with this choice.'

'But the residents . . .' protests Barry.

'We have to stop worrying about them so much. We have to think of ourselves. We aren't getting any younger, either.'

The door opens and Edna smiles sweetly at them. 'Hello, Mr and Mr Grange,' she says.

Garry frowns at her and hurries off. Always in a rush, that one. Barry stands in the doorway. He looks tired but he manages to force a smile. 'Mrs Grey. I hope you're well this morning.'

'Yes, thank you. Mr Grange, I was wondering . . . Mrs Cantle and I are relative newcomers here and the other residents have been talking about a day trip . . . ?'

Barry slaps his head. 'Of course. The Isle of Man. We go every year. A treat on us. Well, usually. Mrs Slaithwaite's daughter is financing it this year. We're to scatter her ashes at the Laxey Wheel.' He frowns, no doubt remembering the conversation he's just had with his brother. 'You will be able to make it, I trust?'

'It sounds a fitting tribute,' says Edna encouragingly.

'Have you ever been? No? It's a marvellous day out. We take the ferry, so we'll set off early, and there we'll see the Laxey Wheel and have a little ride on the steam railway, and have a wonderful fish-and-chip lunch.'

'And are the students invited as well?' queries Edna.

'Ringo and Jenny? Of course! We'll all go. My brother and I, Florin. Should really help to bring people together. Especially after what happened.' Barry pauses. 'Mrs Grey, how are people getting on? I mean, after Mrs Slaithwaite's unfortunate passing, there's bound to be a little disruption, but generally . . . ?'

Edna smiles. 'We're all getting on rather well, Mr Grange.' She gives him a pointed stare. 'I imagine we'll all be happy here at Sunset Promenade for some time to come.'

Barry blows air from his mouth and rubs the back of his neck. 'Yes. Well. I hope so, too. Now, must get on, Mrs Grey . . .'

Edna bids him goodbye and heads to the day room. She was being quite honest with Barry Grange. People are getting on quite well, after the initial friction. She stops herself there, stops herself thinking, You haven't been as happy for sixty years. She cannot afford sentimentality, she thinks ruefully. Not now. Not when it's so close to the final reel.

The night is fuzzy with the haze of distant bonfires, a perpetual glow in the sky inland, the far-off bursts of fireworks crackling in the darkness. Edna, wrapped in her coat and scarf, stands in the long garden at the back of Sunset Promenade with the others and watches Barry Grange throw a match on the petrol-soaked stack of wood, which ignites with a *whuuumpf*.

'Nearly took his eyebrows off, that,' observes Mr Robinson. The wood – broken-up pallets, bits of fallen twig from the trees in the garden, some old timber from the shed at the bottom – catches nicely and begins to throw yellow flames high in the air.

'I do like a bonfire,' says Joe, rubbing his hands together. 'Back in Ibiza they'd light these fires on the beach and dance around them until dawn . . .'

Mr Robinson stares at him. 'Bloody hell, Joe. Sounds like something from bloody *Tarzan*.'

'Would you like a sparkler, Edna?' asks Mrs Cantle. Edna accepts one from her, swirling the sparking tip around, writing her name in the cold air. 'Oh, you are clever,' says Mrs Cantle.

'Are you warm enough, Margaret?' murmurs Edna.

'I've got my gloves, yes.'

'No, Margaret. Are you *warm* enough?'

Mrs Cantle smiles and nods. 'Oh, yes.' She clears her throat. 'I think I'll just go and get my scarf. It's awfully nippy.'

When Margaret has trundled back inside, Edna moves over to Jenny and Ringo, standing together, silhouetted against the bonfire. She can sense a chemistry between the pair, even if they haven't yet noticed it themselves. She wonders if they'll ever get together, if they have time before it's all played out. Jenny turns as she approaches and smiles. She's certainly a lot more relaxed, that girl. For the moment.

'Bonfire toffee, Mrs Grey?' offers Ringo, holding out a tin tray of black goop. 'Florin's done his best but . . . I think it's already clamped Mr Robinson's dentures together.'

'Not for me,' demurs Edna. She lowers her voice. 'But young Florin is to be congratulated for finding something to shut Mr Robinson up for a few minutes. Do you think he could be persuaded to cook up another batch?'

'Are you looking forward to going to the Isle of Man?' says Jenny.

Edna shrugs. 'It will be nice to have a day out. Curious, though, don't you think, that Mrs Slaithwaite's family don't want anything to do with the proceedings?'

'Families don't always get on,' says Jenny, staring into the bonfire. 'Just because you're related doesn't mean you have to like each other.'

Ringo is looking at her a little aghast, as though she's spoken some terrible heresy. Edna hasn't mentioned the fact of Jenny's parents dying ever since the girl got so angry about Ringo telling everyone. That is her prerogative and must be respected. Besides, she has a point.

'It's just . . .' says Ringo carefully. 'Like with Mrs Slaithwaite, you never know when your time is up. Surely it's better to make your peace with people before it's too late?'

There's a long silence, broken only by the reappearance of Mrs Cantle. She tugs at the end of a long woollen scarf. 'Look, Edna, I remembered it.'

'And did you remember everything?' says Edna quietly.

'I did!' says Mrs Cantle. 'It all went wonderfully. I knew those years in the Girl Guides would never be wasted.' She looks at Jenny. 'Were you ever in the Girl Guides, dear? Wonderful organisation. We used to go on camps, sing lovely songs. We learned how to light fires, just like this one.'

'Margaret,' says Edna. 'Would you like some of Florin's bonfire toffee? It's rather chewy, apparently.'

Mrs Cantle ponders, but the decision is taken out of her hands by a sudden piercing shriek from indoors. Barry looks up from where he's been poking the base of the fire with a garden fork. 'That's the smoke alarm!'

'Probably just drifted in from the bonfire,' says Ringo, as they follow the Grange brothers into the house.

Garry Grange grabs a fire extinguisher from a bracket on the wall and starts to mount the stairs. 'It's up on the third floor, I think.'

Ringo and Jenny look at each other. 'That's where we are!'

Edna manages to reach the third floor just behind the young ones, who are already at the door to Jenny's room. White smoke is drifting from the open door, and inside Garry is attacking the wastepaper bin with the fire extinguisher, the white foam killing the last of the licking flames. Barry wafts a tea towel at the smoke alarm until it stops shrieking, and Garry emerges, shaking his head dourly at Jenny.

'A load of screwed-up paper in the bin,' he says. 'You must have put a cigarette out in there.'

'Can I just remind everyone, Sunset Promenade is a no-smoking environment,' calls Barry shrilly as Joe and Mr Robinson finally make it to the top floor, Mrs Cantle slowly following behind.

'But I didn't!' protests Jenny.

'I've seen you smoking,' says Garry accusingly. 'You could have had the whole place up in flames.'

'But I haven't!' says Jenny. She looks on the verge of tears. 'I mean, I did, but I stopped! Days ago! Didn't I, Ringo?'

'I think so,' he says uncertainly. 'I mean, yeah, you said it was your last one, when we were outside, with Mr Robinson . . .'

'Well, no harm done,' says Barry, as his twin pushes past them and stalks downstairs. 'Shall we all go back outside? I think Florin's got a pot of black peas on the go . . . lovely with a spot of vinegar . . .'

As everyone begins to descend the stairs, Edna waits, watching Jenny sit on her bed and stare at the charred remains of her wastepaper bin. Then she looks at the desk, and then at Edna.

'Look at this,' she says softly.

Edna takes this as an invitation and steps into the room, looking to where Jenny is pointing. 'Is that Mr Robinson's missing magnifying glass?'

The glass is propped up on a book, with the desk lamp on and angled right up to the convex lens.

'It's pointing at the bin,' says Jenny numbly, looking at her. 'This is what caused the fire.'

'I've seen that done with sunlight, but can it work with a lamp?' says Edna doubtfully.

'It obviously has!' snaps Jenny.

Edna nods. 'But . . . what are you doing with Mr Robinson's magnifying glass?'

'It wasn't here before! Someone's done this deliberately!' Her eyes widen. '*The Firebugs.* Oh my God. You were right. Someone's copying my grandfather's films. The jewels, locking me in the room, and now this.' Jenny swallows. 'Someone in here is out to get me.'

The girl grabs the magnifying glass and brandishes it at Edna. 'Don't tell anyone about this. I'm going to put it back downstairs.

If Mr Robinson knows it's been in my room it's going to raise awkward questions – we'll have to tell them about everything else.'

Edna nods uncertainly. 'Well . . . all right. But why would someone be doing this to you? What would they have to gain? And more importantly, who is it?'

Jenny stands up, shoving the magnifying glass into the back pocket of her jeans. 'The first two questions, I have no idea. But as to who . . .' She looks at Edna. 'You aren't going to like this, but I think it's Mrs Cantle.'

Ringo's Stars

Mrs Cantle

The picture I remember best of all is happy and sad, really. It's happy because it was the film I went to see when Harry took me out for the first time. Harry was my husband, dear. I was only seventeen, and he was fresh out of the army. He'd been demobbed just the week before. I'd known him from school, you see, and I knew he'd been sweet on me before the war started. He was a couple of years older than me, and he'd done a year in the army after turning eighteen. Burma, they sent him to. I had no idea where it was. I looked it up on a map. Awful long way away. Before he went he said to me, will you wait for me? Until after the war? Then I'll ask you out?

I said to him, I'll wait for you, Harry, but you have to promise not to go and get yourself killed.

So we had a deal, and I waited for him, and he didn't get himself killed, and he came home and we went out for the first time. We went to the pictures and we watched *A Matter of Life and Death*.

Have you seen it, dear? Oh, it is a lovely film. Makes you feel all warm inside. It's about this pilot in the war who gets shot down, and just before he dies he talks to this girl over the radio and they fall in love. David Niven, that's who plays the pilot. But it's too late, isn't it? Because his plane is crashing and then he dies. Except he doesn't die, because something goes wrong. But up in heaven they say it's all been a mistake and he has to die. You'd think that would be the end of it but then he goes to heaven and says, look here, I've fallen in love with this girl and it's not right that I should be dead. So they have this big trial to decide whether he can go back to his life and be with the girl. Lovely film. At the end, Harry held my hand.

After we'd watched the picture, Harry took me for fish and chips and then he kissed me in the doorway to Cattermole's corner shop. A year after that we got married. Oh, we were happy.

Yes, it is a lovely memory, isn't it, dear? But that's not the half of it, you see. Harry died . . . ooh, must be thirty years ago now. Had a stroke. Sad to see him like that at the end. Kept raving on and on about all kinds of stuff. Said he'd killed a man in Burma. He'd never talked about what happened there before, but there he was, his face slack all down one side, his eyes milky, and he was going on and on about this man he'd shot. He looked at me with his funny eyes and said that after he'd done it, he wanted to die himself. And it was only the thought of me that kept him going. He was a right softie, was Harry. He said that it was like that film we watched on our first date, that he loved me so much with all his heart, but he knew that if he did die, then there was no coming back because this was real life and not the pictures, so he had to keep going just for me.

He was at home by then. We'd brought a bed down into the front room. Everybody knew he'd come home to die, really. There wasn't anything they could do for him. I told him to stop being daft, going on about how I'd saved him, and I put the telly on. I was a bit sad, because maybe I really had saved him, if he'd been feeling so bad about shooting that fella. And now I couldn't save him any more. But do you know what was on the telly? That's right. *A Matter of Life and Death*.

Right at the end again, when David Niven is allowed to come back to life, Harry held my hand like he did that very first time in the pictures. And by the time the credits had finished, he'd gone. And I waited an hour with him before I got on the phone to my son, just in case Harry was arguing with them all up in heaven that he couldn't die because he loved me and I needed him. But he didn't come back, of course. Like I said, real life's not like the pictures, more's the pity.

Sorry, Ringo. I don't usually get upset. Do you know if my son's coming to visit yet? No? Ooh, all that talking has made my mouth dry. Have we done? Shall we go and get a nice cup of tea?

✳ 31 ✳

Arsenic and Old Lace

(1944, dir. Frank Capra)

'There it bloody is!' says Mr Robinson, snatching up his magnifying glass from where it sits on top of yesterday's *Daily Mail*, in the stack of newspapers by the television. He brandishes it around. 'Who's had it?'

'Oh, it was probably there all along,' says Joe. 'You didn't see it for looking.'

'Yes, well,' he says, evidently unsatisfied. 'Maybe my medal and your photo will miraculously turn up as well.'

Jenny feels the weight of Edna's stare on her, and when she turns round to where the old lady is sitting by the window, watching the rain from the night sky battering the glass, Edna turns away. Maybe she thinks I took it, considers Jenny. It was in my room, after all. She probably thinks I took the other things as well. She doesn't trust me any more.

But, thinks Jenny, who can I trust now?

As soon as Jenny made the connection with Mrs Cantle in her head, it all became so clear to her. One, the old lady disappeared during the bonfire. Two, she was the one who had opened Jenny's door when she was locked in her room. Three, Jenny is the only person who has actually seen Mrs Cantle's jewels, the only one who knows they are real. This sweet old lady is behind it all, thinks Jenny, at the same time realising just how crazy it sounds. But it all adds up for her. The only question remaining is: why?

Mrs Cantle has been nothing but friendly to her, before, during and after the incidents. Is it all a front? She doesn't seem capable of maintaining that level of deception, doesn't seem that good an actress. Half the time she doesn't seem to know where she is or even what her name is. But perhaps she *is* that good an actress. Maybe the confusion is all part of the performance.

But still, it all comes back to *why*. What has Jenny ever done to Mrs Cantle?

She's spent the last twenty-four hours weighing it all up. If it wasn't Mrs Cantle, that meant it was someone else. And Jenny doesn't know what frightens her more. Knowing that Mrs Cantle is for some reason out to get her, or that someone else in Sunset Promenade is . . . but not who.

After the bonfire, she'd remembered that Mrs Cantle had borrowed her phone to make a call. Jenny had scrolled through the recent calls list. There was a number at the top, one she didn't recognise, made at the same time that Mrs Cantle had borrowed her phone. Googling the number brought up nothing, so Jenny had decided to redial. She didn't know what she was going to say when she got through, but as it turned out she didn't have to say anything. It was an answerphone.

'Hello, you've reached Ronnie Grey. If you know my mobile, try me on that, otherwise I'll get back to you. But be warned, it might be towards the middle of November.'

Jenny had killed the call when the beeps came. A man – mature, middle-aged, older perhaps. How were you supposed to gauge any more from an answerphone greeting? She was no closer to anything. It wasn't until she was lying in bed that it suddenly hit her.

Ronnie Grey.

Grey.

But why would Mrs Cantle be ringing Edna's . . . husband? Son? Brother?

Maybe no relation at all. Grey wasn't that uncommon a surname. But making the call had raised more questions than it answered.

Jenny moves over to sit with Edna at the window. 'I hope the weather improves for the Isle of Man,' she says.

214

Edna nods. Jenny can tell she is perturbed, perhaps even hurt by the suggestion that Mrs Cantle is behind the incidents. They are friends, after all, from before Sunset Promenade. Jenny says, 'Edna, do you have a son?'

Edna gives her a curious smile. 'What? No, no children.'

'Any brothers?'

Edna frowns now. 'I was an only child.'

'Were you not married?'

'Jenny, what is this? I feel as though I'm being . . . interrogated. For your information, no, I have not taken a husband. I nearly married . . . very, very nearly . . . but I didn't. No husband, no son, no brother.' She narrows her eyes. 'No male relatives. Why do you ask?'

Jenny sighs. 'No reason. I'm sorry.' She watches the rain for a while, then says, 'Why did you come here? You and Mrs Cantle? You're friends, right?'

Edna nods. 'We live near each other. Lived. In north London. Winchmore Hill. Do you know it?' Jenny shakes her head. Edna continues, 'We are both old, and our neighbourhood has changed beyond recognition. Friends have died, or moved into care homes, or to live with their families. We decided we should live out our days in a community of like-minded people.'

'London, though?' presses Jenny. 'So why here, up in the wilds of Lancashire?'

'Margaret had lived in this part of the world when she was younger, and moved to London to . . . to be nearer her son. After her husband died.'

'So she does have a son, then,' muses Jenny. 'I wonder why he's never been to visit. She's always going on about him coming.'

Edna looks at her for a while. 'Wasn't it you who said that just because people are related it doesn't mean they have to like each other?'

Touché, thinks Jenny.

Mrs Cantle comes into the room and pauses on the hearth rug. 'Do you think it would be disrespectful to sit in Mrs Slaithwaite's chair?' she ponders.

'She's in no position to complain,' says Mr Robinson. 'Unless she comes back to bloody haunt us. Christ. Imagine that.'

215

Edna smiles at the exchange and turns back to Jenny. 'Do you wish you had got on better with your parents?'

Jenny blinks. She wasn't expecting that. She's never expecting questions like that about her parents. She has to force herself to remember what has happened – the car crash, everything. 'I don't know. I suppose so.'

'What was it that stopped you?' says Edna curiously. Now it is Jenny's turn to feel as though she's being interrogated. 'It can't just be the generation gap. I mean, look at us, now. You seem to get on quite well with most of the residents at Sunset Promenade. Better than most young people of your age would, I think. So it's not that. What is it? Why didn't you like them?'

'They were boring,' says Jenny quietly.

Edna shrugs. 'Most people are, until you get to know them.' She waves at the room. 'I bet you thought we were all boring when you first arrived. Dull old pensioners. Would you say that now? Now you know our stories, or bits of them, at least? Now you've spent time with us?'

Jenny smiles. 'No. Never boring. Not you lot.'

'So what, then? Something else?'

Jenny thinks about it. 'They wanted *me* to be boring,' she says eventually. 'Wanted me to study economics, so I could be an accountant like my dad. Wanted me to stay in a university I hated, because it was a good one, because it was close to home. They didn't even tell me about my grandfather. I found out by accident, found all the scripts and notes and those film canisters in the attic. They knew I'd had an interest in old films since I was really small, and they didn't tell me!'

'Those wonderful film reels,' nods Edna. 'The last traces of William Drake. I can imagine how that must have upset you.' She pauses. 'But perhaps they were just trying to protect you.'

'By making me as nice and inoffensive as them?'

Edna nods. 'Yes. But they probably didn't see it like that. They would say they wanted the best for you. Wanted you to have the best start in life. Didn't want you chasing silly dreams that don't amount to anything.'

'Dreams are never silly,' says Jenny.

Edna looks back at the window, out into the night, her face reflected in the glass. She looks sad. 'Perhaps not,' she says. 'But sometimes it's true that they never amount to anything.'

The door to the day room opens and Ringo steps in, holding it ajar as Florin brings in a tray. 'Cocoa!' he announces. 'And cakes! And there is some of the bonfire toffee left!'

'Keep that stuff away from me,' says Mr Robinson. 'It's more lethal than Bernie's home brew.'

Ringo helps Florin put the drinks out on the coffee table and Joe says, 'Anyone fancy a game of cards before bed?'

'Lovely!' says Mrs Cantle, clapping her hands together.

'I'll shuffle,' says Mr Robinson, holding his hand out for the cards. 'Who's in?'

'Me,' says Ringo. 'Love rummy.' He looks over to Jenny. 'Are you playing?'

She looks from one to the other as they gather round for the game. Edna smiles at her. 'Shall we?'

Jenny shakes her head. 'Not for me. I think I'll just go to my room.'

Ringo gives her a quizzical look as she leaves. But how can she sit around the day room with them, playing cards? When one of them is a crook? She pauses at the door and looks round at them all, her eyes settling on Mrs Cantle.

The old lady smiles at her. Jenny shivers, despite herself, and leaves.

✳ 32 ✳

Vertigo

(1958, dir. Alfred Hitchcock)

The cold November wind blows off the Irish Sea, biting and harsh, as the Isle of Man Steam Packet ferry noses through the slate-coloured waves. Jenny stands on the deck, wrapped in her anorak, eyes on their destination ahead. Everyone else is having a drink and a snack, gathered together around a table in the insulated restaurant, watching the same view as Jenny but from behind thick windows dripping with sea spray.

Jenny prefers to be on her own. She closes her eyes as a shower of salty spray hits her in the face, revelling in its freshness. She almost didn't come at all, but felt that would have been unfair to everyone else, especially Ringo, who seems quite perturbed by her abrupt withdrawal from life at Sunset Promenade.

Douglas looms ahead of them, a wall of white buildings lining the crescent bay, green hills rising gently behind them. Jenny stays on the deck, watching the island grow closer, wondering what she is going to do. Ringo emerges from the innards of the ferry, waving at her.

'Barry wants us all together. He's worried we'll lose someone.'

They were taken to the port of Heysham by Kevin in his minibus, and would be transferring to a local coach on the Isle of Man for a tour of the sights around Douglas. Jenny isn't particularly looking forward to it. She feels suddenly isolated from everyone, suspicious, fearful even. The daylight had brought some measure of ridiculousness to the accusations she has been turning over and over in her head the night before, but she is still unsettled.

At the ferry terminal Barry assumes the role of tour leader, which Garry, engrossed in emails on his phone, seems more than happy for him to do. Mrs Cantle is wearing a bright yellow sou'wester and leaning heavily on a walking stick, while Edna looks as stylish as ever in a pair of long leather boots, a waxed jacket and a tartan woollen scarf. Ibiza Joe is in his customary poncho, the hair that hangs to the sides of his bald pate tied back in a loose ponytail, while Mr Robinson is in his full regimental regalia, complete with blazer and tie.

What a bunch, thinks Jenny, but not unkindly, and the more she looks at them, the more she does indeed feel that she's being stupid.

'Everyone all right after the crossing?' says Barry as the other passengers disembark around them. 'It was quite smooth, wasn't it?'

'Almost missed Mrs Slaithwaite losing her breakfast over the side,' says Joe.

Everyone makes vaguely sympathetic noises about Mrs Slaithwaite, then Mr Robinson says, 'Speaking of food, I'm bloody starving. How long until lunch?'

Barry consults his itinerary. 'We're going straight to the Laxey Wheel to scatter Mrs Slaithwaite's ashes, and then stopping for something to eat on the way back to Douglas.' He looks up. 'There's a bit of a temporary fairground at the attraction, which we'll have a look at. Don't fill yourselves up with hot dogs and candyfloss, though, or you'll not want your fish and chips.'

'It's not a school trip,' mutters Mr Robinson as Barry leads them on to their waiting coach. Barry does a rather unnecessary headcount when they've all sat down, exactly as if it really is a school trip, then takes up a mic and stands at the front of the coach, reading from a pamphlet about their destination.

Joe looks over the back of his seat at Jenny, who's sitting with Ringo. 'Great feat of Victorian engineering,' he whispers with a wink. 'Largest surviving waterwheel in the world. Blah blah blah. Who's up for doing a runner and finding a pub?'

It is rather impressive, thinks Jenny when they get there – a vast red wheel fixed into the white walls of the mine below, connected across the steep hills by a viaduct. In the field under the wheelhouse there is a travelling fairground, waltzers and sideshows and calliope music rising on the cool air.

'Off the viaduct, I think would be appropriate,' says Barry, leading them up. Ringo lets Joe take his arm and helps him walk the path until they're standing on the structure that spans the space between the hills, looking across the glittering sea. At least it isn't raining. Barry reaches into a plastic carrier bag for a small cardboard box: all that remains of Mrs Slaithwaite.

'Well,' he says, speaking up as the wind whistles around them. 'I suppose a few words are in order.' He pauses, gathering his thoughts. 'Mrs Slaithwaite was perhaps not the easiest person in the world to get along with.'

'Hear, hear,' says Mr Robinson.

Barry glares at him. 'But she was a resident of Sunset Promenade. She was one of us. She didn't have a good relationship with her family.' He looks pointedly at Garry. 'They say blood is thicker than water. They also say you can't choose your family. Neither of those things is strictly true. Mrs Slaithwaite, in her own way, chose us. I suppose that means *we* were her family. Maybe the family you choose is as important as the family you're born into. And maybe if we don't get on as well as we should with our blood relatives, it's because we haven't chosen to.' Barry hugs the box and looks out to sea, across the rolling hills. 'Perhaps we just need to remember that we can all choose to get along with everybody, if we want to.'

Mr Robinson nudges Joe and whispers loudly, 'This is one of them whatchamacallits, isn't it? When he says one thing but means another.'

'Analogy?' offers Ringo.

'That's it,' nods Mr Robinson. 'It's all about Europe, isn't it? He's having a go at us for voting out, Joe.'

Barry ignores him. 'That's it, really. All that remains to be said is that Mrs Slaithwaite wanted her ashes scattering here, on the Isle of Man, because this is where she'd been happiest.'

'Even when she was throwing up!' says Mr Robinson.

'I suppose we should be grateful that she was happy when she was with us,' says Barry. He takes off the lid of the box and unwraps the clear plastic bag inside. It looks like fine gravel, thinks

220

Jenny. That's what we end up as. Barry says, 'A little bit of Mrs Slaithwaite will always be with us.'

Then he empties the bag over the side of the aqueduct. Into the wind that blows off the sea, up the hills and over the fields, taking all that is left of Mrs Slaithwaite and making it blossom in the air like a tiny, grumpy cloud.

Into the wind that throws the ashes back at them, right into their faces.

'Oh, Christ!' yells Mr Robinson, spitting loudly as he gets a mouthful of Mrs Slaithwaite.

'Urgh!' says Joe, wiping the grey dust from his face.

'She's in my eye,' complains Mrs Cantle.

'She's in my bloody mouth!' says Joe.

'Ah,' says Barry. 'Maybe we should have scattered her off the other side . . .'

Ringo takes a long drink of water from one of the bottles that Florin is quickly passing round. Jenny empties half of hers into her mouth and spits it over the side.

'You wally,' says Mr Robinson, shaking his head at Barry Grange. 'Well, you were right about one thing. A little bit of Mrs Slaithwaite will always bloody be with us now.'

'Right,' says Barry. 'Who's for a tour of the mine . . . ?'

'Want me to win you a teddy bear on the hook-a-duck, Edna?' says Joe.

'For God's sake,' spits Mr Robinson. 'Like a bloody teenager.'

'I would love a candyfloss,' says Mrs Cantle. 'I haven't had one in years.'

'Hope you're not diabetic; send you doolally,' says Mr Robinson.

'Look,' says Edna to Jenny. 'A Ferris wheel.' There is indeed one rising up from the centre of the fairground, at least the height of the Laxey Wheel that sits higher up the hill, and rather a lot more rickety-looking, in Jenny's opinion. Edna says, 'Be like *The Third Man*, eh?'

They queue for the Ferris wheel, past the metal platform housing the chugging generator that powers the ride. The operator slows the wheel to allow pairs to climb into the gently rocking seats, the safety bars worn smooth from countless hands, the faux leather seats ripped and patched with duct tape. Barry gets on with Mrs Cantle, Joe with Ringo, Jenny with Edna, leaving Mr Robinson to mutter loudly, 'Oh, good grief!' as Florin smiles broadly and gets in beside him. Garry waves his phone at them; he's got business to attend to and can't be distracting himself with fripperies. Then the wheel is full and the operator crunches it into gear, and it begins its jerky revolution.

The seat swings slightly alarmingly, rocking back and forth as the wheel turns. At the apex Jenny looks down the hill towards the Irish Sea. She says to Edna, 'Brotherly love, five hundred years of democracy and peace – and what did that produce?'

'The cuckoo clock,' smiles Edna. 'Very good.'

As they start their second ascent, Jenny says, 'In that movie, *The Third Man* . . . Holly Martins is convinced his friend Harry Lime can't be the criminal everyone says he is.'

'And yet he turns out to be,' says Edna.

'Yes. Sometimes even people we think are friends . . . we don't know them as well as we might.'

'No,' says Edna, looking at the view. 'You still think Margaret is capable of all those things that have happened?'

'Honestly, I don't know. But right now I feel . . . suspicious of everyone. As though I'm waiting for the next bad thing to happen. Like I can't trust anyone.' She looks at Edna. 'I feel like I want my faith in human nature restoring.'

Edna says, 'You sound like you *need* your faith in human nature restoring,' and looks at the view again. From the seat behind, Jenny hears raised voices. She twists round to see Florin with his head in his hands, Mr Robinson red-faced and furious.

'I don't understand!' wails Florin. 'Why do you hate me so much, Mr Robinson? I haven't done anything to you.'

'That's the bloody problem!' shouts Mr Robinson. 'No sense of responsibility. No *culpability*.'

'I do not even know what that means.'

'It means having the good grace to feel bad about something,' says Mr Robinson. 'It means taking blame where it's due.'

Florin shakes his head. 'What am I taking blame for?'

Mr Robinson looks away. 'Killing my father.'

There's a long silence, the wind whistling through the metal struts of the Ferris wheel. Florin looks blankly at Mr Robinson, who glares at him with loathing.

'Not you, obviously. Not personally. I'm not stupid. I'm talking about you *lot*, Eastern Europeans. Oh, don't get me wrong. My father did his duty. He wouldn't have done anything else. And I was proud of him. Proud! But he didn't have to die. Not like he did.'

'How did he die?' asks Florin.

Mr Robinson stares at the sea. 'Have you heard of the Arctic convoys? Back in forty-two, they went out to give support to the Russians. My father was part of what they called Convoy PQ 17. Thirty-five ships, there were, sailing from Iceland for Arkhangelsk, mainly delivering munitions.' He looks at Florin. 'Twenty-four of them were sunk in a week-long attack by submarines and bombers. My father was on one of those.'

'I am sorry,' says Florin miserably. 'But I still do not—'

Mr Robinson shakes his head. 'Of course you don't. You don't understand that we put our lives on the line for you lot. We *died* for you. And now you come over here, and treat us like . . . like a bank, to take money out of! And you just send it all back to bloody God knows where while we're on our arses here! You don't care about us! You'll bleed us dry and then you'll be off to the next set of bloody mugs!'

'Mr Robinson?' says Florin, looking over his feet at the ground far below.

'What?'

'Why have we stopped?'

The seats swing gently in the breeze blowing off the sea and up the hill. Jenny looks down as well; there are people gathering around the bottom of the Ferris wheel, and the engine that drives the ride seems to be pumping out what looks like an awful lot of black smoke. Jenny and Edna have just crested the zenith and started the descent; behind them Florin and Mr Robinson are at the very top of the revolution.

She can see Garry Grange talking animatedly to the ride operator and then he's cupping his hands around his mouth and yelling at them.

'Nobody panic. There's a slight problem. Something's seized up. But this chap reckons he'll get it going again in ten minutes, tops. Just stay where you are.'

'Well, we're hardly going to go anywhere, are we?' says Edna.

'Bloody typical!' shouts Mr Robinson from above. 'Absolutely bloody typical. What is he, that bloke down there? Gypsy? Something like that? What have I been telling you, lad? Is this not exactly what I'm talking about?'

'Mr Robinson, you need to calm down,' says Florin.

'Calm down, my arse!' shouts Mr Robinson. 'I'm stuck up here with you and . . . and—'

'Mr Robinson!' cries Florin, in a tone of such anguish that Jenny has to twist round again to look back and up, to see what on earth can be wrong.

Mr Robinson's face is red and contorted in agony. He's thumping his chest with his fist, and gripping on to the safety bar with his other hand so hard his knuckles have gone white.

'My chest . . . my chest . . .' he gasps. 'Angina attack . . .'

'Mr Robinson!' wails Florin.

'Pills . . .' says Mr Robinson thickly. 'Medication . . . need my medication.'

Florin casts about wildly, making the seat tip dangerously. Then he puts his hands to his head as he sees Barry, far below in the seat, almost at the ground, with Mrs Cantle, waving a small black plastic bag at him.

'Oh!' says Florin. 'Mr Grange has the pills!'

'Bugger,' says Mr Robinson, taking a deep, ragged breath and slumping heavily in the seat, unconscious.

For You I Die

(1947, dir. John Reinhardt)

Jenny twists in the seat to see, causing it to sway precariously. 'Careful, dear,' says Edna, grabbing on to Jenny's arm. 'You'll have us over.'

'Florin!' shouts Jenny. 'What's happening?'

'Mr Robinson, I think he is having an angina episode.'

Jenny turns to Edna. 'Is that bad? I'm guessing it's bad.'

'If he had his pills . . .' says Edna, glancing down at Barry Grange far below. 'Then he might be all right. Without them, there's a risk he could have a full cardiac arrest.'

'Oh God,' says Jenny. She cups her hands around her mouth and shouts to Barry. 'Do you think we should get an ambulance?'

Barry waves the black bag containing Mr Robinson's pills in frustration, then nods and gets out his phone. Jenny turns round to tell Florin and sees him leaning over Mr Robinson, gently trying to shake him awake.

'It's OK, Mr Robinson, the ambulance is coming,' says Florin.

'Tell 'em to bring the bloody fire brigade as well,' gasps Mr Robinson, rolling his eyes and coming groggily awake. 'And the longest ladder they've got. I'd be all right, lad, if I had my pills.'

Florin leans as far forward out of the seat as he can and shouts, 'Mr Grange! Do you think you can throw the bag to me?'

Barry sizes up the distance and shakes his head. Florin smacks the safety bar with the palm of his hand, then says, 'Mr Robinson! Mr Robinson!'

'I'm . . . all right, lad . . . just having a nap . . .'

'I don't think you should sleep, Mr Robinson . . .'

Mr Robinson pats Florin's arm weakly. 'Just forty winks . . . My neck hurts. And my shoulder.'

Jenny looks around at the thin roads snaking out of the valley and across the hillside, but she cannot see any tell-tale blue lights on them yet. She looks over the side to see the Ferris wheel operator leaning into the engine, pulling out greasy components and blackened lumps of metal. It doesn't look like they are going to be moving any time soon.

Then there's a collective scream from the people gathered below and Jenny looks up to see Florin easing himself gingerly out from under the safety barrier across his and Mr Robinson's lap.

'Florin!' cries Jenny. 'What are you doing?'

But Florin has no time to explain. Clutching the side of the seat, he carefully gets into a crouching position and begins to stand, swiftly coming down again as the seat rocks violently. He tries again, more slowly, and when he's on his feet, balancing with arms outstretched like a tightrope walker, he lunges for the thick metal outer rim of the Ferris wheel. Florin stands with his eyes closed, breathing heavily, feet on the seat and arms wrapped around the rim.

'Save yourself, why don't you?' says Mr Robinson weakly.

Florin throws one leg over the rim, following with the other, until he's hugging the cold metal and starting to slide downwards. Jenny shrieks. Then his feet hit one of the spokes that connects the outer rim to the centre, and he reaches down until he's got one hand and both feet on it.

Then he drops. The gasp from the gathering crowd is audible, even from Jenny's seat. But Florin has grasped the spoke with both hands and his feet are firmly planted on the spoke below. He repeats the manoeuvre, now alongside Jenny and Edna's seat, and one more drop brings him to an almost horizontal position.

'I do believe he's going for Mr Robinson's medication,' says Edna.

She's right. Two more spokes bring him in line with Barry and Mrs Cantle. Seeing what he's doing, Barry bunches up the plastic bag and reaches out as far as he can to Florin as he inches towards him.

'I'll hold it in my teeth,' yells Florin, and Barry nods and puts the end of the bag in his mouth. He winks at him and looks up to gauge his journey back. Mrs Cantle breaks out into applause.

In the distance, Jenny can hear the faint sound of sirens. Then she feels a spot of rain on her forehead, and another. Florin is beginning his ascent. The last thing he needs is rain.

The plastic bag in his teeth, Florin negotiates the climb. It's harder for him going up, the force of gravity against him, and he has to haul himself from one spoke to the next. But he's doing it, already level with Edna and Jenny again.

On the next spoke, as he reaches for the one above, his foot slips on the metal and for one awful moment he is suspended in space, feet kicking, the bag dangling from his clenched teeth. Finding his footing, he continues to climb, reaching the top of the Ferris wheel and clambering back into the seat.

The crowd below erupts into cheers and applause as Florin slides under the safety bar. Digging in his own bag, which is hooked over the back of the seat, he pulls out a bottle of water and begins to force pills into Mr Robinson's mouth.

Mr Robinson wipes his mouth with the back of his hand. Florin looks at him, searching his face. 'Mr Robinson? Mr Robinson? Was I in time?'

There's a long silence, during which Mr Robinson breathes heavily, holding his chest. Then he wipes his face with his sleeve and says, 'You know what? I'm bloody starving. I hope we haven't missed the fish and chips.'

Florin reaches into his rucksack again and pulls out a tartan thermos flask. 'Then you are in luck, Mr Robinson.'

'What is it?'

'Cabbage soup!' grins Florin. Then, as the ambulance negotiates its way into the fairground, the Ferris wheel suddenly lurches and begins to move forward again, and everyone cheers.

Mr Robinson, blustering and protesting, is given the once-over by the paramedics in the back of the ambulance and a beaming Florin is swamped by congratulations from friends and strangers alike. As they alight from the Ferris wheel, Edna says, 'Well. What a drama.'

'And it's not over yet,' says Jenny, pointing towards where Mr Robinson, being helped into a wheelchair – or rather, forced into a wheelchair – by the grumbling paramedics, starts to wave frantically at Florin.

'Oh dear,' says Edna. 'I do hope he's not going to cause trouble.'

'Let's get closer, just in case,' says Jenny, taking Edna by the elbow and steering her closer to the ambulance.

'Florin, lad,' says Mr Robinson, buttoning up his shirt as the young carer approaches. He holds his tie in his hand and looks at it for a long time. 'Florin. That thing you did . . . my father would have been proud of you.'

'It is what he would have done. It is what you would have done.'

Mr Robinson shakes his head. 'Not me, lad. I was no good. I need to tell you something.'

'I do not think you should be getting worked up, Mr Robinson. You need to stay calm.'

'I was never in the army,' says Mr Robinson. 'Never made it. Was never Second Lieutenant. That was my father's rank.' He rubs his shoulder and stretches his neck. 'I always told everybody I was because I knew it's what he would have wanted for me. But I couldn't hack it. I did two weeks of basic training and failed.' He looks down at his hands. 'This blazer? The regimental tie? Not even mine. I didn't earn them. Bought them in a charity shop years ago. I'm a failure, lad.'

'It doesn't matter, Mr Robinson,' says Florin.

But Mr Robinson is grasping on to Florin's coat. 'My dad . . . he'd have looked at you, at what you just did, and he'd have been proud of that. When his own son was a failure.'

'I suppose that means you hate me even more, now,' says Florin miserably.

Mr Robinson sits back heavily in the wheelchair. 'I never hated you, lad. Not really. That was something else I was trying to live up to.' He takes a deep breath. 'My dad . . . when he was younger, he saw Oswald Mosley speak. You know who he was, Florin? British Union of Fascists. A lot of people listened to him, back then. Liked what he was saying. About the Jews and the blacks. My dad was one of them. And then the war came along, and my dad went away to fight. I remember saying to him, when I was just a little lad, how come he was going to fight Mr Hitler when him and Mr Mosley said the same things.'

Mr Robinson pauses. 'I suppose I was quite a precocious little boy, really. But it didn't make sense to me.' He looks at Florin. 'My dad whacked me one. Straight across the face. He said that he wasn't going to fight Hitler, he was going to fight foreigners, and there was a difference. He wasn't fighting *ideas*, he was fighting against what Mr Mosley had said was going to happen – that Britain would be overrun with all sorts. My father thought the war was a show of strength, us saying we wouldn't be made a fool of by anyone. And if I knew what was good for me, that whatever happened to him in the war I had to look after my mother and do all I could to fight against the foreigners coming over to ruin our British way of life, because if he died then he was doing it for me, and my future, and I always had to remember that.'

'And he did die in the war,' says Florin. 'Did you do as he said? Did you look after your mother?'

Mr Robinson looks out to sea, at the grey clouds racing over, heavy with rain. 'I didn't have to, lad. Five years after my dad died, she married again.' He turns to Florin. 'I was fifteen. I walked out of the house.' Florin opens his mouth to speak but Mr Robinson holds up one hand to silence him. 'She married a Pole. Load of them came over here in forty-seven, Polish Resettlement Act. He was a nice chap, by all accounts. Engineer. My sister went to the wedding. I never spoke to him, never said one word to my mother for the rest of her life. I know she did it to spite him. To spite both of us.'

Suddenly, Mr Robinson's face crinkles up and he clutches his chest. Alarmed, Florin leans over. 'You need the paramedics again?'

Mr Robinson shakes his head. 'It's not my heart, lad. Well, it is, I suppose. All these years . . . everybody betrayed him, my father. Moved on. Had happy lives. Not me. I was the only one who stuck by him, even after he'd died. The only one who carried on fighting the good fight.' He meets Florin's eye at last. 'Stupid, stupid bastard. Look at me, stuck in a rest home, alone, nobody likes me.' Florin starts to protest but Mr Robinson holds up his hands. 'Nobody bloody likes me! I'm not an idiot, lad. I don't even like me, most of the time. Keeping the flame of my dad's bloody hatred lit, since before I could even try to understand it for myself. Then you, who have every bloody right to sit there and laugh while I die right in front of you, go and do that. Putting your own life on the line. For me.'

Then Mr Robinson begins to sob loudly and unattractively, his face contorted, tears and snot mingling on his chin; the pent-up frustration of, supposes Jenny, decades and decades suddenly exploding out of him. He wipes his nose on the back of his blazer sleeve and sticks out his tongue. 'Urgh. Can I have a drink of water?'

'Do you feel faint?' says Florin, waving at the paramedics as they load up their equipment in the ambulance.

Mr Robinson shakes his head. 'No, lad. I think I've still got a bit of Mrs Slaithwaite stuck in my dentures.'

Edna says quietly to Jenny, 'So. Have you had your faith in human nature restored?'

They have walked away from the crowd surrounding Florin, and are gathering by the doughnut stand. Barry Grange is patting Florin on the shoulder, while Joe and Mrs Cantle are heading over to the ambulance, where Mr Robinson is already losing his patience with the paramedics who are prodding and poking him.

'That was the most awesome thing I ever saw,' agrees Jenny. 'Florin probably saved Mr Robinson's life. I wonder if he'll be grateful.' She looks at Edna. 'Do you think he'll change his ways? Can someone change when they're like that?'

'I don't know,' replies Edna. 'Perhaps it's all too ingrained in him. Perhaps he's just waiting for a chance to change.'

Jenny nods thoughtfully. 'Maybe he needs permission to let go of all those stupid old ideas.'

'We are old, and set in our ways,' sighs Edna. 'But that does not mean we are bad people. We just grew up in a different world than you live in now.'

'I don't buy that. You live in the same world as we do. There's no excuse for prejudice. No reason why people can't change, no matter how old they are.'

They both look for a moment at the ambulance, and at Mrs Cantle. Edna says softly, 'Does it not seem ridiculous that Margaret has done all the things you think she has?'

In the cold light of day, in the aftermath of the very real crisis she has just witnessed, Jenny suddenly thinks it might well do. She surprises herself by smiling. It feels good. 'I'll tell you what,' she says. 'The fourth and final William J. Drake film is called *Off Devil's Head*. It's about a smuggling racket, and a trail of dead bodies that leads the detective to the organised-crime syndicate trying to bring in liquor under the noses of the revenue men.'

'So, by your logic, there should be a crime related to the film to follow,' says Edna. 'What are you expecting?'

'Let's wait and see,' says Jenny. 'But this is the last of my grandfather's films. Either the villain will show themselves . . .'

'Or?'

'Or I'll have to admit I'm wrong. And quite possibly mad.' Jenny sniffs the air and turns towards the food stand. 'Shall we have a doughnut?'

'Yes, let's. But I am curious . . . why do you persist in this idea that there must be a mystery at all?'

'I think because I want there to be,' says Jenny. 'Because without it, I couldn't come up with an excuse not to leave Sunset Promenade and take up a room on campus.'

Edna purses her lips. 'So your head told you to leave but your heart told you to stay. I wonder why?'

Jenny looks at her, and at Ringo helping Joe negotiate a patch of rocky ground, and at Mr Robinson sitting up in the back of the ambulance. At Barry and Garry Grange, quietly arguing about a letter they are poring over; at Mrs Cantle, embracing Florin in her thin arms.

'I have no idea,' she says. 'It's a mystery.'

✳ 34 ✳

Kiss Me Deadly

(1955, dir. Robert Aldrich)

'I think this calls for a celebration,' says Mr Robinson, when they are all firmly ensconced back in the day room of Sunset Promenade. He has retrieved a carrier bag from his room and produces from it a brace of two-litre Pepsi bottles filled to the brim with dark liquid.

'Bernie's home brew!' says Joe happily. 'But I thought you'd cleared it all out before the inspection.'

'As if,' sniffs Mr Robinson. 'Florin, lad, get us some glasses, will you?'

'Are you quite sure you should be drinking, Mr Robinson?' says Barry Grange gingerly. 'I mean, after everything that's happened . . .' He pauses, and frowns. 'Do we even allow alcohol in here?'

'Nonsense, I'm fit as a fiddle,' says Mr Robinson. 'Those paramedics said so. In fact, I'd probably feel worse if I didn't have a drink.' He looks pointedly at Barry. 'So it's medicinal, in a way. You're not going to stop us, are you? Do you really want that on your conscience, if anything happens to me?'

Barry sighs, and smiles. 'Get the glasses, Florin. One for everyone. I think it's about time I sampled Bernie's home brew for myself.'

It feels to Jenny as though some sort of corner has been turned in Sunset Promenade. She is even beginning to feel a little silly at what looks to her now to be her own mild hysteria about Mrs Cantle. Even if the old lady did start the fire, even if she did lock Jenny in her room . . . she's a little confused at times, but harmless, really. It's not worth dwelling on. She's lost her jewels and she's absent-mindedly picked up Mr Robinson's medal and Joe's photograph, and that's that.

And as soon as Jenny allows herself to believe this, it's like a weight is lifted from her shoulders. She doesn't have to be the detective, just like she didn't have to be the femme fatale. For the first time in her life, she thinks, she isn't trying too hard to be someone, or not be someone. She's just being herself, being Jenny Ebert. It feels good.

When everyone has a glass of Bernie's home brew poured for them, Barry stands up and clears his throat. 'Well,' he says, looking around the room. 'We've had quite an eventful day, haven't we? I just wanted to say . . . I'm sure we're all grateful to Florin for his bravery today.'

There's a round of applause and Mr Robinson stands up as well. 'Hear, hear. And there's nobody more grateful than me.' He looks towards Florin, who's standing by the door, and raises his glass. 'I might not be standing here now without the actions of this young lad.' Mr Robinson takes a mouthful of beer. 'Look, I know we might not have seen eye to eye on everything, and I don't want anyone thinking I've suddenly gone soft. I have my views and I can't say a lot's changed, to be honest. But.' He looks around the room. 'But . . . sometimes you have to take people as you find them. I admit I've not been very good at that. I've tended to . . . well, I suppose you'd say prejudge people. Based on where they're from or what they look like. But there's good and bad no matter who you are, I reckon . . .' He tails off. 'That's it, really.' He raises his glass. 'To Florin.'

'To Florin!' echoes everyone else, and they all take a gulp of their drinks. Jenny grimaces; it really is foul stuff. She can't see what everyone is excited about. She glances at Ringo, sitting next to her on the sofa, and beyond him to the dark rectangle of the window, the curtains still open, and the clear sky beyond.

'Wow, look at that. I can see stars,' she says.

'A good omen, perhaps,' says Edna, sitting on the other side of Ringo. She appraises the pair of them for a moment. 'A good evening for your astronomy, perhaps, Ringo?'

He looks at Jenny, then down at his drink, cradled in his hands

233

on his lap. 'Yeah, I might go and do a bit . . .' Ringo looks up at Jenny again. 'I don't suppose . . . ?'

The rest of the room has lapsed into its own conversations, Garry showing around the photos on his phone of Florin's dramatic climb on the Ferris wheel. 'Ooh,' says Mrs Cantle. 'You can see right up my skirt on that one!'

'I'd love to,' says Jenny quietly to Ringo.

He breaks out into a wide grin. 'Ace! I'll go and get it set up. See you up there in five minutes.'

'It's a Newtonian reflector with an eight-inch aperture,' says Ringo proudly, as Jenny inspects the telescope poised at his window.

'I love it when you talk dirty,' she says, then immediately blushes. Ringo's eyes widen for a moment, then he looks at his feet and gives a short, awkward laugh.

'It's a beginner's telescope, really,' he says. 'But it's pretty good at what I need it for. I can focus on the stars and the planets, and the moon looks brilliant.' He looks at her. 'Mr Robinson was like a little boy when I showed him the moon through it. He was almost in tears. I don't think he's had a good life at all, you know, Jenny.'

'It doesn't excuse his attitudes, though.'

Ringo shrugs. 'It might explain them a bit.'

'Hmm,' says Jenny. She points at the smaller telescope sprouting from the thick barrel of the main body. 'What's that?'

'The focus finder – that's what you look through,' says Ringo. 'Here have a go.'

Jenny closes one eye and leans over the viewfinder. Suddenly the sky becomes a black tapestry inlaid with glittering jewels. 'Wow,' she says.

'See that really bright star? That's Vega in Lyra. Look just to the left of that . . . what do you see?'

'Two stars close together . . .' says Jenny. 'Wait. Each one is two stars . . .'

'The Double Double,' says Ringo with satisfaction. 'Epsilon Lyrae. It's a binary star system, but each star is actually a double star. It's quite rare. This is the best time to see it. You're really lucky.'

'Yes,' says Jenny, straightening up and looking at Ringo in the darkness. 'I suppose I am.'

And for the first time she *does* feel lucky. Lucky that she came here, to Sunset Promenade. Lucky that she's had these experiences, met these unconventional friends. Lucky that she knows Ringo. She says, 'How did you get into all this stuff?'

He waves a hand dismissively. 'I've always been into space and astronomy, I suppose,' He shrugs and then says, 'When my mum . . . when she was near the end . . . she said to me that I should choose a star, any star, and when she'd gone that I was to look up at it at any time, and that's where she'd be. If I ever needed her.' He gives a small laugh. 'Bit silly, really. Don't know why I'm telling you that.'

'It's lovely,' says Jenny, the words suddenly choking her. 'Which star?'

Ringo looks into the focus finder and repositions the telescope. 'Take a look.'

There's a bright star, glowing almost orange. 'Albireo,' says Ringo softly. 'It's in a constellation called the Northern Cross. It's also called Cygnus, or the Swan. Albireo forms the head of the swan.'

Jenny looks at the star for a long moment, then back to Ringo. He's staring out of the window, seeing – what? She doesn't know. 'When I was little I used to say she was like a swan because she had this thin, graceful neck.' He looks at Jenny. 'And then, when I was older, I heard that thing about swans looking all graceful and serene on the surface, but paddling furiously under the water, out of sight. That was like Mum.'

Jenny puts a tentative hand on Ringo's shoulder.

'Anyway,' he says briskly. 'Here's an awesome thing. When we're seeing the sun, we're seeing what it was like eight minutes ago, right, because that's how long it takes the light to get to us.'

'I hated physics at school,' mutters Jenny.

'Listen,' chides Ringo. 'This is interesting. Our next nearest star is in the Alpha Centauri system; it takes more than four years for the light from that to reach us.' He waves his hand at the vista of the night sky, stretching above them and down to the distant sea. 'See those stars up there? That light's taken thousands of years to get to our eyeballs. Tens of thousands, sometimes.' Ringo looks at Jenny. 'If one of those stars died now, we'd never know about it, not for millennia. We're looking at the distant past. It's time travel, yeah?'

Jenny thinks about this. She says carefully, 'In a way it's like my old films. The light from those movies . . . it's dead light. The people are dead, the films are half forgotten. We're looking through a window into the past.'

Ringo smiles crookedly. 'We're both obsessed by things from a long time ago. We're both focused on the past.'

Jenny realises she still has her hand on him. She puts her other hand on his shoulder, gently turns him to face her. 'Perhaps we should think about the here and now a bit more.'

Then she's pulling him closer, putting her lips against his, and pulling his T-shirt up and over his head. He shrugs it on to the floor and moves to close the curtains.

'No,' she whispers, and takes him by the hand to his bed, the pair of them shedding clothes as they walk, until by the time they lie down together their bodies are naked and painted with silver starlight.

It's gone nine when Jenny wakes to a low rumble of thunder and distant, raised voices. Rain is lashing against the window from a sky so grey and dark it barely offers any more light than the previous night. Just no stars. She is naked and Ringo is, too, his limbs draped over hers in a tangle of cool skin.

Oh my God, she thinks. Then grins. Then blushes.

'Hello, you,' he says, making her jump.

'How long have you been awake?' she says.

He smooths the hair from her face. 'Half an hour, maybe. Just watching you.' He pauses. 'Is that weird?'

Jenny wants to kiss him again but her mouth is dry and cottony and sour from the glass of home brew. 'Not weird,' she says, considering. 'Maybe a little bit.' She gives him a chaste, closed-mouth kiss on the cheek. 'I feel bleurgh; I really need to have a shower and clean my teeth.'

'Are you in lectures today?'

She retrieves her phone from the pocket of her jeans, which lie crumpled on the floor. 'Oh God, yes. In a couple of hours.'

Jenny pulls her knickers from the jumble of clothes and awkwardly slides into them under the duvet, then does the same with her bra and T-shirt, only emerging to quickly pull her jeans on. She doesn't want to rush away and appear harsh and uncaring, but by the same token she doesn't want to gush and come on too strong. Ringo sits up in bed, his thin arms behind his head.

'So,' he says. 'What happens now?'

She looks at him. 'What do you think should happen now?'

'I think we should get married!' he says happily.

Jenny's eyes widen. 'Are you joking?'

'Yes,' he grins. 'Look, let's take it as it comes. Here and now and all that, right?'

She smiles. 'Sounds like a plan. I'll see you later, right?'

'I'm not going anywhere,' says Ringo. He stretches like a thin cat. 'In fact, I might really not go anywhere. I might just stay here all day.'

However, as Jenny emerges cautiously from his room, looking up and down the corridor to make sure no one sees her on the short dash between his place and hers, she hears commotion from downstairs.

'If everyone can be quiet, I'll explain fully,' Barry Grange is shouting. 'We need everyone to be here for this. Has anyone seen Ringo? Jenny?'

She dashes back to her room and closes the door, mussing up her neat sheets and duvet just in time for Florin to knock on her door.

'Jenny,' he says, his face serious. 'We have a house meeting in the day room. Right now.'

'Barely had my bloody breakfast,' says Mr Robinson, folding the paper and tucking it under his arm. 'I'm not a well man, you know. I shouldn't have shocks. What's going on?'

Barry and Garry Grange are standing together in front of the blank television. Garry begins to speak. 'We have some important news for you. It affects you all.'

'*Us* all,' says Barry, glaring at him. 'A couple of you might have heard my brother and I having a . . . a heated conversation this morning . . .'

'Blazing row,' says Joe in a stage whisper, nudging Ringo. 'Surprised they didn't wake you up.'

'We've had some news,' says Garry.

'Is it about the inspection?' asks Mrs Cantle. 'The one poor old Mrs Slaithwaite slept through?'

Barry blinks. 'Oh, that? We had news on that yesterday. Passed with flying colours. The inspector was very impressed with the integration between our older residents and the students.'

'For as long as it lasts,' mutters Garry.

Edna says, with evident impatience, 'What do you mean by that? Is someone going to tell us just what's going on?'

Garry says, 'You all know that Sunset Promenade is unusual, and possibly even unique, in its business model. We keep your fees at the absolute minimum, and we achieve this through a combination of grants and funding from a variety of sources. Most of it comes through several funds set up in the European Union to finance the care of the elderly, especially via non-traditional or innovative means.'

Everyone looks at Mr Robinson and he glares around the room. 'What? I never said *everything* about Europe was *all* bad, did I?'

'On quite a few occasions, yes,' says Joe mildly.

Barry sighs and pinches his nose. 'We've had a communication this morning from the body that administers most of these grants. It's . . . not good news.'

Garry continues, 'What my brother is prevaricating about telling you is that the plug is being pulled on the funding. As of now.'

Jenny stares at him. 'All of it?'

'Enough of it to make a difference,' says Garry. 'A big difference. Essentially, we can't afford to run Sunset Promenade any more. We're not getting another penny from them.'

Mr Robinson slaps the newspaper on the carpet. 'I knew it. You're going to put our rates up, aren't you?'

'If only it was as simple as that,' says Barry softly. 'Without this money . . . well, we've got your contributions, and of course we've saved a little, but running a place like this costs so much. And unless we can prove that we're a solvent business . . . we'll lose our licence, good inspection or not.'

'Sunset Promenade as you know it is over,' says Garry briskly. 'We've not many options facing us. Either we sell the business as a going concern to the Care Network, as many of you know I've been advocating for quite some time now, or . . .'

'Or what, dear?' says Mrs Cantle.

Barry and Garry look at each other, then Barry says, 'Or we close down Sunset Promenade. Permanently.'

A heavy silence blankets the room. Edna breaks it eventually. 'If you do sell to this other company, what will that mean for the residents?'

Barry has gone pale. 'Well, they'll want to charge you the going rate for residency here. Which, according to their current tariff . . .' He swallows, then says, 'It would be more than forty-five thousand pounds a year. Each.'

There's a hubbub of startled conversation, and Barry holds up his hand. 'Added to that,' he says, 'in buying us out it would mean Garry and I would have no further involvement in Sunset Promenade. And Florin would have to take a pay cut of . . . of roughly fifty per cent, if he were to be kept on. Which is highly doubtful. The Care Network would more likely want to bring in their own staff anyway.'

'Isn't there anything we can do?' says Joe helplessly.

'Not unless you've got a secret fortune in the bank you can give us,' says Garry with a humourless laugh. 'That would see us through for a while. But otherwise . . . even you lot and your madcap schemes aren't going to save Sunset Promenade, I'm afraid.'

✳ 35 ✳

Off Devil's Head

(1950, dir. William J. Drake)

It feels like a hollow gesture, but Jenny doesn't know what else to do, so suggests a final meeting of the Lonely Hearts Cinema Club, and a viewing of her grandfather's last film, *Off Devil's Head*.

'We might as well,' says Joe listlessly. 'Be a shame for this place to close down without us having seen the full set.'

Everyone has been letting the idea sink in that they are going to have to leave Sunset Promenade, and thinking about looking at alternative plans. The options for the residents seem limited, given their financial situations. Barry has arranged for someone from social services to come in, to go through likely scenarios. There are care homes available, but places are scattered across Lancashire, and since none of the residents has capital or savings, then they'll basically have to go where they're put. They'll be split up, that much is certain.

'I feel quite bad,' Jenny confides in Ringo. 'At least we can go to the new hall of residence. I'm going to the accommodation office to see if those places are still open.'

'I'm not,' says Ringo. 'I'm going to stick it out until the bitter end.' He looks at Jenny. 'Don't you feel part of this? It feels wrong to just run away.'

'We'll have to leave sooner or later,' she says, feeling a little stung. 'What will we do if we can't get accommodation?'

'Here and now, remember?' says Ringo. 'It isn't over until it's over. Something might happen.'

She smiles at his optimism, but knows nothing will happen. Nothing good, at any rate. Last night, the two of them . . .

that suddenly seems a long time ago. That happiness she felt has evaporated. Restless, she walks the stairways and landings of Sunset Promenade, touching the wooden banisters, running her fingers down the panes of rain-sluiced glass, committing the place to memory. Eventually she finds herself a reception and the already yellowing and curling print-out of that story from the local newspaper on the noticeboard, talking in such bright terms about the wonderful new initiative at Sunset Promenade, bringing senior citizens and students together – how fabulous it was going to be.

The door to the office is open and she sees Barry Grange brooding behind his desk, poring over papers spread out before him. He glances up and sees her, and smiles sadly. 'It doesn't matter how many times I go over these figures, I can't make them add up to what I want them to.'

He beckons Jenny in and she sits on the chair beside his desk while he leans back and stretches. His blue bow tie is ragged and loose. He looks tired.

'I suppose you have to take comfort from the fact that you've kept this place running the way you wanted it to for so long,' Jenny says slowly. 'It's an achievement, isn't it?'

Barry walks round the desk and to the door, looking out into the lobby. 'And now it's over. After twenty years, it's come to an end.' He turns back to Jenny and there are tears in his eyes. 'But we did a good thing, I hope. Do you think so?'

'Yes, I do. I think you've done a wonderful thing. I wish there was some way to help.'

Barry smiles. 'You have helped, just by being here. You've helped them realise that just because they're old, it doesn't mean they aren't people. I imagine you and Ringo will be leaving us, soon. I hope you'll continue to engage with the old people until then.'

'They're not old people,' says Jenny, standing up. 'They're just people.' She pauses at the door. 'They're my friends.'

'Welcome to what I suppose is the last meeting of the Lonely Hearts Cinema Club,' says Jenny, standing by the TV. There's a chorus of boos, whistles and cheers. 'It seems quite fitting that the last film we'll see is the final movie made by William J. Drake.

I hope you haven't been disappointed in not watching films you might have been more familiar with.'

'They're brilliant pictures, love,' says Joe. 'And when you get to our age, it's nice to see something you haven't seen before. Makes you feel alive.'

'This is called *Off Devil's Head*,' says Jenny. 'It's not only appropriate because it was my grandfather's last film, but also because it's got a coastal flavour. It's about smuggling and organised crime. It was filmed in Cornwall and Devon, and released in nineteen fifty.'

'Why was it his last film?' asks Edna. 'What happened to him?'

Jenny smiles tightly. 'He was told his dreams were stupid. He took the nice, safe option.' She looks at Ringo. 'He was really bright, for a time, like one of those stars . . . what is it, Ringo, a supernova? But a supernova is just what happens when a star dies, am I right? Sometimes they explode, sometimes they just fade away. William J. Drake did both.'

Jenny looks at all of them in turn, at Edna and Mrs Cantle, Joe and Mr Robinson, Ringo. At Florin, at the Grange twins. At the empty chair still dimpled with Mrs Slaithwaite's impression. Jenny says, 'I worried I was going to just fade away as well. But I think we can all go out with a bang, if we want to.'

There's a spontaneous round of applause that quite embarrasses Jenny, and she quickly starts the film and settles down on the sofa between Ringo and Edna, while Florin dims the lights. She feels a thrill as Ringo quietly takes her hand in his in the darkness, and the last ever film of the Lonely Hearts Cinema Club gets underway.

Afterwards, she takes Ringo to her room and they lie together in the gloom, legs entwined. She feels sad, suddenly; like it's the end of a holiday romance. She wonders what will happen to them, to her and Ringo. Will they move to rooms on campus? Will they stay together? Are they even together? Here in the rarefied atmosphere of Sunset Promenade, life has taken on an almost unreal varnish. Out there, in the real world . . . can things ever be the same?

Ringo begins to sing softly into her hair. She laughs at first, because the vibration of his voice is tickling her ear, but then she listens to him, her eyes closed. He's not got a bad voice. He's singing 'Eleanor Rigby'. She says quietly, 'So, did you save me then?'

'I don't think I needed to,' he says. 'I think you saved yourself.'

She smiles in the darkness. 'I did, didn't I?'

They lie there in silence for a moment, then he says, 'You never talk about your mum and dad, though.'

She feels herself stiffen. She wishes he hadn't said that. 'I don't want to.'

Ringo kisses her hair. 'When you do, I'm here, you know.'

'I know,' she says. She lies there, staring at the dark ceiling until Ringo's breathing becomes regular and heavy, and she knows he's fallen asleep.

'How. Fucking. Dare. You,' she breathes, though she's not talking to Ringo. She's mouthing the words spoken in anger all those months ago, sitting in the back of her father's car.

'Jenny!' snaps her father. 'I won't have language like that in front of your mother!'

'Turn this car around,' says Jenny levelly. 'I'm not going to Loughborough.'

'You'll do what you're told, young lady. You'll do what's best for you.'

'Jenny,' says Barbara. 'We only have your own interests at—'

'Turn around!' screams Jenny, lunging forward into the space between the front seats before her seatbelt snaps her tight. Her father tries to push her away with his left arm and she grabs on to it, screaming, 'Turn around turn around turn around!'

'Simon!' shrieks Barbara, and Jenny's father forces her off him, pushing her away into the back seat, but he's pulling down at the steering wheel with his right hand and the car is spinning off the road and on to a grass verge lined with trees and there's a squealing of brakes and a smell of burning rubber and a sudden crumple of metal and that's all that Jenny Ebert remembers.

The following morning Jenny takes the bus into Morecambe and heads straight to the accommodation office. The next hall of residence is set to open soon, and with a heavy heart, as though she's committing some strange act of betrayal, she puts her name down for a room.

'The second stage will be ready in a couple of weeks,' says the accommodation officer. 'So you'll be in well before this term ends.' She smiles encouragingly. 'Just in time for all the Christmas parties, eh? Be a bit livelier than that old folks' home. Bet you'll be glad to be among the living again.'

Outside she sees Amber and Saima, sharing an umbrella and both peering intently at their phones as they dash past. Jenny smiles but they hurry on without stopping. Not deliberately ignoring her, decides Jenny; just caught up in their own lives. She wonders if, come Christmas, she'll be like that. A normal student. Maybe Sunset Promenade will weaken and fade in her memory the longer she's away from it; maybe she'll look back in years to come and it will barely register; maybe it'll just be a few strange weeks in her life, hardly worthy of comment.

Jenny goes for a coffee in the refectory, looking around at the faces of her peers. She was so aching to be one of them, not long ago – so desperate to be accepted and welcomed. Now she wonders if she'll ever truly fit in. Back when she wanted to become a new Jenny Ebert she was cautious and shy about these clusters of other people her age; now that she's reconciled herself with the Jenny Ebert she always was, she feels just as separate from them.

Ringo bringing up her parents has coloured her mood, she realises, as she stares into the depths of her coffee. They still hang around her like ghosts, Simon and Barbara Ebert, as if to say, *Enjoy it while you can, Jenny, because our blood still flows through your veins – every chromosome in your body comes from us; we are your future.*

Then again, the blood of William J. Drake flows in her veins as well, albeit diluted. Maybe there's hope for her yet.

'Maybe he was a failure. But at least he tried,' Jenny remembers saying to her father.

'He didn't care about anyone! Just like you! It looks like the worst of him skipped a generation!' Simon Ebert shouts back to her across the months.

But he was wrong, wasn't he, her father? She does care about people. She's proved it. Maybe it was her mother who was the anomaly; maybe the true character is William's and Jenny's. That makes her smile a little, and she heads off to her lecture, where she sees Amber and Saima sheltering under the umbrella outside the hall.

'Are you moving into halls soon?' asks Saima.

Jenny makes a non-committal noise. 'I've just been to the office. So, yes I suppose.'

'No need to sound, like, ecstatic,' sniffs Amber.

'Hey, there was an old lady here looking for you,' says Saima.

'We told her you were at the accommodation office,' says Amber.

So they did see Jenny, then; just didn't bother to say hello. But . . . old lady?

'How old?' asks Jenny. She can only think it's Edna or . . . or Mrs Cantle.

Amber shrugs. 'Old old.'

'Was she . . . glamorous, would you say?' presses Jenny. 'Like, platinum-blonde hair? Well dressed?'

Saima snorts. 'I don't think so.'

Jenny breathes heavily. So, not Edna. And there's only one other old lady she knows. Mrs Cantle. But what's she doing here, so far from Sunset Promenade? Why has she come?

Then all the suspicion and paranoia come flooding back. The jewels. Being in her room. The fire. One after each film. And now the fourth and final film has been shown, and here, once again, is Mrs Cantle.

What does Mrs Cantle want?

She thinks about Eddie Monk in *Off Devil's Head*, investigating the smugglers off the Cornish coast, lured to an old fisherman's cabin on a remote beach at midnight.

'What did you bring me here for?' asks Monk.

'To shut you up,' says the bad guy. 'To stop you asking too many questions.'

'And how the hell are you going to do that?'

'The only way we know,' says the baddie. 'We're going to kill you.'

✳ 36 ✳

Phantom Lady

(1944, dir. Robert Siodmak)

Jenny rushes through the rain back to the accommodation office, so intent on her destination that she doesn't notice until he's pulled down the hood of his black coat that she's run right into Ringo.

'Hey, slow down, where are you going?'

'Come with me,' she says fiercely. 'I need you to see this. It's *her*. She's here. Now people will have to believe me.'

'Who's here?' says Ringo, putting a hand on her arm, which she shrugs off violently. 'What's going on?'

'Mrs Cantle,' says Jenny. 'Ever since I got here . . . I don't know why but she's . . .' Then it all pours out: the jewels, the locked room, the magnifying glass. Jenny is exhausted by the time the words have tumbled out. 'I told Edna but I don't think she believed me.'

Ringo is staring at her. 'Jenny,' he says gently. 'Think about what you're saying . . . why on earth—?'

'That's what I've been asking myself since this started,' she interrupts. 'But she's up to something, even if I have no idea what it is. And now you're coming with me and we're going to find out for ourselves.'

Ringo puffs up his cheeks and blows air out, hard. 'I'll come with you, of course I will. But you know how this sounds, right?'

She ignores him and stalks off towards the office, Ringo in her wake. She's approaching fast when she sees a figure – grey hair, in a camel raincoat – sheltering under a blue umbrella, with her back turned. Jenny begins to slow down.

Ringo catches up and says, 'Where is she?'

The woman turns round, looks at Ringo and raises an eyebrow.

'Hello, Jenny,' she says.

Jenny stops, the wind knocked out of her. Her arms drop to her sides. She's like a ship, suddenly becalmed. She can almost feel the weight of Ringo's quizzical stare on her.

Jenny says, 'Hello, Mum.'

Ringo's mouth falls open in a way she would find endearingly amusing if it wasn't done in the glare of Barbara Ebert's thin, pinched face. He says numbly, 'I thought your parents were dead.'

Barbara's eyebrow is still raised but otherwise her face remains impassive. She says, 'Dead. Is that what you've been telling everyone, Jennifer?'

Jenny closes her eyes. She says quietly, 'I'll speak to you about this later, Ringo.'

'But the crash,' he persists.

The corners of Barbara's mouth twitch. 'You said we died in a crash? *That* car crash?'

There's a squealing of brakes and a smell of burning rubber and a sudden crumple of metal and that's all that Jenny Ebert remembers as the seatbelt digs into her shoulder and chest and she is flung back against the seat, banging her head. She thinks she might have passed out for the briefest of moments, and when she opens her eyes again Simon Ebert is out of the car, standing with his hands on his head and inspecting the crushed front of the vehicle against the tree, smoke and steam pouring from under the bent bonnet.

'Are you all right?' shouts Barbara Ebert, releasing her seatbelt and turning to the back seat. 'Jenny? Are you all right?'

'I'm fine,' she mutters, pressing the button on her belt and climbing out of the car. It is a wreck. Barbara joins Simon and they stare in horror at the smashed front end.

'Jesus Christ!' he shouts finally. 'Jesus. Christ. Look at it. It's a write-off. I bet the insurance won't even pay out. I bet I'm not covered for . . . for . . .' He turns to glare at Jenny in fury. 'For acts of petulance by bloody stupid little girls!'

It is the first time Jenny has heard her father swear like that. She doesn't know what to say. Then the car suddenly slumps, and the front wheel nearest Simon Ebert springs off and rolls past him down the grass verge. He turns to watch its progress, incredulity on his face, until it gently bumps against a hedge and topples over.

Jenny starts laughing.

Barbara frowns at her and Simon's eyes widen in incandescent fury. 'She's laughing,' he says, to no one in particular.

'I guess we're not going to Loughborough after all,' says Jenny through her manic, uncontrollable laughing.

'You can do what you want to!' scowls Simon Ebert. 'Go to bloody Timbuktu for all I care.'

'Simon,' says Barbara mildly. 'Perhaps you should call the AA . . . ?'

He makes a snorting noise, gets out his phone and begins to jab at it. Jenny reaches into the car and gets the box of DVDs, then starts to walk away, back the way they came.

'Where's she going now?' snarls Simon.

'Jenny!' shouts Barbara. 'Jennifer! You can't walk home! It's miles. Come here at once and wait for the AA man.'

But Jenny keeps walking and with every step she puts between herself and her parents, she feels lighter, as though she's finally shaking off the shackles they've had on her since birth. But how far will she have to walk to be utterly free of them, of the boring, dull chromosomes they built her from? Is there a place far away enough in the world? In the universe?

'Jennifer Ebert!' shouts Barbara, ever more distantly. 'Where do you think you're going?'

'Timbuk-fucking-tu!' she cries, and clutching the box of precious William J. Drake DVDs to her chest, she begins to run down the country lane as fast as she possibly can.

'Wow,' says Ringo. He looks very confused, bless him, thinks Jenny. She puts a hand to his face.

'I'll talk to you later. I promise.'

He looks at her. 'You lied to me,' he says in a small voice.

'Later,' she says insistently. She kisses him on his unyielding lips. 'Go home. I'll be back soon.'

He shakes his head and looks at Barbara as though he can't quite believe she's standing in front of him. 'You said they were dead. What sort of messed-up person does that, Jenny?'

Barbara looks at Jenny, 'Yes. What sort of messed-up person says those sorts of things?'

'Go. Home.' Jenny stares pointedly at Ringo.

He nods, as though in a daze. 'Yeah. I think I will.' He hesitantly holds out a hand towards Barbara, then withdraws it, as though he is worried she actually is dead. 'Well. Nice to meet you. I'm, uh, glad you're alive.'

'More than some people are, apparently.'

Ringo shakes his head and glances one last time at Jenny. Her heart sinks at the unfamiliar look in his eye. Something like fury tempered with sadness.

'Where is *home*, anyway?' says Barbara as Ringo walks uncertainly away. 'I've been all over this campus looking for you.'

'Sunset Promenade,' says Jenny. 'I chose it because you'd never have found me in a million years. They put me in an article in some local newspaper piece, which I wasn't happy about, but they spelled my name wrong. So even if you'd have bothered to try to google me, you wouldn't have found me.' She looks curiously at Barbara Ebert. 'But why now? Why have you come?'

Barbara says, 'Because you're our daughter, Jenny. Because we're family, and we miss you.'

Jenny takes Barbara to a coffee shop in town, a long walk through the rain from the campus. They sit in a booth at the back, hanging their rain-wet coats from hooks on the wall, and Barbara leaves her umbrella, still opened, by the table to drain. Jenny orders a latte, Barbara has a cup of tea. Typically dull and boring.

'So,' says Jenny. 'Why are you here?'

Barbara stares into the depths of her tea. She doesn't say anything for a long time. Then she looks up at Jenny. 'When I was young, I wanted to be an artist.'

Jenny frowns at her. And this is relevant how . . . ? But she says nothing, and her silence is an invitation to her mother to continue.

'I was good at art in school. Better than good. I was exceptional. All my teachers said so. They wanted me to go to art college. I wanted to go.' She meets Jenny's eye. 'My father wanted me to go, too. Your grandfather. William J. Drake. But just like my mother had turned him away from his film-making, she persuaded me that there was no future in pursuing art.' Barbara smiles thinly at her daughter. 'And I listened. Just like my father had listened to her. And I didn't go to college at all, didn't go to university. I abandoned art. I did a few middle-of-the-road jobs until I met your father and we got married. Needless to say, my mother approved wholeheartedly of Simon.'

'Do you remember what Dad said to me?' says Jenny quietly. 'He said that the worst of William Drake had skipped a generation. Had skipped you and had settled in me, he meant.'

Barbara's eyes are shining and wet. 'Yes, he did say that. He was wrong. And it wasn't the worst of your grandfather. It was the best. Dreams and ambitions. How can that be the worst of someone?'

'You let them knock it out of you.'

Barbara nods. 'Yes, I did. And I was going to let it be knocked out of you as well. Because I've had a happy life, Jenny. I'm satisfied. There's nothing wrong with a life that is . . . ordinary, you know. Billions of people have ordinary lives.'

Jenny sips her coffee. It has gone cold. She says, 'Why did you hide my grandfather's films from me?'

'Because he hid them away himself,' she says. 'After he married my mother, after he married Joan. She didn't want them around the house, didn't want them to be a reminder of the life he gave up. He showed them to me once, when I was a little younger than you. I'd had no idea before that of what he did when he was younger. I thought . . . I was worried . . .' She pauses, gathers herself. 'I thought if you knew about them then nothing could stop you from following your own path.'

Jenny stares at her. 'And that would be a bad thing?'

'No,' says Barbara finally. 'No. I was secretly delighted when you found them. William Drake gave up his dreams, and so did I. And I think I'd started to believe that ambitions were a bad thing, that because William had ultimately had a not-unhappy life, and I'd had a not-unhappy life, then maybe they just got in the way.'

Jenny leans forward. 'A not-unhappy life is not the same as a happy life.'

Barbara nods. 'That's why I'm here. We were worried about you, Jenny. Your father said to give you space, that you'd come round. And I did give you some space. But now I'm here to tell you that . . . that it's fine. That I approve. That I want you to follow your star.'

'And Dad? What does he think?'

Barbara smiles. 'He still thinks you should do economics. But he's a bit resigned, to be honest.' She digs in her handbag for her purse. 'There's something else as well . . . your father knows this chap at his golf club. They were talking about my father's films, and . . . well. It appears those thirty-five-millimetre reels are valuable. Very valuable, in fact. This friend of your father knows a collector of such things, and he's spoken to him and . . .' Barbara pushes a business card across the table. 'That's his number. And on the back is the price he would be willing to pay for all the William J. Drake memorabilia. The films, the scripts, the notes. Though I imagine that's a low opening offer, and he could be pushed higher.'

Jenny takes the card and flips it over, and her eyes widen. 'That's . . . wow. That could pay for all my university fees. Twice over. And then some. Wow.' She narrows her eyes. 'You've told him he can have them?'

'I told your father that they're not mine any more, they're yours,' says Barbara. 'He grumbled a bit, of course, but I was quite firm. They are yours, Jenny, and furthermore I said that I doubted you would sell them.' She nods at the card. 'But it's entirely up to you. He also wants to discuss buying or leasing the rights to release them on DVD or license them to TV. I've checked, by the way, and the rights to them were owned by my father. And now they're yours. But that's a whole different negotiation to be had. There's apparently quite an appetite for old films again these days, especially ones that haven't been seen very often.'

Jenny looks at the card again, then puts it in her pocket. Her cup is empty. She says, 'I'm sorry I said you were dead.'

Barbara shrugs. 'I'm sorry we gave you reason to say that.'

'So you're not going to try to persuade me to come home? Go back to Loughborough?'

'Go back to Loughborough, no. If you're happy here then I want you to stay.' She stands up and puts on her coat. 'But as for coming home . . . it is still your home, Jenny.'

Barbara gathers her things, then says, 'I thought I knew who I wanted to be, Jenny, and I let people tell me otherwise. That's not going to happen to you.'

Jenny feels a tear rolling down her cheek. 'But I'm not even sure I know who I want to be.'

Barbara pats her hand. 'You're young. There's plenty of time for that.'

Then Jenny throws her arms around her mother and holds her tighter and tighter, and she feels Barbara's arms around her, and she wonders to herself what this feeling is that makes her warm and shivery at the same time. She can't understand why she can never remember her mother's arms around her so tightly before, and hopes that she doesn't have to go through the rest of her life without a hug from her like this again. She buries her face in her mother's shoulder and cries and cries and cries, and to her utter astonishment it's because she's so unexpectedly happy.

37

Kill Her Gently

(1957, dir. Charles Saunders)

Jenny has no real idea how she gets back to Sunset Promenade, she's in such a daze. She stands in the lobby, sopping wet, a puddle forming beneath her squelching shoes. She feels full to bursting, as though she might throw up. Edna emerges from the day room and looks at her impassively. 'You're wet through.'

'I'll catch my death,' says Jenny, and giggles, horrifying herself. She looks down at her sodden clothes. 'Have you seen Ringo?'

Edna nods. 'Hmm. More than that, I've spoken to him. The poor boy's in shock.'

Jenny stares at her. 'He's told you?'

'Oh, he didn't come running in telling tales, don't worry. I found him in the living room, looking like he'd been hit by a train. He didn't want to tell me but I coaxed it out of him. He says he saw your mother today. The one that you'd told him died in a car crash.'

'Where is he?' says Jenny impatiently.

'I'd be surprised if he wanted to speak to you,' observes Edna frostily.

'Please don't judge me,' says Jenny, her voice wavering. 'I've had a bit of a shock myself today.'

Edna raises one eyebrow, invites her to go on.

'My mum . . . my mum's not who I thought she was.'

Edna shrugs. 'I think you'll find many people are not who you think they are,' she says pointedly. 'If you really want to see Ringo, he's probably down on the beach.'

✳

'Hi,' says Jenny. 'Building pebble towers?'

Ringo says nothing for a while, just stares out to sea. Then he says, 'Building towers is when you want to make something permanent, or at least that might last.' He draws back his arm and lets loose a flat stone that bounces once, twice, three times across the dark water. 'Skimming stones is for when you want to escape.'

'And that's what you want, is it? To escape?'

Ringo bends down and selects another stone from his pile, turning it over this way and that in his hands. 'Maybe.'

She watches him skim the stone, then puts a hand on his arm. He shrugs her off. She says quietly, 'Let me explain.'

'Fire away.' He still hasn't looked at her.

She looks curiously at him. 'Why are you so upset?'

Finally he turns and meets her gaze. 'You lied to me, Jenny. About something so serious. You said your parents were dead.'

She sighs. 'It wasn't intentional. It was just a story. It was . . .' She casts around for the right analogy. 'Armour. A shield. To stop people asking too many questions about me. So I didn't have to talk about my boring life. To make me sound more . . . interesting.'

There's something in his eyes that upsets her. It could be hatred. It could be pity. 'So you made up a story that your parents had died in a car crash? Do you know how screwed up that is?'

'Once I'd said it, I didn't know how to unsay it,' she says, lamely. 'It was the whole Lauren Bacall thing, the femme fatale . . .' She realises how stupid it all sounds, and shuts up.

Ringo is silent for a while, rubbing his fingers over a flat stone. He tosses it into the water.

'I thought we had something.' Another stone, four bounces.

'We did. We *do*, don't we? Have something?' She pauses. 'Or do you mean you thought we had something in common? Dead parents? Is that what drew you to me? Is it the whole "Eleanor Rigby" thing again?' Her eyes widen. 'Did you think if you saved me you could in some way save yourself? Is that what this was all about?'

'No!' says Ringo fiercely. 'It was nothing like that! In fact I think I might . . . might have . . .'

'What?' she says, willing him to say it. *Fallen in love with you.* 'What?'

'Doesn't matter.' He sounds like a petulant child. Another skim. 'What did she want, anyway, your dead mother?'

Jenny looks out to sea. 'I think she came to remind me that she was still alive.'

By the time she has finished her story, Ringo has stopped skimming stones and has been absently building a new stack of rocks, from widest to smallest, in front of her. She doesn't know what this means, or if it means anything.

'Wow,' he says eventually. 'Just goes to show, I suppose. You never know who people really are.'

Jenny smiles. It feels weird and right and wrong all at the same time. 'I suppose.'

He places a stone that wobbles then settles on the stack. 'So what are you going to do? Sell your grandfather's stuff?'

'I don't know. I'm still processing it. What would you do?'

He breathes out for a long time. 'I've no idea. You could be rich, relatively. Depends on how important it all is to you.' Another stone. The stack topples over.

Jenny thinks about it. 'It's important, I suppose.' She's set so much store by her maverick film-maker grandfather, thought he was the ideal she should aspire to. She never knew about her own mother's dreams. Never thought to ask.

The sky is darkening above them. 'We should get back,' says Ringo. 'We don't want to get stranded.'

'The tide's going out,' counters Jenny. She pauses and says, 'Are you still angry with me?'

Ringo nods. 'Yes. Yes, I am. You lied to me and I don't care what the reasons were. You lied to me and you didn't need to. And if there's one thing I hate, it's lies.' He looks at her. 'My mum told me she'd never leave me, you know. Even when she knew she was dying.'

He turns and walks back up the wet sand. Jenny feels like she wants to take his hand, but doesn't know how he'll react, doesn't know if things have changed so much between them that it would be a weird, unwelcome thing to do. She watches him go for a while then follows him, catching him up at the road.

'I wonder what's for dinner,' says Ringo as they cross the road to the stone steps leading up to Sunset Promenade.

Jenny grimaces. The very thought of eating ties her stomach in knots. 'I think I'll give it a miss. I'm going to get out of these clothes, have a bath.' She pauses, the words she wants to say feeling like stones in her mouth. 'If you wanted . . . maybe you could come to my room later . . . ?'

They climb the steps in silence. Ringo turns to her at the door. 'Maybe you need to be on your own for a while. You've got a lot to think about. Maybe I have, as well.'

He stands still for a minute, then turns back to her. 'I don't think you realise how shitty a thing it is you've done, Jenny. Not just to your parents, though God knows what they think. But to me, to everyone here. We've all lost people, Jenny. You haven't. Having people you love dying on you . . . it's not a story to hide behind. It's something that can take over your entire life, if you let it. It's like Mrs Cantle told me. Real life's not like the pictures. When bad things happen, they're really bad. You've made it something small and convenient, when it's totally the opposite.'

She watches him head into the dining room, shaking the rain off his jacket. Being on her own is the last thing she wants right now. As she begins to climb the stairs she wonders how it is that with so many people in her life, she can feel so alone.

Soaking in the bath warms her chilled bones through, and she wonders if there are baths in the new accommodation block on campus. Unlikely. She's not even sure they have en-suite shower rooms. All this is going, she thinks, Sunset Promenade all around her; all this is falling down like one of Ringo's pebble stacks. Everything disappearing under the rolling tides.

She sinks under the water, holding her breath, eyes tight shut. She's been in the bath an hour now and the water is, at best, tepid. She inspects her fingertips, wrinkled like prunes, and wonders if your fingerprints are the same when your skin is like that, ridged and etched by the water.

Jenny feels hungry, finally, but can't face the others. She dries off and moisturises and puts her wet hair in a ponytail, wrapping herself in her dressing gown. Then she pads quietly down the stairs and into the dining room, cleared after dinner, and then the large kitchen beyond. In the fridge she finds a clingfilm-covered plate of cold chicken. Contemplating the effort of making a sandwich, instead she just wolfs down three of the slices and washes them down with a mouthful of orange juice straight from the carton.

Back in the hall, she listens for a moment at the door to the day room. She can hear Ringo's voice. They're all playing cards. Life is going on at Sunset Promenade, even after Barry's bombshell.

Climbing the stairs again, Jenny ponders Ringo. He's angry and he's every right to be. God, her mother ought to be even more angry, come to that. Jenny told everyone they were dead. True, she wanted a clean start, wanted to be different from the Jenny Ebert who was at Loughborough. A nice, untroubled family life didn't fit with the femme fatale character she was trying to be. But did she have to go that far? The chicken suddenly weighs heavy in her stomach, makes her feel like she's going to throw up. She said they were dead. Ringo's right. What sort of person does that?

Jenny tries to read for a while, then listens to music, then puts on a DVD and watches Humphrey Bogart in *The Big Sleep*, hoping for some inspiration from the title at least. But she can feel no sleep approaching any time soon. She watches the movie to the final credits and looks at her phone. Ten. She can hear footsteps on the stairs and the sound of voices as Sunset Promenade folds itself into the night and people go to bed.

Jenny turns off the light and kills the TV, and lies there for a while in the darkness. She's left the curtains open, in the hope that the sky will clear and she can see the stars. Funny how things so far away can make her feel connected to someone just a couple of doors down the corridor. She wonders if Ringo's looking out as well, waiting for a break in the clouds.

She hears a footstep creak on the floorboards outside her door.

Jenny holds her breath.

Someone is turning the doorknob, ever so slightly. She listens to it squeak, then fall silent.

Come in, come in, she wills him. For God's sake, Ringo, come in.

Jenny lies flat on her back and closes her eyes. Her skin feels on fire at the thought of Ringo, at the idea of him standing outside her door, wondering what to do. She wants to scream at him, wants to throw open the door and drag him inside. But there's nothing.

Jenny's bed suddenly feels very large and very empty. She smooths the front of her nightdress, rubs her stomach. Where do you want him? she asks herself. Is it here? She touches her heart. Here? Her head. Here? Does it matter?

Then she hears the floorboard shift again. Finally. Thank God. She thinks she might explode if he doesn't get a move on. The doorknob rattles again and there's a click, and a sliver of light appears around the doorframe.

Jenny closes her eyes and waits. She hears the door swing open and then close again. She smiles as he walks with small, light steps across her carpet, around to her side of the bed. Jenny stifles a giggle. She can hear Ringo breathing.

'Come on,' she says, low, throaty.

Nothing happens. Jenny opens her eyes and sees Ringo silhouetted against the faint glow of the pale moonlight filtering in through the window as there's a sudden break in the clouds.

It's not Ringo.

But she knows who it is.

'Mrs Cantle,' says Jenny, suddenly breathless. 'What are you doing?'

Mrs Cantle lifts the pillow she's holding in her thin hands and the black, shadowy figure of her says, 'What do you think I'm doing, dear? I'm killing you.'

Then Mrs Cantle puts the pillow firmly over Jenny's face.

* 38 *

Murder, My Sweet

(1944, dir. Edward Dmytryk)

After a long moment, Jenny says, 'Mrs Cantle? I think one of us should probably move the pillow now.'

Mrs Cantle sighs and takes away the pillow that has really just been resting on Jenny's face. 'You're quite right, dear,' she says, lowering her thin frame on to the chair by the desk.

Jenny sits up and turns on the bedside light. Mrs Cantle looks sad and a little confused, but also strangely . . . relieved?

'What's going on, Mrs Cantle?'

'I suppose it's all just a game, really. Is that it, now? Is it over?'

'Was it really you all this time?' says Jenny. 'Did you hide your jewels? Did you lock me in my room? Did you try to start the fire in my wastepaper bin?'

'I suppose so, mostly,' nods Mrs Cantle. She smiles enthusiastically. 'It was the films, you see.' She begins to count them off on her fingers. 'Jewels and imprisonment and arson and murder!'

'Just a game,' says Jenny hollowly. She cannot bring herself to be angry at Mrs Cantle, and she's no longer afraid of the old woman. She just feels an incredible sadness.

'I'm glad that's an end to it now,' she says. 'It was quite against my nature, you see. I would much rather have gone on a cruise.' She looks at the pillow in her hands. 'I think I'd like to go to bed now.'

Jenny slides out from under the duvet and accompanies Mrs Cantle down the stairs to her own room. At the door the old lady says, 'Thank you, dear. And I'm sorry for any inconvenience.'

'You're not going to try to kill me again or anything, are you?' cautions Jenny. 'I don't have to lock you in your room, do I?'

Mrs Cantle stifles a yawn and shakes her head. 'I'll be out for the count as soon as my head touches the pillow.' She brightens. 'Like you were supposed to be, dear!'

When Mrs Cantle has closed the door, Jenny stands there for a long moment, pondering, then shakes her head and returns up the stairs. She pauses outside her room, then carries on down the corridor and knocks on Ringo's door.

'Are you decent?' she whispers. 'It's me.' Then she opens the door anyway. Ringo is sitting up in bed, his thin, birdlike chest bare.

'Jenny?' he says. 'I don't think you should really be here. I've been thinking a lot and I'm not sure we can really come back from this.'

She closes the door and walks over to the bed. 'Budge over,' she says. 'And before you say anything, don't. Mrs Cantle's just tried to kill me and after everything that's happened today I don't really want to be on my own.'

As she slides under the covers, Ringo's eyes goggle as he processes everything she's saying. 'Mrs Cantle tried to *kill* you?'

'I'll explain later,' says Jenny. 'I'm sorry for telling you my parents were dead. It was horrible and wrong and I feel really bad. Now tell me you forgive me, then shut up and kiss me.'

The next morning, under the hot spray of the shower in her en-suite, Jenny wonders what she's supposed to do now. Should she go to the Granges and tell them everything? The only reason she held off about the supposedly missing jewels in the first place was because it might have put Sunset Promenade in jeopardy, but that's a moot point now that the place will have to be sold anyway. What will she achieve? Mrs Cantle is obviously very confused. Does that necessarily mean she's harmless, though? What if Jenny had been asleep? What if Mrs Cantle had been stronger? Did she really intend to kill her?

So, here we are again. It was all true; all her suspicions were real. Mrs Cantle had been out to get her. She had done everything that Jenny thought she had. Towelling off, Jenny wipes the condensation from the mirror with her hand. Stares at her reflection. She should be happy, should feel vindicated. Instead she just feels sick to her stomach. It's like the bubble she'd surrounded herself with has burst. Ringo, her mother appearing just that little more human, the value of William J. Drake's body of work, the friendships that have blossomed in the rest home. Even with the imminent end of it all, the closure of Sunset Promenade looming on the horizon, it still felt as though everything was heading towards a vaguely satisfying conclusion. It was like the bittersweet ending to a movie; some sadness, but also some closure. None of the main players left broken or dead. A new day would dawn, as always, leaving people changed but perhaps the better for it.

Mrs Cantle's confession has thrown confusion over everything. The third act is in disarray. This was not how it was supposed to end.

Jenny wipes the re-forming condensation away again and brushes her teeth. Maybe because things don't end, she thinks. Maybe because real life isn't the movies. Maybe because there's no neat three-act structure. Things can just keep happening. Good things, bad things. Mediocre, boring things. These are just the actions of a confused old lady.

She isn't going to tell anyone else. What's the point? To hasten the demise of Sunset Promenade, already tumbling over the edge of the abyss? To get Mrs Cantle in trouble? To sow suspicion and fear among the residents?

She'd told Ringo, of course, and asked him not to say anything until she'd decided what she was going to do. He believes her, she thinks. Or at least he says he does. Which is a start. So what she's going to do, she decides as she pulls a brush through her damp hair, is go down to breakfast and sit with Ringo and say nothing about Mrs Cantle, and they'll all see out their time in Sunset Promenade and they'll all go their separate ways and hope-fully, everyone will find some measure of happiness, or at least not unhappiness. And while it is true that not being unhappy is not quite the same as being happy, Jenny can only hope that Joe and Mr Robinson, Edna and Mrs Cantle, Florin and the Granges . . . she can only hope that they'll be as fine as they possibly can be.

From under the bed, her grandfather's last will and testament – the only surviving copies of his movies – seems to glint at her in the light from her lamp. Jenny glares at them. 'What?' she demands.

But they don't *say* anything, of course. They are just nitrate-based cellulose, their stories trapped on them until released by light and motion, after all. Still, they seem to be speaking to her nonetheless.

But Jenny ignores them, and plugs in her hairdryer. After all, what can she do?

When she has dressed and done her make-up in the dull light of the grey day that sits heavily outside her window, Jenny heads downstairs for breakfast and to think some more. As she reaches the ground floor she hears a hammering on the front door. Probably Bernie with another grocery delivery. He'll be sad to see this place sold off and the residents go. She can't imagine the owners of a major care home corporation having much truck with his Pepsi bottles full of home brew.

Neither Florin nor the Grange brothers seem to be around, so Jenny opens the door herself. It isn't Bernie, however; it's a tanned, fit-looking man in his late fifties, wearing a pink polo shirt and a pair of chinos and an angry look on his face.

'Let me in,' he demands. 'Do you work here? I want to see the manager. I've come to collect someone.'

Jenny steps back as he pushes past her and looks around the reception hall, shaking his head. 'Bloody hell. Heads are going to roll for this, I can tell you.'

'I don't work here, I live here,' says Jenny.

The man frowns and looks her up and down. 'What?'

'Never mind, I'll find someone,' she says. 'What did you say your name was?'

'Grey,' he says, folding his arms. 'Ronald Grey. And I want to know why my mother Edna is being kept here.'

Her mind racing, Jenny runs to the kitchens to find Florin, who calls Barry Grange on his mobile. Within five minutes Barry is there, nodding and frowning as he listens to Ronald Grey.

'This is quite . . . irregular, Mr Grey.'

'You're telling me,' says Ronald. 'I work away a lot – I've been in the Middle East for the past two months – and it was only when I got home late last night that I had a message on my answerphone from my mother saying she was here and she wanted to go home.' He rubs the back of his neck. 'I thought she was supposed to be on a cruise with that friend of hers, Margaret Cantle.' He looks around. 'And she's in a care home on the Lancashire coast. This is like some kind of surreal farce.'

'More of a rest home than a care home,' says Barry. 'But I take your point. Florin, I think you'd better go and get Mrs Grey.'

'Don't bother, she's here,' says Ronald Grey, looking towards the stairs. 'Mum!'

'Ronald!'

Barry looks to Florin, who looks to Jenny, who looks back at Florin, as Ronald Grey's mother descends the stairs. Jenny is the first one to speak.

'That's not Edna Grey,' she says slowly. 'That's Mrs Cantle.'

39

Strange Impersonation

(1946, dir. Anthony Mann)

It is Florin who speaks next. 'So if Mrs Cantle is really Edna Grey
. . . who is Edna Grey?'

Mrs Cantle – or the woman formerly known as Mrs Cantle –
laughs. 'Oh, Florin. That's Margaret Cantle. It's all quite simple,
really. I am really Edna Grey but I was pretending to be Margaret
Cantle, and Margaret Cantle was pretending to be me, who is
Edna Grey.' She pauses. 'I think that's right.'

Barry decides that this business will be best conducted in the
privacy of the office, especially as Ronald Grey is bandying about
the names of lawyers with whom he's on close personal terms. At
the door, Barry smiles at Jenny. 'Thank you, I'll take it from here.'

'Oh, let her stay,' says Mrs Cantle – or Mrs Grey, Jenny supposes,
confused – 'it's all really about her, anyway.'

'Will someone please tell me what's going on?' demands Ronald
as Florin brings in a tray of coffee.

Barry begins to speak but closes his mouth and blinks as Jenny
says, 'Suppose you tell us what you think is meant to be going
on, Mr Grey?'

Ronald takes a deep breath. 'I live in London. Winchmore Hill.
After I got divorced a couple of years ago, I built an annexe for Mum
to come and live in. I'm an aerospace engineer and my work takes me
away for long stretches – I've just done two months in Saudi. To be
honest, I was getting a bit worried about Mum . . .' He smiles at the
woman Jenny can't stop thinking of as Mrs Cantle but now knows is
really Edna Grey. 'You've been getting a bit confused, haven't you?'

'Don't talk to me as though I'm a child, Ronald,' chides Edna.

'I was concerned about leaving her, but then Mrs Cantle rode to the rescue.'

'So you do know Ed— the other Mrs Cantle,' says Barry.

Ronald nods. 'The real Mrs Cantle. The *only* Mrs Cantle. She's lived close to us for years. Lived there much longer than me.' He blows a low whistle. 'She and Mum had become friends recently, and when Mrs Cantle suggested they both go on a three-month round-the-world cruise for the period I was away – all paid for by Mrs Cantle – it seemed the perfect solution.'

'She paid for the cruise for both of them?' says Barry, frowning. 'She has a house in Winchmore Hill? So she's rich?'

Ronald shrugs. 'She's not poor, that's for sure.'

'Wait,' says Jenny, clicking her fingers. 'Did you say cruise? The postcards!'

Ronald nods. 'That was what I couldn't understand. When I got home last night there was a pile of postcards on the mat. Egypt, Cyprus, Eilat . . . having a lovely time, all that, weather's a bit hot, saw dolphins today.'

'That was Margaret's idea,' says Edna proudly. 'She really did think everything through. She bought the foreign stamps off the internet and everything.'

Ronald says, 'Then I got the message on the answerphone.'

'That was my phone,' says Jenny. 'Your mum asked to borrow it. I didn't know why.'

Ronald shakes his head. 'I was up all night trying to find out where this place was and got here as soon as I could.' He points at Barry. 'You're lucky I didn't bring the police with me. Now it's your turn. Speak.'

Barry opens his hands wide. 'I don't know what to say. The woman I thought was Mrs Grey got in touch, said she and her friend wanted to relocate here and had heard good things about us. We had rooms . . . Mrs—The *other* Mrs Cantle paid upfront, in cash, for the first three months.'

'Didn't you run any checks?' says Ronald in disbelief.

'We asked for all the usual identification documents,' protests Barry. 'Birth certificates, pension books, that sort of thing. They were all in order.' He pauses. 'I thought, anyway.'

'We just swapped them!' says Edna delightedly. 'It was very easy. Nobody looks that closely at old ladies, you know. Then Margaret pretended to be me and I pretended to be her. I had to remember a lot of things, it was quite difficult sometimes.'

There's a long silence in the office, then Ronald shakes his head. 'But why?'

Edna points at Jenny. 'It was all to do with her. Margaret never gave me the full details.' Edna looks around the room with a serious expression. 'It's about something that happened a long time ago. And Margaret wanted her revenge.' She screws her eyes up. 'It was very clear that I had to pretend to be Mrs Cantle, in case Jenny somehow found out why that name was important. So it would not link Margaret to everything if it all came out.'

Ronald pushes his coffee cup away. 'Mum, get your things. I've heard enough. I'm taking you home.' He looks at Barry. 'You haven't heard the last of this.'

'Oh, he hasn't done anything wrong,' says Edna.

Barry nods vigorously. 'Quite. In fact, I'm the victim here.'

Jenny stands up. 'Mr Grey. Don't do anything rash yet. Let me deal with this. Let me have it out with Margaret Cantle. It's all to do with me for some reason, anyway.'

Ronald shrugs. 'I'm still taking my mother home.'

Edna stands up as well, and digs in her handbag. She brings out Mr Robinson's medal and Joe's photograph and hands them to Barry. 'Could you make sure these get back to their proper owners? And apologise from me. It was all part of the game, you see.' Then she opens her arms to embrace Jenny. 'It was lovely meeting you, dear. I'm sorry about everything, especially trying to murder you.'

Ronald and Barry stare at each other, wide-eyed, as Jenny races from the office. 'Murder?' says Ronald hollowly.

'I'll explain on the way home,' says Edna. 'But all told, I think it's probably best to let sleeping dogs lie for now.'

Jenny finds the woman she now knows to be Margaret Cantle outside, standing by the taped-off chasm that still hasn't been filled from when the access road washed away, before any of this even started. She is wearing a long raincoat, though the downpour of earlier that morning has stopped and the clouds appear to be thinning. She's standing with her back to Sunset Promenade, considering the wet sand and rocks far below. Clutched in her hands is a rectangular paper bag.

'Hello, Jenny,' she says, without turning round.

'Hello, *Mrs Cantle*,' says Jenny.

At last, she turns. 'Ah. Then it's all come out, has it?'

'Edna's son has turned up to collect her,' Jenny says. 'I was wondering why she had called the person I thought was your son when she borrowed my phone. I'm glad I never mentioned that to you. You'd probably have got to him first, and none of us would be any the wiser.'

Margaret smiles thinly. 'Quite the little detective, aren't you?'

'It was all you, wasn't it? You put poor old Mrs Grey up to everything. The thefts. Locking me in my room. The fire in the bin. To get at me. But why?'

Margaret considers this. 'Are you going to turn me in?'

Jenny stares at her. 'You had her put a pillow over my head last night! That's . . . that's *incitement*, at the very least. She could have killed me!'

Margaret turns to look at the sea. It is an almost invisible grey thread on the horizon, acres of damp sand between it and them. 'Edna is a very confused old lady,' she says. 'I'm not sure how viable her testimony would be. Besides, the pillow was all her own doing. She decided to think for herself. Got a little bit carried away, I'm afraid.'

'But why?' says Jenny, bewildered. 'Why me? What have I ever done to you?'

Margaret hands the paper package to Jenny. Inside is a DVD case. She says, 'You have a choice. Turn me in to the Granges now, and I will sit quietly and await my fate. Or take this and watch it, then come and find me.'

'You'll do a runner!'

Margaret shakes her head. 'I won't, dear. I'll be here. Nearby. You'll find me if you know where to look.'

Jenny stares at the DVD case, then cracks it open. There's a disc inside, unmarked. She looks at Margaret. 'What is it?'

'That,' says Margaret Cantle, 'contains the rushes for *Dark Retribution*, the only surviving footage.'

'A film?' says Jenny. 'I've never heard of it.'

'You wouldn't have. It was never completed. Had it been finished . . . it would have been William J. Drake's crowning glory. It would have been your grandfather's fifth, and greatest, movie.'

Jenny looks at the disc. 'How did you get this? I never even knew it existed.'

'I've had it for a long time. On thirty-five-millimetre film. Thank you for your advice on getting it transferred to DVD, I found a place not far from here. I thought that would make it easier.'

Jenny stares at the blank DVD case in her hand. The fifth film of William J. Drake. She feels her heart racing, the hairs on her arms prickling. The lost, unfinished, final movie by her grandfather. She looks at Margaret Cantle. 'You know I can't resist this.'

Margaret says, 'Find me when you've seen it. First, give me your phone.'

Jenny hesitates. 'Why?'

'Phone.'

Jenny frowns. Margaret raises an eyebrow in challenge. Jenny shrugs. 'Fine. Take it. I'll watch this. Of course I will. I couldn't not, could I? But then you're going to tell me exactly what's going on.'

It's a rough and largely unordered series of scenes, only about half an hour's worth. It's magnificent. At the end there are some make-shift title screens. *STARRING GEORGE STORM*, they say. *WITH EDGAR TEAGUE*. And *INTRODUCING MAGGIE LORELEI*.

When the screen goes blank, Jenny stares at it for a long time. Then she races to Margaret's room, which is of course empty. There's no sign of her in the day room, or the dining room, or the kitchens. Jenny goes back to her room and only then notices the handle of the green bag she'd stored under her bed flopping on to the rug. She pulls it out and sees it's empty. The film canisters have gone. The scripts, the notebooks, the DVDs. Everything relating to her grandfather. All gone. And she knows who has them. The final theft. The last crime.

The villain unmasked.

Jenny rushes downstairs to the terrace and looks out to sea. Right on the shoreline there's a tiny dot of a figure.

You'll find me if you know where to look.

Jenny heads back inside and hammers on Ringo's door, bursting in as he sits on his bed, tapping away on his laptop.

'What's going on?' he says. 'Mrs Cantle's son was here, only Mrs Cantle's not Mrs Cantle, she's Mrs Grey. Or something.'

'Later,' says Jenny, heading for the telescope. 'Can you point this at the beach?'

Ringo shrugs and aims the telescope, peering into the focus finder. 'What are you looking for?'

Jenny shoulders him away and puts her eye to the telescope, swinging it around the shoreline until she finds the figure, standing at the water's edge, her back to the beach and Sunset Promenade. It's Margaret.

'Gotcha,' breathes Jenny.

'Are you going to tell me what's going on?' says Ringo.

She plants a quick kiss on his lips. 'I will, I promise. But not now.'

Then she's running out of the room. Ringo shakes his head and puts his eye to the focus finder, trying to see what's got Jenny so excited.

* 40 *

The Unfaithful

(1947, dir. Vincent Sherman)

There's a sliver of blue sky up there in the breaking clouds. A nice day for it, thinks Margaret Cantle, standing on the damp sand. The sea laps at her boots, crawling back up the beach inch by inch. Margaret, she says to herself. Maggie. It feels so good not to be Edna Grey any more, like finally taking off a shabby and ill-fitting dress. She feels like herself again. And not a moment too soon.

She turns away from the chill wind blowing off the sea to watch Jenny walking across the beach, alone, towards her. It's a good half-mile from the road, but Maggie is patient. She has to be. She's waited six decades for this. She can afford to wait a few minutes longer. She hefts the big green sports bag higher on her shoulder.

Jenny finally reaches her and stops, hands in the pockets of her anorak, watching her. 'You have my things,' she says. 'My films. The notes. Everything.'

'Yes,' Maggie says. 'You watched it? The DVD?'

'Maggie Lorelei,' says Jenny. 'That was you. God, you were so beautiful.'

Maggie inclines her head slightly. 'Thank you.'

'And so talented. You shone out of those rushes. You were amazing. What happened? What happened to Maggie Lorelei? She should have been a star.'

'She went back to being just plain old Margaret Cantle.'

Jenny shakes her head. 'But why? What happened?'

Maggie fixes her stare on the girl. 'Your grandfather happened. William J. Drake happened. Or rather, he stopped happening.'

Jenny takes a step forward. 'Tell me.'

Maggie sighs. 'It's a long story, and it all happened so long ago. Are you sure?'

Jenny looks at the sea. 'Tell me.'

'I started off as a dancer,' says Maggie. 'When I was very young, sixteen. I got work in C. B. Cochran's revue shows in London: *Big Ben*, *Bless the Bride*, *The Ivory Tower* . . .' She pauses, gathering her thoughts, assembling the memories that are as vibrant as images on a cinema screen, untarnished by time. 'My big plan was to go to drama school, but my family had no money. My father was a fishmonger at Billingsgate, my mother worked in a post office. So I did little jobs, and then landed a role dancing in the chorus of these big music hall shows, saving up every penny so I could put myself through school.

'It took longer than I anticipated. What's that they say? Life is what happens to you while you're making plans. First my father died, then my mother not long afterwards. I was an only child, and the only person with any money, so first I had to pay for his funeral, then look after my mother, then pay for hers.'

Maggie looks at the sand. 'It was a whirlwind time, working the revues. There was drink and fun. Then I got pregnant, and it didn't seem so much fun any more.'

'My grandfather?' asks Jenny.

Maggie shakes her head. 'I hadn't met him yet. I can't even remember the chap's name, nor see his face. It was one long round of parties, back then.' She takes a breath. 'Abortion was illegal, so I had to go to what they called a back-street practitioner. It cost a lot of money, and it wasn't the most hygienic of places. I developed an infection and couldn't work for several months.

'One good thing about working the revue circuit was that you met a lot of actors, producers, that sort of thing. Now I think about it, perhaps the man who made me pregnant might have been a director or producer, or at least he might have said he was. There was a lot of that sort of thing happening back then. Girls gave up almost everything in the hope of a shot at stardom. A lot of them ended up like me.'

'So how did you meet William Drake?' says Jenny.

'At a funeral,' says Maggie sadly. 'Eddie Monk's. He used to come to the revues sometimes, and I got to know him. Probably slept with him. It was a long time ago. He'd been in a couple of movies by then, was quite the star. He died in nineteen fifty.'

'The plane crash,' nods Jenny. 'It had just taken off from Shoreham Airport, hadn't it? Bound for Paris?'

'Poor Eddie. His funeral was vast, though, a huge party. Everyone was there. Joyce Palermo upstaging everyone with her black Christian Dior dress made especially for the occasion. And Jacky.'

'Jacky?'

'Your grandfather. That's what everyone knew him as. It was his middle name. He only used William J. Drake as his official director's name because he thought it sounded impressive.'

'Jacky,' says Jenny, rolling it around her tongue. 'And you got together?'

'He said later that he'd been unable to take his eyes off me at the funeral,' smiles Maggie. 'I wasn't in a custom-made Dior dress, of course. Just something I'd stitched together myself. But Jacky . . . he said he was bewitched. Said I had star quality.'

'You did,' says Jenny softly. 'Those rushes . . .'

Maggie shakes her head. 'We girls used to hear that sort of thing all the time back then. It was usually just a shortcut to getting you into bed. But I knew of Jacky, of course, he'd just brought his fourth film out, *Off Devil's Head*.' Maggie smiles. 'But I don't need to tell you anything about that, of course. He was starting scripting work on his next feature, *Dark Retribution*. First he asked me to try out for the lead role, then he took me to dinner, then I got the part . . . and then, halfway through filming, he asked me to marry him.'

Jenny's eyes shine. 'Oh my God. How romantic!'

'It was,' agrees Maggie. 'He said he loved me, and I believed him. Because I loved him too, loved him with all my heart.'

Jenny's hands fly to her mouth. 'I've just remembered something my dad said, when we were arguing. He said that Jacky was just about to get married when he met my grandmother . . .'

Maggie's face darkens. 'Yes. You know how close we were to getting married?'

Jenny shakes her head.

The projectionist in Maggie's head changes the reel, and the next act takes a more sombre tone. 'He left me at the altar. Everyone was there, and I had to drive round the church twice, and when I finally demanded to know what was going on, they told me. Told me that Jacky hadn't turned up, that he wasn't coming.'

'Oh my God.'

'Yes. I cursed God and I cursed the devil and I cursed Jacky so very, very deeply.' She goes silent for a moment, remembering. 'I went round to his flat in my wedding dress. I had a gun.'

'A gun!'

Maggie gives a bitter little laugh. 'It was just a prop from the set. But I don't think Jacky realised that. I put it to his head and demanded to know what was going on. I was a little out of my mind at that point, I think. He told me everything. Told me that he was almost bankrupt, that he owed his creditors a pile of money, that he wasn't even sure he could finance the rest of *Dark Retribution*. His first four films had done all right, but Jacky was useless with money. He'd been going cap in hand to anyone he could think of, and at one of the distribution companies he dealt with he met a girl, Joan, in the accounts department. He didn't get the financing he wanted but he had his head turned. Not just by her, but by her father, who offered him a nice steady job if he gave up the whole film business. So he did it. He walked away from *Dark Retribution*, walked away from me, walked away from his career. And in doing so ruined mine.'

'But why?' says Jenny eventually. 'Why would it ruin your career as well? He was an idiot. He was worse than that. But I've seen those rushes . . . you could have made it.'

Maggie shakes her head. 'The fire went out of me. I had no desire to do anything other than lock myself away and mourn. I was too shamed to show my face to anyone I knew. I'd been abandoned at the altar, Jenny. I don't think you can understand what that meant, back then. If I'd been brave enough I think I would have killed myself.'

'So what did you do?'

Maggie shrugs. 'Wept until I was a shrivelled husk. Locked myself in the house I'd bought with the money I'd made from the film, though it was never finished. Scrubbed my face clean of make-up and wore my hair down and flat, made myself look as innocuous as possible. Took a boring job in a boring company and led a boring life.'

She looks at Jenny. 'Quite the Miss Havisham, eh? And, eventually, many years later, I plotted my revenge.'

And suddenly the girl understands. She looks at the sea, at the bag filled with William J. Drake's legacy, then back at Maggie. 'Your revenge. All this, everything that's happened to me . . . it was you having your revenge for what my grandfather did.'

Maggie feels the tide washing around her boots and steps up on to a raised bank of sand. 'Yes. I didn't know what form my revenge would take, not for a long, long time. So I played what you might call a long game. Very long indeed. I had to choose my moment. Nothing presented itself when Jacky was alive, and his wife died not long after he did. I watched his daughter for a while, your mother. Kept tabs, you might say.' Maggie smiles. 'I went to her wedding to your father.'

'What were you going to do?' says Jenny.

Maggie shrugs. 'Nothing *bad*. I wasn't going to hurt anyone. In fact, over the years I almost gave up. And then I saw something. On your Twitter feed.'

Jenny blinks. 'You follow me on Twitter?'

'No, but I looked at it, now and again. Just to see what Jacky's family was up to.' She looks at the grey water. 'It was perhaps like looking through a window at a life that was almost mine.'

'What did I say on Twitter?'

Maggie pats the bag on her shoulder. 'You put photographs on there of the things you'd found, Jacky's films. The only surviving copies. And his notes. And I thought, if I can't get at him, perhaps I can destroy his legacy. Wipe him from memory. But I could think of no way to access your things. Until, over the summer, I saw something on the internet: a mention of Sunset Promenade, and your name. I've become quite adept at using computers over the years – monitoring your family, waiting for a way in. Then it presented itself.'

Jenny just stares at her. 'You've been nursing this . . . this hatred since . . . what, nineteen fifty-two? All these years?'

'It has consumed me,' says Maggie sadly.

Jenny shakes her head. 'But they didn't even spell my name right in that piece about me moving into Sunset Promenade.'

Maggie smiles. 'I told you. I had become quite the detective myself. I set up searches, alerts, anything with your family name in it. And because I know how slapdash people can be, I searched for variations, too. Ebert, Herbert, Hibbert . . .'

'You're crazy,' says Jenny.

'You might think so,' says Maggie mildly. 'But I assure you, a madwoman could not have planned this. Nor tutored poor old Edna Grey into posing as me. It was easy for me to be her, of course – I'm an actress. Many times I thought she was going to blow it all, though.'

'I don't understand that,' confesses Jenny. 'Why bring her into it?'

Maggie shrugs. 'To have someone to blame.' She taps her temple with her forefinger. 'Edna is not in the best of mental health. Getting her to do everything would mean that there was no obvious link to me, that it was just the work of an addled old woman. I'd intended her to steal those canisters, destroy them. I would be as shocked as everyone. And if there was any mention of my name buried in your grandfather's journals . . . then you wouldn't suspect me.'

Jenny frowns. 'But all the thefts . . . the fire in my room! You know how flammable old film is? She could have burned Sunset Promenade to the ground.'

Maggie grimaces. 'Edna did get a little . . . carried away. She got into her part rather better than I anticipated. But that had something of a bonus side effect that I did not forsee.' She pauses. 'Tell me, Jenny, how did you feel when you thought you were being targeted, being hunted, being singled out?'

'Afraid,' says Jenny. 'Angry. Like I didn't know where to turn, like I couldn't trust a single person around me.'

'You had that for a couple of weeks,' says Maggie with a satisfied smile. 'That was just a taste of what I have lived with for sixty-five long years. After I was abandoned at the church by Jacky, I became a laughing stock. You can't imagine, these days, the shame of that. I became a pariah. No one wanted to talk to me – it was as if my tragedy was contagious. I couldn't show my face in public, and certainly not in the film industry. It effectively destroyed my whole career, brought all my dreams crashing down around me.' Maggie pats the bag over her shoulder. 'I need closure. I need revenge. I can't hurt Jacky for what he did to me, but I can destroy his legacy. A legacy only you seem to care about these days.' She shrugs. 'So I suppose that means hurting you as well.'

Jenny takes a step backwards and her shoe splashes into a puddle of seawater. She looks around her at the wet sand, then back to Maggie. 'So what, then? You're going to throw everything into the sea? Destroy it?'

'I suppose so,' says Maggie.

Jenny looks at her. 'I'm sorry. I'm sorry Jacky did that to you. It was an awful, shitty thing. If it's any consolation, I wish he'd married you. You would have been a star. I'm sure things would have worked out.'

'Yes, I was sure too. I begged him to reconsider. But Jacky had chosen another path. A safer life. And I was not to be a part of it.' She thinks for a moment. 'What will you do, Jenny? Are you going to turn me in? What will you say I have done?'

'The jewels . . . ?'

'Mine in the first place, so nothing has been stolen. I merely left them in Edna's care until I was sure you'd seen them.'

'Locking me in the room . . .'

'No evidence,' says Maggie. 'At worst, the actions of a confused old lady.'

'The fire.'

Maggie shrugs. 'Nothing to link it directly to me.'

Jenny backs away from her, feet splashing in the water. The tide is lapping around them. She says, 'Last night. Edna Grey tried to kill me.'

'As I said, she got rather carried away with it all,' sighs Maggie. 'A pillow over your face indeed.'

'It didn't even fit in with the theme,' says Jenny. 'After we watched *Off Devil's Head* I thought . . .' Her voice tails off as she looks around. 'Oh. Right. That was your masterstroke. Destroy everything in the sea.'

While Maggie has been talking the tide has been insinuating itself around them. Tendrils and channels of water have crept up the beach, circling back on themselves. They are standing on a slightly raised sandbank surrounded by water. Maggie says, 'Very curious, the tides around here.'

'Can come in faster than a horse can gallop,' says Jenny. She looks at Maggie. 'Are you expecting me to try to stop you?'

'I imagine you will,' says Maggie, slipping the bag off her shoulder. 'But all I have to do is drop this in the water and everything's ruined.'

Jenny looks at her for a long time, then says, 'Fine. Do it. I don't care any more.'

Maggie frowns. This is not what she was expecting. 'What?'

Jenny shrugs. 'Do it. They're only *things*. They're not important.'

Maggie looks at her quizzically. 'Really? I thought these were your treasures. Your only link to your beloved grandfather.'

Jenny pauses for a moment, then says, 'I used to admire my grandfather. I wanted to be him, to have his spark, his creativity. Now, well . . . he was just like everyone else. He let people take his dreams from him. And treated other people like rubbish. Treated *you* like rubbish. There was nothing special about him. He was as boring and greedy and *ordinary* as anyone. So do what you want. I'm going back to Sunset Promenade.'

Jenny splashes into the moat surrounding them, the cold seawater rising up over her ankles, then stops. She tugs at her leg, then at the other, and when she turns round there is real fear in her eyes. Maggie frowns.

'I can't move,' says Jenny.

✳ 41 ✳

Quicksand

(1950, dir. Irving Pichel)

'This is serious, you know,' says Jenny. The water is up to her calves now, and rolling quickly up the beach. She has shouted herself hoarse, but there's not a soul on the sand as far as she can see in either direction, and ahead is only the shape of Sunset Promenade, its blank windows looking blindly out to sea. There hasn't been a car on the road above all the time she's been stuck. For one glorious moment she reached into her pocket for her phone, then realised she'd handed it over to Maggie. 'Have you got my phone?'

Maggie shakes her head. 'I left it in my room. I just didn't want any distractions.' Jenny strains one leg, and then the other. Maggie says, 'It's quite useless. It's quicksand. The bay's notorious for it.' She tries to move her own legs, the water lapping around the hem of her skirt. 'I'm stuck too.'

Jenny begins to cry, which just makes her more furious. 'Oh God, we're going to die.' She looks at Maggie, an awkward manoeuvre as she's behind her now. 'Did you plan this, too?'

Maggie seems to hesitate. 'Ah, no. This was not part of the plan. It is a bit unfortunate.'

Jenny stares at her. 'Unfortunate? Is that what you call it? Unfortunate?' She looks up at the sky. The clouds are clearing. At least it's not raining. Then she laughs out loud at the ridiculousness of the thought. 'What a lovely day to drown.'

'The water's cold,' observes Maggie.

'Oh, God!' wails Jenny. 'I'm only nineteen. I can't die here.' She turns to Maggie again. 'I've actually taken some steps towards making peace with my parents.'

'I'm sorry.'

'And Ringo! I think I've got a proper boyfriend for the first time in my life!'

'I really am sorry.'

'You don't sound sorry!' screams Jenny. 'Do you actually want to die here?'

'I have nothing, Jenny. Not since Jacky abandoned me. I never married, never had children. I have a big house, and nice things, but it's all so . . . hollow,' says Maggie. 'I honestly thought I was going to die a bitter, lonely death.' She looks across the sand. 'I never thought I would have such a nice time at Sunset Promenade.'

Jenny narrows her eyes and looks round at Maggie. 'You know, you actually do sound sorry.' She gives a sharp intake of breath as the icy water washes over her. 'You sound like you're regretting everything.'

Maggie furrows her brow. 'You know . . . I rather think I am.'

Jenny stares at her, then takes a deep breath. 'Well that's just fucking GREAT!' she screams.

Maggie blinks and shies backwards a little.

Jenny shakes her head. 'It's great.' She begins to applaud, slowly and sarcastically. 'Absolutely brilliant. You spend, what, sixty-five years nursing this frankly crazy desire for revenge and you orches-trate all this . . . this *madness*, just to track down Jacky's films and destroy them, and then you get us stuck in quicksand as the tide's coming in, and' – Jenny smacks her palm against her forehead – 'and now you *rather think* you are sorry.'

Maggie holds out her hands in supplication. 'I . . . I suppose I didn't think . . .'

'You've had all that time to do nothing else but think!' shouts Jenny. 'You've wasted your life, do you realise that? All those years, you could have been happy. You could have actually used your time to be a good person. To help people. Instead you just wallowed in your own self-pity.'

Jenny folds her arms and stares back at the beach. 'And you old people say *we* are self-obsessed. We've got nothing on you.' She pauses, squinting at the road, and a tiny black shape.

'A car!' says Jenny. She begins to wave her hands in the air. 'Help! Help! Over here!'

Suddenly she's aware of Maggie waving frantically too. 'Help!' cries Maggie. 'Help!'

But the car continues past until it's lost around the bend. Jenny turns viciously to Maggie again. 'Why couldn't you have realised an hour ago that you were sorry, that you hadn't thought this through? Why couldn't you have met me in the bloody garden, instead of on this stupid beach? You've got everything and you didn't even realise it. You've got friends, people who think highly of you, a wonderful home here . . .'

'I thought it was far too late for all that for me,' says Maggie quietly.

'It's never too late!' snaps Jenny. The water swirls around her knees. 'I was going to go and see Mum and Dad. I was going to spend time with Ringo, enjoy all the things he enjoys, his music and his star-gazing and his . . . his . . .'

She stops. Her eyes widen. 'Ringo. He might still be in his room! With his telescope!'

Maggie hitches the bag of film canisters higher on her shoulder and joins Jenny in gesticulating wildly at the distant Sunset Promenade. After five minutes Jenny sighs and stops. 'Even if he can see us he probably thinks we're only messing around. He's probably just lying on his bed, listening to his stupid Beatles records . . .' She pauses, eyes widening as she remembers the poster on his wall. 'Maggie,' she says urgently. 'I've got an idea. A last-ditch idea. But I want to strike a deal with you.'

Maggie winces as the water laps at her stomach. 'What deal?'

'Your house is in Winchmore Hill. It's got to be worth a few quid, right?'

'I'd imagine so,' says Maggie.

'What about the jewels? Are they real?'

'Of course. Most of them were gifts from your grandfather. He was very generous with his money. It's no surprise he ended up broke.'

'So they're valuable? What are they worth?'

Maggie shrugs. 'I'm sure I don't know. A considerable amount, I suppose.'

Jenny slaps her hands to her face, her eyes shining. 'We could save Sunset Promenade! You could sell your house, sell your jewels, and I could sell my grandfather's films. I've been offered a substantial sum for them. We could give it all to the Granges.'

Maggie raises an eyebrow. 'And what would I do? Live in the gutter?'

'No! You'd live at Sunset Promenade, forever! As . . . as a partner, an investor, whatever you wanted! You could be with everyone, you wouldn't be on your own. You'd never have to be lonely, or angry, or bitter, ever again.'

'But . . . but all this,' says Maggie, flapping her hands at the rolling waves. 'Everything I've done.'

'That's my part of the deal,' says Jenny. 'You do that, save Sunset Promenade, and this information goes no further.'

Maggie takes a deep breath, then nods.

'OK,' says Jenny. 'Do what I do. I'm not sure if this will work but it's the best chance we've got.'

She faces Sunset Promenade, the water almost around her legs, and holds her arms outstretched by her sides, angled slightly downwards. Checking over her shoulder to make sure Maggie is following suit, she then raises her arms to just above her shoulders. Then lifts her right hand directly up in the air, her left pointing straight out from her side. Finally, her right hand still in position, she points her left hand down.

'Again!' she says. 'Do it again, and keep doing it!'

Ringo sits on his bed and picks up his phone for the umpteenth time. Jenny's been gone two hours now, and he's had no calls from her. Her phone is ringing out and he's followed the sound of it, which has led him, surprisingly, to the room of the real Margaret Cantle, the woman everyone had thought of for so long, as Edna Grey, where it just sits on the desk. He's already paced around his own room, explored Sunset Promenade for her and got the whole story about Mrs Cantle and Mrs Grey from Barry Grange. Or at least as much of it as he understands. He's got a weird, itchy feeling in the back of his head, like something's going down, something really serious.

He stands at his window, gazing out to sea. The tide is coming in at a fair lick now. And it's clearing up. He looks at the sky. Might get a nice bit of star-gazing in later, if this carries on. Ringo picks up Jenny's phone again. Where is Jenny? Why did she come in here, looking for his telescope? Where's she gone?

He stares at the telescope for a moment, still in the position where Jenny left it. Ringo puts his eye to the focus finder, bringing the image there into sharp relief. He lifts his head up, blinks and looks back. It's Jenny. And Mrs Grey . . . or Mrs Cantle, he supposes. It's all really confusing. But what are they doing? Paddling in the sea at this time of the year?

Jenny's doing something with her arms. They both are. Maybe it's some new water aerobics thing that Mad Molly's got them into. Ringo watches for a moment, then frowns. Arms out to the side, arms raised . . . he looks up at the window, then to the wall where his Beatles poster hangs.

Help!

'Bloody hell, they're in trouble,' breathes Ringo, diving on to the bed for his phone.

'Maggie, are you all right?' says Jenny.

'Cold,' says Maggie. 'Very cold.'

'Shit,' says Jenny, and continues to signal maniacally. Maybe Ringo's not in his room. Maybe he's gone out. Maybe all this is for nothing.

'Jenny,' says Maggie, her teeth chattering. The water is around her waist now, the sports bag over her shoulder. 'Jenny.'

'Don't talk,' says Jenny. 'Save your energy.'

Maggie shakes her head. 'You've been a proper friend to me, Jenny. Right to the end. I can see a lot of Jacky in you.'

'Don't say that,' says Jenny. 'He was a bastard.'

'Jenny,' says Maggie. 'Look!'

Jenny gets a splash of water in her face and wipes her eyes. Then she sees a pipe-cleaner of a figure tearing across the road, jumping up and down on what's left of the beach.

'It's Ringo!' she says. 'Thank God!'

But is it too late? Then Maggie says, 'What's he pointing at?'

Jenny turns to her left, where Ringo is gesticulating distantly, and lets out a ragged sigh of relief as the sound of an outboard motor rises on the breeze and an orange shape cleaves the grey waves, bouncing towards them.

'It's the inshore lifeboat,' says Jenny, furiously pumping her arms above her head.

The dinghy is on them in seconds, pulling up alongside. A familiar face, clad in a white helmet and life jacket, beams at her. 'You can't get a taxi out here, love.'

'Kevin!' exclaims Jenny. 'Oh, you won't believe how glad I am to see you! What are you doing here?'

'Funny, that's what they all say,' he laughs. 'Volunteer crewman for the lifeboat, aren't I? Now let's get you two out of that mud and back on dry land, eh?'

'Good job that young man back there raised the alarm,' says one of Kevin's colleagues. 'Way this tide's coming in, I reckon you'd have been underwater in another ten minutes. What were you two doing out here, anyway?'

As they gently pull Maggie from the mud and sea and into the boat, Jenny smiles raggedly. 'Oh, you know. Just a couple of girlfriends hanging out at the beach. And can you be careful with that green bag, please? Don't let it get wet.'

'What's in it?' says Kevin, hauling the bag into the boat. 'Oh, I remember this. Family silver, I said, didn't I?'

Jenny nods as strong arms grab her and pull her from the quicksand. 'I just didn't know back then how big a family I was going to find.'

* 42 *

Second Chance

(1947, dir. James Tinling)

Barry and Garry Grange sit at the desk, both looking over copies of the typed documents in front of them. They simultaneously frown, adjust their glasses, fiddle with their bow ties, then look at each other.

And break out into wide grins.

'Mrs Cantle, Miss Ebert,' says Garry. 'All this seems in order.'

Jenny grins broadly and looks at Maggie, who says, 'I've kept in reserve a small amount for myself, of course. For clothes and cosmetics. Perhaps the occasional holiday. But the rest of it I'm prepared to invest in the business.'

'And Jenny . . . this is incredibly generous of you. Are you sure you want to donate the proceeds of the sale of these items belonging to your grandfather . . . ?'

'Yes,' says Jenny firmly. 'They are just things. People are more important.'

'Well,' says Garry. 'In that case . . . I think you have yourselves a deal.'

Jenny can't help applauding. 'We did it! We saved Sunset Promenade.'

Barry takes out the contract from the Care Network that's been sitting in his desk drawer and gleefully tears it to pieces, throwing them up in the air like confetti.

'It's a lot of money,' says Garry, 'but we're still going to have to be quite frugal, and invest it wisely.'

'We have every confidence in you both,' smiles Maggie.

After Kevin and the rest of the lifeboat volunteers had rescued them from the sands, Maggie and Jenny were taken to the hospital in Lancaster. Jenny was released after a quick check-up; Maggie had been kept in for three days, suffering from mild hypothermia. The police had become involved, but Jenny had stuck to her word and said nothing about what had happened.

'I'll instruct my solicitors straight away,' continues Maggie. 'I'll get the jewellery valued and auctioned. My house will go on the market as soon as possible. It's a sought-after location, so I don't think there will be much delay.'

'Without wanting to muddy the waters,' says Barry, 'won't you miss it? Your own home?'

Maggie shakes her head. 'If there's one thing my stay at Sunset Promenade has taught me, it's that there's nothing more important than good friends. And I seem to have some very lovely friends here indeed.'

'Well,' says Barry, clapping his hands. 'Shall we go and tell the others?'

They file out of the office, past Jenny's bags assembled in the reception hall and into the day room, where they are all gathered: Florin, Mr Robinson, Ibiza Joe and Ringo. They all turn expectant eyes towards them. Everyone knows about the rescue, of course; the details as to why Mrs Cantle is now Mrs Grey and vice versa are still cause for some discussion and confusion.

'We have news,' says Barry. 'Mrs Cantle . . .'

Maggie holds up a hand. 'Actually, just before we get into that, I have a favour to ask. A long time ago I was known by another name—'

'Bloody hell,' mutters Mr Robinson. 'How confusing is this going to get?'

'I was known as Maggie Lorelei.' She glances at Jenny, who grins, then continues, 'That was a name I buried along with the person I used to be. The more I think about it, the more I want to be that person again. So I'd appreciate it if you'd all get used to me being "Ms Lorelei" now . . .' She pauses. 'Actually, though, I think Maggie will do.'

Barry nods. 'Right. Well, Ms Lorelei . . . Maggie . . . basically, she's pulled us out of the fire. She's investing in Sunset Promenade, becoming a director and full-time resident, and you can all keep your jobs and your home.'

There's a stunned silence, then a babble of voices and applause. Barry raises his hand. 'There's more news. Florin . . . he's been to see us. He's concerned about his future, with Brexit and everything, and he's missing his family, as you can all understand. He's indicated to us his desire to return to Latvia.'

'Oh, no!' says Joe.

'Lad,' says Mr Robinson. 'Are you sure? I mean, is there work for you back there . . . ?'

'No,' says Florin. 'But Mr and Mr Grange have had an idea . . .'

'We're going to bring his wife and daughter over here,' says Barry. 'We are going to employ Irma as a co-carer with Florin. We're going to try to fill the empty rooms, you see, and we've already had some interest. Things might be looking up for us all round. We don't know what will happen in the future, whether they'll be allowed to stay, but . . .' Barry shrugs. 'We all do what we can, right?'

'Bloody marvellous!' Mr Robinson says. 'Florin, lad, I've got a couple of bottles of Bernie's in my room . . . you couldn't get it for us, could you?'

As Florin is leaving, the doorbell sounds. 'I will get that first,' he says happily.

Ringo jumps up from the sofa and joins Jenny. 'So, you all set?'

She nods. 'I think so.'

'What's the schedule?'

'Home. See my parents.'

Ringo gently brushes a stray strand of hair from her face. 'I wish you were coming back to Sunset Promenade, though.'

She wrinkles her nose. 'Me too, in a way. But I think it's also best if I take up that room in the halls of residence. You're staying here – and I must say, I think you're mad – and if I was here too . . . I don't know. Maybe we'd get fed up of each other, living in each other's pockets.'

'Never,' he says, and plants a kiss on her cheek. 'But I respect your wishes. I'm just worried that now I've found you, I might lose you again.'

286

Jenny touches her face. 'Let's not worry too much about what might happen, eh? Here and now, remember? Here and now.'

He smiles. 'Hey, I handed in my project. "Ringo's Stars", remember? My tutor loves it.'

Jenny pulls an impressed face. 'So you do actually go to lectures, occasionally?'

He swipes at her playfully. 'I do, and I saw Ling and Bo, as well. They've settled into the new halls. You'll probably see them around when you move on to campus. They're going to come up to Sunset Promenade – we're going to have a bit of a party the week before Christmas. You'll be back for that?'

'Only if you keep me away from Bernie's home brew.' Then she leans in close and whispers, 'My taxi isn't coming for another hour. Want to go and say goodbye to my room properly?'

Before they can sneak out, the door opens and Florin walks in with the tanned, frowning figure of Ronald Grey. He looks around the room, grimacing at Maggie, then turns to the Grange brothers.

'Ah,' says Barry. 'Mr Grey. I was hoping we might have smoothed everything over . . . ?'

'I told you that you'd hear from me again,' says Ronald. 'I still have barely the faintest idea of what's been going on here, and I've tried to get some sense out of my mother, but the more I hear the more fantastical it all sounds.'

'Perhaps we need to go into the office,' says Barry.

Ronald shakes his head. 'No need. This won't take long. I've someone here who wants to speak to you.'

'Is it a lawyer?' asks Barry, his voice quivering.

'No, dear, it's me!' says a voice, and from behind the tall figure of Ronald emerges the woman formerly known as Mrs Cantle: Edna Grey.

Ronald shakes his head. 'I've a beautiful house with a custom-built annexe in one of the most sought-after parts of London. But she's decided she wants to come back and live here. Can we talk terms?'

'Margaret!' says Edna, embracing her old friend. 'I'm glad we can use our real names at last.'

'She's bloody called Lorelei or something now,' grumbles Mr Robinson. 'It never gets any less bonkers, this place, does it?'

As Florin enters the room with the two bottles of Bernie's home brew, Jenny winks at Ringo, takes his hand and quietly leads him out through the door.

'Well,' says Maggie. Jenny has said her goodbyes and it's just the two of them now, standing on the terrace at the front of Sunset Promenade. A cold wind whips off the sea and Jenny pulls her scarf tighter around her neck. On the coast road below, Kevin's Astra waits to take Jenny and her luggage to the train station.

'Well,' agrees Jenny. She cocks her head to one side. 'You were the very first person I met at Sunset Promenade. You quoted *Alice in Wonderland* at me.'

'Seems such an awfully long time ago now.'

'I'll miss you all,' says Jenny.

'We'll all miss you too. But I expect we'll see you again soon? Ringo will be quite bereft if not.'

'Try and keep me away,' smiles Jenny. 'I just have some things to attend to, and then I'll be moving on to campus. I think it's for the best.'

'If it's meant to be, it'll be,' says Maggie. 'You and Ringo, I mean.'

Jenny narrows her eyes. 'Do you believe that? Really?'

'No. Sometimes you make your own destiny, sometimes things happen that are beyond your control. There's no point dwelling on it, letting it eat you up. You just have to get on with life.'

'I bet you wouldn't have said that a few days ago,' smiles Jenny.

Maggie clears her throat, then says, '"I could tell you my adventures – beginning from this morning," said Alice a little timidly: "but it's no use going back to yesterday, because I was a different person then".'

'I'm still not sure who I'm supposed to be,' says Jenny.

'There's nothing at all wrong with choosing who you are,' says Maggie. 'No one's life is set down on train tracks. It is a young woman's prerogative to invent the best possible identity for herself.' She pauses. 'Be that person when you know who she is. You have plenty of time to find out. What's important is that you run towards who you want to be, not away from who you don't.'

Jenny nods. 'That's good advice. And from one of the best actresses of her generation, to boot.'

'You're too kind. But we are all actors, in some way. We all play a part. Just make sure that whatever happens, you're the leading lady in your own movie, Jenny.'

Jenny laughs, and leans in to kiss Maggie on the cheek. 'I'll be back before you know it. I've been given a leave of absence for a couple of weeks, after what happened. Then it'll be nearly Christmas. Your first one at Sunset Promenade.' She goes to the edge of the steps and waves at Kevin, who hurries up to carry her bags down for her. 'I'm actually looking forward to spending Christmas with my mum and dad for the first time since I was a child.'

'Be kind to your parents, Jenny,' says Maggie. 'They only want the best for you, even if they might have gone about it in the wrong way.'

Jenny nods. 'I'm sure by Boxing Day we'll be ready to kill each other, but . . . well, like Mrs Slaithwaite's daughter said, it's not that hard to be nice. It doesn't cost anything.'

'Ready, love?' says Kevin.

Jenny nods and embraces Maggie again. 'I'll see you soon.'

Then she walks down the steps behind Kevin and pauses at the car, taking a last look at Sunset Promenade. She climbs into the passenger seat and puts on her seatbelt.

'Station, is it?' says Kevin, turning on the engine and performing a three-point turn on the deserted coast road. They drive in silence, Jenny watching the distant sea and the pale blue November sky. Eventually Kevin says, 'Back to the old mum and dad? Bit of a rest from all the excitement? Be quite boring after all this, I expect.'

'I suppose,' says Jenny. They're turning off the coast road, heading towards town. In front of them she can see the statue of Eric Morecambe silhouetted against the sky. 'But being old doesn't have to mean you're boring, does it?'

'My mum was a right old bore,' says Kevin. 'My old man, though? Couple of pints inside him, it was like having your own cabaret show. Still, you can't choose your family, can you?'

No, thinks Jenny, you can't choose your family. But you can choose your friends. And maybe you can choose to be friends with your family. Maybe. As they pass the statue, Kevin starts to sing. 'Bring me sunshine, da-de-dah. Bring me sunshine, do-de while.' He nudges her. 'I must say, you know, you look a lot more relaxed than you did when I first brought you here.'

'Looking at yourself in a mirror isn't exactly a study of life,' she says.

'That sounds like a quote. Who said that?'

It was Lauren Bacall, but Jenny doesn't tell him that. Instead, she says, 'Just somebody I tried to be, before I knew who I really was.'

'And who's that?' says Kevin, turning in to the station.

'Jenny Ebert,' she says. 'Whoever she turns out to be.'

THE END

Acknowledgements

Around the time I started writing *The Growing Pains of Jennifer Ebert*, I had a lot of contact with various agencies and organisations who help and work with older people. Not for research, but because of family. It was enlightening in many ways, mainly for the dedication and hard work put in by these people, especially on the frontline, but also to see first hand the pressures that the NHS particularly is under on a day to day basis. I hope I'm lucky enough, if I ever need to, to end up in a place like Sunset Promenade, but I doubt that will be the case. It's my fervent hope that the NHS and the social care budget gets the funding it – and we – deserves from some forward-thinking government in the very near future. That doesn't have to be the wishful thinking of an over-imaginative author; it's something that needs to happen.

As ever, while the life of an author is necessarily taken up by a lot of solitary working, a book like this doesn't come into being without a huge team of people. I'd like to thank everyone at Trapeze and Orion for their hard work in making this happen, especially (but not limited to) my editor Sam Eades, and the Robin to her Batman, Mireille Harper; Krystyna Kujawinska and her super-human rights team; the living supernova that is Richard King; marketing and PR supremo Alex Layt; Mark Stay, who I want on my side when the robots invade, and everyone who's made magic happen.

*

Thanks also to my agent, John Jarrold, for his boundless enthusiasm, endless support and words of encouragement at every step of the way.

Finally, a huge thank you to my wife Claire for always believing in me, even when it looked like things were never going to happen, and to our children Charlie and Alice for managing to look mildly impressed every time I finish a new book. Anyone with teenagers will know that's high praise indeed.

David Barnett, West Yorkshire, 2018

Reading Group Guide

Topics for discussion

1. What are your first impressions of Jenny? Do you like her?

2. Describe how the Sunset Promenade rest home becomes a character in the book. What do you think of the residents? Are they likeable?

3. How do Jenny's feelings towards Ringo change as the novel goes on? Did your feelings change towards him too?

4. How does the author ratchet up feelings of loneliness throughout the novel? Were there particular moments when you felt empathetic towards the characters?

5. Did you suspect who was behind the missing jewellery? Were you surprised by the revelation of the culprit?

6. Did the reveal about Jenny's parents shock you? Or could you see the cracks in her story?

7. Jenny's past has left her feeling isolated and withdrawn. What are her coping mechanisms? How do the Sunset Promenade residents become her support network?

8. Were you surprised about Margaret's family history? Or did you suspect there was more to her story?

9. What does life hold in store for Jenny, Ringo and the residents of Sunset Promenade at the end of the novel? Will they get their happy ever after?

10. The relationship between young people and elderly people has often been explored. Share your favourite films, TV programmes and books on this theme.

Author Q and A
Katherine May interviews David Barnett

The Growing Pains of Jennifer Ebert **is brimful of references to the Golden Age of cinema. Does this reveal you to be a movie buff yourself?**

I am an inveterate consumer of old films, or 'Hobnob Specials' as I like to call them (other biscuits are available). Like Jenny, I do love a good film noir, but there's a certain luminous magic to all old black and white films, and often such a depth of storytelling that we don't always get these days with modern movies.

What would be your own first choice of film to show at the club?

Depends on the time of year. I do love *It's A Wonderful Life* and *Bell, Book and Candle* at Christmas, but I think I'd go with a classic such as *The Third Man* or *The Maltese Falcon*, maybe. Then again, I am a sucker for the old Universal monster movies, such as *Frankenstein*, *Dracula* and *The Mummy*.

One thing that Jenny and Ringo have in common is that they're young people who like old things - film noir and the Beatles. You seem to be picking up on a 'retro' trend here. What makes so many young people nostalgic for eras they don't remember?

That's a good question, and I'm not sure all young people are nostalgic. And perhaps they shouldn't be . . . certainly, when you're quite young you should be forging your own art and culture, and appreciating what's around you right there and then. But at some point you do start to investigate what led to the things you like now, what the influences were on your favourite band or author or movie director, and that does open you to a whole world of hitherto undiscovered material. The Beatles especially is always a major discovery for a young person into their music.

What were you like when you were Jenny and Ringo's age? Please tell me you were having more fun than them!

Oh, I would hope so! Actually, when I was 19 I'd just started my first job as a journalist, so didn't do the university route at all, apart from a one-year journalism course. That meant I had money in my pocket (but not much – I was a trainee journalist!) and really just embarking on adulthood and all that entails. This was 1989, so it was a pretty interesting time, culturally and politically.

Would you have taken up the offer to move into a retirement home for cheap rent?

I think I'd have been quite intrigued to live in an old folks' home though . . . maybe for a few weeks, anyway. Especially if the residents were as quirky and interesting as the ones at Sunset Promenade. I think old and young have a lot to learn from each other, if they can get over their initial and probably quite natural generational prejudices.

Central to the novel is the theme of loneliness and isolation that unites both young and old. Do you feel optimistic or pessimistic about your own old age?

Hmm. We live in an odd world where people are living longer, and being more active into old age, but there's not the infrastructure or resources from the state to actually cope with this very well. Which basically means if you're rich you'll be all right, but as for the rest of us . . . we risk creating an even more polarised society of the haves and the have-nots than we already have, unless someone takes the whole health and social care issue by the horns fairly quickly.

The spectre of Brexit looms large over your book, but it's great to see the two sides of the debate sharing their perspectives. Do you think the EU is a line in the sand between old and young – or will there be a rapprochement eventually?

I think Brexit was the most divisive thing this country has seen for generations – that's evident in how close the referendum vote actually was. It seems almost astonishing now that we went into something so monumentally important without the full facts to hand, and there does indeed seem to be a generational divide. Whether everyone comes together eventually remains to be seen, and I suppose that depends on how well – or badly – the process goes when we get fully into it. You always have to have hope that everything will turn out well, but sometimes it's difficult to see how that's going to happen.

You've now tackled Bowie and the Beatles – do you have any more musical heroes that you're dying to share with the world?

Funnily enough, the piece I'm currently in the very, very early stages of planning will be, if it comes to fruition, taking us back to the mid-nineties, so will be against a backdrop of Britpop, Blur vs Oasis, and the Spice Girls. I'm also currently writing a comic book for an American publisher, IDW, called *Punks Not Dead*, which features the ghost of a punk rocker called Sid who might be very familiar to some people, so that's another musical box ticked! As for the future . . . well, the eighties seems ripe for casting my beady eye over.

Katherine May is the author of *The Whitstable High Tide Swimming Club*, published by Trapeze.